PRAISE FOR
FABLEHAVEN

"Like Harry Potter, *Fablehaven* looks like a book for kids, but, like Harry Potter, *Fablehaven* can be read aloud in a family with as much pleasure for grownups as for children. . . . Do yourself a favor, and don't miss the first novel by a writer who is clearly going to be a major figure in popular fantasy." —ORSON SCOTT CARD, AUTHOR OF *ENDER'S GAME*

"Every bit as much a 'page-turner' as the Harry Potter books! This story is so compelling and so well written that you'll find its magic working on you as well, completely taking over your ability to put the book down, even for a moment." —*COLUMBIA DAILY TRIBUNE*

"*Fablehaven* is a fantastical, wonderful book. Look out, J. K. Rowling; the fantasy genre has an outstanding new author to embrace!" —BOOKREVIEW.COM

"Imagination runs wild in *Fablehaven*. It is a lucky book that can hold this kind of story." —OBERT SKYE, AUTHOR OF *LEVEN THUMPS AND THE GATEWAY TO FOO.*

FABLEHAVEN
SECRETS OF THE DRAGON SANCTUARY

BRANDON MULL

ILLUSTRATED BY
BRANDON DORMAN

ALADDIN PAPERBACKS
NEW YORK LONDON TORONTO SYDNEY

For Chris Schoebinger, the original caretaker of Fablehaven

If you purchased this book without a cover, you should be aware that this book is stolen property. It was reported as "unsold and destroyed" to the publisher, and neither the author nor the publisher has received any payment for this "stripped book."

This book is a work of fiction. Any references to historical events, real people, or real locales are used fictitiously. Other names, characters, places, and incidents are the product of the author's imagination, and any resemblance to actual events or locales or persons, living or dead, is entirely coincidental.

ALADDIN
An imprint of Simon & Schuster Children's Publishing Division
1230 Avenue of the Americas, New York, NY 10020
Text copyright © 2009 by Brandon Mull
Illustrations copyright © 2009 by Brandon Dorman
All rights reserved, including the right of reproduction in whole or in part in any form.
ALADDIN is a trademark of Simon & Schuster, Inc., and related logo
is a registered trademark of Simon & Schuster, Inc.
For information about special discounts for bulk purchases, please contact
Simon & Schuster Special Sales at 1-866-506-1949 or business@simonandschuster.com.
The Simon & Schuster Speakers Bureau can bring authors to your live event.
For more information or to book an event contact the Simon & Schuster Speakers
Bureau at 1-866-248-3049 or visit our website at www.simonspeakers.com.
The text of this book was set in Goudy Old Style.
Manufactured in the United States of America 0210 OFF
2 4 6 8 10 9 7 5 3 1
The Library of Congress has cataloged the hardcover edition as follows:
Mull, Brandon, 1974—
Fablehaven: Secrets of the Dragon Sanctuary / Brandon Mull.
p. cm.
Summary: When Kendra and Seth go to stay at their grandparents' estate,
they discover that it is a sanctuary for magical creatures and that a battle
between good and evil is looming.
ISBN 978-1-60641-042-4 (hc)
[1. Magic—Fiction. 2. Grandparents—Fiction. 3. Brothers and sisters—Fiction.] I. Title.
PZ7.M9112Fa 2006
[Fic]—dc22 2006000911
ISBN 978-1-4169-9028-4 (pb)

Contents

CHAPTER 1   Journal 1

CHAPTER 2   Stingbulb 14

CHAPTER 3   Impostor. 25

CHAPTER 4   Captive. 43

CHAPTER 5   Mourning 61

CHAPTER 6   The All-Seeing Eye 75

CHAPTER 7   Sabotage. 103

CHAPTER 8   Knapsack 120

CHAPTER 9   Hall of Dread 138

CHAPTER 10   Hotel 158

CHAPTER 11   Gate-Crasher 176

CHAPTER 12   Grunhold 194

CHAPTER 13   Shadow Charmer 214

CHAPTER 14   Heart and Soul. 230

CHAPTER 15   Horns 251

CHAPTER 16   Moving Out 268

CHAPTER 17   Wyrmroost 293

CHAPTER 18   Blackwell Keep 315

CHAPTER 19   Dragon Tamer 338

CHAPTER 20   Griffins 356

CHAPTER 21   Giant Problem 380

CHAPTER 22   Raxtus 394

CHAPTER 23   Shrine. 414

CHAPTER 24   Temple 434
CHAPTER 25   Slayings 452
CHAPTER 26   Ambush 476
CHAPTER 27   Navarog 494
CHAPTER 28   The New Knights. 518

CHAPTER ONE

Journal

Kendra Sorenson briskly scraped the head of a wooden match against the rough strip on the side of a rectangular matchbox. Cupping her hand to shield the new flame, she held the burning match against the blackened wick of a candle stub. Once the flame spread to the wick, she shook out the match, thin strands of smoke winding upward.

Seated at the desk in her bedroom, considering the remains of the match, Kendra was struck by how quickly the fire had consumed the wood, leaving the top third fragile and charred, the substance transformed into an unrecognizable state. She contemplated the plague at Fablehaven that had swiftly turned many of the inhabitants of the magical preserve from beings of light into creatures of darkness. She and her family and friends had managed to reverse the plague before it destroyed the preserve, but their efforts had cost the life of Lena the naiad.

Snapping out of her reverie, Kendra set the spent match off to one side, slid three keys into a locked journal, opened the book, and began hurriedly leafing through the pages. This was her last umite candle—she could not afford to waste any of the special illumination that made the words on the pages visible.

She had brought the Journal of Secrets home from Fablehaven. It had once belonged to Patton Burgess, a former Fablehaven caretaker whom Kendra had unexpectedly met when he had traveled forward through time at the end of the previous summer. Written in a secret fairy language, the words inside were further disguised by being inscribed in umite wax. Only under the light of an umite wax candle would the characters glow into view, and only by virtue of her status as fairykind could Kendra decipher them.

Reading and speaking fairy languages were only some of the abilities granted to Kendra after hundreds of giant fairies had mobbed her with kisses. She could see in the dark. Certain magical mind tricks failed to affect her, allowing her to penetrate the illusions that concealed most magical creatures from mortal eyes. And fairies had to follow any command she issued.

Kendra checked over her shoulder, listening for a moment. The house was quiet. Mom and Dad had taken to jogging at the rec center on weekday evenings, hoping to make it a habit before the New Year. She doubted the resolution would survive more than a couple of weeks, but for now it provided her an opportunity to peruse the journal unsupervised. Her parents were blind to the magical world she and her brother had discovered. As a consequence, when they had caught her reading a book full of strange symbols by candlelight, they thought she was getting involved with some bizarre cult. There was no way to explain that the book contained the secrets of a former Fablehaven caretaker. Not wanting her parents to confiscate the journal, Kendra pretended to have returned it to the library and had started reading it only when she could be sure of prolonged privacy.

Because the presence of her parents reduced her reading time, and because she had a limited supply of candles, Kendra had not yet read every word from cover to cover, although she had skimmed the entire volume. The voice in the journal was familiar—she had read many entries in some of Patton's less secretive journals at Fablehaven. While browsing the Journal of Secrets, Kendra had found where Patton described at length the story of how Ephira had become a spectral menace, omitting none of the dismal details, along with passages where he expressed his innermost fears about his relationship with Lena. Kendra had also learned about a passageway to a grotto beneath the old manor, various stashes of treasure and weapons concealed around Fablehaven, and a pool at the base of a small waterfall where an intrepid fortune hunter could catch a leprechaun. She found information about a secret chamber at the end of the Hall of Dread in the Fablehaven dungeon, along with the passwords and procedures needed to gain entry. She read about journeys abroad to India and Siberia and Madagascar.

She absorbed information about various preserves at the far corners of the globe. She scanned theories regarding possible threats and villains, including many alleged plots by the Society of the Evening Star.

Tonight, with the umite candle burning low, she turned to her favorite entry in the journal and read Patton's familiar handwriting:

Having returned scant hours ago from a singular adventure, I now find myself unable to suppress the urge to impart my thoughts. I have seldom considered whom I intend to read the covert information compiled in this record. Upon the occasions when I have paid heed to the matter, I have vaguely concluded that I was jotting these notations for myself. But I am now aware that these words will reach an audience, and that her name is Kendra Sorenson.

Kendra, I find this realization both thrilling and foreboding. You face challenging times. Some of the knowledge I possess could aid you. Regrettably, much of that same knowledge could usher you into unspeakable danger. I keep staging vigorous internal debates in the attempt to discern what information will grant you an advantage over your enemies and what information might further imperil your situation. Much of what I know has the potential to cause more harm than good.

Your enemies among the Society of the Evening Star will balk at nothing to obtain the five artifacts that together can open Zzyzx, the great demon prison. At the time I left you, to our knowledge, they had acquired only one artifact, while your able grandfather retained another. I have information about two of the artifacts that you lack, and could probably acquire more knowledge with some effort. And yet I hesitate to share. If you or others try to pursue or guard the artifacts, you might inadvertently lead our enemies to them. Or you could be harmed in the attempt to retrieve them. Conversely, if the Sphinx is in avid pursuit of the artifacts, I am inclined to believe that he will eventually succeed. Under certain circumstances, it would benefit our cause for you to have my knowledge in order to keep the artifacts out of his grasp.

Therefore, Kendra, I have elected to rely on your judgment. I will not include the specifics in this journal, for who could resist such temptingly convenient access, regardless of that person's integrity? But in the hidden chamber beyond the Hall of Dread I will disguise further details regarding the hiding places of two of the artifacts. Unearth that information only if you find it becomes absolutely necessary. Otherwise, do not even mention that such knowledge exists. Use discretion and patience and courage. My hope is that the information will lie dormant for your whole lifetime. If not, information about the location of the hidden chamber awaits elsewhere in this journal. Go to the chamber and use a mirror to find the message on the ceiling.

Kendra, I wish I could be there to help you. Your loved ones are strong and capable. Put your trust where it belongs and make smart decisions. Keep that brother of yours in line. I am grateful to have such an exemplary niece.

Drumming her fingers on the desk, Kendra blew out the candle. Enough of the waxy lump remained to light it again, but the flame would not last long. Grandpa probably had more umite candles at Fablehaven by now, but getting them would be a hassle. She leaned back in her chair, pinching her lower lip. Between school and her volunteer day-care job, she had hardly found time to give the matter the contemplation it deserved.

She had not yet shared the message from Patton with anyone. He had trusted her judgment, and she was in no hurry to betray that trust. Patton was right that once the information about the location of the artifacts got out, people would want to pursue them. And he was also right that the Sphinx would be watching for a chance to exploit any such attempt. Unless information about the hidden artifacts became essential, she would let it be.

Throughout that fall season, Kendra had kept in touch with her grandparents. They did not talk openly about secrets on the phone, but they had found ways to pass needed information without getting too specific. Ever since the Sphinx had been revealed as the leader of the Society of the Evening Star, all activity by the Society had seemed to cease. But they all knew that the Sphinx was out there, watching and plotting, waiting for the opportune moment to strike.

Two members of the Knights of the Dawn kept Kendra and Seth under constant surveillance and smuggled them information when necessary. So far there had been no alarming incidents. Although the individuals assigned to protect Kendra and Seth rotated, at least one of their bodyguards was always a trusted friend like Warren, Tanu, or Coulter. For the past four days, Warren had been watching them, along with a supposedly trustworthy girl named Elise.

Kendra sighed. After all the subterfuge during the past couple of years, she wondered if she would ever fully trust anyone again. Perhaps that was another reason she kept Patton's message to herself.

Something rustled faintly behind her. She turned to see that a folded sheet of paper had been slipped under her door. She crossed to the doorway, picked up the white piece of paper, unfolded it, and scanned the typed list. The more she read, the narrower her eyes squinted. She stalked out of her room, down the hall, and stopped in Seth's open doorway.

"Do you honestly expect to get a hang glider for Christmas?" Kendra asked her younger brother.

Seth glanced up from the desk where he had been doodling lizards on his math homework. "I certainly won't if I don't ask."

Kendra held up the list. "Who else got this?"

"Mom and Dad, of course. Plus I e-mailed copies to all of our relatives, even some distant ones I tracked down online. And I mailed a copy to Santa, just to cover all of my bases."

Crossing the room to stand beside her brother, Kendra wiggled the page in front of him. "You've never made crazy requests like these before. A set of custom golf clubs? A hot tub? A bullet bike?"

Seth snatched the list from Kendra. "You're only naming the big-ticket items. If you can't afford to get me a massage chair, you could get me a kite, a video game, or a movie. You'll find ideas on my wish list for any budget."

Kendra folded her arms. "You're up to no good."

Seth stared at her with the wide-eyed, mildly offended expression he typically used when hiding something. "Limiting what I *get* for Christmas is one thing. Limiting what I *ask* for is another. Who are you, the Grinch?"

"You normally use a strategic approach to Christmas, asking for a few presents you really want—and it usually works. You've never campaigned for anything that costs more than a bike or a video game system. You keep your wish list realistic. Why the change?"

"You're overanalyzing, Professor," Seth sighed, handing back the list. "I just figured it couldn't hurt to aim high this year."

"Why send the list to relatives so distant they don't even know you?"

"One of them might be a lonely billionaire, who knows? I have a hunch that this could be my lucky year."

Kendra regarded her brother. Even since the summer, he looked less like a kid. He kept getting taller, all gangly arms and legs, and his face looked slimmer, his chin more defined. They had not spent much quality time together over the fall. He had his own friends, and she was busy getting accustomed to high school. Now the holiday break loomed less than a week away.

"Don't do anything stupid," Kendra warned.

"Thanks for the brilliant advice," he said. "Do you mind if I quote you in my diary?"

"Are you keeping a journal?"

"I'll have to start if you keep dispensing such precious pearls of wisdom."

"I have the perfect first entry," Kendra suggested, glaring. "Dear diary, today I bought myself fancy Christmas presents with gold I stole from Fablehaven. I tried to pretend the gifts came from distant, billionaire relatives, but nobody was fooled, and the Knights of the Dawn have hunted me down and locked me in a grimy dungeon."

Seth's mouth opened and closed soundlessly as he commenced and then abandoned several possible responses. After clearing his throat, he finally managed, "You can't prove that."

"How did you sneak out gold?" Kendra exclaimed. "I thought Grandpa confiscated the treasure you and the satyrs took from the nipsies."

"We're not having this conversation," Seth insisted. "I don't know what you're talking about."

"You must have had multiple stashes, and Grandpa didn't find them all. But how are you converting gold and jewels into cash? A pawn shop?"

"This is nonsense," Seth maintained. "Sounds to me like you're the one with the criminal mind."

"You have your guard up now, but I saw through it a minute ago. That gold wasn't Newel's or Doren's to give you! After all that happened last summer, how did you walk out the front door with stolen treasure in your pockets? How shameless are you?"

Seth sighed in defeat. "Grandpa and Grandma weren't using it."

"Right, Seth, because they're the caretakers of Fablehaven. They're trying to protect the creatures and items hidden there. You might as well steal from a museum!"

"Kind of like you taking the rain stick from Lost Mesa? Or Warren keeping the sword he found there?"

Kendra flushed. "Technically, Painted Mesa wasn't part of the Lost Mesa preserve. Plus, I'm not hawking the rain staff to buy a WaveRunner! And Warren isn't trying to trade the sword for a snowmobile! Part of why we have those items is in order to protect them, not to sell them for a fraction of their value!"

"Settle down, I still have all of the gold."

"Maybe you should give it to me for safekeeping."

"Not likely," Seth snorted. He eyed her reluctantly. "But I'll return the treasure to Grandpa the next time we go back."

Kendra relaxed. "I can live with that."

"I don't have much choice since I live with the world's biggest tattler. What if I pay you off? Would you keep quiet? I could buy you some awesome Christmas presents."

"I'm not in the market for a hang glider."

"It could be anything," Seth offered. "Dresses, jewelry, a pony—whatever stupid girly junk you want!"

"The main thing I want this year is for my little brother to develop some integrity so I can stop baby-sitting him."

"I could always use some of the gold to hire some thugs to kidnap you and hold you captive until after the holidays," Seth considered.

"Good luck with that," Kendra said, crumpling the typed list and tossing it at the wastebasket beside the desk. The irregular ball of paper bounced off the lip of the wastebasket and landed softly on the floor.

Seth leaned down from his chair, snatched up the crumpled paper, and dropped it into the trash. "Nice aim."

"Nice list." Kendra strode into the hall and returned to her room. The scent of candle smoke still lingered so she opened the window, admitting a cold draft. She waved her hands to disperse the smell, then shut the window and flopped down on her bed.

Even far from Fablehaven, at their own house, with constant supervision from hidden bodyguards, Seth was still finding ways to cause unnecessary trouble! Part of her wished she could share the message from Patton with her brother. These days, he was the only person she could talk to about this type of problem. But she would not dare allow him access to the information in the Journal of Secrets. He would undoubtedly find a way to put that knowledge to bad use.

Her secrecy about the journal had caused some friction between them. When they discussed the subject, he knew by her vague answers that she was withholding information. But unable to translate the arcane writing himself, there was nothing he could do about her reluctance to share.

Rolling over onto her stomach, Kendra slid a hand under her mattress and pulled out five envelopes bound together by a rubber band. There was no need to read the letters from Gavin—she had the content memorized. But she enjoyed holding them.

He had promised that he would try to take a turn as one

of her guards, but he had yet to show up. As a dragon tamer, he had unusual skills that had recently been required in some distant parts of the world. At least he had sent letters, delivered by bodyguards. In the notes, he shared details about his dealings with dragons: cutting skin tumors out of the slimy hide of a long, slender dragon; studying a rare dragon that lived underwater and used dense clouds of ink to confuse her prey; rescuing a team of magical plant experts from a small but ferocious dragon that spun webs like a spider.

Interesting as the dragons were, Kendra had to admit that her favorite parts of the letters were any mention of him missing her or looking forward to seeing her again. When she wrote him back, she made it clear that she was looking forward to seeing him as well, hopefully without sounding too overanxious. Closing her eyes, she pictured him. Was he getting better-looking in her memories?

Content to have held the letters for a moment, she slipped them back under her mattress. She had done her best to keep Seth from noticing the correspondence. He already loved to tease her about having a crush on Gavin. Imagine if her brother found evidence that it was sort of true!

From downstairs came the rumble of the automatic garage door opening. Her parents were home. Kendra sprang from her bed and snatched the journal and the candle stub from her desk, placing them on a high shelf in her closet and moving folded sweaters in front of them. She unzipped her backpack and put a notebook and a pair of textbooks on her desk, although her homework was already finished.

Kendra took a deep breath. She only had to make it through two more days of school, and then winter break would allow her to relax and think through some of the issues that had been troubling her. She left her room and walked to the stairs, trying to compose her face into a casual expression with which to greet her parents.

CHAPTER TWO

Stingbulb

Crunchy, dirt-flecked snow covered the ground outside of Wilson High School as Kendra proceeded down the steps toward the curb. Jagged, crusty mounds flanked the street and irregular piles bordered the sidewalk. Although the walkway looked clear, Kendra stepped carefully for fear of ice patches. A hazy ceiling of light gray clouds added monotonous shade to the cold day.

Idly swinging her backpack, Kendra peeked at the spots where her bodyguards normally loitered and noticed Elise leaning against a parked car across the street, penciling a word into a crossword puzzle. The woman did not make eye contact, but Kendra knew she was slyly watching. Elise appeared to be in her thirties—thin, medium height, with ruler-straight bangs. Kendra wondered if Warren thought she was pretty.

As Kendra turned left at the sidewalk that paralleled the street, she continued to survey the area. Most of the time she could spot Warren, but she did not try hard today, since he was probably off guarding Seth.

At the crosswalk, Kendra hustled to the other side of the street and then walked past the library to the huge rec center. The boxy brick structure housed a swimming pool, an exercise room, a basketball court, three racquetball courts, locker rooms, and a spacious day care. Kendra volunteered at the day care every day after school until five. It was an easy job, and there were even occasional windows of time when she could get some homework done.

The closest elementary school got out before the high school, so when Kendra entered the day-care area, kids were already coloring, building with blocks, squabbling over toys, and running around. Some of the kids near the door greeted her as "Miss Sorenson." None of them knew her as Kendra.

Rex Tanner stood across the room coaching a young freckled boy as he sprinkled fish food into the aquarium. An olive-skinned, middle-aged man from Brooklyn, Rex ran the day care and maintained a relaxed atmosphere. He had a natural, easy way with the kids. Nothing ever seemed to fluster him.

When the boy finished with the fish, Rex noticed Kendra and waved her over, his smile wider than usual. His curly hair, thick mustache, and lightly tinted glasses meant he always looked like he was wearing a corny disguise. When Kendra got close, she could smell that, as usual, he had gone heavy on the Old Spice.

"Hey, Rex," she said.

"Kendra, good to see you, good to see you." Whether addressing kids or adults, Rex normally spoke like he was hosting a show for young children. He clapped his hands, rubbing them together. "We're going to explore the five senses today. I came up with a very exciting exercise. Come see what you think."

She followed him to the counter at the back of the room where five square cardboard boxes stood in a row. Each box had a hole cut in the side.

"Am I supposed to feel what's inside?" Kendra asked.

"Bingo," Rex said. "Try to guess what you're touching. Go left to right."

Kendra reached into the first box, her fingers sliding off the surfaces of small, greasy spheres. "Slimy eyeballs?" she guessed.

"Peeled grapes," Rex revealed. "Try the next one."

Kendra reached inside the second box. "Intestines?"

"Noodles."

The third box contained rubber erasers of various sizes, which she guessed correctly. The fourth felt empty at first, then she found something that felt like a potato. She was opening her mouth to guess when she felt a stabbing pain in her thumb. Yelping, Kendra withdrew her hand. "What was that?" she cried.

"You okay?" Rex asked.

"Let me guess, cactus?" Kendra sucked the pad of her thumb, tasting blood.

"Close. A cactus fig. Edible fruit. I could have sworn I'd removed all the sharp spines!"

Kendra shook her hand. "Missed one."

Rex blinked, looking off balance. "Let me get you a Band-Aid."

Kendra checked her thumb. "No, it's just a little prick."

"Maybe we'd better limit the exercise to four boxes," Rex decided.

"Probably. What's in the last one? Rusty razors?"

"Damp sponges."

"Did you use any of them to wipe up broken glass?"

Rex chuckled. "They should be safe." He picked up the box with the cactus fig inside. "I'll stow this back in my office."

"Good idea," Kendra said.

As Rex took the box away, Ronda came over. The overweight mother of three worked part-time at the day care, mostly during the afternoon shift. "You all right?" she asked.

"Rex had me feeling cactus fruit. Stuck me pretty good. I'm fine, though."

Ronda shook her head. "For such a nice guy, he can be a real knucklehead."

"It's no big deal. I'm just glad the victim wasn't a five-year-old."

The rest of the afternoon went smoothly. Kendra had no urgent homework, so she was able to relax and enjoy the kids. She ran a game of musical chairs and a couple of rounds of Simon Says. Rex read a story, Ronda played her ukulele for singing time, and the touch exercise went over big. Soon the clock over the sink read 4:55 and Kendra began gathering her things.

She was shouldering her backpack when Rex came up behind her. "We have a problem, Kendra."

Kendra turned, her eyes darting around the room, searching for what had broken or who was injured. "What is it?"

"I've got an irate parent on the phone in my office," Rex apologized. "I need you for a minute."

"Sure," Kendra said, trying to guess what might have provoked the call. Had she treated any of the kids unfairly in recent days? No incidents came to mind. Perplexed, she followed Rex into his office. He shut the door and pulled the blinds closed. The handset of the phone was off the hook, resting on his desk. He motioned toward the phone. "Who is it?" she stage whispered.

Rex jerked his head toward the far corner of the office. "For starters, take a gander behind the filing cabinet."

Furrowing her brow. Kendra moved toward the tall metal filing cabinet. Before she arrived, a girl emerged from behind the cabinet. A girl who looked exactly like Kendra. Same height, same hair, same face. It could have been her twin, or some trick with a mirror. The Kendra replica cocked her head, smiled, and waved.

Kendra froze, trying to process the bizarre sight. She had seen some impossible things in the past couple of years, but nothing more surprising.

Taking advantage of the stunned pause, Rex attacked from behind. One of his arms reached around Kendra's torso, roughly pulling her against him. A pungent rag covered her nose and mouth. She bucked and squirmed, but the fumes from the rag quickly made her light-headed. The room swayed, and her sense of urgency faded. Senses muddy, she sagged against Rex and slipped into unconsciousness.

※ ※ ※

Kendra returned to consciousness by degrees. First she heard a distant babble of kids and parents. As she lazily tried to stretch, she became aware that her arms and legs were bound. Her alertness increasing, she remembered the mirror image of herself and how Rex had inexplicably attacked her. When she tried to call out, Kendra noticed the cloth wadded in her gagged mouth.

Only then did she open her eyes. She was on the ground behind Rex's desk, trussed to a long piece of plywood. A pounding ache pulsed behind her forehead. She struggled, but her bindings were snug, and the board kept her immobilized. Panicked, she concentrated on breathing through her nose and listened as the prattle of kids and parents diminished to nothing.

Disorganized thoughts flashed through Kendra's mind. Could she somehow call fairies to her aid? She hadn't seen a fairy in months. Did her fairykind status grant her any advantages in her present predicament? Nothing came to mind. She needed a Tylenol; her head was really throbbing. Maybe Warren would rescue her. Or Elise. Kendra wished that Gavin had been here watching over her. Where was he? The most recent letter had come from Norway. Why had they crammed so much cloth in her mouth? One of the fluorescent lights in the ceiling was dying. Would Ronda miss her and come looking for her? No, that would be the purpose of the duplicate Kendra. The impostor would probably fool Warren and Elise as well. Where had the impostor come from? Could Rex be a member of the Society of the Evening Star? If so, he must have been some kind of undercover sleeper agent—he had worked at the day care for years.

The door to the office opened. Desperate hope surged inside of Kendra until Rex came and stood over her. "Just you and me, kid," he said pleasantly, crouching.

Kendra uttered muffled complaints, pleading with her eyes.

"Don't like the gag much?"

Kendra shook her head from side to side.

"Can you keep your trap shut? Believe me, I'll put you right back under." He opened a desk drawer and withdrew a small bottle and a rag. Unstopping the bottle, he moistened the rag and set it aside. "Cry out and you'll be sorry. If you think you have a headache now, just wait until after a second dose. You with me?"

Eyes wide and glistening, Kendra nodded.

Rex peeled the duct tape from her mouth and tugged out the saliva-soaked cloth. Kendra smacked her lips. Her tongue felt dry. "Why, Rex?"

He smiled, eyes squinting behind lightly tinted lenses. "Rex wouldn't do this to you, kiddo. Haven't you caught on? I'm not Rex."

"Are you some kind of shape shifter?"

"You're getting warmer."

"There were two of you," Kendra guessed. "Just like there was another me."

Rex sat down on the chair by his desk. "Want the lowdown? Honestly, I came from a tree. I was originally a fruit. A stingbulb. We're not supposed to exist anymore, but here I am."

"I don't get it."

A small smile tugged at the corners of his mouth. "When you reached into the box, playing the touch game, a stingbulb pricked you. Stingbulbs must be handled carefully. They become the first living thing they sting."

"That clone of me used to be the cactus fig?"

"We're amazing fruit. Takes about ninety minutes for the metamorphosis to occur. Throughout the transformation, we continue to draw matter and nutrients from the tree we were plucked from. Then the remarkable connection breaks, we survive for three or four days, and poof, we die."

Kendra stared at Rex, thinking through the implications. "So the Kendra stingbulb is going to pose as me."

"She is a remarkable duplicate. She even has most of your memories. She'll do a good job imitating you. Your guardians will be none the wiser."

Kendra scowled. "If she has my personality, why isn't she helping me?"

Rex placed his palms together, tapping his fingers. "Not your personality. Your memories. The majority of them, anyhow. Like any stingbulb, she has her own consciousness. So do I. Just because I can access Rex's memories doesn't mean he gets to run the show. We stingbulbs follow whatever commands we are issued after our transformation. My course is set. Rex was complicated. I'm not. I was created for the purpose of abducting you. While Ronda was leading singing time, I was issuing instructions to your duplicate."

"Why not disobey your instructions and let me go? The people who made you are evil! You don't want to help the bad guys, do you?"

Rex chuckled, smiling broadly. "Don't waste your breath. Stingbulbs are single-mindedly loyal, Kendra. Our awareness functions differently from yours. We accomplish what we've been programmed to do. Despite the fond memories of you that Rex possesses, I can only perceive you as my enemy. Tough luck. I'll only exist for another day or two. I must fulfill my assignment."

"What are you supposed to do with me?" Kendra whispered.

"Deliver you to my creator."

"Who created you?"

His eyebrows went up. "You'll see."

"Are we going far?"

He shrugged.

"Is the Sphinx behind this?"

"Is that a name I should know?"

Kendra pressed her lips together. "What was the mission of the other stingbulb?"

"Posing as you is her main task. If your guardians suppose you are snug in your bed, imagine how simple it will be to smuggle you away."

"What other tasks does she have?"

Rex nodded, leaning forward. "They said you would be full of questions, and that you would try to persuade me to help you. They said I should help you understand what had happened, that it would calm you. They didn't tell you much more than I needed to know, and I have told you all that I can."

"Who programmed you?"

"We're done talking for now."

"Rex, don't do this—you know me, you don't want to hurt me. Rex, they'll kill me. They'll hurt my family. Rex, please, don't give in to them, this is life or death. They're trying to destroy the world."

He smiled as if the plea were cute and pathetic. "Enough chitchat. I'm pretty well oriented—been in this skin for more than a day. I can't be confused or persuaded. Let's enjoy some music. I really like music. I've never had ears before. Don't scream, don't try anything. It will only make matters worse."

Rex switched on the radio atop his desk and turned up the volume. Kendra assumed the classic rock was meant to help mask any sounds she might dare to make. The blaring guitars and screaming vocals made it harder for her to think.

Would anybody catch on to this ruse? Would Warren come rushing to her aid? Or Elise? Or Seth? How could they possibly guess that somebody else had taken her place? Until he had revealed himself, it had not even crossed Kendra's mind that Rex could be a fake. If the counterfeit Kendra had her memories, what information might she share with their enemies? What might she steal? Who might she harm?

Rex remained beside Kendra in the chair, patiently watching her, occasionally beating an imaginary drum set. He showed no sign of letting his guard down. Try as she might, she could envision no way out of the predicament. It was a perfect, unforeseeable trap. The Sphinx had to be behind it. Would Rex take her to him? When? Closing her eyes, trying to tune out the rock music, Kendra yearned hopelessly for a plan.

CHAPTER THREE

Impostor

Chewing on a bite of toast, Seth watched his sister shake an impressive pile of Cocoa Krispies into her cereal bowl. When she added milk, the mound of cereal rose, rice bits spilling over the edge of the bowl onto the table. As the cereal crackled, she brushed the fallen rice bits into her palm and popped them into her mouth. Then she dug in with her spoon.

"Hungry today?" Seth asked.

Kendra glanced over at him. "I love this stuff."

"That's your third bowl. Are you on some sort of anti-diet?"

She shrugged, spooning up another heaping mouthful.

"You're probably just in mourning," he teased, taking another bite of toast. "Last day of school until next year. No tests, no assignments, what will you do?"

"There's not much going on today. Maybe I'll skip."

Seth laughed. "Nice. Good one. Where are you heading instead? Over to the movie theater? Burn up some quarters at the arcade?"

Kendra shrugged.

Seth studied his sister. "What's your deal today? You hardly ever touch my Cocoa Krispies."

"Guess I forgot how tasty they were."

He shook his head in amused disbelief. "You know, you're almost to the bottom of the box, where all the chocolate dust is hiding. It's really good. Might as well."

Kendra looked into the box, sniffed it, then dumped the cereal remnants into her bowl. She stirred the cereal with her spoon and resumed eating. Her eyes widened. "You're right."

"Make sure you drink the milk at the bottom. Whatever is left will be delicious."

Kendra nodded, gulping down another mouthful.

Seth glanced at the clock. "I should get out to the bus stop, unless you're serious about ditching. If you were, I'd stick around to witness the miracle."

Kendra stared at him as if tempted, then rolled her eyes. "You know me better than that."

"Do I? You almost had me going. Dad already left for work, Mom went to her painting group. We could pull this off."

"Better hurry. There's nobody here to drive you if you miss the bus."

Seth snatched his backpack and headed for the door.

"Don't just leave your junk on the table!" Kendra called.

"Could you grab it for me? I let you have the best part of the cereal."

"You're such a pest!"

Seth walked out the door. He still felt frustrated that Kendra had foiled his plans for a gold-funded Christmas. All of that work—hauling the batteries to Fablehaven to trade with the satyrs, collecting his payment from the nipsies, returning only part of the gold to Grandpa before sneaking the rest out—had gone to waste. Then again, he could still set aside a little gold and pretend to return it all the next time they visited Fablehaven. But with Kendra around, who knew when he could find a chance to convert gold into cash undetected?

His sister had sure been acting odd this morning. He had walked in on her smelling the decorative soap in the bathroom. Not just taking a whiff—she had been cupping the lavender rosebuds in her hands and inhaling with her eyes closed. And he knew from experience that consuming three huge bowls of sweet cereal would lead to a serious stomachache. Kendra normally ate a smallish, healthy breakfast. Furthermore, what was with her comment about ditching? Even as a joke, that was out of character. He wished she hadn't planted the idea of skipping school in his brain. The possibilities were attractive.

When Seth saw the yellow bus lumber around a corner down the street, he hustled to the bus stop, taking care not to slip and fall with an audience watching. He arrived just in time, and his thoughts turned to horsing around with his friends.

※ ※ ※

As he descended the bus steps after school, Seth felt as though an enormous weight had been taken from his shoulders. Winter break was nothing compared to summer, but it was still long enough to pretend that school would never happen again. Walking to his house, he kicked chunks from the crusty snowbanks, scattering an icy spray with each impact. He found the front door locked. Mom had mentioned that she might be off running errands. He took out his key and let himself inside.

In the kitchen, Seth foraged for snacks in the cupboards. They were out of the best stuff, so he settled for Doritos and chocolate milk. After the snack, he plopped down in front of the TV and flipped through the channels, but of course nothing was on but talk shows and worse. He hung in there for some time, skipping around, hoping variety might substitute for quality, but eventually he surrendered. When he turned off the TV in despair, inspiration struck.

Mom was gone. Dad was at work. And for perhaps the last time in a while, Kendra was absent. He knew that she occasionally received letters from Gavin. Back in October, while hunting for the Journal of Secrets, Seth had found two notes buried in her sock drawer. Each had contained all sorts of awesome information about dragons. But then

Kendra had chosen a new hiding place. He was sure that she had received more letters, but he had not recently found an opportunity to search thoroughly.

Hurrying up the stairs, Seth felt exhilarated and a little guilty. He trotted to Kendra's room and peeked between her bookshelf and the wall. Nothing. She used to keep the Journal of Secrets there. Like the letters, she had apparently moved it to a less obvious spot.

He started opening drawers, pawing carefully through the neatly folded clothes inside. Part of him wished he could accelerate the search by dumping her junk on the floor and kicking over furniture, but obviously it was crucial that he leave no evidence of his intrusion. Why did his sister have so many drawers, so many clothes? As the process began to feel painfully slow, he started to reassess how badly he cared about seeing the letters.

He went to the center of the room, hands on his hips, eyes scanning high and low. Kendra was no moron. Where might she have chosen to hide the letters? Where was a really tricky spot? Maybe she had taped them under her desk? Nope, nothing there. Inside the vent in the wall? Not there either. Between the pages of her mammoth dictionary? No dice.

Seth began working his way through her closet. Inside a shoebox? Inside a shoe? On a shelf? Behind and beneath some sweaters on a high shelf, he found the Journal of Secrets and the umite candle stub.

He was surprised that she still kept something so important in a fairly obvious place. He would have hidden it behind the insulation in the attic or somewhere else truly out of the way.

Unbeknownst to Kendra, Seth had found the Journal of Secrets before. He had lit the umite candle, pondered the undecipherable symbols, realized he would never know what the book said without her to translate, and carefully replaced it behind her bookcase.

Seth flipped open the journal, in case she had stashed the letters inside. Nope, just blank pages. He considered hiding the journal in a different spot to demonstrate that she needed to keep it in a smarter place. The exercise would serve as a reproachful object lesson. But of course if he did that, his sister would know he had been snooping around her room, which would only lead to trouble.

And then, without warning, Kendra entered the room.

Seth stood frozen, his eyes dropping from his sister to the journal in his hands. What was she doing home? She should be at the day care for another hour!

"What are you doing?" Kendra accused sharply.

Seth tried to appear calm while he struggled to recover from the surprise and devise a plausible response. Meeting his sister's stern gaze, he resisted the urge to try to conceal the journal. It was too late. She had seen it. "I wanted to make sure you'd hidden the journal in a safe place."

"You have no right to come in here and go through my stuff," she stated flatly.

"I wasn't hurting anything. I was just bored." He held up the journal. "You didn't hide it very well."

Kendra's clenched fists quivered at her sides. When she

spoke, she sounded barely in control. "Don't try to pretend you're my watchdog. For starters, Seth, you need to admit that what you did was wrong. You can't pretend that this was okay."

"I was invading your privacy," he admitted.

She relaxed a tad. "Was that right or wrong?"

"Wrong to get caught."

Her face reddened. For a moment it looked like she would charge him. Seth was startled by the extent of her reaction. "Have you done this before?" she asked, voice strained.

Seth knew he should placate her. But when people got this mad at him, even if they were right, it made him feel belligerent. "Would you believe that the first time I ever snuck into your room happened to be the one day you came home early? Talk about terrible luck!"

"I know you think that everything is a big joke. That no rules apply to you. But I'm not going to let this slide."

He tossed the journal on her bed. "Settle down. It isn't like I can read it."

She huffed. "I'm surprised you would read anything on purpose."

"You know what I like to read? Love letters. Those are my favorites."

Kendra trembled with rage. He noticed her eyes flick to the bed. Seth tried not to smile. What was with her today? She was normally more clever than this. And less angry. "Get out," she seethed. "Just wait until Mom and Dad get home."

"You're going to bring Mom and Dad into this? Are you

planning on telling them about Gavin's letters and your secret Fablehaven journal? Grow a brain."

Face contorted with rage, Kendra rushed at him. Seth was taller than his sister, but not by much, and he found himself staggering away from her, blocking ferocious punches. What was with her? She was aiming at his face with closed fists! They had often wrestled around when they were younger, but she had never gone after him like this. He didn't want to try to pin her down or push her away—that would just enrage her even more. Instead, he deflected the onslaught as best he could, maneuvering around so he could retreat out the door.

Fortunately, Kendra did not follow him into the hall. She lingered in her doorway, eyes fierce, hands gripping the door frame as if holding herself back from further violence. From below came the grumble of the automatic garage door grinding open. Kendra's expression melted from angry to worried and perhaps ashamed. "Stay out of my room," she said numbly, shutting the door.

In his room, Seth examined the bruises forming on his forearms. Something was definitely out of whack with his sister. Was she having trouble at school? Getting a B in some class? Maybe she had received bad news from Gavin. Whatever the cause, he definitely needed to go easy on her for a few days. Clearly, something had upset her enough to drastically alter her personality.

Seth awoke late that night to a gentle tapping at his window. He sat up, blinking, and squinted at his digital clock—3:17 A.M. The only light in the still room came from the face of his clock and the moonlight seeping in through the softly glowing curtains. Had he really heard a tapping sound? He plunged back into his pillow, curling up and snuggling into his comforter. Before sleep could enfold him, the tapping was repeated, faint enough that it might be only a twig scraping his windowpane as a branch shifted in a gentle breeze. Except there was no tree near his window.

More alert now that he realized the tapping had not been hallucinated, Seth scooted out of bed and crossed to the window. Pulling a curtain aside, he found Warren, looking a bit haggard, crouched on the narrow shelf of roof beyond the glass. He had already removed the screen.

Seth reached to unlock the window, then hesitated. He had been burned before by recklessly opening a window. There were creatures in the world that could disguise themselves with illusions.

Warren nodded, acknowledging the hesitation. He gestured toward the street. Leaning his cheek against the cool glass, Seth could see where Elise stood beside one of the cars they had been driving. She waved.

It might not be concrete proof, but Seth felt convinced. He opened the window. Shockingly cold air flowed past him.

Warren crept inside. As far as Seth knew, this marked the first time any of his bodyguards had entered the house.

Back when Tanu was watching them, he and Seth had talked quite a bit, but it had always been outside. Only something extraordinary would have motivated Warren to drop by like this.

"You're not going to turn into a goblin and try to kill me?" Seth whispered.

"It's really me," Warren said quietly, "although you probably shouldn't have let me in, even after seeing Elise. The Society would stop at nothing to get to you."

"Should I get Kendra?" Seth asked.

Warren held up both hands. "No, I approached you like this so we could talk in private. Elise and I are concerned about your sister. Have you noticed any odd behavior recently?"

Guilt surged through Seth. "She wasn't herself today. Mainly it was my fault. She caught me snooping around her room and went ballistic."

Warren eyed Seth thoughtfully. "Did her reaction seem extreme?"

Seth paused. "I shouldn't have been in there. She had a right to be mad. But yeah, it was really extreme."

Warren nodded as if the description fit his expectations. "Kendra snuck out of the house earlier tonight, a little after one. She went over the back fence. Elise was on watch. She spotted Kendra and followed from a distance."

"Kendra knows she isn't supposed to go anywhere without you guys," Seth interrupted. "Why would she try to give you the slip? It isn't how she operates."

"You're right, it doesn't fit her behavioral pattern, but

it gets much worse. Elise followed your sister to a public mailbox, where Kendra deposited a letter. You understand, Seth, our mission is to protect you from outside influences, and part of that mission includes protecting you from yourselves. Once Elise made sure that Kendra was safely back in the house, she verified that I was on guard and returned to the mailbox. She got inside, located the envelope Kendra had mailed, and checked to see what information it contained."

"You guys go through our mail?" Seth asked, unsettled.

"Routine screening," Warren assured him. "We have to make sure you don't accidentally leak compromising information. Especially when a letter is mailed under such suspicious circumstances. We don't check the mail you send through us to your grandparents—just communication to outside parties."

"I assume Kendra messed up?"

Warren held up an envelope. "The message she sent was no mistake. Have a look."

Seth accepted the envelope. Warren clicked on a flashlight. The envelope was addressed to T. Barker at a post-office box in Monmouth, Illinois. "Any idea who this is?" Seth asked.

"No clue. Doesn't ring a bell?"

Seth considered the question. "I can't think of any Barkers. As far as I can recall, we don't know anybody in Illinois."

"Read the letter."

The envelope had been expertly opened. Nothing ripped, no evidence of intrusion. It could easily be resealed and mailed. He removed the folded paper inside and read the following:

Dear Torina,

They keep a close watch on me here. I'm not sure if I'll find another chance to forward more info. I'm unsure whether they have the phones tapped, so I'll probably stick to mail. By the way, so far so good. Nobody suspects, although Seth has been a pain.

I have key information. They found one of the artifacts! The Chronometer is in their possession at Fablehaven! They also have a journal from Patton Burgess. He claims to know the location of other artifacts. Those locations are not described in the journal, but are hidden at Fablehaven in a secret room beyond an area in the dungeon called the Hall of Dread.

I'll try to write again if I learn anything essential. Before I finish here, I will try to hide Patton's journal near the old tree house at the creek along Hawthorn Avenue.

Faithfully yours,

Kendra Sorenson

Seth looked up at Warren. "What is going on?"

"Good thing we screen letters, although we never expected a note like this. Imagine the consequences if this message fell into the wrong hands."

"It looks like her handwriting."

"I'm confident that Kendra wrote it."

"Is Vanessa out of the Quiet Box? Maybe she was controlling Kendra in her sleep."

Warren shook his head. "I considered the possibility and

contacted your grandfather. He checked. Vanessa remains in her prison. But that sort of thinking may be along the right lines."

"Somebody must be blackmailing her or controlling her. She would never just betray us! Not on her own!"

"I can't imagine that she would. Yet it is tough to read this letter and not see a deliberate attempt at crippling betrayal. Elise doesn't know Kendra very well. She wants to take her into custody."

Seth stood up. "She can't lock up Kendra!"

"Simmer down. I'm not saying that is the only option. But whatever the method, given all that is at stake, immediately silencing Kendra has become necessary. I don't want to incarcerate your sister, but we have to get to the bottom of this."

"Do we confront her?" Seth wondered aloud. "Spring this on her and watch how she responds?"

"I'd love to hear an explanation. I haven't managed to conjure up a reasonable one."

"Unless somebody is using mind control."

Warren shrugged. "After reading that letter, nothing would shock me. Whatever we do, we mustn't disturb your parents."

"You want to confront her right now?"

"We can't wait on this. Besides, moving now should catch her off balance. If she's a little groggy, it may help us extract honest answers."

"Okay." Seth led Warren to his door. "You're right that we don't want to wake Mom and Dad."

"They don't appreciate strange men visiting their home in the middle of the night?"

Seth chuckled darkly. "It wouldn't be a good scene."

"Let's go find out why your sister is mailing potentially disastrous letters."

Seth led Warren into the hall and tiptoed to Kendra's door. He gently tried the knob. "Locked," he mouthed. He leaned close to Warren. "We don't need a key. Just a pin or a paper clip. Something skinny to poke in the hole and pop the lock."

Holding up a finger, Warren removed what looked like professional lock-picking gear from a pocket. He quietly inserted one of the slender instruments into the tiny hole by the doorknob, and the lock clicked. Pocketing the tools, Warren swiftly opened the door and strode into the room with Seth right behind him.

Kendra sat cross-legged on her bed reading a letter. She looked up, annoyed at first, then perplexed as she recognized Warren. "What is it?" she asked.

Seth closed the door.

"You're up early," Warren said.

"I've had trouble sleeping," Kendra replied, folding the letter.

"We need to talk," Warren said.

Kendra shifted uncomfortably. "Why?"

Warren held up the envelope she had mailed earlier in the night.

For a moment her face betrayed pure terror. Then she scowled. "How dare you go through my personal—"

"Don't even try it," Warren cut her off. "I need honest answers right now or we're carting you away. There was nothing personal about this note. It was naked treachery. Why, Kendra? We need an immediate explanation."

Kendra's eyes darted around the room as she flailed for a response. "I wasn't sending it to an enemy."

"I never said you were," Warren replied. "Sending this type of information to anyone outside our circle of trust would qualify as a major betrayal. I have never heard of Torina Barker. Who is she?"

"Please, Warren, you have to trust me, you know I would never—"

"'I will try to hide Patton's journal near the old tree house at the creek along Hawthorn Avenue,'" Warren read. He lowered the letter. "You're right, Kendra, I would never have suspected you capable of this kind of disloyalty. Explain yourself."

Her mouth opened and closed wordlessly. Suddenly her eyes filled with pain and worry. "Please, Warren, don't ask more questions, I had to do it, they made me, I can't explain."

Warren studied her shrewdly. "This feels like an act. Seth?"

"She's lying," he agreed.

Abruptly Kendra looked angry. "I can't believe you would treat me like this."

"What I can't believe is how clumsily you keep jumping from tactic to tactic," Warren said. "Who am I speaking with? I'm not convinced that Kendra's mind is behind these words."

"It's me, Warren, of course it's me. Remember how I helped restore you from being an albino? Remember how we faced that three-headed panther with Vanessa? Ask me anything."

"Why did you forget the combination to your locker?" Warren wondered.

"What?"

"I was watching you at school today. You had to go get help from the office to open your locker. Why?"

"Why does anybody forget anything?" Kendra protested, her voice unsteady. "The numbers just slipped my mind."

"Why did you come home early from day care?" Seth asked.

"Rex was out sick. The lady replacing him said she didn't mind if I ducked out early."

Seth took a step toward his sister. "That is not a very Kendra-like thing to do. You're right, Warren. This isn't her. I don't think it has been her all day."

"I'm your sister," Kendra insisted, eyes pleading. She jammed her hands into her pockets.

Seth waved a finger. "No. You are definitely not my sister. Know what you are? You're a pig! I've never seen anyone down so many Cocoa Krispies!"

Warren grabbed Kendra's arm. "I need you to come with me, whoever you are, until we can ensure you have released your hold on Kendra's mind." He spoke harshly.

Kendra slapped her free hand to her lips and swallowed. Warren pushed her back onto the bed, trying to swab her mouth with his finger. Kendra laughed. "Too late, Warren," she said around his intrusive finger. She started to cough. "Quick-acting, leaves almost no trace. Everyone will think it was a stroke."

"That was poison?" Seth asked, looking stricken.

Kendra pouted at him and nodded. "No more big sister. Hope you two are," she started gagging and then recovered, "are proud of yourselves."

Her body began to convulse.

"Do something!" Seth urged.

Warren leaned forward, gripping Kendra's chin. "Whoever you are, you will pay for this."

"Doubtful," Kendra choked.

The convulsing stopped. Warren checked for a pulse in her neck. "She's not breathing." He pressed an ear to her chest, then started CPR.

Seth watched in horror, his legs weak beneath him, as Warren relentlessly attempted to revive his sister's body. He wished she was awake and angry and punching him, whether her mind was in control or not—anything but this!

After several minutes, Warren finally backed away from the dead body. "Seth, I don't know what to say."

"You better leave," Seth sobbed, cheeks soaked with tears. "Mom and Dad can't find you with her like this."

"I should have . . . I didn't realize . . ."

"Who could have seen that coming?" Seth said hoarsely. He approached his sister, trying to find a pulse, caressing her face, searching for any sign of life. There was none.

Warren helped Seth tuck her in under her covers. Mom and Dad would think she had passed away peacefully in her sleep. Seth could not stop crying.

Finally Warren helped Seth back to his own room and into bed, then slipped out the window and replaced the screen. Seth found he could not sleep. Soon his pillow was drenched. He could not stop obsessing about the lifeless body in his sister's room. After all they had been through together, Kendra was gone.

CHAPTER FOUR

Captive

When the minivan eased to a stop in the darkness, Kendra had no idea whether they had reached their final destination. Bound and gagged in a cramped, enclosed trailer hitched behind the maroon vehicle, she had surrendered to the dismal theory that she might spend the rest of her life being shuttled from campground to campground.

Kendra had spent the previous day tethered to a tree in a remote, wooded camping area, eating applesauce, baked beans, and canned pudding. A modest campfire had held off the chill, but it occasionally became almost unbearable when the smoke wafted her way. This was after being transferred from the day care to the trailer in the dead of night, then driving for hours on highways and winding roads.

The phony Rex did not converse much, but he had tried to keep her relatively comfortable. Multiple quilts currently bundled her, and she rested on several pillows. The stingbulb impostor made sure she remained fed and hydrated. But there were plenty of inconveniences. She had not been able to use a real restroom, the gag was obnoxious, and her bindings had proven frustratingly secure.

Suddenly, the door at the back of the trailer rolled up and two figures shone flashlights at Kendra. She blinked and squinted into the light as the figures approached, wrapped her up in one of the quilts that surrounded her, and lugged her out of the trailer. Kendra opted not to squirm. What was the point? Bound and gagged, the most she could accomplish by resisting was to get dumped on her head.

As the strangers carried her, part of the quilt fell away from her face and Kendra found herself gazing up at a big, run-down house against the backdrop of a starry sky. Inside her cocoon, she traveled up the porch steps and through the front door. Though the house was unlit, no amount of darkness could blind Kendra, and she saw that the interior was better furnished than the exterior would have suggested. She tilted as the strangers toted her up a staircase, then leveled out as they hauled her through a set of double doors and deposited her on the glossy wooden floor of a brightly lit room.

Glancing up, Kendra saw that one of the men lugging her had been the Rex impostor, the other a heavyset, bearded man wearing dark glasses. The two men withdrew, and Kendra shifted her attention to the room. Vibrant abstract art adorned the walls, tastefully illuminated by tracks of lights on the ceiling. A stylishly designed clock accented with neon hung above an ornate mantel. Dynamic metal sculptures of various sizes added further personality to the room.

"So you're what all the fuss has been about," a feminine voice declared.

Kendra rolled over to face the speaker. Apparently in her fifties, the woman had a slender figure and wore an elegant red gown. Her heavy makeup was well applied. The hand resting on her hip glittered with rings. She wore her blond hair short and curly, the style seeming a tad too young for her age.

The woman walked toward Kendra, high heels clicking, and pulled a switchblade from her handbag. The blade snapped into view. Kendra stared with wide eyes. Wearing an unreadable expression, the woman bent over and cut the gag away without scratching Kendra's cheek.

"Don't you dare scream," the woman chided breezily. "No one will hear you, and my nerves can't abide it."

"Okay," Kendra said.

The woman smiled. She had full lips and a broad mouth. Perfect teeth. Her light blue eyes were wide-set, her nose a bit thick, her ears small, her face shaped a little like a valentine. Even though some of her individual features almost seemed unfortunate, overall her face retained an undeniably striking beauty. The years were trying to steal her looks with creases and lines, but she was successfully retaliating with cosmetics. "Am I the kidnapper you expected?"

"What are you going to do with me?" Kendra asked boldly.

"Untie you, if you promise not to make a ruckus. I must

look like a rusty old relic to you, but please believe me that under no circumstances could you possibly fight your way out of this room. I'll make you sorry if you try."

"You don't look old," Kendra said. "I won't try to escape. I know you have henchmen."

"You are in serious danger of getting on my good side," the woman said, bending down with her knife. The keen blade whispered through the cords.

Sitting up, Kendra massaged where the bindings had left marks. "Who are you?"

"I'm Torina," the woman said. "Your host, your captor, your confidante—however you prefer to think of me."

"I think *kidnapper* probably nails it."

Torina tilted her head, absently fingering her pearl necklace. "I'm glad you have some spunk. I'm keeping a low profile these days, which means I'm slumming in a small Midwestern town breathing the same air as goats and hogs and cattle." She closed her eyes and shuddered. Her crystal blue irises reappeared, locking on Kendra. "Maybe you can relieve some of the blandness."

"Are you some kind of witch?" Kendra guessed.

Torina smirked. "I can stomach audacious if you keep it polite. Fortunately for you, I've met some smoking hot witches in my day, so I take no offense. I'm not a witch, per se, though I know my fair share of magic. Inside these walls my identity is no secret. I'm a lectoblix."

"The type that can suck away the youth of other people?"

"Not bad," Torina said, impressed. "Yes, I drain vitality from others in order to remain young. Before you start formulating smart comments, no, I have not done so in quite some time, which explains my haggard appearance. I prefer not to gratuitously abuse my ability."

"You don't look haggard," Kendra assured her.

Torina regarded Kendra through lowered eyelids. "You have a knack for imitating sincerity. How old would you peg me?"

Kendra shrugged. "Late forties?" She deliberately guessed a little young. Early fifties would have been more honest.

Eyes suspicious, Torina uttered a brief, amused laugh. "My body is currently sixty-two."

"You're kidding! You really look much younger," Kendra said, noticing that Torina could not resist looking pleased. "But if you've drained vitality from others, you must be older than sixty-two."

"Goodness, yes, child! I would never divulge my actual age! You'd think you were conversing with a mummy!"

Studying her stylish captor, Kendra took a shuddering breath. "Are you going to suck away my youth?"

Torina chuckled. Her smile suddenly appeared brittle, and though the laugh was meant to dismiss the possibility as ridiculous, it carried a predatory undertone. "No, Kendra, you silly thing, the Sphinx would have my head! Besides, I live by a code. I am opposed to draining children. It stunts their growth, turns them into freaks. Too unfair." Torina paused, briefly scraping the corner of her lips with a long fingernail. "Then again, should you try to escape, I would have no choice but to hinder the attempt by those means which are available to my kind." Her eyes glittered.

"You don't have to worry about that," Kendra claimed.

"No, I don't," Torina agreed. "The windows are all barred. The bars are invisible, so as to avoid unwanted attention. The doors are locked and powerfully reinforced. I could leave you unsupervised and you would have no hope of escaping. But I have guards, and my whisper hound."

Grandma and Grandpa Sorenson had a whisper hound guarding the prisoners in the basement. Kendra did not know too much about it. "What does a whisper hound do?"

"Funny you should ask," Torina remarked, crossing to the door through which Kendra had entered. She opened the door and spoke a command in a foreign tongue. A gust of cold wind rushed through the doorway. "Keep very still, Kendra."

Kendra sat rigidly on the wood floor as frosty air swirled around her. The air settled, stirring mildly, and became even colder, a penetrating chill that made her teeth chatter. She held her breath as the frigid air caressed her strangely. Torina issued another unintelligible command, and the cold pocket whisked away, gushing out the door.

"Now that the whisper hound has your scent, escape is out of the question," Torina said, closing the door. "Bars on the windows are a needless redundancy. As are my associates who will assuredly keep a sharp eye on you. As are the spells I have in place on the doors."

"I get it," Kendra said glumly.

"For your sake, I hope you do. Now, dearest, I know it is no fault of yours, but you reek of wood smoke and tree sap. I am sorry to have subjected you to the outdoors. Such torture is cruel and unusual, but poor Rex was doing his best to keep a low profile. Our first order of business will be to restore you to a presentable state. You'll find a fresh outfit in my bathroom along with such amenities as you may require."

Beckoning for Kendra to follow, Torina clicked across the floor, through a doorway, and into a tastefully decorated bathroom. Kendra traced a hand across a granite countertop, taking in the groupings of expensive-looking cosmetic products. The heady aromas of fine soaps and lotions mingled in the air. Soft lights lined the mirror above the counter. Kendra thought her reflection looked unusually pretty.

"Amazing what proper lighting will do for a complexion," Torina observed airily. "Here are your things." She stroked a thick, soft towel and gestured at a green-and-white checkered dress. "You can use the jetted tub or the roomy shower. As for shampoos and body wash, what is mine is yours. I'll leave you with some privacy. I'll be nearby should you need anything."

"Thanks," Kendra said.

Torina exited, closing the door behind her. Kendra locked it. The bathroom had a window with opaque glass. It was large enough for a person to fit through. In case the invisible bars were a ruse, Kendra opened the window. It appeared to offer easy access to the roof, but when Kendra extended her hand, as Torina had promised, she could feel metal bars blocking any exit into the cold night. She closed the window with a sigh.

Folding her arms and leaning against a wall, Kendra considered the opulent bathroom. She would almost have preferred confinement in a dingy cell. It would have felt less treacherous. She did not appreciate the illusions of friendliness and comfort. To Kendra, Torina came across like an alluring tropical plant poised to devour unsuspecting insects.

Yet here she was in a lovely bathroom, and she did need a shower, so she might as well. Kendra disrobed. Beneath her bare feet, the floor was tacky with hair-spray residue. The warm stream of the shower felt good, as did the perfumed body wash. After she had washed, Kendra lingered in the shower with her eyes closed, breathing steam, enjoying the sensation of the water running down her back, reluctant to end the solitary interlude.

Finally she shut off the water and toweled dry. She put on fresh undergarments and the checkered dress. Everything fit her just right.

Hair still damp, Kendra unlocked the door and returned to the trendy bedroom. Torina hastily pulled off a pair of reading glasses and tossed aside a celebrity magazine. Folding the glasses awkwardly and tucking them into her handbag, she stood up. "I was beginning to worry that you would never emerge."

"The shower felt good."

"The dress looks darling. Twirl for me."

Kendra obliged her.

"Very nice," Torina approved. "We should do something with your hair."

"I'm not really in the mood."

"Just style it a smidge? Or we could roll up our sleeves and have some real fun. Red and gold highlights? No? Another night, perhaps. I'm no amateur."

"I believe you. I'll take a rain check."

Torina smiled. "Shall we have a look around? Or should I just show you to your room?"

"I'm kind of tired."

"Of course you are, dear. But you must also feel unsettled, a stranger in a new place. Let me at least show you the aquarium, then I'll let you get some rest."

"You're the boss."

Torina led the way into the hall, heels clicking, hips swaying. Kendra followed, impressed by the décor. What would it cost to furnish such a large house so lavishly?

"Our aquarium is unique," Torina commented, pulling open an ornate pair of doors. "It doubles as our library."

Kendra halted in the doorway, astonished by the sight before her. Bookshelves lined the walls from floor to ceiling, interrupted by an occasional niche displaying antique scientific instruments. Bulky leather sofas and recliners offered plenty of places for a reader to relax, accompanied by a variety of handsome tables for added convenience. Aside from the lights in the ceiling, plentiful lamps contributed to the even illumination. But none of this held Kendra frozen in the doorway.

Dozens of fish drifted through the air, as if swimming in water. The more Kendra stared, the more details registered. Rays of various sizes patrolled the room, winglike fins flapping gently. An octopus clung to the side of an ottoman. Exotic fish with vivid stripes and splotches swam in synchronized schools. Crustaceans crept across the floor, antennae probing. A spotted, six-foot shark prowled the library in ominous circles.

In contrast to the bizarre vision before her, Kendra inhaled what seemed like normal air. Nothing in the room was even damp.

Torina sashayed into the spacious, fish-infested library. "Isn't it a marvel? Come on in!"

"What about the shark?" Kendra asked.

"Shinga? He's a leopard shark. We've never had any serious trouble out of him. The eels can get nippy—just stay away from the globe."

Kendra hesitantly stepped into the room, enchanted by the fish swimming all around her. "Can I touch one?"

"Sure. Try the big one with the yellow stripes."

The fish drifted within reach, fins flowing as if in water, and Kendra brushed a fingertip along its side. It felt slightly slimy, and surprisingly solid. "Are these real?"

Torina grinned. "Absolutely."

Kendra noticed an orange fish with an elaborate series of spines nearing the doorway. "Should we close the doors?"

"They can't get out."

Kendra crouched down beside the octopus, tipping her head so she could see some of the suckers on the tentacles. The body of the octopus flexed, pulsing strangely, and Kendra hastily stepped away. Three seahorses hovered nearby. Off to one side, beside a lamp, small fish gobbled up tiny fragments of floating matter. "This is so cool. How does it work?"

"The easy answer?" Torina asked, manicured hand on one hip. "Magic." She compressed her lips thoughtfully. "How could I put this in layman's terms? Imagine that in an adjacent reality, this library is full of water. A sturdy container holds all of it in place. Then imagine that these fish are able to inhabit both realities at once. They are fully interacting with both realities, while we remain oblivious to the water. That description isn't exact, but it conveys the proper idea."

"Unbelievable," Kendra breathed, warily watching the sleek shark glide by almost within reach.

"We may be surrounded by barnyards and outnumbered by livestock, but not even countless miles of farmland can deny us at least a few truly sophisticated amenities."

"How do you feed them?"

"Sometimes they devour one another, though we have some magical deterrents in place, particularly on the shark. Normally we just do to their food what we did to them, leave it floating in both realities, and they find it without much trouble." Torina clapped her hands. "I have tested your patience long enough. Allow me to escort you to your room."

Kendra let Torina usher her back into the hallway. Stealing a few backward glances at the surreal aquarium, she wondered how anybody would get any reading done in there. Torina directed Kendra up some stairs to a third level, where numerous doors flanked a narrow hallway. Kendra glimpsed an old man peering from one of the doorways, but he ducked away as they approached. Paying him no heed, Torina escorted Kendra to the third door on the right.

Beyond the door awaited a frilly trundle bed, a dresser, a bookshelf, a pair of nightstands, a modest desk, and a small private bathroom. The simple room had a single window and unadorned walls.

"This will be your room while you remain here," Torina said. "You're welcome to explore this floor. Please do not wander the rest of the house except by invitation. I would rather not resort to less comfy accommodations."

"You've been pretty nice for a kidnapper," Kendra said. "Too nice. It's really weird. Are you going to fatten me up and eat me?"

Torina pursed her lips and gently scratched at the corner of her eye. "The witch references are getting tiresome, dear."

"What will you do with me? You mentioned the Sphinx."

"You answered your own question. I'll do what the Sphinx tells me."

Kendra's mouth felt dry. "Will he be coming here?"

A sly smile crept onto Torina's lips. "I am not his keeper, but I expect he will, sooner or later. Look, darling, I have no desire to make your situation harsher than necessary. Believe me, you can't escape, and nobody will find you. Don't rock the boat, and I'll keep things bearable."

Kendra doubted she could get more useful information out of Torina. "Okay. I'll try to be good."

"Sleep well, Kendra."

Torina closed the door.

Kendra sat on the edge of the bed. What would the Sphinx want? Information? Cooperation? Would he torture her? Could she resist torture? Ancient as he was, he probably knew a million ways to get people to talk. There were plenty of secrets that she needed to protect. Would he want to use her fairykind ability to recharge spent magical objects?

Would he find ways to use her abilities to harm the people she loved?

She pictured the false Kendra currently sleeping in her bed. What was the impostor doing? Would she harm Seth or her parents? Supposedly the impostor had access to her memories. Was she already divulging secrets? Kendra lowered her face to her hands. By the time the Sphinx arrived, whatever secrets she possessed might be irrelevant.

There came a soft knock at the door. Kendra scooted off the bed and opened it. A pair of elderly men waited outside, one in a wheelchair, the other pushing.

"Welcome," said the man in the wheelchair. His white hair was disheveled. He wore thick horn-rimmed glasses, plaid pajamas, and felt slippers. A folded newspaper rested on his lap.

"Can we come in?" asked the man pushing the chair. Liver spots dotted his bald scalp.

"What do you want?" Kendra asked, not moving out of the way.

"To introduce ourselves," said the man in the chair. "We're your new neighbors."

The man behind the chair lowered his voice. "We know some things that might be of service." He winked.

Kendra stepped aside. "Isn't it late?"

"What do we care about late?" griped the man in the wheelchair. "Too many days are the same here. You get sick of it. A new face is front-page news." The bald man guided the wheelchair into the room.

"I'm Kendra."

"Haden," said the guy in the wheelchair. "The other geezer is Cody."

"We're not really geezers," Cody said. "I'm thirty-two. Haden is twenty-eight."

"Oh, no," Kendra said. "She drained you! What was it like? Can I ask?"

"The first bite is quick," Cody said. "It leaves you paralyzed. Then she really latches on, and you can feel your life ebbing away. Your body withers. Deflates. It doesn't hurt. It's dreamlike. Hard to describe."

"Torina can put on quite an act," Haden warned. "Don't trust her. Not for a second."

"Why do you guys live here with her?" Kendra wondered.

"We're prisoners," Haden said. "Torina chooses her victims wisely. I don't have any close relations. Even if I somehow busted out of here, old duffer like me, I'd have no place to go."

"Ditto," Cody echoed.

"So we cooperate," Haden said, resignation in his tone. "It beats the alternative."

"You don't want to end up in the basement," Cody cautioned. "Some of the other guys in our situation ended up down there. Not pleasant. They don't always return."

"How many of you are there?" Kendra asked.

Haden inflated his cheeks and exhaled slowly. "Seven, right now. Two in the basement. One on his deathbed. One mostly keeps to his room. Quiet type. And Kevin is her lapdog. Hangs on her every word. Steer clear of Kevin."

"Two others have died since I've been here," Cody added.

"That doesn't add up," Kendra complained. "You're talking about hundreds of years of vitality. Are there lots of lectoblixes here?"

"Just her," Haden said. "She's an old one, and she's slipping. Like a reusable battery that doesn't hold a charge anymore. Every year she ages, what, at least twenty-five?"

"Closer to thirty," Cody asserted.

"She steals forty or fifty years from us and consumes them in less than two."

"How terrible," Kendra said.

"She tries not to overindulge," Cody said. "She hates to show any wrinkles, but too many disappearances and she'll have to move the whole operation, find a new lair. She's been here close to twenty years, near as we can figure."

Haden lifted the newspaper from his lap and began unfolding it. "She's on the prowl for new blood. Been running this ad in all the nearby counties for a week now." He directed Kendra's attention to a certain want ad:

Wealthy Dowager
Seeks Young Male Companion
autumnalsolace@gmail.com

"This is how she nabs victims?" Kendra exclaimed.

Haden and Cody exchanged an uncomfortable glance.

"We were dumb enough," Cody said.

"Sounded like easy money," Haden admitted. "I was curious."

"She has something of a conscience, you see," Cody said.

"Especially when she gets on a talk-show binge," Haden interjected, rolling his eyes.

"She tells herself she's just sapping years from gold diggers. Taking from takers. 'Course, we never got a chance to take anything. And she didn't bother to find out what kind of guys we were."

"No worse than most. No malice. We just stumbled across the wrong ad."

"As some other poor fool will shortly."

"And then we'll have *another* new face."

Cody raised his eyebrows. "Misery loves company."

Despite the actual ages the men claimed, the duo sure acted like crotchety old fogies. It made Kendra wonder how much their aged bodies affected their personalities. "Speaking of new faces," she said, "what were you guys going to tell me? You know, to help me?"

Haden adjusted his glasses. "Don't trust her. Don't disobey or you'll end up in the basement. Don't make her angry."

Cody's face became solemn. "I saw her suck the last years out of a guy who didn't know when to lay off the insults. She got younger and he got . . . dead. She normally leaves her prey with some final years. She feels enough guilt to leave most of us something. But don't cross her. She's capable of ugliness like you can't imagine."

"You're scaring the girl," Haden complained. "Here's the best tip—flattery works wonders. Even when she knows you're laying it on thick, Torina can't help but respond to generous remarks. Pathetic, really. Way I see it, deep down she so desperately needs to feel admired, she absolutely treasures sugary words, especially about her looks."

"She's extra vulnerable right now, while her age is showing," Cody agreed.

Haden harrumphed. "Old or young, she's always a sucker for compliments. Not so much that she'd let you go or anything. But she'll make your life easier if you play to her vanity."

"Word to the wise," Cody said, adding a wink for emphasis.

"Now that we've made our introductions," Haden announced, "we had better leave this young lady in peace."

"Don't be in such a hurry," Cody complained. "One last question. Kendra, tell us, what did you do to earn her attention? Why did Torina bring you here?"

"Don't press her to spill her guts on a first meeting," Haden growled.

Cody shushed him.

"I think it's mainly because I have information she wants," Kendra said.

"You're part of her world," Cody confirmed. "Not some girl off the street."

"I know there are magical creatures hidden among us, along with other dangerous people like her," Kendra confirmed.

Haden and Cody nodded in silence.

"We don't know much about the supernatural," Cody said. "Only what we've gleaned since living here."

"Tread carefully," Haden advised. "We'll try to watch out for you, keep our hearing aids to the ground."

Cody wheeled Haden out the door.

"See you tomorrow, Kendra," Cody said.

"Good night, guys. Sorry you're in here."

Haden twisted in his chair and pointed at her. "Same to you but more of it."

CHAPTER FIVE

Mourning

The crusty snow gleamed beneath the winter sun, refracting the light in dazzling patterns, as if the graveyard were flooded with diamonds. Eventually the rising breeze pushed the vanguard of a fleet of threatening clouds across the sun, reducing the glare, leaving the cemetery cold and bleak. Here and there, flowers and tiny flags added splashes of color to the snow-choked graves.

Dressed in a dark blue suit, hair neatly combed, Seth sat with his back against an eight-foot obelisk, resting his wrists on his knees. The suit coat offered only flimsy protection against the chill, but he hardly noticed. His sister had recently been laid to rest in the family plot near his Grandma and Grandpa Larsen. He had quietly told his parents that he needed a few minutes by himself.

No tears pooled in Seth's eyes. He figured he had used up his lifetime allotment over the past few days. Now he felt numb and dry, as if all emotion had been wrung out of him.

Footsteps crunched through the icy snow, approaching from the side and behind. A moment later Grandpa Sorenson stood over him, hands in his pockets. "How you holding up, Seth?"

Seth kept his eyes on Grandpa's shoes. "I'm okay. How about you?" They had not found a chance to really talk yet. Grandpa and Grandma Sorenson had barely arrived in time for the services.

"You can imagine," Grandpa sighed. "The whole situation is an unbearable nightmare. We've been scrambling to piece together what happened."

Seth's head snapped up. "Find any leads?" This was what he needed. Everyone kept wallowing in the loss. He needed answers.

"Some. When you feel ready, we can—"

"I'm ready right now," Seth assured him. "I need to know how and why."

Grandpa nodded. "Some of our friends broke into the morgue and conducted an informal autopsy on Kendra. Seems to really be her. Not a changeling, at least. We still can't fathom what species of mind control may have been at work here."

"She wasn't herself," Seth stated. "It wasn't Kendra calling the shots."

"I'm sure of that," Grandpa agreed. "So is Warren. The man who ran the day care where she volunteered, Rex

Tanner, turned up dead in his condo over the weekend. What do you know about him?"

"Nothing. But that is really suspicious."

"A safe guess is that whatever happened to Kendra originated at the day care. But the trail is cold." Grandpa looked around, then motioned with one arm. "Your folks are gone. I told them I would bring you home. They were in no condition to argue. I want you to meet someone."

Seth heard more footsteps approaching, these much stealthier than Grandpa's. They rustled the snow rather than crunched. A bald black man wearing a long leather coat and dark, glossy boots came around the obelisk. Snowy gravestones reflected in his sunglasses.

"Seth, this is Trask," Grandpa said. "He's a detective and a Knight of the Dawn. He'll help us get to the bottom of this."

"You look the part," Seth said. "Do you ride a motorcycle?"

Trask stared down at him. "I'm sorry for your loss." There was a no-nonsense tone to his voice.

"Have you found out anything yet?"

Trask glanced at Grandpa, who gave a nod. "I spent the last couple of days in Monmouth, Illinois."

"Where the letter was addressed," Seth recalled.

"Kept an eye on the post office box. Spent some time at the local college, got to know the town and the outlying areas. Nice place. So far, we have nothing. I left a man watching the post office."

"I'm glad you guys followed up on the letter," Seth said.

"We're nowhere near done," Trask promised. "I want to

hear firsthand about any oddities you noted regarding your sister's behavior."

Seth recounted how Kendra had acted at breakfast, how she had come home early from the day care, how she had overreacted when she found him in her room, and the final tragic confrontation with Warren.

"All of this happened on the same day," Trask confirmed.

"Yep. Except the scary part with Warren was technically early the next day."

"No strange behavior the day before."

"Well, she kept to herself more than usual the evening before. Stayed shut up in her room."

"After she got home from the day care," Trask said.

"Right," Seth said. "She seemed very much herself the day before."

Trask turned his head toward Grandpa. "Everything points to the day care. Elise checked in the windows multiple times while Kendra was there. Nothing appeared amiss. I interviewed Ronda Redmond, a woman who works overlapping hours with Kendra. I presented myself as a private investigator. She claimed that the only time Kendra was out of her sight on the day in question was when Rex brought Kendra into his office for a minute or two to respond to a call from a parent. We've kept Ronda under heavy surveillance and have dug deep into her past. Whatever transpired, she seems to be an oblivious bystander."

"That brings you up-to-date," Grandpa said to Seth.

"I want to help find out more," Seth said. "Maybe you can use me as bait."

Grandpa shook his head. "We can't risk anything like that until we better understand what we're dealing with."

"Warren and Elise are no rookies," Trask said. "Neither am I. This was done with an unthinkable level of finesse. We'll get to the bottom of it, but time will be required. Unless fresh details come to mind, Seth, you could best serve our needs by returning to Fablehaven with your grandfather."

"To Fablehaven?" Seth asked.

"Tanu is already prepping your parents," Grandpa said. "Given their agitated condition over the loss of Kendra, and his skill with potions, they will soon arrive at the conclusion that you should spend Christmas with your grandmother and me."

"No," Seth protested softly. "I want to be here, helping the investigation."

"We can't protect you as well here," Trask said. "There are many causes for concern. We can't be certain the letter was the only communiqué sent to our enemies by whoever was posing as your sister. Who can say what they may have already learned? We need to assume a defensive posture until we have a more complete grasp of the situation."

"On your feet," Grandpa said, extending a gloved hand.

Seth took it and let Grandpa haul him up. On his feet, he gained a better appreciation for Trask's impressive height. They began walking across the snowbound cemetery.

"Have you kept track of Kendra's belongings?" Grandpa asked Seth.

"I hid the journal and the letters, like Warren told me. And I found the rain stick from Lost Mesa. She actually hid it really well, behind the drywall in her closet. She cut a small opening and slid it in, then sealed it up pretty good. It took some time to figure it out."

"We'll bring those belongings home with us," Grandpa said.

"Grandpa," Seth said hesitantly. "I took some gold from Fablehaven last summer. I felt I'd earned it doing business with the satyrs, so I didn't return all of it to you. Kendra caught me. Before she wasn't Kendra anymore. She isn't here to make me, but I wanted you to know I'll return it all."

Grandpa's eyes grew moist. He patted Seth on the back and nodded.

❖ ❖ ❖

The last time Seth had driven to Fablehaven, he had streaked through the night in the back of a flashy sports car piloted by Vanessa. The pace was considerably slower with Grandpa Sorenson at the wheel of a bulky SUV.

Grandpa and Grandma had spent two days consoling Seth's heartbroken parents while Tanu assisted Warren, Elise, and Trask with the homicide investigation. The days were frustratingly uneventful. No new clues were discovered. No enemies made a move. And they could find no ties between Rex and the Society of the Evening Star. The day-care supervisor appeared to have been an innocent victim.

Trask, Warren, and Elise had stayed behind to keep working. Unusually quiet and thoughtful, Tanu rode beside

Seth, the seat belt barely long enough to stretch across his massive Samoan frame. Grandma sat up front with Grandpa.

Seth tried to sleep, but could never quite get comfortable. His imagination refused to stop inventing scenarios to explain what had happened to Kendra. He tried to keep an open mind, even to the point of questioning whether magical mind control had actually been employed. If somebody had used brutal blackmail, the stress alone might have altered her personality. But what leverage could have motivated Kendra to betray her family? Maybe she thought she was protecting them from something worse. But what?

The cell phone rang, and Grandpa answered. After a moment, the SUV accelerated briskly. "Have you told Dougan?" Grandpa said. "Keep trying. Right, do what you can for him, we'll hurry." Grandpa set the phone aside.

"What was that?" Grandma asked, alarmed.

"Maddox showed up in the attic," Grandpa said. "He's a mess. Skinny, dirty, injured, sick. Coulter and Dale are doing what they can."

Although he was thrilled to hear that the fairy trader had returned, it saddened Seth to picture the robust adventurer sickly and weak. At least Maddox was alive. "He came through the bathtub?" Seth asked. The previous summer, he had learned that Tanu had taken a large tin washtub to the fallen Brazilian preserve in order to give Maddox a portal home. The washtub shared the same space as an identical washtub in the attic at Fablehaven. After an object had been placed in one washtub, the object would appear to be in both, allowing an accomplice to remove it from the other. When the washtubs were far apart, the linked space allowed items to be instantly transported over great distances.

"He did," Grandpa said. "After all this time. Well done, Tanu."

"Sounds like Maddox will need some healing," Tanu said.

"Which is why I'm stepping on the gas," Grandpa replied.

"When it rains, it pours," Grandma remarked.

❧ ❧ ❧

As the SUV turned off the road, Seth gazed out the window at the skeletal forest, amazed at how far he could see with the leaves gone and the undergrowth reduced to tangled twigs. He had previously only seen Fablehaven in summertime. Everything was now brown and gray, with a few snow patches lingering among the crumbling dead leaves.

The SUV raced down the driveway, through the gate, and up to the house. The gardens surrounding the house remained incongruously in bloom. Seth realized that the fairies must be responsible for the improbable verdure.

When they skidded to a stop, Tanu vaulted out of the car and dashed into the house. Ever since the call, he had been sorting through his potions and ingredients. Seth jogged inside after him.

Dale stood in the entry hall. "Hi, Seth."

"Where's Maddox?" Seth asked, unable to tell which way Tanu had gone.

"Up in your grandparents' bedroom. The nearest bed to the washtub."

"How is he?"

Dale whistled softly. "He's seen better days, but he'll pull through. You keep getting taller."

"Not as tall as you yet."

Grandpa and Grandma came through the front door together. "Where is he?" Grandma asked.

Dale led them up the stairs and down the hall to the room where Tanu sat in a chair beside the bed, rummaging through his potion bag. Coulter leaned against the wall in the corner. Maddox rested on the bed, lips dry, cheeks flushed, a filthy red beard hiding half of his face. "Good to see you, Stan," he croaked, craning his neck forward.

"Lie still," Tanu admonished. "Save words for later." The Samoan turned to look at Grandpa. "He's feverish, malnourished, and badly dehydrated. Probably has parasites. Broken wrist. Sprained ankle. Mild concussion. Cuts and bruises everywhere. Give me some time with him."

Grandpa shepherded the others out of the room. Coulter came with them. They gathered not far down the hallway.

"Has he divulged anything?" Grandpa asked in a hushed tone.

"He doesn't have the artifact, nor does the Society," Coulter said, passing his hand over his mostly bald head, matting down the tuft of gray hair in the middle. "He knows the location of the vault where the artifact is housed. I don't have details. Dale and I were trying to make him rest."

"Still no leads on the room beyond the Hall of Dread?" Grandpa asked.

Coulter shuddered. "Just a blank wall. I've spent some real time investigating, even though it isn't my favorite environment."

"You haven't found the room from Kendra's letter?" Seth asked. "I figured as caretaker you would already know all about it."

"The secret was not handed down," Grandma said.

"We aren't even convinced that we want to learn the possible artifact locations," Grandpa explained. "For now we just want to know we have access to the information should the need arise."

"What exactly is in the Hall of Dread?" Seth asked. "You guys never get very specific."

"Dangerous creatures that require no upkeep are jailed there," Coulter said. "They need no food or drink. Beings like the revenant we met in the grove."

"Do they radiate fear?" Seth asked.

"Some of them do," Coulter said. "Makes working down there a pain and a half. I'd normally prefer to stay far from those cells."

"Maybe I could help search for the room, since magical fear doesn't bother me."

Grandma shook her head. "No, Seth, in some ways that makes it more perilous for you. The threat posed by those creatures is real. Fear can be a good thing. It keeps us respectful of their power. Many of those entities could destroy Fablehaven if loosed."

"I wouldn't free them! I'm not a nut job!"

"But it might be interesting to see what they looked like," Grandpa suggested.

"Have you seen them?" Seth asked. "What do they . . . wait a minute, you're testing me."

"Curiosity killed the cat," Grandpa said. "And it has almost leveled Fablehaven in the past, if I recall accurately."

"I'd follow your rules," Seth said. "If the rule is no peeking, I won't even consider it."

"If we find a need for your special immunity, we'll make use of it," Grandpa promised.

"*If* you find a need," Seth muttered. "I bet you won't be looking very hard. Say, Coulter, how did you know Maddox had come through? I mean, he could only exit the bathtub he entered, isn't that how it works? To come out on our side, somebody needed to physically lift him out."

"That's exactly right," Coulter explained. "We posted Mendigo as a permanent sentry, watching the tub. Truth be told, we probably wouldn't have kept the overgrown puppet stationed there much longer. After all these months, there was scant room for hope."

Tanu opened the bedroom door and poked his head out. "I have him stabilized. He responded well to the treatments. I've advised him to sleep, but Maddox insists he wants to speak with you sooner rather than later. All of you."

"Is he up to it?" Grandma asked.

"He'll be all right. He's determined. He'll rest better after we give him a chance to be heard."

Grandpa led the procession back into the bedroom. Maddox sat propped up by pillows. His skin shone with perspiration, and his lips already looked less chapped. His eyes regarded them alertly.

"You don't have to stare like I'm in my coffin," Maddox said, his voice stronger than before. "Inviting as the mattress feels, this isn't my deathbed. I'd already be up and about if Tanu would allow it."

"You must have quite a tale to tell," Grandpa prompted.

"Aye, and I've learned a lesson or two. First and foremost—never accept assignments from the Knights of the Dawn." He winked at Seth. "Where's your sister?"

All of the other adults exchanged awkward glances.

"She's dead," Seth said flatly. "The Society got to her."

Maddox blanched. "My apologies, Seth, I had no idea. What a tragedy."

"Wasn't your fault," Seth assured him. "You've had plenty of your own trouble."

"How did you survive?" Grandpa asked.

"Hiding in caves, mostly. Wet, dark, narrow places. I found chambers where Lycerna couldn't reach me. Lived off terrible food, insects and fungus and the like. I lost track of time. Could hardly poke my head outside without something trying to bite it off. All openings to the cave remained heavily guarded, night or day, rain or shine. So I tunneled my own exit, made a break for the house, and found the washtub. If I hadn't found a coded message from Tanu informing me about my free ride home, I'd still be sloshing through half-flooded caverns."

"I'm glad my mission served a purpose," Tanu acknowledged.

"Then he saves me twice over, administering miraculous potions. I'm doubly indebted, my friend."

"Nonsense," Tanu said dismissively. "You were risking your neck for us in the first place."

"We're glad you made it out alive," Grandpa said. "We were beginning to lose hope."

Maddox winked. "Never count me out. I've survived some close scrapes in my time."

"Coulter mentioned that you have an idea where the artifact is located," Grandma said.

"That I do," Maddox replied. "I could draw a map, or even lead a team back there."

"A map would suffice," Grandpa said. "We'll want to move on this swiftly, and you're in no condition to go afield."

"I'm surprised you didn't return with some fairies in tow," Coulter said.

"Almost did," Maddox said, eyes brightening. "Came across some exotic specimens. I have a few patented methods for luring and befriending fairies, even under those dismal conditions. Without some help from the fairies, I could not have survived in the caves. I wanted to bring some with me, but in the end, I barely got out of there with my own hide intact. Wasted opportunity."

"You should rest now," Tanu urged.

"What about the map?" Maddox complained.

"We'll bring you materials soon enough," Grandma promised. "Close your eyes, recover some strength."

Maddox looked around the room, at each person in turn. "Thanks for pulling me out of there and giving me a place to land. I owe you all."

"On the contrary," Grandpa said. "We owe you for undertaking such a perilous mission. Get some rest."

Maddox closed his eyes and settled back into his pillows.

CHAPTER SIX

The All-Seeing Eye

"Okay, Kendra," Haden said, picking up a cunningly sculpted queen between a finger and a thumb. "Knowing how the pieces move and capture is only a small part of the game. Understanding position and values is crucial. I know a point system that ranks the values of the pieces in a useful way. Think of this queen as nine points." He set it down and touched the other pieces as he named them. "Rooks are five, knights three, bishops three, and pawns one. That should help you calculate if a sacrifice is worthwhile."

"What about the king?"

"Think about it."

"Right. Top priority. You can't really give it a number."

"Good. White moves first, so it's your turn."

Kendra studied her row of pawns. She could move one of eight pieces a square or two forward. "Is there a best first move?"

"The early moves establish a lot about the game. Just experiment."

Kendra bit her lip. "Isn't chess sort of a game for old fogies?"

Haden raised his eyebrows. "Do I look like a young guy to you? My legs don't work. Sort of limits my options. This keeps my mind agile. I'm excited to train a new opponent."

Kendra picked up the pawn in front of her queen and moved it ahead two squares.

Haden's door opened and Cody entered. "We have a visitor," Cody announced.

"Who?" Kendra asked.

"The latest fly has landed in Torina's web," he replied.

Kendra stood up. "The next person she wants to drain!"

Haden mirrored Kendra's move, his pawn blocking hers from moving further forward. "You'll get used to it," Haden murmured.

"We have to warn him," Kendra declared.

"That may not go over too well," Cody said. "We'd just rile Torina and make life worse for everyone, the new victim included."

"Have you guys totally given up?" Kendra accused.

"We've accepted the unavoidable," Haden soothed. "Have a seat."

"No thanks," Kendra said, storming from the room. Cody stepped aside to let her pass.

"Hardheaded," she heard Cody mumble behind her. She was walking too quickly to discern Haden's response.

She reached the end of the hall and started down the stairs. What was the worst that could happen? Torina might suck away her youth? Kill her? Lock her in the basement? Kendra clenched her fists. She was already a prisoner. What was the use of pretending to be a guest? At least this offered a chance to help somebody, and maybe in the process help herself. If she didn't take advantage of opportunities like this, she would never get away.

Kendra reached the second floor. A broad goblin dressed in a suit barred access to the stairway down to the ground floor. His gaunt red skin stretched over jutting cheekbones and a prominent jaw. Veins corkscrewed grotesquely at the sides of his bulging forehead. "Get back upstairs," he growled, baring uneven teeth.

"I need to talk to Torina," Kendra demanded. "It's an emergency."

"No games," the goblin snarled.

"I've never met you before," Kendra said. "I have no reason to obey you. I have to speak with Torina. It's urgent."

"What makes you think she's down there? The mistress is occupied. She will come to you later. You belong upstairs."

Kendra tried to step around him and descend the stairs, but the thick goblin seized her arm with a rough hand.

"This is none of your business," Kendra spat. "I have to go downstairs. You know I can't leave the house. Let go of me or the Sphinx will turn you into ground beef." They glared at each other for a moment. After a hesitant pause, the calloused fingers abruptly opened, releasing her arm.

"I'm not sure the Sphinx is yours to command," the goblin chuckled.

Kendra rushed down the stairs. Obviously the goblin had some doubts, but she did not bother to point that out. She trotted through the entry hall, pausing when she saw a young man standing in the parlor, admiring a large painting in a gilded frame. A battered suitcase and an overstuffed duffel bag leaned against a sofa not far from him.

"Who are you?" Kendra asked from the doorway.

The young man turned. He had dark hair that hung to his shoulders and a scraggly mustache. A few pimples dotted his pale face. He wore a black T-shirt and tight jeans. "I'm Russ. Have you seen Torina?"

Kendra entered the room. "Are you here responding to the ad?"

"You got it. Are you a relative?"

"I've been kidnapped. Torina is holding me prisoner. You have to leave immediately!"

Russ snickered. "Good one. I like it. Should I run off screaming and call the cops?"

"I'm serious," Kendra said. "Come on."

She raced to the front door. Russ followed, displaying only mild curiosity.

Kendra tugged at the door. It was locked. She jiggled the handle desperately. "Help me break it down."

"That will make a great first impression," Russ chuckled. "They need to put you in the movies."

Tears of frustration gathered in Kendra's eyes. "I'm

not acting, Russ. She's a psycho. She keeps old men and kids locked up here. There's no time! Please help me. Get away and contact Scott Michael Sorenson or Marla Kate Sorenson. They live outside of Rochester. My name is Kendra. I'm a missing person."

Through her tears, Kendra saw that Russ finally looked uncomfortable. He started chewing one of his fingernails.

"What are you carrying on about, my dear?" a silky voice inquired. Torina strolled down the stairs, her black evening dress shimmering with sequins. "Your mother won't be back until four."

Russ glanced from Kendra to Torina.

"Run, Russ," Kendra pleaded.

"Kendra, go easy on poor Russ, he isn't used to your antics. Why not run along and go play out back? Aunt Torina has arrangements to discuss with our new friend."

Kendra had been caught in the act. She couldn't see how she would get into worse trouble. It was all or nothing. "Russ, come out back with me, I need to show you something."

"He'll follow along in a minute or two. We have grown-up things to discuss." Torina clicked across the floor to Russ, taking his hand. "Shall we adjourn to the parlor?"

"Don't let her bite you, Russ, she'll suck you dry," Kendra warned. "Together we can take her, fight our way out of this."

Torina's radiant smile faltered ever so slightly. "Am I a vampire now? How novel! Young lady, I value a healthy imagination, but your behavior is bordering on impertinent. Jameson? Would you escort Kendra to her room?"

"Certainly, madam," answered a rough voice. The goblin in the suit strode down the stairs. He glowered at Kendra. Glancing at Russ, Kendra realized that he could not recognize the goblin's true form. To him, the monstrosity probably looked like an ordinary human butler.

Kendra raced for the back of the house, but the goblin intercepted her, gripping her shoulders painfully. The goblin steered her toward the stairs as Kendra screamed and writhed and tried to kick him.

"Such a display!" Torina exclaimed. "Your mother will hear about this, young lady."

"Look at them!" Kendra shrieked. "Locked doors, people dragging me away! Get a clue, Russ!"

"What's going on?" Russ asked, his voice nervous.

"The girl is mentally disturbed," Torina purred. "Let me tell you a secret."

The goblin heaved Kendra over his beefy shoulder. Staring back at Russ, she saw Torina nuzzle his neck, then catch him as he slumped to the floor, one leg twitching. As the goblin mounted the stairs, the pair passed out of sight.

☈ ☈ ☈

Kendra crouched over the desk in her room, refolding a piece of stationery. The note already had so many creases that it was almost useless. She had tried once again to improve on the only design that had sort of worked, and once again the result had been unsatisfactory.

She folded the paper into the familiar basic shape,

pressing hard on the creases, hoping the form would hold. When she finished, she held up the paper airplane, inspecting it from various angles. It would win no contests for beauty or function. She could almost hear Seth laughing at the pathetic attempt.

Why had she never learned to fold a proper paper airplane? Her brother could produce at least six varieties, all excellent flyers. They were sleek and simple, and he would add little extra tears or wrinkles to produce acrobatic effects.

The airplane she had designed after several miserable failures flew only a little better than crumpling up the paper and throwing it. She transported her ugly little plane to the window, opened it, and passed her hand between the invisible bars. Cold air flooded into the room. Experience had shown that a quick, gentle flick of the wrist was the best way to send the plane soaring. The dark night would conceal the flight, and hopefully some passerby would find one of the notes in the morning.

My name is Kendra Sorenson. I have been kidnapped. Please contact the police. Then contact Scott Michael Sorenson or Marla Kate Sorenson. They live outside of Rochester, New York. This is not a joke.

Not long after the goblin had locked Kendra in her room, she had decided to start an airborne letter campaign—the aeronautical equivalent of letters in bottles. Kendra debated about which way she should angle this next toss.

A key rattled in the door.

Kendra threw the plane and hurriedly shut the window, turning to face the doorway. Torina entered, exuding confidence. She wore the same flashy dress from earlier, but filled it out differently, her body now curvier. Her arms and legs were firm and toned, her skin soft and healthy. She wore much subtler makeup, relying on the natural radiance of her stunning features. Gazing triumphantly at Kendra, she looked like a prom queen ready for her big night.

After an awkward pause, Kendra realized that Torina was awaiting a compliment. "You look amazing," Kendra said.

"People can say what they want," Torina remarked casually, placing a hand on her slim waist. "Diet, exercise, pharmaceuticals, surgery, spa treatments, cosmetics—there is simply no substitute for youth."

"You drained him?"

"Much more ruthlessly than I would have without your intervention," Torina stated, eyes hard.

"Why?"

She closed the door and sauntered into the room. "The way I live grants me limited pleasures, Kendra. Toying with my prey is perhaps the most satisfying. I already had to settle for a less than adequate specimen. Then you soaked all the fun out of the whole encounter, forced me to rush it."

"I'm so sorry," Kendra apologized. "That must be rough when sucking someone's life away isn't super fun."

"Don't you dare mock me, missy," Torina hissed. Outrage tightened her youthful features. Tendons stood out in her neck.

"You're so beautiful when you're angry," Kendra said dramatically.

Torina's fury transformed into fierce laughter. "Even though you're joking, Kendra, you thought to say it, which means it must be true at some level." She wiped a tear from the corner of one eye and crossed to the desk, gathering up the papers there and opening drawers to collect any extra stationery. "No more airplanes. We gathered the ones you've thrown so far. Origami isn't your strong suit."

"They weren't very good," Kendra admitted.

"Understatement of the year," Torina murmured. "Look, normally I would relocate you to the basement for the stunt you pulled today. I gave you a lot of leeway and you burned me for it. But there is a certain euphoria that comes with regaining my youth, and the Sphinx will be here tomorrow, so you can just stay locked in here until he's ready for you."

Kendra's legs suddenly felt wobbly. "The Sphinx?"

"Why do you think I settled for a subpar specimen like Russ?" Torina said emphatically, snapping her fingers as if to get Kendra's attention. "Read between the lines. I wanted to look my best for a reason. Impress the boss. Aren't you the same girl who supposedly took down Vanessa Santoro?"

"You know Vanessa?"

"Knew Vanessa. Past tense. As you're well aware, the Sphinx's little pet bit off more than she could chew. She's out of the picture. Word was you had something to do with it. I can't fathom how. I mean, Vanessa was overrated, but the girl wasn't completely incompetent!"

"What does the Sphinx want with me?" Kendra asked.

Torina flashed a predatory grin. "Great question. I'll let you mull that one over until he sends for you tomorrow. Sweet dreams." She strode to the door. "By the way, dear, don't lose sleep planning a daring escape. The whisper hound was under orders to let you roam the house. Until instructed otherwise, it will now keep you confined to this floor. Once the hound has your scent, you can't fool it."

"Wait, can I just—"

Torina cut her off by firmly closing the door. Kendra heard the lock click. She returned to the window, staring out into the gloom, unsure how she would possibly sleep.

❊ ❊ ❊

Somebody was knocking on the door. Kendra squinted at the bright light pouring between her half-drawn curtains. She had rested poorly, waking many times in the night, plagued by unsettling dreams that evaporated under conscious scrutiny. And of course, once she had finally slipped into a deep sleep, somebody was pounding at the door.

"I'd invite you in, but the door is locked," Kendra called, still groggy.

"I have a key." It sounded like Cody. "And I have breakfast."

Kendra rubbed her eyes. She had slept in her clothes. "Come in, then."

The door opened and Cody entered with a tray. "Scrambled eggs, sausage, bacon, toast, yogurt, and juice," he announced, setting the tray on the desk. "You barge down the stairs, infuriate Torina, and end up with a first-rate breakfast. Maybe I should start acting a little less compliant!"

"Don't get too jealous. This may be my last meal."

Cody shrugged. "They're expecting visitors. They told me to deliver this. I'm supposed to suggest that you be on your best behavior. So I've suggested it."

"You want some bacon or something?"

He hesitated. "I couldn't take your food."

"Have a strip. And some sausage, too. How am I supposed to eat all that?"

"Personally, I'd use the toast to make a breakfast sandwich. If you're willing to part with a strip and a link, I'll call it my tip." Cody placed some bacon and sausage on a napkin and exited the room. She heard the lock reengage.

Kendra sat at the desk. Molten cheese glued chunks of ham to the fluffy eggs. The sausages glistened with grease but tasted good, and the bacon had a pleasant crunch. As she was sipping some juice, the door unlocked and Torina entered, wearing a flirtatious sundress and sandals.

"He's here," she announced, girlishly flustered. "Did you sleep in those clothes? Really, Kendra, we need to get you washed up and presentable." There was an edge of excitement to her expression and voice, as if she were about to greet her favorite rock star.

"Is he really going to care what I'm wearing?" Kendra replied, munching on a bite of toast.

"I care," Torina said. "How's breakfast? I made it for you."

"I'll be sure to let the Sphinx know how domestic you are."

"I am going to miss the music of your sarcasm," Torina pouted. "Done eating?"

"You didn't give me much time."

"He's early."

"Why don't we skip the shower?"

Torina giggled nervously. "Seriously, come now, or I'll have Jameson scrub you down."

Kendra drained the last of her juice. "You win." She stole a final bite of toast as she rose and followed Torina down to the lavish bathroom. Soon she stood under a warm spray, wondering how the upcoming encounter would play out. She had not seen the Sphinx since he had hidden behind a mask at a Knights of the Dawn gathering the previous summer. Now that he had been exposed as an enemy, what would he do with her?

She tried not to dwell on the possibilities. Worrying would just leave her rattled. She needed to relax and stay ready to deal with whatever problems actually materialized.

After finishing her shower and toweling off, Kendra put on the black slacks and blouse that Torina had laid out for her. In the mirror, the outfit actually looked pretty cute. She returned to Torina's room, and the blond lectoblix insisted that Kendra let her style her hair. Kendra reluctantly sat in a chair in front of the bathroom mirror while Torina added some curl.

"What do you think?" Torina asked at last, adding a final squirt of hair spray.

Kendra swiveled her head from side to side. The end result actually looked fabulous. "Guess I'm ready for my date."

"I'm glad you can still joke. You have now officially passed my inspection. Shall we?"

Kendra followed Torina down the stairs to the main level. On her way to the rear of the house, Kendra became peripherally aware of a group of adults conversing in the living room, but her focus remained on where Torina was heading. Stopping in front of a heavy wooden door, Torina rapped twice, then opened it, favoring Kendra with a sugary smile that silently conveyed, *you are no longer my problem*.

When Kendra entered the study, the Sphinx rose to greet her. The last time she had seen him unmasked had been outside the Quiet Box at Fablehaven. He was dressed simply, his maroon shirt untucked over dress pants, his feet bare. Short, beaded dreadlocks framed his ageless face. Dimly, Kendra heard the door shut behind her.

The Sphinx took her hand, clasping it affectionately in both of his. "I am so happy to see you again, Kendra," he said, his voice mellow, the accent prompting Kendra to envision tropical islands. The greeting was so warm and gentle that she almost found herself relaxing.

"I wish I could say the same," Kendra responded cautiously, removing her hand from his grasp.

"Please," he said, motioning to one of two chairs positioned to face each other. They both sat down. "You have ample reason to feel frustrated."

"You're a traitor," Kendra said. "What is it with people

pretending to be nice as they hold me prisoner? Torina has the same personality disorder. What do you want with me?"

"I mean you no harm," the Sphinx replied, unruffled. "I need to have a conversation with you. Cornering you has been a difficult task, now that I have fallen out of favor with your dear ones."

"You mean since you stole the artifact from Fablehaven, released a demon prince from captivity, torched Lost Mesa, and got Lena killed?"

The Sphinx leaned forward, fathomless eyes intent. "I always admire spirit, Kendra. I do not blame you for perceiving me as your enemy. I am aware of the pain my actions have caused. However, your comments raise a question. Why do you label the prisoner from the Quiet Box a demon prince?"

Kendra silently admonished herself for the outburst. She needed to say as little as possible. The Sphinx had no reason to suspect they knew that the occupant of the Quiet Box before Vanessa had taken residence there had been a demonic dragon named Navarog. Every tidbit that Kendra offered the Sphinx about what she and her family knew could potentially give him an advantage. "No reason."

He considered her in silence. "Not important," he finally decided. "How has Torina treated you?"

"She did my hair today. I think she has a crush on you."

"Did she show you her aquarium?"

"That was actually really cool."

"Agreed. How is Seth?"

"You tell me," Kendra said. "Hasn't the Kendra clone been reporting?"

"Remarkable fruit, the stingbulb. Almost everyone who knows of stingbulbs believes them to be extinct. But having lived many years and visited many places, I know where one stingbulb tree still grows. The tree does not bear many fruit in a year. They must be used within a narrow window of time or they are rendered useless."

"Is the phony Rex gone?"

"The forms the stingbulbs adopt survive only for a few days. He served his purpose."

Kendra looked away from the Sphinx's gaze. "What about the real Rex?"

"I honestly like you, Kendra. Unfortunately, we are on different sides of a heated struggle. You would be surprised if you knew all those who side with me on this issue. The conflict boils down to this: you and those you have aligned yourself with believe that magical creatures should be held captive at all costs, while I believe they should be free. Rex was an unfortunate casualty of that disagreement. There have been many before him, on both sides. He will certainly not be the last."

"Am I the next?" Kendra wondered.

"I don't think so," the Sphinx said. "I hope not. I need to perform an experiment. And I require information from you. Help me find answers to my questions and you will go home. Immediately and unharmed. Some profess to see courage in enduring hardship for a cause. This only makes sense when victory is possible. I have the means to involuntarily extract the required information from you. I see wisdom in graciously accepting the inevitable. Kendra, where is the artifact that was hidden at Lost Mesa?"

His sultry voice invoked a sort of trance, and Kendra found herself on the verge of answering the question. Gripping the arms of her chair, she kept her mouth clamped shut.

"Kendra, I am convinced that you either have the Chronometer or know where it is."

Kendra closed her eyes. His stare was too penetrating, as if his eyes could bore inside her mind and uncover the truth. "I don't know what you're talking about."

"You need to share every lead you have regarding the missing artifacts. Give me the information I require, and you will soon go free. Refuse to share the information, and, believe me, Kendra, I will take it."

Kendra opened her eyes. "There is nothing to take. There was no artifact at Lost Mesa. When I got back to Fablehaven, a demon was trying to destroy the preserve, so we killed him. End of story. Try and take what you want. I have nothing to give."

The Sphinx watched her closely. A small smile produced a pair of dimples. "You have more to give than you know, Kendra. Allow me to introduce two of my associates."

The door opened. A chubby man with pink skin and a black pompadour entered the room. An ancient brown lady with wiry gray hair rested her pruned hand on his elbow. Her shabby, homespun shawl contrasted with his pinstriped suit.

"Kendra, I would like you to meet Darius and Nanora," the Sphinx said.

"Charmed," Darius sniffed, looking Kendra up and down disapprovingly. Nanora stared silently. Was she drooling? "I understand you are reluctant to share what you know about the artifacts."

"There is nothing to share."

"Let me be the judge of that," Darius said. It seemed like he was trying hard to appear debonair. He laid a thumb beside his temple. Nanora raised her arthritic hands, twisting her fingers into a complex pattern and peering through a gap with one eye. Darius scowled and took a step closer. Nanora took a step back.

Apparently they were trying to read her mind. With all the force she could muster, Kendra mentally transmitted the message, "You are both idiots."

Darius glanced at the Sphinx, who nodded slightly. "Keep still, Kendra," the Sphinx said.

"Don't think about the artifacts," Darius cooed, leaning forward and placing the tip of one finger against Kendra's forehead. His eyes squeezed shut. Kendra stared at the thick gold ring on his pudgy pinky. Nanora tottered closer, her gaping mouth revealing a squishy lack of teeth.

"Too bright," Nanora rasped. Her mouth sounded full of saliva.

Darius stepped away, looking perplexed. "Nothing. You're right. She would be an interesting candidate."

"I'm unsurprised," the Sphinx said. "Have Mr. Lich bring the object."

"If you want, we could try——"

The Sphinx cut him off by raising one hand.

"Right," Darius said, withdrawing from the room.

"You have an unsearchable mind, Kendra," the Sphinx said. "Psychics are not my only recourse to unlock your secrets, just the least tedious."

"At least they came in on cue without you calling for them," Kendra said. "That part was sort of impressive."

Darius returned accompanied by Mr. Lich and a figure in a mask. Mr. Lich reverently carried a small red pillow. A silken square of pink cloth concealed an object on the pillow. The Sphinx gestured at a low table. Darius pulled it between Kendra and the Sphinx; then Mr. Lich set the pillow down.

The Sphinx reached out and removed the handkerchief. Upon the pillow sat a spherical crystal with countless facets. "Behold the Oculus."

"Looks expensive," Kendra said.

"Kneel beside the table," the Sphinx instructed, "and lay a hand on the sphere."

"Do you need it recharged? Is it going to suck out my secrets?"

Pointing at the crystal, Mr. Lich let out a brief grunt. The tall Asian man towered over Kendra, his long face humorless. Even back when she had thought the Sphinx was an ally, Mr. Lich had made her nervous.

The Sphinx held up a hand. "What Mr. Lich is trying to say is that if you refuse to comply, we will force you to touch the crystal. That would not be as safe for you as voluntary compliance."

"What is it?" Kendra asked.

"The Oculus. The Infinite Lens. The All-Seeing Eye. The prototype all seeing stones and scrying tools are hopelessly patterned after. It is the artifact from the Brazilian preserve."

"You found another one!" Kendra cried.

"When we first spoke, I discussed the topic of patience. I have exercised great patience for many centuries—learning, preparing, infiltrating. But patience proves futile without the will to take decisive action when the opportune moment arrives. My long-awaited window of opportunity has come at last. I will possess all of the artifacts sooner than you can guess."

"I won't charge it for you."

The Sphinx laughed softly. "The Oculus does not require energy from you. The artifact is functional. We want to see whether you can survive using it."

Kendra looked around the room at the many faces regarding her. "What do you mean?"

"This is the artifact of sight, Kendra. With it, you can see anywhere, everything."

"So why don't you use it to find the remaining artifacts yourself?"

"Most minds cannot handle the vast sensory input available through the Oculus. It has already put four of our best people into catatonic stupors. Given how your status as fairykind shields your mind from certain magic, we want to see if you fare any better than our colleagues."

"I refuse," Kendra said.

"If we force your hand onto the sphere, Kendra, it will surely overpower your mind. But if you participate voluntarily, and I guide you, there is a chance you will survive."

"If you fry my brain, you'll never learn what I know about the artifacts."

"We already know so much," the Sphinx said. "We received an extensive e-mail from the stingbulb facsimile we created of you. She felt suspicious she had been followed on her way back from the mailbox, so she risked electronic surveillance and sent the e-mail as a backup. She explained that your grandfather has the Chronometer at Fablehaven and that Patton Burgess left clues regarding some of the remaining artifacts. We know those clues wait in a hidden room beyond the Hall of Dread in the Fablehaven dungeon. We already have a plan in motion to recover the information. Our facsimile could not recall exactly how to access the room. They never remember everything. I'd love that information, if you have it—the password or trigger— but we'll get into the room with or without you. I'd love your help translating the journal, but we'll find someone who reads the required tongue with or without you. What I really want is to see if you can survive the Oculus. It is arguably the most powerful of the five artifacts. Mastering it is my highest priority. I am optimistic that you can survive."

Kendra had no idea what to say.

"Consider this, Kendra," the Sphinx continued. "If you succeed in mastering the Oculus, you can look anywhere, discern anything, and we will be none the wiser. You might find knowledge that will help you escape us, or beat us to the next artifact. There are plenty of self-interested reasons for you to look. The possibilities are endless."

"Then why give me a chance?" Kendra asked. "So you can torture the information out of me later?"

"Right now, a man in this town is at the local post office watching box 101 in hopes of intercepting a murderer. This man is here on behalf of your grandparents, hoping to catch the people who killed their granddaughter. I know what the man looks like. I want you to use the Oculus to describe him to me in detail. That is the first test. Will you try voluntarily?"

"You wish," Kendra spat.

The Sphinx glanced at Mr. Lich. The tall henchman grabbed Kendra's arm just below the elbow, dragged her out of her chair, and lowered her unwilling hand toward the Oculus.

"Wait," Kendra yelled. "I'll do it! Don't force me! I'll do it."

"Now?" the Sphinx asked.

"Now."

The Sphinx nodded and Mr. Lich released her. Kendra knelt beside the table, considering the intricate facets of the crystal globe. "You will want to close your eyes," the Sphinx instructed. "The Oculus will become your organ of sight. Many visions will compete for your attention. Your task will be to ignore the massive interference and focus your gaze on the post office. Find the man. It will be visually disorienting. If you lose control, you have permission to remove your hand from the crystal. Describe what you see, and I will help talk you through it."

"And if it blows my mind and I go insane?" Kendra asked.

"Another casualty of our conflict. I wish you well. Relax and focus."

Kendra took a deep breath. Unable to dream up another option, she extended a trembling hand toward the crystal. Tiny rainbows winked inside the glimmering sphere. When her fingers were almost there, she closed her eyes.

The instant her fingers came into contact with the cool surface, it looked like her eyes had opened, even though she could clearly feel that they were still closed. She stared at the Sphinx. Then she realized that she could also see Mr. Lich standing behind her, as if she had a second pair of eyes in the back of her head. No, more than that. She could see forward and backward, up and down, left and right, all at the same time. There were no blind spots.

"I can see in all directions," Kendra said.

"Good," the Sphinx encouraged. "Keep looking and your vision will broaden."

He was right! Now not only could she see in all directions, she could also see herself, as if she had eyes outside of her body. She could see the Sphinx from the front, back, top, and sides. She could see the room from hundreds of different angles, not fragmented or compartmentalized, but part of a single seamless mind-warping image. Trying to ponder the perspective made her feel dizzy.

"Now I can see the room from every direction," Kendra said.

"You can also see beyond the room," the Sphinx said.

Kendra tried to move her vision out into the hallway, and the view expanded suddenly, hitting her with a sensation like vertigo. She could now see every room in the house from multiple vantages. It was like her mind was hooked up to thousands of security cameras, but instead of looking from one screen to the next, she was seeing through all of the cameras simultaneously. There was the leopard shark prowling the library. There was Torina fussing over an elaborate lunch in the kitchen. There was Cody playing chess with Haden. There were imps scurrying through the walls of the house like rats. It was hard to focus on anything specific, because she perceived too much. "I see Torina in the kitchen. I see the whole house."

"Move your vision outside. Examine the town. Find the post office. Find the man."

As her vision expanded beyond the walls of the house, the feeling inside Kendra was similar to taking the first drop on a roller coaster, except she was falling in all directions at once. Her viewpoint extended so that she was looking at the town from high above, peering down on tiny rooftops, while also staring up into the cloudy sky. And gazing down busy streets. And inside houses and shops. She saw into dank sewers, dusty attics, dim garages, and cluttered closets. All at once, she observed every person in town from every angle. Every room in every building. The exterior and interior of every car. And the brain-tingling vision kept stretching outward, unstoppable now. She looked down on land masses and cloud formations from space. She saw sprawling cities and everyone in them. She observed every cubicle in every skyscraper. She penetrated caves and forests and oceans. She saw cows, deer, birds, snakes, insects. Gophers burrowed in the ground. Dragons perched on lofty crags. She saw inside hospitals and circus tents and prisons. She saw the barren surface of the moon.

Kendra was no longer aware of her body, the crystal, or the Sphinx. She had been rendered powerless by the flood of sensory input, everything viewed at once, all of it in motion. There was too much—it was impossible to even begin to try to process this staggering view of everything. In this moment she was witnessing so much more than she had experienced over the entire course of her life. She couldn't bring anything into focus. She couldn't even think clearly enough to try. Conscious thought had ended, drowned by incomprehensible overstimulation.

Then she noticed something so new and brilliant that it distracted her from everything else. A beautiful face suffused with light. A physical embodiment of purity. The face gazed at Kendra. Not merely in her direction—Kendra somehow knew that, unlike anyone else within her endless view, the radiant woman could see her.

Release the crystal.

The thought came to her mind in a familiar way. Not with words for her ears. It was communication through thought and feeling, mind to mind. Kendra realized that she was seeing the Fairy Queen.

Release the crystal.

What crystal? Then Kendra remembered that she had a body. She was in a room with the Sphinx conducting an experiment. She still saw everything from every angle, but the vision became distant. She concentrated on the brilliant, beautiful face. Faintly, using forgotten senses, she could hear a voice calling her name, and she could feel her fingers touching something.

Release the crystal.

Kendra pulled her hand away from the cool, glassy surface. The vision ended as though somebody had pulled a plug. Kendra fell back on her elbows, blinking, astonished by how limited her sight seemed. She actually had to turn her head to take in the surprised faces around her.

The Sphinx crouched over her, grinning, his teeth white. "Welcome back, Kendra," he said. "You know me, correct?"

"Never again," Kendra gasped.

Everyone in the room murmured. They sounded amazed.

"I thought that perhaps you would see nothing. That your nature as fairykind would totally shield your mind from the vision. But you saw everything and made it out."

"Barely," Kendra said. "I lost all sense of where I was, who I was. There was too much."

"You seemed to slip away once you looked beyond the house," the Sphinx coaxed.

"It was like trying to drink from a tsunami," Kendra said. "How long was I gone?"

"Ten minutes," the Sphinx said. "You were convulsing gently, like the others. We had lost hope that you would return on your own. What brought you back? Once the seizures struck, I expected you to end your days in a vegetative state."

Kendra did not want to tell him about the Fairy Queen. Her realm had to stay hidden. "My Grandma saw me. Grandma Sorenson. She saw me seeing her and told me to release the crystal."

The Sphinx studied Kendra. "I had no idea Ruth was clairvoyant."

Kendra shrugged. "Bottom line? You want me to touch that thing again, you will have to force my hand onto it, and please don't pretend you're doing anything besides erasing my mind. There was no way I could control what I saw. No way to focus. I was nothing."

"You did well, Kendra," the Sphinx said. "If not an outright success, the experiment was instructive. I am convinced the Oculus is beyond your capacity to wield. Having witnessed the others who have tried, I feel there was no way you could have imitated their state of agitation so precisely. We could all tell when the Oculus overpowered you. It was earlier than with any of the others."

Kendra shifted her gaze to the Oculus, glittering innocently on the pillow, like nothing more than a sparkly bauble from a museum collection. Yet never again would she see it as a glimmering work of craftsmanship. The Oculus was a gateway to insanity.

The Sphinx locked eyes with the others in the room

one by one. "We are essentially done here. Tomorrow we will move out. Kendra, you may return to your room. Thank you for your cooperation. Get some rest. Plan on departing with us at daybreak."

CHAPTER SEVEN

Sabotage

As the hammock swayed back and forth, Seth stared up at the naked branches overhead, stark against the hard blue sky. A satyr reclined on a similar hammock to his right, softly playing a flute fashioned from reeds, shirtless despite the cold. A second satyr with redder fur and longer horns lay on a third hammock to the other side, a long striped scarf dangling from his neck to the ground.

"You're right," Seth admitted. "This is the most comfortable bed in the universe."

"Did you doubt us?" Newel blurted, adjusting his woolen scarf. "And we're in view of the yard, so Stan won't be able to come down on you."

"You've fed me and made me really comfortable," Seth said. "I'm guessing you want to ask me something."

"Ulterior motives?" Newel gasped. "I'm shocked and appalled! Can you only conceive of us helping a longtime friend relax if we were buttering him up for a proposition?"

Doren stopped piping. "We're out of batteries again."

"Thought so," Seth said. "Haven't you guys heard of conservation? I gave you a mountain of batteries last time."

Newel folded his arms across his hairy chest. "Have you ever used batteries to power a television? Even a small one? They don't last."

"Plus we watch it nonstop until we run out," Doren added, earning a glare from his comrade.

"This could be another *golden* opportunity for you," Newel enticed.

"I had to bring back the gold I earned last time," Seth said. "They won't let me keep it. And they're right. It isn't yours to give me. We're stealing from the preserve."

"Stealing?" Newel sputtered. "Seth, hunting for treasure is not stealing. You think trolls like Nero got their hoards through legitimate channels? You think wealth does any good piled in crypts or caves? If currency isn't exchanged, the economy stagnates. We're heroes, Seth. We're keeping the gold in circulation for the benefit of the global marketplace."

"And so we can watch more TV," Doren clarified.

"I really don't feel good about taking any more gold," Seth said. "Removing treasure from Fablehaven is like robbing a museum."

"What about something other than gold?" Newel

suggested. "We have loads of wine. We make it ourselves. Top-notch stuff, worth a hefty sum. If you sold it, you'd make money, and you wouldn't be stealing."

"I'm not going to become a wine dealer," Seth said. "I'm barely thirteen."

"What if we recovered treasure without an owner?" Doren said. "Not stolen. Salvaged."

Newel tapped the side of his nose. "Now you're thinking, Doren. Seth, we've been doing some fishing in the lake of tar by where Kurisock lived. Ever since Lena got rid of him, his domain has become neutral territory."

"Wasn't like he left a will," Doren joked.

"We've found some interesting objects. Stuff has collected in the sludge over the years. Some of it worthless, some of it surprising."

"Any bones?" Seth asked.

"Bones, weapons, armor, trinkets, equipment," Newel listed. "We've been stashing away the interesting stuff. No actual gold yet, but we've only been trawling the tar at our leisure. If you'll accept treasures from its depths, we'll spend more time there."

"I'll have to check what Grandpa thinks," Seth said.

"Stan?" Newel cried, exasperated. "Since when are you Stan's lackey? He'll put a damper on our dealings no matter what! He's against us watching TV in the first place!"

"What happened to you, Seth?" Doren asked. "You don't quite seem like yourself."

"It's hard to explain," Seth said.

"Doren, you missed your vocation!" Newel exclaimed.

"You should have been a therapist. There it was right in front of us but we missed it. Something is troubling the boy. What is it, Seth? What's taken the wind out of your sails?"

"The Society killed Kendra," he said reluctantly.

Both of the satyrs fell silent, their expressions melancholy.

"It wasn't very long ago. I can hardly think about anything else. We don't even really understand what happened. I have to figure it out."

"Sorry to hear it, Seth," Doren said gently.

"Don't mention it to Verl," Newel cautioned. "He might dive into a chasm. Kendra's all he can talk about these days. The poor guy is hopelessly smitten. I keep reminding him that she's Stan's granddaughter. He doesn't care that she's too young. Says he'll wait. I tell him satyrs don't tie themselves down to one maiden. He says he's not tying himself down. He says she captured him against his will, and he's forever her prisoner. Those exact words."

Seth chuckled.

"The phase will pass," Doren said. "Verl is a nut."

"We'll give you some time," Newel relented. "We can talk business when you're feeling more like yourself again."

"Guys, I know how much those batteries mean to you. Maybe I could just go and get a bunch of them and bring them to you without any—"

Doren sat up swiftly, setting his hammock rocking. "Something is coming."

"Something big," Newel confirmed, cupping a hand to

his ear. "Coming fast. But Seth was sharing an idea. About batteries?"

Seth propped himself up on his elbows. He could now barely hear the distant thump of heavy footfalls. "Hugo?" Seth guessed.

"Must be," Newel said. "But why is he coming so fast?"

"Who knows?" Doren replied. "The big guy has been acting strange lately."

Hugo bounded into view, a humanoid conglomeration of rock, soil, and clay. The last time Seth had seen him, the golem had been enlarged and outfitted for battle by the fairies. Now he looked like his old self, except perhaps a bit taller and thicker.

Hugo took a final tremendous leap, landing solidly near the hammocks, the impact making everything tremble. "Hugo . . . miss . . . Seth," the golem declared in a voice like a rockslide. The words were enunciated more clearly than Seth had ever heard the golem manage.

"Hi, Hugo!" Seth said, rolling out of the hammock. "It's good to see you too! You're talking so well!"

The golem gave a craggy smile.

"Looks like our party has officially been crashed," Newel lamented.

Hugo stared at Seth.

"Want to play?" Seth asked.

"Yes," Hugo said.

"You know a fun game?" Newel murmured softly to Seth. "Pulling treasure out of the tar pit."

"Newel, that's really far from the yard," Seth whispered.

"Keep . . . Seth . . . safe," the golem rumbled.

"Right," Newel said. "Just an idle thought. I was brainstorming. You two run along."

"We'll have another hammock party soon," Doren promised.

"Okay, sure, guys," Seth said. "What do you want to do, Hugo?" The simple question was something of a test. The golem was still getting used to having a will of his own. He typically struggled to come up with an activity without some suggestions.

"Come," Hugo said, extending a stony arm.

Seth grabbed on, and Hugo hoisted him onto his shoulder. Seth liked the satyrs, but he felt relieved to escape their company. The conversation had become too serious once the subject of Kendra came up. He wished he could make a general announcement to everyone he had ever known that his sister was dead and that he needed some time to cope with it in his own way. Recounting the tragedy to new people inflamed the pain too much. Maybe while hanging out with Hugo he could finally ignore the loss for a while.

The golem tromped over to the unseasonably green lawn of the yard and approached a large tree in the far corner. Seth recognized it as the former site of the tree house before he had infuriated the fairies and they had torn it down with him inside. The rubble had been cleared away long ago, but now Seth saw that a new tree house had been constructed, bigger and sturdier than the previous one, buttressed by a pair of heavy stilts.

"Make," Hugo said, pointing at the tree house.

"You rebuilt it?" Seth asked. How could those big hands manipulate tools with the skill necessary to construct something like a tree house?

"Seth . . . see," Hugo said, lifting Seth and setting him on the narrow wooden ledge outside a door in the side of the tree house.

Seth went inside. There were few furnishings, but the room was spacious. The floor felt solid, and the walls were thick. An old iron stove sat in the middle of the floor, with a pipe that extended through the roof. Since the golem was much too big to enter, Seth didn't stay inside very long. He uncoiled the rope ladder by the door and climbed down.

"Hugo, that is the awesomest hideout ever!"

"Happy," Hugo said.

Seth hugged the earthy creature, his arms barely reaching halfway around Hugo's waist. The golem patted his shoulder.

Seth stepped back. "Did you do that on your own?"

"Hugo . . . idea. Stan . . . help."

"Let's go over to the house. I want to thank Grandpa too."

Hugo picked up Seth and trotted to the house, setting him down near the deck. Seth charged inside. "Hugo is talking so well!" he called, not seeing anyone from where he stood by the back door. "He showed me the tree house! Guys?"

He heard a faint banging. The sound seemed to come from the basement. Was everyone down in the dungeon?

When Seth opened the door to the basement, the banging became much louder. Somebody was hitting the door beyond the bottom of the stairs. He heard a female voice shouting, muffled by the heavy door into the dungeon. "Dale! Stan! Hello! Ruth! Tanu! Help! Someone? Hello!"

Seth charged down the stairs. "Vanessa?"

"Seth? Get your grandparents. Hurry!"

"What are you doing out of the Quiet Box?"

"No time to explain. You have a spy among you. Hurry, bring them here quickly!"

Seth turned and ran up the stairs, his head spinning. What could possibly explain Vanessa's being outside the Quiet Box? Was she no longer being kept there? Had his grandparents lied? Could she have been the person controlling Kendra? That was ludicrous, right?

He dashed through the kitchen, reached the entry hall, and raced up to the second floor. "Grandpa! Grandma! Hello?"

Still no answer.

He ran through his grandparents' room and pulled open a door in their bathroom. Instead of a bathroom closet, a steel door awaited, with a large combination wheel. Seth dialed in the numbers he had memorized the previous summer, yanked a lever, and the heavy door clacked open.

"Hello?" Seth shouted up the stairs to the secret side of the attic.

"Seth?" called Grandpa.

"Vanessa is out of the Quiet Box," Seth announced. "She wants to talk to you."

He heard footsteps. Grandpa, Grandma, and Tanu rushed down the stairs.

"What were you doing?" Seth asked.

"Having a meeting," Grandma said. "Where is she?"

"At the door to the dungeon," Seth said. "She's banging on it and calling for you guys." The three adults charged past Seth. Grandma held a crossbow. Tanu scrabbled in a pouch for potions. "Where is everybody else?"

"Dale went to the stables to check on the animals," Tanu said. "Maddox went into the dungeon to help Coulter search for the hidden chamber in the Hall of Dread."

Tanu took a detour to his room to grab a flashlight and handcuffs. Seth trailed after his grandparents as they descended the stairs to the entry hall, and then down to the basement. Tanu caught up as they arrived at the bottom of the stairs.

Grandpa approached the door to the dungeon. "What are you doing out of the Quiet Box?" he called through it.

"Open the door, Stan," Vanessa answered. "We need to talk."

"How do I know every prisoner in the dungeon isn't at your side, ready to storm past us?"

"Because I called you," Vanessa replied. "If this were a trap, I would have used surprise to my advantage."

"You have to do better than that," Grandma said. "Where is Coulter?"

"In the Quiet Box."

Grandpa and Grandma shared a concerned glance.

"What about Maddox?" Tanu asked.

"He's the problem," Vanessa said. "Look, I have a key,

Stan. I'm contacting you this way only to reduce the shock and avoid a fight. I'm on your side."

A key rattled in the lock and the door opened. Vanessa stood alone beyond the doorway, holding a flashlight. A dark corridor lined with cell doors extended behind her. Even wearing one of Grandma's housecoats, she was strikingly attractive with her long black hair, dark eyes, and smooth olive complexion. "Maddox released me," she said. "He wanted me to help him subdue the rest of you and access a secret room beyond the Hall of Dread."

"What?" Grandpa cried.

"He's not really Maddox, Stan," Vanessa said. "I put him to sleep with a bite. Come with me."

The three adults followed the narcoblix down the dreary corridor. Seth brought up the rear, relieved that nobody had forbidden him from tagging along.

"What do you mean it wasn't Maddox?" Grandma asked. "Who was it?"

"A stingbulb," Vanessa said.

"There are no more stingbulbs," Tanu protested. "They've been extinct for centuries."

Vanessa glanced back at him. "The Sphinx has access to stingbulbs. I knew that even before this phony version of Maddox confirmed it."

"He confessed?" Grandma asked.

"He assumed I was on his side," Vanessa said. "He was enlisting my help."

The corridor ended, branching left or right. Vanessa turned right.

"The Quiet Box is the other way," Grandpa pointed out.

"Maddox is this way," Vanessa said. "I extracted as much information as I could before incapacitating him outside the Hall of Dread."

"Does this mean the real Maddox is dead?" Tanu asked.

"He was alive when they made the copy," Vanessa said. "Stingbulbs can only replicate the living. But Maddox was in bad shape, as was reflected in the copy. The stingbulb maintained that Maddox was alive the last he saw."

"What exactly is a stingbulb?" Seth asked.

"A species of magical fruit that can extract a sample of living tissue and then grow into an imitation of that organism," Vanessa explained. "The copy is almost exact, even duplicating most memories."

Seth furrowed his brow. "So they could impersonate somebody pretty good. But they might be a little off."

"Right," Vanessa said.

"What if that explains what happened to Kendra?" Seth gushed. "Maybe she was replaced by a stingbulb!"

Grandpa stopped walking, and the others paused along with him. He slowly turned to face Seth, two fingertips resting on his lips, his expression unreadable. "That could be," he murmured. "That fits really well."

"She could still be alive," Grandma gasped.

Seth made a choked little sob as he tried to fight back the tears of hope and relief that sprang unbidden to his eyes.

"What happened to Kendra?" Vanessa inquired.

"We thought she was dead," Grandpa said. "We caught her trying to leak secrets to the Society, and when Warren confronted her about it, she poisoned herself. Our best guess was that she was under the influence of some kind of mind control."

"You're right," Vanessa said. "Sounds like a stingbulb. The Sphinx would be in no hurry to harm Kendra. He knows how valuable she could be. Come."

They started walking again, and turned a corner.

"What do we do?" Seth asked.

"We'll get this info to Trask," Grandpa said. "Vanessa, if the Sphinx sent the stingbulb to free you, why tell us?"

"The Sphinx only sought to free me once I regained strategic value," she said coldly. "He didn't think the stingbulb could access the hidden room unaided, so suddenly Vanessa Santoro deserved to be rescued. I should have secured that loyalty long ago. For years, I functioned as one of his top operatives, risking my neck time and again, succeeding in mission after mission. He discarded me at the first moment I might have become an inconvenience. The stingbulb had an entire speech memorized, explaining how my incarceration was always planned to be temporary, a tactical necessity. In his pride, the Sphinx thinks I'll come whimpering back at the first opportunity. He is in for a surprise. I no longer trust his character and, by extension, I no longer believe in his mission. I won't rest until I take him down."

Up ahead, the flashlights illuminated a form sprawled on the floor of the hallway. The group jogged forward, staring down at Maddox.

"Can you revive him?" Grandma asked.

Vanessa crouched over Maddox, her hands probing his

head. He flinched, crying out. She stepped back and he sat up, blinking into the flashlight beams. His eyes flicked to Vanessa, his expression guarded.

"What is this?" he asked, rubbing his head. "Stan? What happened?"

"We have reason to believe you're not Maddox," Grandpa said.

Maddox chuckled incredulously. "Not Maddox? You're kidding. Who am I, then?"

"A stingbulb," Grandma said.

Maddox glanced at Vanessa. "Is that what she told you? Stan, don't be so hasty to trust a liar like her. Coulter thought it might be smart to consult Vanessa about what happened to Kendra. You know, see if she knew anybody in the Society who lives in Monmouth. We thought we could handle her together, but she shot out of the Quiet Box like a tornado and overpowered us. That's all I remember."

"Monmouth, Illinois?" Vanessa verified. "Is that where they took Kendra? Stan, that must be Torina Barker. She's a lectoblix who works closely with the Sphinx."

"Do you know where she lives?" Grandma asked urgently.

"I've never seen her lair," Vanessa said. "I just know of her."

"Stan, give me the cell phone," Grandma said. "The reception down here is lousy. I had better go call Trask."

"Wait, you believe *her*?" Maddox spluttered. "You think I'm some kind of talking fruit?"

Grandma accepted the cell phone and started down

the hall. Grandpa glowered at Maddox. "Yes, I do. And you had better start doing some serious talking. What's the news from Brazil? What's really happening at Rio Branco?"

Maddox chuckled silently, eyes down, face flushing. "You're taking her word over mine," he mumbled to himself. He raised his head. "Stan, I know you're torn up because of Kendra, but I can't help you. I'm Maddox. Remember that night in Sri Lanka? You won that ring-tailed sparkler off me with a full house?"

"We'll go release Coulter from the Quiet Box," Grandpa said. "If his story fails to match yours, I'll make you very sorry for wasting more time."

"Don't bother," the stingbulb spat, glaring at Vanessa. "There will be consequences," he threatened, holding her gaze.

"I've never been a big fan of rotten fruit," Vanessa commented calmly.

"Your mission is over," Grandpa stated. "What can you share with us?"

"There isn't much to say," the stingbulb replied.

"Search your memories," Grandpa invited. "You're aware of some wonders that Tanu can work with potions. Or, beyond the door behind you, I could introduce you to a wraith. Ever meet a wraith, friend?"

"You misunderstand me," the stingbulb replied. "I know very little. Do you suppose they would risk sending me here with my head full of sensitive information? I have a small amount of knowledge specific to my mission, nothing more. The Society is aware of the secret room at the end of the

Hall of Dread. They want me to recover coded messages from Patton Burgess about where certain artifacts might be hidden. They explained where Vanessa was imprisoned and how the Quiet Box worked. They told me that I should be able to rely on her for assistance. I came into being inside the main house at Rio Branco, beside the washtub that brought me here. The memories I have from Maddox at Rio Branco are mostly of hiding in a cave, much as I described, until he was captured. They have him in custody. With my consent, they added to my injuries so I would look authentic. I know nothing else."

"That could be true," Vanessa said. "They wouldn't want to risk a stingbulb divulging their schemes."

Tanu rolled the stingbulb onto his belly, crouched over him, and cuffed his hands behind his back. When Tanu stepped away, the stingbulb did not move.

"Do they have the artifact?" Grandpa asked.

"I have no idea," the stingbulb said. "But I told them where it was hidden. Maddox knew that much."

"What now?" Grandpa asked Vanessa.

"We could stash him in the Quiet Box," Vanessa proposed. "Get Coulter out of there."

"I was afraid you might say that," Grandpa said. "Having bitten most of us, you can control us in our sleep. The Quiet Box is the only place we can hold you to curb that power."

"Haven't I earned any credibility?" Vanessa asked.

"Without a doubt," Grandpa said. "But you could still be setting us up for a greater betrayal in the future. We can never let you see the information beyond the Hall of Dread."

"I hear you," Vanessa said. "What do I care about some stingbulb? Turning him in could be a ruse to earn your trust. Except, if I'd meant to betray you, that is not how I would have done it. I would have followed the script the stingbulb brought me. It was a golden opportunity. Coulter was already out of play. With keys to the dungeon and help from the stingbulb, it wouldn't have been difficult to use the element of surprise to capture the rest of you. Then I could have proceeded to seek out the desired information at my own pace."

"And she wouldn't have told us about the lectoblix in Monmouth," Seth added.

"You don't need to place full trust in me," Vanessa said, hands on her hips. "Keep your secrets. Just let me assist you. I know things. And I have bitten many people in my time, including several inside of the Society. Let me use my abilities, and I'll help you recover Kendra."

"You make a compelling argument," Grandpa sighed. "Tanu?"

"Ruth won't like it," Tanu said. "But Vanessa is right that turning in the stingbulb was unwise unless she's on our side. Simply knowing that the Sphinx has stingbulbs is invaluable intelligence."

"Seth?" Grandpa asked.

Seth was so flattered that Grandpa was asking his opinion on the matter that it took a moment to collect his thoughts. "I think we should stick the stingbulb in the Quiet Box and have Vanessa spy for us."

Vanessa arched an eyebrow. "Stan?"

"Tanu has it right about Ruth," Grandpa said. "She won't want us to give you an inch. We'll have to keep you down here in a cell, at least at first. We'll try to make it comfortable. Vanessa, let me be clear. If you take control of any of us in our sleep, I will consider it irrefutable evidence of your allegiance with our enemies, punishable by death."

"Understood," she said evenly.

Grandpa nodded. "We could use your help. As soon as possible, I want you searching for sleeping members of the Society who can help us locate Kendra." Grandpa bent down and helped the stingbulb to his feet. "Let's go release Coulter."

CHAPTER EIGHT

Knapsack

The room was dark, but, as always, Kendra could see. Unable to sleep, she stared at the ceiling, watching a tiny spider progress across the featureless white expanse. She wondered what the room looked like to the small arachnid, inching along upside down. Knowing that spiders had many eyes, she felt new empathy for how they viewed the world.

It still made her dizzy to recall her encounter with the Oculus. Half a day later, she found that she could not recreate the experience in her mind. The vision had been too disorienting, too distinct from the way she had always seen and the way she saw now. She could only hazily recollect the sensation of observing the world from billions of perspectives.

What if the Sphinx or someone else in the Society

mastered the use of the Oculus? It would mean no more secrets. The Society would be able to see everyone, everything, everywhere.

The thought made her shiver.

Tomorrow she would leave with the Sphinx and his freaky entourage. Where would they take her? Would the journey offer any opportunities for escape? Could she possibly get away with the Oculus? What a coup that would be!

The door to her room eased open. She had not heard the lock disengage, but caught the motion out of the corner of her eye. Her body went rigid. A hand reached inside and placed something on the floor.

"Hello?" Kendra called softly. "Who's there?"

The door closed.

Kendra swung her legs out of bed and crossed to the door. She opened it, peering up and down the dim hall, but saw no one. Had her door been unlocked all night? Had the stealthy visitor unlocked it silently?

On the floor just inside her door sat a tan leather knapsack. A piece of paper leaned against it. Kendra picked up the paper and read these words:

You must escape tonight. The knapsack contains an extra-dimensional storage compartment. You can easily fit inside. Once you're inside, the knapsack can be flattened, jostled, or dropped and you will feel none of it. You'll find a stingbulb in the front pocket. Prick yourself, wait for the duplicate to take form, and then issue instructions. Leave the decoy behind, and get as far from here as you can. Hurry!

The note was unsigned. Kendra was glad that she could read it without turning on a light. No need to draw attention to her room now that escape was suddenly an option. Her heart pounded. She opened her door, wandered over to the top of the stairs, and listened. The house was quiet. If she didn't disturb anyone, she should have at least a few hours to herself.

She returned to her room and examined the knapsack. Could this be some kind of trick? Was the Sphinx playing mind games? Or was the note legitimate? Maybe somebody really was lending her aid. What need would the Sphinx or Torina have for mind games? She was their prisoner. Subtlety was no longer required. If the note was genuine, she should move quickly.

Kendra opened the small flap that covered the front pocket of the leather knapsack. Thrusting her hand inside, she felt a stinging prick that reminded her of when she had reached into the mystery box at the rec center. Instead of pulling away, she closed her fingers around the fruit and removed it from the pouch.

The stingbulb was a dull, purplish color, with an irregular shape and a rough, fibrous texture. She was no expert, but the fruit seemed authentic. The sting had felt right. She placed the fruit by the wall near the window and returned to the knapsack.

Would she really fit inside? Kendra unbuckled the big flap that covered the top, pulled it open, and looked inside. Instead of seeing the inside of a knapsack, she was peering through an opening down into a room with a dingy slate floor and cracked adobe walls. Weathered crates and barrels were stacked along two of the walls. Iron rungs descended the wall near the opening, granting easy access to the unlikely space.

Kendra gaped at the room in amazement. Were there no limits to the wonders possible through magic? She tried to guess who might have given her such an incredible gift. Nobody came to mind. What could the Sphinx gain by giving her false hope? What if she really had a secret ally?

Kendra glanced at the fruit. How long would the transformation take? She certainly did not want a second Kendra wandering around without instructions. The process seemed to be advancing slowly so far. Surely she had enough time to slip down and investigate the room.

Kendra poked her head into the knapsack. What cargo did the barrels contain? Might she find other useful materials inside? Pulling the mouth of the knapsack open wide, Kendra slithered through the opening and climbed down the ladder.

An unlit lantern waited on the floor at the bottom. Kendra ignored it—her enchanted vision would suffice. The room was about ten feet tall, fifteen feet across, and twenty feet long. She noticed small vents on three of the walls near the ceiling. She approached the goods stacked against one wall. Everything looked timeworn and cobwebby. Random items were scattered among the heaped containers: a folded rug, an outdated tennis racket, the mounted head of an antelope, a clear jar of marbles, a few fishing poles, torn work gloves, several filthy rolls of wrapping paper, a damaged wicker chair, some framed pictures, rotting coils of rope, unused candles, and a battered chalkboard.

Nothing looked useful. Kendra tried to open a crate, but the top felt nailed down. She found a rusty rake and used it to pry the top off. Inside she found bolts of gray cloth.

She tried a barrel, but stopped attempting to pry it open once she caught a whiff of the contents. Whatever food had been in there had spoiled long ago.

Kendra set the rake aside and stepped back. This felt like rummaging through a long-abandoned garage. She supposed if useful items had been included within the knapsack, the note would have mentioned them.

Returning to the ladder, Kendra climbed up and shimmied through the mouth of the knapsack back into the dim bedroom. She checked on the stingbulb and found that it was now the size of a football and had taken on a more elongated shape.

Kendra changed her clothes, trying to select an inconspicuous outfit that could withstand the cold. She settled on the clothes she had worn to talk to the Sphinx, plus the jacket she had been wearing when she was abducted. She bundled the rest of her clothes and chucked them into the knapsack.

Sitting cross-legged near the knapsack, Kendra reread the note. Obviously she would enter the knapsack and have the stingbulb duplicate slide it through the invisible bars of her window. Once on the snowy ground, she would exit the knapsack and run for it. Where would she go? She supposed she could stash the knapsack under a bush and hide inside it until morning. Could she find a phone and call home? Might be tough in the middle of the night in a small town.

Would the duplicate fool the whisper hound? Torina had talked as though the creature used scent to identify targets, so if the duplicate smelled just like Kendra, the hound should be satisfied. Kendra's scent would never leave the house. Of course, there might still be trouble if the hound could somehow sense her scent outside. Apparently whoever had left the knapsack felt the ruse would work. In her desperate circumstances, it was worth the risk.

Kendra scooted across the floor so she could lean against her bed. The stingbulb expanded so gradually that she could not discern the change unless she looked away for a few minutes and then looked back again.

Should she invite Haden and Cody to run away with her? If they ratted her out, she would lose her only opportunity to escape. The prematurely aged men were bitter about what Torina had done to them, but they seemed resigned to their fate. They might have no interest in breaking out. After all, Torina was providing them with a free retirement home, an option they might not find elsewhere.

But was it fair to deny them the option to decide for themselves? The men might quietly long to rejoin normal society. They could certainly fit inside the capacious knapsack, although Haden might have a tough time getting down the ladder. They had both treated her well. It would be wrong to simply abandon them.

She didn't need to share the specifics of how she planned to flee. She could wait to tell them how the escape would be accomplished until they agreed to join her. If they chose not to accept the offer, she didn't have to mention the duplicate or the knapsack. They wouldn't even know she had escaped—they would assume she had changed her mind.

The stingbulb continued to slowly grow. Kendra wondered at what point it would begin to look human. So far it looked like a big purple yam. Settling back against the bed, Kendra rested her eyes, assuring herself that she would not doze. How could she sleep with the prospect of a desperate escape looming? But it sure felt nice to close her eyes! Before long, the silent house, the dim room, the eventful day, and the late hour conspired against her, and she slipped off to sleep.

Kendra was aroused by a crunching, cracking sound like green wood splitting. Still an irregular shape, the stingbulb was now larger than Kendra. Fingers had broken through the purplish husk of the fruit and were peeling it away. Kendra crawled over to the oversized fruit and helped widen the hole as quietly as she could manage.

Soon Kendra sat back and watched an identical copy of herself squirm out of the fibrous husk. The duplicate was even wearing the same clothes Kendra had been wearing when she was pricked!

"I'm Kendra," Kendra informed the newcomer.

"I can't see you," the duplicate said.

"Can't you see in the dark?"

The duplicate paused before answering. "Nope. I should be able to. I can remember seeing in the dark. Now I can't."

"I guess my powers aren't transferrable," Kendra mused.

"Apparently not," the duplicate agreed. "What am I to do?"

"I've been imprisoned by an evil lady," Kendra said. "I need you to pose as me."

The duplicate thought about this for a moment. "No problem."

"You know you're a fruit," Kendra said.

"I'm perfectly aware of what I am."

"Where did you grow?" Kendra asked.

"Far from here. I couldn't think very clearly back then. I love this body!" She flexed her fingers, then took a deep breath. "So many sensations!"

"Can you remember being a fruit?" Kendra wondered.

The duplicate furrowed her brow. "Vaguely. Nothing was as sharp or immediate as it is now. There was an awareness of light and heat, a sense of growing, of being nourished by the mother tree. And later a sense of being separated from the tree. A tenuous connection remained until I exited the husk. By that connection the mother tree nourished me from afar so I could grow into a replica of you."

"You even have my clothes. How is that possible?"

"Who knows? Magic, I guess. The same way I started thinking like you from the first instant I sampled you."

"Weird," Kendra said.

"So all you want me to do is imitate you?"

"I guess I have a few more instructions."

"I exist to follow them," the duplicate pledged.

"First, don't divulge any sensitive information to the

Sphinx, Torina, or anyone. Keep the secrets you know at all costs. Second, learn what you can about their plans, and then try to escape and notify me." She recited Grandpa's cell phone number. "The Sphinx will take you away from here in the morning."

"I remember."

"Keep your eyes and ears open. Take whatever opportunities you can to harm the Society of the Evening Star."

"I will. You can count on me. Are you going to invite Haden and Cody to join you?"

"What do you think?"

The duplicate shrugged. "Seems like you think you should."

"Right," Kendra said. "When I return, after I'm inside the knapsack, I'll need you to put it through the window bars and toss it to the ground."

"Gotcha."

"You'll only follow my instructions, right?" Kendra verified. "The others would love to find you out and change your allegiance."

"I'll only obey you. I'll do a good job. Unless *you* mess up, the Sphinx will never know I'm an impostor."

"Unless they try to get you to use my powers," Kendra said. "You'll have to make up excuses."

"Leave it to me."

"What time is it, anyhow?"

"I can't see, remember? Isn't there a clock on the desk?"

"Oh yeah," Kendra realized. "It's almost 3:30 A.M. I'd better hurry." She went to the door. "I'll be right back."

Tiptoeing into the hall, Kendra crept over to Haden's room. She tried the door and found it unlocked. Easing it open, she slipped inside and crossed to the adjustable bed where Haden snored softly. She shook his bony shoulder. "Haden, wake up," she hissed.

Haden bunched up his covers and rolled away from her. She gave him another shake. Huffing and sniffing, Haden sat up. "What is it?" he asked.

"It's Kendra."

"Kendra? What time is it?" He was gazing in her general direction, but his eyes weren't quite looking into hers, a reminder that although she could see, he could not.

"Late. Haden, I think I have a way to sneak out of here. I'm wondering if you want to come with me."

He considered the proposition for a moment. "You're serious."

"Yes. I discovered a sure way to escape. Something safe and reliable."

"When?"

"Now or never."

He cleared his throat. "I'd better stay. I would just slow you down."

"You really wouldn't slow me down. Don't stay behind for my sake."

He scratched the side of his nose. "I never expected an opportunity like this." He patted his chest, frowning. "All things considered, I think I'd better stay. I'm not sure where else I'd go, what else I'd do. I guess I won't be able to complain about being held captive anymore."

"You're sure?" Kendra checked.

"Yes, I'm sure. I wish you the best. Do you need my help?"

"Just for you to keep quiet about this," Kendra said.

"My lips are sealed. Good luck."

"Thanks, Haden."

"Did you invite Cody?"

"Not yet."

He looked troubled. "Okay. Okay. Even if he goes, I had better stay. That is my final word."

"Who knows," Kendra said, backing toward the door, "maybe it won't work out. But I think I have a solid plan."

"From what I hear, either way you'll be moving on tomorrow."

"Which is why I have to duck out tonight."

"Good luck."

"You too."

Kendra exited and closed his door, then slipped down the hall to Cody's room. She quietly eased the door open.

"Who's there?" Cody called, alarmed.

"It's just Kendra."

"Kendra?" Cody repeated, his voice only somewhat quieter.

Kendra shushed him gently. "Not so loud. I don't want to get busted. I have to ask you something that couldn't wait until morning."

"Sure, come in," he whispered. "Sorry. You startled me."

"I have a sure way out of here. I'm leaving tonight. You could come if you'd like. Should be easy."

Sitting up, Cody switched on a reading light. He shielded his eyes until they adjusted. "I know you're worried about leaving with the Sphinx tomorrow. But there is no way out of this place. Trying to bust out will only make matters worse in the morning."

"It isn't wishful thinking," Kendra insisted. "I've had some outside help, and I now have a guaranteed way to escape. I'm talking immediately. You won't slow me down and it shouldn't be too tough. Do you want to come or not?"

"Have you asked Haden?"

"He turned me down."

Cody picked up a mostly empty glass of water from the low table beside his bed. He took a sip and set it down. "I suppose if the getaway is as sure as you make it sound, I wouldn't mind leaving this place behind. If I manage to find a comfortable place for Haden on the outside, I could always come back for him."

"So you'll come?" Kendra said.

"If I agree that your method of escape looks sensible, yes, I'll join you."

"Get dressed and come to my room. Be quick and quiet."

Cody slid his legs out from under the covers. They looked white and thin. "I'll be close behind you," he assured her.

Kendra jogged down the hall. The disappearance of Cody would raise questions. There was no stingbulb to replace him. They would certainly interrogate Haden, since he and Cody were so close. Could it lead them to suspect the authenticity of the Kendra duplicate? Possibly, but if Cody wanted to come, leaving him behind was not an option.

Returning to her room, Kendra found her duplicate sitting on the bed. The husk from the overgrown fruit was gone. "What did you do with the husk?" Kendra asked.

"I cleaned it up and dropped it into the knapsack," the duplicate replied. "Are the old guys coming?"

"Cody," Kendra said. "His disappearance will raise questions. You'll have to be ready to act oblivious."

"I'll make you proud," the duplicate said. "They won't suspect."

Kendra felt confident that she could rely on the duplicate. It was like relying on herself. "Thanks, I'm sure you'll do great."

Kendra sat down on the bed next to her duplicate. She had to wait longer than she liked for Cody to show up, and was just getting ready to return to his room when he entered quietly. Diffused light from his room illuminated him faintly. He wore a dark green topcoat and a matching homburg hat with a brownish band and an upturned brim.

"You look sharp," Kendra remarked.

"Torina got me the outfit," Cody said. "You're right about Haden. I went by his room and gave it a shot, but he's set on staying. How do we escape?"

"We climb into this knapsack," Kendra said.

"The knapsack?" Cody said incredulously. "I'm sorry, Kendra, I can't see a thing in here."

Kendra clicked on a light.

"Two of you?" Cody gasped.

KNAPSACK

"Long story," Kendra said. She lifted the flap of the knapsack. "This backpack has a magical compartment. Climb down the ladder. I'll take care of the rest."

"Now I've seen everything," the old man muttered, peeking into the knapsack.

It took some twisting and some steadying from Kendra, but eventually Cody got his feet onto the rungs and started down. The generous mouth of the knapsack stretched as his shoulders squeezed through. Had Cody been a heavyset man, he might not have fit very easily.

"Just chuck the bag out the window," Kendra reminded the duplicate. "I'll call up from the bottom when I'm ready."

"I'll wait for your signal," the duplicate confirmed.

"'Bye," Kendra said. "Thanks."

"I exist to execute your will. Thanks for the intriguing mission."

Kendra descended through the mouth of the knapsack into the unlit room below. When she reached the bottom, she gazed up at the duplicate peering down at her. Kendra gave a thumbs-up. "We're ready."

The mouth of the knapsack closed. Kendra waited. There was no sense of motion.

"What's happening?" Cody asked. "I can't see my hand in front of my face in here."

"She'll throw the knapsack out the window."

"Out the window? We're three stories up!"

"We won't feel it in here." She hoped it was true.

From up above, Kendra heard the window slide open. A

[133]

moment later, she heard the knapsack hit the ground. The room didn't tilt or tremble.

Kendra retrieved the damaged wicker chair from among the goods heaped against the wall. "You can sit here," she offered.

The wicker creaked as Cody took a seat. Despite the numerous broken, missing, and protruding fibers, the brittle chair looked like it would hold him fine. Kendra rushed over to the rungs in the wall and climbed up to the closed mouth of the bag. Reaching up, she pushed open the flap.

"Where are you going?" Cody inquired.

"I'm going to take the knapsack someplace safe," Kendra said. "Sit tight."

"You're the boss."

Kendra climbed up through the opening, into the side yard of the big house. Above her, the bedroom window she had fallen from was dark. The house remained quiet. There was no sign of pursuit from the whisper hound. Kendra closed the knapsack, picked it up, and hurried away across the crunchy snow. Fortunately the snow looked pretty chewed up, so leaving footprints probably wouldn't be a problem. Just to be sure, she dragged her feet so that whatever footprints she did leave would look misshapen.

She reached a sidewalk and started down the road. Slipping on a patch of ice, she fell hard, banging her elbow. She remained on the ground for a moment, breathing icy air, feeling the cold from the concrete seeping through her clothes, before rising carefully and continuing. She had seen enough of the neighborhood to know it consisted of large, old houses on good-sized lots. Her first goal was to put some distance between herself and her enemies. She turned down a couple of streets, heading for what she thought was the center of town. Not much after four in the morning, the chilly streets were quiet. No light seeped down through the cloudy sky.

As she progressed, the houses were getting smaller and closer together. Most needed some upkeep. A few were really run-down, with weedy yards, cluttered porches, and sagging roofs. From a pen at the side of one house, a big dog barked, prompting Kendra to walk even faster.

The house she had escaped from was well out of view. She kept glancing over her shoulder, unable to believe she had made a clean getaway. How far did she need to get before she stashed the knapsack and hid inside until morning?

Up ahead, a car came around a corner and drove toward her. The headlights flashed onto her, and Kendra knew she would look even more suspicious if she tried to hide. If she stayed calm, the car would almost certainly just drive on by. Except that the car was slowing. Was it a Good Samaritan wanting to make sure that this teenage girl walking alone at night was all right? Or could it be some psycho who really liked the idea of girls on their own in the dark? Or could somebody from the house have noticed already that Cody was missing?

As the car pulled to a stop near her, Kendra made a break for it, running for the gate into the backyard of the nearest house.

"Kendra," a voice called from behind in a hushed shout.

Kendra glanced over her shoulder and glimpsed a black man getting out of the silver sedan. She crashed into the gate, rattling the entire wooden fence, but couldn't figure out how to open it. She grabbed the top, splinters pressing into her palms, and boosted herself up.

Strong hands seized her sides, yanking her off the fence. As her feet hit the ground, a hand covered her mouth. The other arm pinned her arms down and held her close. "I'm a friend of your grandfather's," the man whispered. "I'm a Knight of the Dawn."

A light turned on inside the house. Kendra had rammed the fence pretty loudly.

"Come on," he said, guiding her toward the sedan. "You're safe now."

"How do I know I can trust you?" Kendra asked, coming with him half-willingly.

"You don't," he said. "The name is Trask. I've been driving around town all night. So have Warren, Elise, and Dougan. You know them, right?"

He opened the back door and Kendra ducked into the sedan. What else was she supposed to do? The stranger was fast and strong. If she tried to run again, he would catch her even more easily this time. She desperately wanted to believe him. Trask slid in behind the wheel. The car was still running. Judging by the leather seats and the fancy instrument panel, the sedan seemed expensive.

"How did you find me?" Kendra asked.

Trask pulled forward, accelerating smoothly. Kendra glimpsed a squinting male face in the lighted window of the house, his thinning hair standing up in messy clumps. "Stan Sorenson got a tip that you might be wandering the streets of Monmouth tonight. And here you are."

"Somebody helped me get away."

He nodded. "Fits the tip."

"You've been looking for me?" Kendra asked.

"I'm a detective. I was called in to investigate your murder. We didn't suspect you were alive until earlier today."

"Where will you take me now?"

He took out a sleek cell phone. "We'll rendezvous with Warren and the others, then get you straight to Fablehaven."

CHAPTER NINE

Hall of Dread

"Hike," Hugo rumbled, backing away from the line of scrimmage.

Seth and Doren began their routes, struggling to keep their footing in the deepening snow. Newel defended Doren well, staying with him when he cut left. Verl shadowed Seth, playing him too closely. When Seth faked a cut, Verl bought it, so Seth went long.

Hugo was the all-time perfect quarterback. The golem adhered religiously to a six-second time limit for releasing the ball, negating the need for a rush. There were no constraints to how far he could throw, the passes were always accurate, and he showed no favoritism.

Seth looked up and back. Blinding swirls of snow swept through the air, obscuring his view. He kept his legs pumping hard. Verl trailed two steps behind him. Seth could no longer see Hugo or the other satyrs. How far had he run? Fifty yards? Sixty?

A dark shape appeared amid the whirling flakes, hissing through the air. Seth extended his arms. Although the football hit him in stride, it was like trying to catch a meteor. Only Hugo could throw a long bomb with so little arc on the ball!

Seth lost his footing and fell in a spray of snow but managed to hang onto the football, trapping it against his chest. He lay for a moment in the furrow he had plowed through the snow, feeling an icy prickle on the back of his neck, hesitant to get up because he knew that snow had collected inside his collar and would disperse chillingly down his back.

"What happened?" Newel called.

"He caught it," Verl replied. "Touchdown."

"Again?" Newel complained. "I'm taking Seth next time."

"Please do," Doren said excitedly. "I want Verl covering me."

"This game is rigged!" Newel protested.

Verl brushed away some of the snow from the back of Seth's neck and gave him a hand up. The good-natured satyr had wooly white legs with brown spots, stubby horns, and a more childish face than Newel or Doren. He wore a thick brown turtleneck, while the other satyrs played bare-chested.

"Thanks," Seth said.

"I can't believe you held on to that one," Verl said. He had dropped several similar passes.

"Me neither," Seth admitted. "Hugo throws hard."

"I guess losers walk," Verl sighed, trotting away to get ready for the next kickoff.

"Seth!" Grandma shouted from the porch. "We have a car pulling into the driveway."

"Kendra!" he exclaimed, dropping the football. "I have to go, guys."

Verl came hustling back, smoothing his hands down the front of his half-soaked turtleneck. "How do I look?" he asked anxiously.

"Like a prince," Seth said. "Remember, no guts, no glory." He had informed Verl that Kendra would be arriving today, and had encouraged his hopes of winning her affection. Ever since learning that his sister had been recovered, Seth had felt much more like himself.

"I don't know," Verl whimpered, eyeing the woods. "Newel and Doren warned that Kendra is way too young. They said Stan would skin me alive if he knew about my ardent admiration."

"Just be a gentleman," Seth said. "This is the moment you've been waiting for."

"I'd rather do this on my terms," Verl hedged, backing away. "Perhaps in a hot-air balloon. With a picnic lunch. And a top hat."

"Suit yourself," Seth said, jogging toward the porch. He had convinced Grandpa to grant the satyrs permission to enter the yard in order to play snow football with him. He had needed something to occupy his mind while waiting for his sister to arrive. The snowstorm had slowed her arrival by more than an hour.

"You look like you've been making snow angels," Grandma said.

When he reached the covered porch, Seth flapped his arms and stamped his boots, shedding clumps of snow. "Verl was guarding me, so I got the ball a lot," Seth said. "Verl isn't much of a tackler, but Newel hits hard. He made me fumble twice."

"You shouldn't roughhouse with satyrs," Grandma chided.

"The snow breaks the falls, and the jacket cushions everything," Seth assured her. "Doren and I were up 49–35."

Grandma helped him brush himself off. As Seth entered the house, he removed his boots and jacket. He heard the front door open and raced to the entry hall.

Kendra and Warren were coming through the door. A red seam slanted across Kendra's cheek—evidence that she had dozed in the car. Eyes teary, Seth ran to her and gave her a big hug.

"Whoa," Kendra said, hugging him in return, taken aback by the enthusiastic affection.

"I'm so glad you're all right," Seth said, blinking away the embarrassing tears. "We buried you."

"I heard. Feels weird to know I have my own tombstone."

"I'd keep it in my room if it was mine," Seth said. "Maybe

make it my headboard. Can you picture it? 'Here lies Seth Sorenson.'"

"I hear you guys have a stingbulb copy of Maddox," Kendra said, changing the subject.

"Yeah, he quit talking once we found him out. Vanessa says if we let him out of the Quiet Box, he'll die pretty quickly. His kind don't last long."

"How weird is that? Vanessa out of the Quiet Box!"

"She helped us find you," Seth said. "She used her powers to get info that somebody would help you escape last night. That was why everybody was patrolling the streets all night."

"Wait a minute," Kendra said. "Vanessa gave them the tip I'd be escaping? Who told her?"

"She won't say much. She would only reveal that the person who supplied the information was quietly on our side and had to remain unknown. All we know for sure is that Vanessa traveled into a sleeper somewhere and got the info. Must have been somebody who knew you'd be getting that knapsack."

"Trask found me. I didn't know him, so I was freaked. Warren said they weren't sure exactly where I was being held."

"Vanessa claimed not to know the precise location," Seth explained. "She knew Torina was in Monmouth, and she had a tip that a traitor was going to help you escape. She wouldn't share who supplied the tip. Can I check out your knapsack?"

"How much do you know about the knapsack?"

"Quite a bit. Your escape was all we could talk about this morning!"

Kendra took the knapsack off her shoulder.

"You fit in there with an old guy?" Seth asked.

"Cody is actually thirty-two. But he looks at least seventy. Torina drained away his youth. She's a lectoblix. I think he wants some revenge. He stayed behind with Trask." She opened the main flap of the knapsack and Seth peeked inside.

"No way! How do you always end up with the coolest stuff? This would be the ultimate emergency kit!"

"I'm surprised that anyone would part with such a valuable object," Coulter said, coming up behind them. "The art of creating extra-dimensional storage has been lost. The knapsack is a rare and valuable item. Somebody went well out of their way to free you."

"Hi, Coulter," Kendra said.

He hugged her. "We'll have to examine all the contents, just in case your unknown benefactor had a secret motive of smuggling unwanted guests into Fablehaven. You don't know who gave it to you, correct?"

"No idea."

Grandma, Grandpa, Dale, and Tanu had held back while Kendra spoke with Seth, but now they swarmed in, welcoming her and expressing their relief at her safe return. Seth backed away, waiting for the flood of good wishes to abate.

Grandma ushered Kendra to the kitchen, offering her a variety of food choices. All Kendra wanted was hot chocolate, so Dale placed a pan of milk on the stove.

"What are we going to do with Vanessa?" Kendra asked, now seated at the table.

"Don't get me started," Grandma griped. "I'm sure she had reasons of her own for helping us. That woman cannot be trusted. She has lied to us so sincerely and betrayed us so deeply that I can't believe Stan is permitting her any degree of freedom. She should go right back into the Quiet Box."

"She protected us from the impostor to her extreme disadvantage," Grandpa reminded his wife. "And she helped us recover Kendra. If we're careful, we may be able to use her."

"She's already concealing information from us," Grandma said. "Who knows who she spoke with while in that trance of hers, or what she may have revealed? Go ahead, Stan, keep using her. Boys love to play with fire. Just don't come crying when you get burned. We'll see who ends up using who."

"Vanessa has good reason for hating the Sphinx," Warren observed.

"How convenient for her," Grandma replied.

"I have some important information," Kendra announced, staring at her hands. "Stuff I didn't want to say in front of Trask or Dougan or Elise. Stuff I didn't want to discuss over the phone."

"You were holding out on me?" Warren said. "That was a long, boring drive!"

"I thought I should wait until we were all together at Fablehaven," Kendra apologized. "I met with the Sphinx. He has the artifact from Brazil. It's called the Oculus."

Grandpa winced. "I was afraid the presence of the Maddox stingbulb meant the Society had already captured the artifact."

"Are they able to use it?" Coulter asked tentatively.

"I don't think so," Kendra said. "They made me try."

Grandpa banged a fist down on the counter, his face reddening. "The Oculus is the most dangerous of all the artifacts," he growled. "What do you mean, they made you try it?"

"They forced me to put my hand on it," Kendra said. "At first I could see in all directions, like I had extra eyes. Then it was like I had eyes all over the room, showing me dozens of perspectives at once. Then I had eyes all over the house, then the town, then the world."

"What did you see?" Seth asked eagerly.

"Everything and nothing," Kendra said, her voice haunted. "It was too much. I couldn't really focus on anything. I forgot where I was, who I was."

"How did the vision end?" Grandma asked.

"I couldn't think clearly enough to take my hand off the crystal," Kendra explained. "I saw into the place where the Fairy Queen lives. I managed to focus on her. She commanded me to take my hand off the Oculus. With her help, I escaped."

"You could have lost your mind," Grandpa seethed.

"I don't think any of them have mastered it yet," Kendra said. "If they do, we'll have no secrets. The Sphinx seems determined."

"Does this mean we need to enter the chamber beyond the Hall of Dread?" Tanu asked.

"Absolutely," Grandpa said. "The Society is gaining too great an advantage. We must work under the assumption that they will soon be empowered to see anywhere. We need to learn all we can to even the odds."

"Can't we use the Chronometer somehow?" Seth asked. "Wouldn't time travel come in handy?"

"I've been studying the device," Coulter reported. "I've made a little headway, but the Chronometer is both complex and dangerous."

"There is little available knowledge on the subject," Grandma added. "We don't have an instruction manual."

"They have an artifact that heals any wound, and another that could let them see anywhere," Seth said. "They'll use the Oculus to find the others. We know about the Chronometer. What do the other two artifacts do?"

"One grants power over space," Coulter said. "The other offers immortality."

"If they collect all five, they can open the demon prison," Kendra said.

"Zzyzx," Seth breathed.

"Which would mean the end of the world as we know it," Grandpa said. "The Society of the Evening Star would fulfill their self-proclaimed mission and usher in the night."

Grandma poured warm milk into a mug, added chocolate powder, and stirred. She placed the mug in front of Kendra.

"Thanks," Kendra said. "Warren mentioned that you guys brought the Journal of Secrets."

"It's in the attic," Seth said. "On our side."

"It has the passwords for opening the secret room," Kendra said. "I'll need an umite wax candle."

"I stocked up," Grandpa said. "We have plenty."

Kendra took a sip from the mug. "We might as well do it now."

"You should rest first," Grandma urged.

Kendra shook her head. "I slept in the car. I doubt the bad guys are resting."

❀ ❀ ❀

The dismal dungeon corridor stretched to the left and right, lined with cell doors on both sides. But none were comparable to the door before Seth, composed of blood-red wood bound with black iron. Coulter stood on one side, Grandpa and Kendra on the other. After considerable begging, Seth had been permitted to tag along.

Coulter held a flaming torch. Grandpa carried a key and a mirror. Kendra clung to the Journal of Secrets. Seth had a flashlight.

"Stay away from the doors in the hall," Grandpa reminded them. "Each door has a peephole. Resist any urge to peek. You do not want to gaze into the eyes of a phantom. Do not touch any of the doors. Violate this rule and you will be removed from the Hall of Dread immediately, never to return." He was looking at Seth. So were Coulter and Kendra.

"What?" Seth said.

"You often ask for chances to prove yourself," Grandpa said. "Don't blow it."

"You'll barely know I'm here," Seth promised.

"Many of these creatures can radiate fear and other disturbing emotions," Coulter warned. "The special cells that hold them help dampen the effects. Speak up if the sensations get overwhelming. Kendra, watch out for feelings of depression, desperation, or terror. Seth, I'll be interested to see how well your immunity to magical fear holds up in here."

Grandpa inserted a key into the door. He placed a palm against the red wood and muttered a few unintelligible words as he turned the key. The door swung inward.

Coulter entered the dark hallway first, using his torch to ignite others hanging on the walls. The wavering firelight cast an ominous glow over the stone walls and floor. As Seth followed Grandpa inside, he noticed that the air was palpably colder than elsewhere in the dungeon. His breath plumed in front of his face.

The hall was not long—the torchlight already glimmered against the far wall. There were eight doors on either side of the corridor, equally spaced, each crafted from solid iron and embossed with archaic symbols and pictograms. Every door had a keyhole and a closed peephole.

"You're right," Kendra said, her voice hushed. "This place feels wrong."

"You can *feel* the darkness," Coulter whispered. "You all right, Seth?"

"Just a little cold." Aside from the inherent creepiness of the heavy doors bathed in torchlight, and the unsettling guesses of what might be imprisoned behind them, he sensed no sinister emotions.

Grandpa led the way toward the end of the hall. Coulter hung back at the rear. As Seth passed the second set of doors, he began to hear faint, spidery whispering. He glanced back at Coulter. "Do you hear that?"

"The silence can play tricks on your ears," Coulter replied.

"No. Don't you hear voices whispering gibberish?"

Coulter paused. "All I hear is the torch crackling. It's quiet as a tomb. Are you squirreling around with me? We're falling behind."

They picked up their pace, catching up to Kendra. Seth concentrated on the babbling whispers. As he focused, he began to catch words.

"Alone . . . thirsty . . . pain . . . hunger . . . agony . . . mercy . . . thirst."

The words were tangled, many voices overlapping. When his concentration lapsed, the sounds reverted to gibbering nonsense.

Seth glanced back at Coulter, who motioned for him to keep walking. Why couldn't the older man hear the voices? The eerie babbling wasn't just in his head. He could hear the jumbled whispers as distinctly as his footsteps.

Soon they reached the final set of doors at the end of the hall. The wall ahead of them was a blank expanse of stone blocks interrupted by three brackets holding torches. Seth saw no evidence of a door.

Kendra opened the Journal of Secrets, and Grandpa lit an umite candle. Coulter watched over her shoulder.

"It says to light the torches on the left and right. Then

place one hand on the center sconce, and the other on the block with the silver vein in it."

Coulter brought his torch close to the wall. He and Grandpa started to examine blocks.

"Do you hear the voices whispering?" Seth asked Kendra.

She punched him on the arm. "Cut it out. You might not feel the fear, but I'm kind of freaked right now."

"I'm not kidding," Seth said.

"Save it."

Seth stepped away from her. The whispering sounded clearer than ever. He began picking out forlorn phrases. "I hear you," Seth whispered in his quietest voice, barely more than mouthing the words.

The overlapping whispers ceased. A chill ran down his spine, making the hairs on the back of his neck bristle. The tingle was not a reaction to magical fear. It came because of a certainty that the voices had clammed up in response to his words. During the menacing silence, Seth felt sure that all of the beings in the Hall of Dread were aware of him.

"Help me, Great One, please, please, help me," a single voice hissed, breaking the silence. The silky whisper was coming from the cell to his left.

Seth clenched his jaw. Grandpa and Coulter were debating about which of three blocks had the most obvious silver streaks. Kendra had her head bowed and her eyes closed. No one else seemed to have noticed the slithery voice.

"Who are you?" Seth whispered.

"Free me and I will serve you for all time," the voice vowed.

Seth stared at the door. He wanted to see who was addressing him. But Grandpa would skin him alive if he peeked.

"Yes, yes, look upon me, grant me mercy, pardon me, Wise One, and I will serve you well."

Grandpa had one hand on a block and the other on a sconce. Kendra stood beside him, telling him what to say.

The ghastly voice became more intense. "Behold me, Mighty One, pity me, speak to me, answer me."

"Seth!" Coulter said, approaching with the torch and snapping his fingers. "What's your interest in that door?"

Seth wrenched his gaze away from the iron door. "I hear a voice."

Grandpa turned away from the wall. "A voice? The fiend in that cell doesn't speak."

"It speaks to me," Seth said. "It wants me to free it. It says it will serve me."

"He said he was hearing whispers as we entered," Coulter said. "I didn't take him seriously."

"You were really hearing voices?" Kendra said.

The voice from the cell continued to implore him. "Help me, Great One, free me."

"You guys really hear nothing?" Seth checked.

"I'm not sure what this means," Grandpa said, studying Seth intently, "except that you had better leave this place immediately."

Seth nodded. "I think you're right."

Grandpa blinked. He shot Coulter a worried glance. "Take him upstairs."

"Right." Coulter took hold of Seth's elbow and guided him back toward the blood-red door.

"I will wait," the voice from the cell promised. "Please."

Seth pressed his hands over his ears as he exited. He began to hear faint, pleading voices from other cells, so he started humming to himself until he was back in the regular part of the dungeon.

As they walked toward the stairs to the kitchen, Seth uncovered his ears. "What was going on back there? What's the matter with me?"

Coulter shook his head. "I keep remembering how you were the only one who could see us when we were shades, back when the plague was overcoming Fablehaven."

"Graulas said that was because of removing the nail to defeat the revenant. I thought once the nail was destroyed and the plague reversed, there wouldn't be any more shadow creatures left to see."

Coulter stopped walking. The torch threw strange highlights and shadows across his features. "Whatever explains your condition, if I were in your shoes, I would steer clear of shadowy creatures."

"Makes sense," Seth said, trying to keep his voice steady.

❋ ❋ ❋

Standing beside Grandpa, Kendra stared at the door through which Coulter and Seth had departed. She felt deeply worried for her brother, but it was hard to tell how much of that concern was a reaction to the dark emotions stirred by the atmosphere of the hall.

"Have you heard of anything like this?" Kendra finally asked.

Grandpa looked at her, his expression suggesting he had momentarily forgotten she was with him. "No. I'm not sure what it means. I know I don't like it. You didn't hear anything, did you?"

"Not a word," Kendra said. "I *feel* plenty. I feel scared and sad and alone. I have to keep reminding myself the emotions are false."

"We should retrieve the information we need and get out." Grandpa placed one hand on the sconce and the other on the stone block he had decided contained the clearest vein of silver. "What do I say?"

Kendra read from the journal. "'Nobody deserves these secrets.'"

Grandpa solemnly repeated the words.

The entire center portion of the wall dissolved in a cloud of dust.

"Look at that," Grandpa murmured.

"'Those who came before me were wiser than I am,'" Kendra read, coughing softly.

Again Grandpa repeated the words.

"That second part disarms the traps," Kendra explained, closing the journal.

Grandpa took a torch from the wall and led the way through the mist of dust. Kendra placed a hand over her nose and lips as she followed, squinting to keep the gritty particles out of her eyes.

After about fifteen feet, the dust cloud ended abruptly. A hall stretched ahead of them. To the left and right stood a final set of iron doors. Kendra tried not to envision what might lurk inside those secret cells.

Grandpa led the way down the hall, eventually descending a flight of two dozen stairs. At the bottom of the stairwell, they passed through an archway into a spacious room. The smooth floor, walls, and ceiling were composed of white marble swirled with gray. A stone fountain dominated the center of the chamber. No water flowed, but the basin was full. Diverse objects lined the walls: full suits of armor, upright sarcophagi, ornate jade sculptures, grotesque masks, laden bookshelves, colorful marionettes, statues from various cultures, archaic maps, painted fans, framed scrolls, antique carousel animals, elaborate urns, bouquets of glass flowers, the skull of a triceratops, and a heavy golden gong.

"Many of these items would be priceless museum pieces," Grandpa remarked, surveying the room, torch held aloft.

"Did Patton bring all of this here?" Kendra wondered.

"He and others before him," Grandpa said. "I'm most curious about the books." He approached the nearest bookshelf. "Lots of German and Latin. No English. Some languages I don't recognize. Some might be fairy dialects."

"I don't see any words I recognize," Kendra said.

Grandpa turned, eyes scanning the room. "The message from Patton is on the ceiling?"

"I'm supposed to use the mirror to read it."

Footsteps resounded from outside the room, slapping down the stairs. Coulter trotted into view, bearing a torch and Seth's flashlight. "Would you look at this," he murmured, shining the flashlight beam around the room.

"We're looking for a message on the ceiling," Kendra informed him. "Probably a fairy language written backwards."

"Watch for elaborate patterns," Grandpa instructed.

The three of them separated and roamed the room, eyes on the ceiling. Kendra held the flashlight, the others carried torches. With her eyes upward, she stumbled against the edge of the fountain, nearly tumbling into the glassy water of the basin. After almost taking a plunge, she proceeded with greater caution.

Patches of unusual markings decorated several portions of the ceiling. Each time one of them found a suspicious cluster of designs, Kendra stood below the markings and viewed them in the mirror from various angles. After several disappointing attempts, Coulter spotted a particularly elaborate pattern of symbols above the gong. When Kendra viewed the symbols in the mirror, she beheld a lengthy message seemingly inscribed in plain English.

"I've got something," Kendra said.

"What does it say?" Grandpa asked.

Kendra read silently at first.

The Oculus is located at the Rio Branco preserve in Brazil. The caretakers have the key to the vault, which is located near a point called Três Cabeças, where three huge boulders overlook the main river. You will have to climb to reach the entrance.

She recited the words to the others.

"We're a little late on that one," Coulter complained.

"There's more," Kendra said.

"Read on," Grandpa prompted.

The Translocator can be found at Obsidian Waste in Australia. The caretakers know the location of the vault. Since the vault is virtually impregnable without the key, I took extra measures to make this artifact more difficult to recover. I hid the key to the vault at Wyrmroost, one of the three dragon sanctuaries closed to human interference. I have a false grave there. Below the headstone you will find a clue to the location. Wyrmroost is inaccessible without a key to the main gate, and is protected by the most potent distracter spell I have ever encountered.

The key to the gate at Wyrmroost is the first horn of a unicorn. I know of only one such horn, and I presented it to the centaurs of Fablehaven. They guard it as their most prized talisman.

"Is that all?" Grandpa asked after Kendra finished relaying the words.

"Yes," Kendra said.

"Sounds like the best way to keep the Translocator hidden might be to leave it alone," Coulter grumbled.

"You're probably right," Grandpa acknowledged. "Patton created some serious obstacles."

"What is the Translocator?" Kendra asked.

"The artifact with power over space," Coulter replied. "Most likely some sort of teleportation device."

"Read the inscription again," Grandpa said.

Kendra complied.

Grandpa and Coulter stood in silent contemplation after she finished.

"What does he mean about Wyrmroost being closed to humans?" Kendra asked.

"Four of the dragon sanctuaries are open to human visitors," Grandpa said. "Few know about them, and fewer would actually take the opportunity to enter one, but those few are generally welcome. The other three sanctuaries are considerably less hospitable."

"But the three worst ones can't be totally closed to humans," Kendra said. "Patton went there."

"In theory, humans could visit if they managed to get past the gate and secure permission from the caretaker," Coulter said. "I can't imagine what unspeakable dangers would await. Dragon sanctuaries make Fablehaven look like a petting zoo."

"Then I'm with Coulter," Kendra said. "Even if we recovered the artifact, how could we hope to hide it in a better place?"

"We couldn't," Grandpa said. "We now have our information. Let's go check on your brother."

CHAPTER TEN

Hotel

Snowflakes flung by shifting gusts silently assailed the attic window. Powdery drifts covered the lower panes. Seth paced the room, bouncing a rubber ball, unable to stop wondering about the ghostly prisoners who spoke only to him. It was tough to decide whether he should be afraid or intrigued.

Seth heard footsteps coming up the stairs. The bedroom door opened and Grandpa entered.

"Did you learn anything about the artifacts?" Seth asked.

"Yes. One message concerned the Oculus. The other discussed an artifact that remains hidden. How are you feeling?"

Seth bounced the ball. "Fine. Weird. I don't know."

"Let's sit down." Grandpa took a seat on one of the beds. Seth plopped down on the other. "What happened in the dungeon clearly rattled you."

Seth bounced the ball, tossing it forward with a spin that brought it back to him. "You could say that."

"Hearing spectral voices strikes me as an experience that would normally excite you." Grandpa stared at him searchingly.

"It does. I mean, it's really cool that I could hear them. They offered to serve me, and part of me would love to have a zombie servant. Who wouldn't? But it felt wrong. Too creepy. Grandpa, what if destroying the revenant made me evil? I don't fear deadly creatures. I can see invisible shadow people. I hear whispers from your freakiest prisoners."

"Recognizing dark elements imperceptible to others doesn't make you evil," Grandpa said firmly. "Neither does having courage. We all possess different gifts and abilities. How we use those gifts determines who we are."

"I didn't feel any fear," Seth said. "Not the paralyzing kind. The voices were freaky, but I could get used to it. That's what scares me. The voice kept flattering me, calling me wise and powerful. I don't want phantoms to admire me! I'm sure it was setting me up for some nasty trick. I don't know if I can trust myself, Grandpa. I wanted to peek in the cell. If you guys weren't there, I probably would have!"

"You've always been more curious than most," Grandpa said. "Curiosity doesn't make you evil. Neither do flattering words from sinister entities. The wraith hoped to use you to get free. Nothing more. The fiend would have said anything to convince you."

"The worst part is, I really am curious. Sick as it sounds, I'd love to go hear more of what the wraith has to say. Not because I intend to let it out. It's just interesting. See why I can't trust myself? I'd go down there because I'm interested, and then that thing would probably find a way to trick me or hypnotize me, and pretty soon Fablehaven would be under attack from evil wraiths."

"But here you are instead, anticipating the possible dangers," Grandpa said. "You're doing what any sane and responsible person should do. Just don't succumb to your curiosity."

"Why exactly can I hear them?"

"I honestly don't know. But I do know that there is a difference between hearing and listening. You can't always help what you hear. But you can control what holds your interest, what you choose to dwell on."

Seth tossed the ball up and caught it. "I guess that makes sense. The whole thing still creeps me out."

"Now that we're aware of this ability, we'll keep you away from similar circumstances. In fact, that is part of the reason I came to speak to you. Do you know what day tomorrow is?"

"I was wondering when you'd bring this up. Tomorrow is the winter solstice."

Grandpa held up a hand. Seth tossed him the rubber ball, and he started bouncing it. "I didn't want to mention it too early and get everybody flustered. Things have been hectic enough without fretting about tonight being a festival night."

"Don't we have to make preparations? Carve pumpkins and all that?"

"The jack-o'-lanterns are an extra precaution, and not a very convenient one in this weather. I was thinking more along the lines of having your grandmother take you and Kendra to a hotel for the night."

Seth motioned for the ball, and Grandpa bounced it to him. "Isn't it dangerous to leave the preserve? The Society could come after us."

"We've weighed the pros and cons. I don't relish the idea of putting you beyond the protections offered by Fablehaven, but festival nights seem to be getting increasingly violent. If the Society intends to hit us where we live, it will probably happen tonight, when sinister creatures are free to cross boundaries and enter the yard. The voices you heard in the Hall of Dread have made the decision easy. Too many apparitions and shades roam the preserve on festival nights. I won't have you here if their voices can reach you. We'll send along Warren and Tanu to make sure you stay safe. You'll pay cash. It'll be just one night."

Seth nodded. He bounced the ball off the wall, missed the catch, and watched it roll away across the floor. "I can live with that. I'm not up for a whole night with monsters whispering crazy stuff to me. Speaking of Tanu and Warren, where are those guys?"

"While we were pursuing the messages from Patton, they were interrogating Vanessa with your grandmother."

"About what?"

"We're trying to decide what to do with her. She has shared some information about possible traitors within the Knights. Nobody you know. She still claims to have some enormous secret that she won't share unless we release her."

"We can't let her go," Seth said. "Grandma is right that she could be playing us."

"True. At the same time, if she truly has abandoned the Sphinx, Vanessa could be a valuable ally. She has already volunteered a great deal of information. I can hardly blame her for keeping some leverage available while we hold her prisoner."

"Do we ever go on the offensive?" Seth asked. "We should hunt down the Sphinx and take the artifacts back."

"We're trying. Trask has kept the house where Kendra was held under constant surveillance. Kendra's friend Cody supplied all the details he needed. We believe that the Sphinx remains inside. A strike force will mount a raid tonight. I wish I felt more optimistic. The Sphinx is slippery."

Seth got up from the bed. "When do we leave for the hotel?"

"Vanessa keeps asking to talk to Kendra, and your sister has shown interest. Your grandmother will oversee the conversation. After they chat, we'll get you guys ready."

* * *

Kendra knew that her old friend waited behind the cell door. She had wanted to speak with Vanessa ever since the woman had been locked in the Quiet Box months ago. Most of the others had spoken with Vanessa already and had relayed information from those conversations. But Kendra hadn't been around when they took place. Her last direct communication from Vanessa had been a note scrawled on the floor of a cell.

"You don't have to do this," Grandma said.

"I want to speak with her," Kendra affirmed. "I'm just a little nervous."

"You're sure?"

She wasn't. But she nodded anyhow.

Holding her crossbow ready, Grandma inserted a key and opened the cell door. Vanessa was reclining on her cot, dressed in a stylish outfit. A battery-powered lantern rested on a table cluttered by novels. A mirror hung above a dresser topped with various cosmetic supplies. An obvious effort had been made to provide some comfort.

"Hello, Kendra," Vanessa said, rising.

"Hey," Kendra replied.

"I'm sorry."

"You should be."

Vanessa looked grave. "I owe you a great deal."

"You nearly killed us."

"Kendra, you deserve a colossal apology. You healed me. I was burned beyond repair, minutes from death. After the betrayal I committed, nobody could have blamed you for letting me perish. Including me. For years I faithfully worked for the Sphinx. How was I repaid? The villain stabbed me in the back the instant I became inconvenient. In contrast,

I deceived you, betrayed you, and put your loved ones in danger. Yet you showed me mercy. I want you to know that my loyalty is not completely blind, nor is my reason utterly bankrupt. I'll never betray you again."

Kendra shifted uncomfortably. "Thanks, Vanessa. I'm sure you can see why your apology might be hard to believe. But I appreciate it, and I hope it's true."

"I'd be a fool to blame you for doubting me. I'll patiently prove my sincerity."

Grandma snorted bitterly. "Or patiently bide your time until the opportunity for another truly crippling betrayal arrives."

"Which is why I can't begrudge your decision to keep me in this cell for the moment," Vanessa conceded. "I could be more effective roaming free, but I can see that it would place too great a strain on your trust. Rightfully so."

"You wanted to see me to apologize?" Kendra asked. The conversation was harder than she had expected. She simultaneously liked and hated Vanessa too much. She wanted to leave.

"Chiefly," Vanessa said. "I also want to share some information with you."

"They said you're withholding some secrets."

"My biggest secret must not yet be divulged," Vanessa said. "Good people on your side of this conflict would be endangered if this truth became too public. For the moment, my keeping it will benefit your cause. The day may come when that changes. Conveniently, this final secret also provides me with a little leverage to perhaps get out of incarceration at some point. I'm on your side now, but I have no desire to end my days in a cage."

"They said you helped me escape," Kendra said.

"I seized control of a sleeper and learned that the Sphinx had you in his custody. I also learned about a plan to free you. The Knights have spies as well. I discovered where you were being held and alerted Stan. I didn't personally facilitate your release. Who accompanied the Sphinx?"

Kendra told Vanessa about Torina and Mr. Lich, then described the other people she had seen with the Sphinx as best she could.

Vanessa nodded. "I'm not surprised they tried to use psychics to test the Oculus. Let me guess. They also tried to read your mind."

"Yes."

"And they failed?"

"They seemed really puzzled."

"I bit you, Kendra, but I could never take control of you. Your mind is shielded. None of those enemies are of serious interest except for the Sphinx and Mr. Lich. Despite her delusions, Torina is really just a minor player. I'm curious about the person in the mask. Could it have been the prisoner from the Quiet Box?"

"It could have been anyone," Grandma said.

"I have a warning for both of you," Vanessa said. "The Sphinx is a supremely patient man. He would not have dropped all pretenses like this unless he saw a clear path to his destination. Count on the fact that he has a plan to secure all of the artifacts. Beware. He is very good at anticipating contingencies. As you move to stop him, you may find yourselves playing into his hands."

"We're aware of the dangers," Grandma assured her.

"Let me fill you in on some history. For centuries, the leader of the Society of the Evening Star has been a brilliant mastermind named Rhodes. Over the years, rumors abounded as to his actual identity. A cunning blix lord. A wizard. A demon. At times, the Society thought he had died or lost interest, but he always resurfaced. He was patient. And immensely secretive. None of us ever stood in his presence.

"Over the past decade, Rhodes became more active than ever. As did our great archenemy, the Sphinx. With my talent, I am always uncovering information. Not long before I was assigned to recover the artifact from Fablehaven, bits and pieces began to add up, and I found myself among a small group of Society members who suspected that the Sphinx and Rhodes might be the same person.

"Having now confirmed that the Sphinx and Rhodes are indeed one and the same, and that he was working for the benefit of the Society, the members of the Society will be enthused as never before. Many members have grown dormant over the years, but this news will swell the ranks of the active. Clearly, after centuries of waiting, the end is near."

"I've never heard of Rhodes," Grandma said.

"Like I said, he was very secretive," Vanessa replied. "Much more so than even the Sphinx. We could only utter his name under certain conditions."

"Torina called him the Sphinx," Kendra mentioned.

"I'm not surprised," Vanessa said. "We used to call Rhodes the Lodestar. But he will now be using his surprise identity as the Sphinx to build morale. Ruth, Kendra, he has spent centuries researching how the artifacts work so that when he found them he would be ready. Count on the fact that he will move swiftly to recover the other artifacts, and shortly thereafter he will unlock the demon prison."

"Thank you for the warning," Grandma said. "Is that all?"

"I just want to make sure you understand that I intend to use my abilities to spy on the Society," Vanessa said. "I'll share information as I learn it. I won't take control of any of you while you sleep. If I do, you would be welcome to kill me."

"What if you share secrets with our enemies while you're off inhabiting sleepers?" Grandma challenged.

"First, don't give me secrets to share. Second, you desperately need information—the threat posed by the Sphinx is both real and immediate. Third, to a minor extent, yes, you need to trust me a little. I won't disappoint you."

"You've already sold Stan," Grandma sighed. "You know my suspicions about your pretenses at reform. I would love to be proven wrong." Grandma opened the cell door.

"Wait," Kendra said. "Do you know who placed the knapsack in my room?"

Vanessa regarded her thoughtfully. "I have some suspicions. But they are part of the secret I must keep. Take heart knowing that we have secret allies."

"Come on, Kendra," Grandma huffed. "We'll find few answers here. Don't waste your breath with more questions."

"Good-bye for now," Vanessa said.

"See you," Kendra replied.

✻ ✻ ✻

Snow no longer descended from the murky sky, and snowplows had mostly cleared the roads, but Grandma pulled into the parking lot of the Courtesy Inn cautiously. Even at moderate speeds, the SUV had slid several times on the icy streets.

The Courtesy Inn was a large wooden lodge with a mostly vacant, halfway cleared parking lot. Grandma piloted the SUV into a stall. Tanu went inside to check in and scope out the place while the others waited in the car. Seth wished Grandma would turn down the heater, but the vents kept gushing warm air.

"I'm going to die of heatstroke in the snow," he mumbled. It was his third complaint about the temperature. Grandma ignored him. He briefly considered taking off his shirt in protest.

"It is a little warm," Warren remarked.

"This vehicle is not a democracy," Grandma replied.

A few minutes later, Tanu returned with two keycards. They collected their bags and entered the inn. Flames danced in the lobby fireplace, and the air carried the odor of lemon-scented cleansers. They rode up an elevator to the second floor and marched down a carpeted hall to a pair of neighboring doors.

Warren entered first, checking the room thoroughly while the others lingered in the hallway. After what seemed like a long wait, Warren exited and unlocked the second room. Grandma, Tanu, Kendra, and Seth went into the first room.

"I'll take the rollaway," Tanu offered.

"I'm smaller," Kendra said.

"I'm security," Tanu countered. "Don't argue."

The plan was for Grandma, Kendra, and Tanu to sleep in here while Seth and Warren took the adjoining room. Seth unwrapped the tiny bar of soap beside the sink. There came a brisk knock on the door that internally connected the two rooms.

Seth hustled over. "What's the password?"

"Passwords are for sissies," Warren's muffled voice responded.

"Works for me," Seth said, unlocking the door and opening it.

"The rooms look clean," Warren pronounced. "Hopefully we'll have a long, dull night."

Seth grabbed his suitcase and took it into his room. It was a mirror image of the first room, minus the rollaway. As he heaved his suitcase onto the bed, he caught a flicker of motion in the far corner by the window.

He turned, staring at the empty corner. Was the window open? Had the curtain blown sideways? Everyone else was in the other room.

Staring hard, he abruptly caught another flicker, a hand flashing briefly into view along with part of a leg. The body parts appeared out of nowhere and disappeared just as quickly. Seth cried out and stumbled away from the corner.

Warren raced into the room. He stopped short, looking around. "Was that a drill?"

Seth narrowed his eyes, staring hard. "I think there's something in the corner."

"That corner?" Warren asked.

A full body pulsed temporarily into view—a tall, thin goblin with a knobby head, a shriveled nose, and jutting tusks. His skin was all shiny pinks and oranges, like burn scars. "See!" Seth yelled, jumping back again.

"I didn't see anything," Warren said, producing a pair of knives, one longer than the other.

Tanu stood in the doorway, a blowgun in his hand. "I don't see anything either."

"Either there is a goblin standing in that corner, or I'm going nuts," Seth insisted, voice quavering. The goblin was not currently visible.

Holding both knives ready, Warren advanced toward the corner. The goblin flashed back into view, irregular nostrils flaring, glaring at Seth. "I see him again," Seth announced, pointing.

Warren hurled the smaller knife at the corner. Twisting, the goblin sprang sideways, barely dodging the blade. The knife lodged in the wall. Wrenching the knife free, the goblin charged Warren.

"The knife vanished!" Warren said.

"Here he comes!" Seth warned. The goblin no longer pulsed in and out of view. Seth saw the creature clearly.

Tanu came up beside Seth. "Where is he?"

Warren backed away, blindly swinging his long knife. The goblin avoided the desperate swipes and slashed Warren across the chest. Warren lunged forward, but the goblin sidestepped the knife thrust and used Warren's momentum to hurl him to the floor.

"There," Seth said, pointing.

Tanu exhaled powerfully.

The goblin paused, staring at the small feathered dart protruding from his wrist. He staggered, swayed, steadied himself, then toppled to the floor, landing hard.

"Is that Vanessa's blowgun?" Seth asked.

"Yeah," Tanu said. "I sweetened the sleep potion on the darts to a nearly lethal dosage."

Seth gestured at the fallen goblin. "Can you see him now?"

"Nope."

Warren staggered to his feet, probing the bloody stripe across his chest.

"Deep?" Tanu asked.

"I have leather armor under my shirt," Warren said. "The freak still gave me a good scratch. I keep my knives sharp." Warren crouched, recovering his throwing knife from where it had fallen.

Vicious snarling erupted out in the hallway. Tanu tossed Seth a potion. He pulled out two more potions and stepped into the adjoining room. "Go gaseous!" he instructed Grandma and Kendra.

Seth had used the gaseous potion over the summer. It would transform him into a vaporous version of himself. As a gas, nothing that he knew of would be able to harm him, but he would also lose the ability to assist Warren and Tanu.

Instead of drinking the potion, he knelt beside the goblin. What was making it invisible to the others? Seth guessed it had to be some sort of magical item, like Coulter's glove. The goblin wore simple clothes: a black silk shirt, loose black shorts, and sandals. Tucked in his belt were a pair of long, sharp knitting needles and a strangle cord. A conspicuous silver bracelet adorned one sinewy forearm.

Seth tore the bracelet free and put it on. The goblin remained visible, as did his own body. In the past, when Seth had worn Coulter's magic glove and held still, his body had become transparent, even to himself. But since his eyes somehow saw through the goblin's trick, he had no way to gauge whether he had cloaked himself from view or merely stolen a gaudy piece of jewelry.

Warren and Tanu had charged into the hallway, and Seth heard more snarling. He raced out of the room and gawked at the scene down the hall where Tanu and Warren were confronting a gray wolf nearly the size of a horse. The overgrown canine already had three feathered darts visible in its fur, along with Warren's throwing knife. The ferocious wolf snapped repeatedly at Warren, who was barely holding the animal at bay by gradually retreating and slashing its muzzle with his long knife. Tanu fired another dart from the blowgun, then dropped the weapon to scrabble through his potion bag.

Grandma emerged from her room, crossbow in one hand, the potion Tanu had given her in the other. Seth grinned. Apparently he wasn't the only person unwilling to go gaseous and miss the action. Grandma stared right through Seth at the combat with the wolf, then raised her weapon, taking careful aim. Seth lurched aside. Behind Grandma, the window at the end of the hall exploded in a shower of jagged shards as a muscular, winged creature crashed through it.

Grandma whirled as the horned gargoyle, body scratched and bleeding, scrambled to its feet and raced down the hall, trident in hand, wings folded. She held the crossbow level and let a quarrel fly. When the projectile disappeared into the creature's head, the gargoyle lurched backward and collapsed to the floor as if he had bashed his face against an invisible beam.

Seth turned around to see the wolf backing away from Warren, legs wobbly, muzzle torn and wet. Tanu held a potion near his lips. Warren brandished the long knife. The wolf's legs buckled and it slumped heavily to the floor, a motionless heap of fur and blood.

The bracelet on Seth's arm felt steadily warmer. He removed it just as it was becoming unbearable to touch. Tossing the bracelet aside, he saw it disappear in a flash before hitting the floor.

"Seth?" Grandma exclaimed. "Where did you come from?"

"The goblin had some kind of invisibility bracelet. It got hot and disintegrated."

"It may have run out of energy," Grandma said. "Or it

may have been protected by a self-destruct spell in case it was stolen."

Warren and Tanu conferred briefly. Warren trotted down the hall toward the lobby, while Tanu came toward Grandma and Seth. "Thanks for dropping the gargoyle, Ruth," Tanu said. "It must have tracked us from the air when we left Fablehaven. We aren't safe here. We should collect our things. Warren is going to make sure the coast is clear."

A wispy, ethereal version of Kendra drifted out of her room. She gazed at the fallen gargoyle and wolf.

"Don't worry, Kendra," Seth said, swiping a hand through her insubstantial body. "I'll grab your suitcase."

CHAPTER ELEVEN

Gate-Crasher

K endra awoke tucked between crisp sheets. She had a
kink in her neck from sleeping on too many pillows.
With the shades drawn, the hotel room was mostly dark, but
she could hear the shower running. She sat up to check the
clock. The display read 8:23 A.M.

Stretching, she groaned. They had driven for more than
an hour the previous night before choosing a new hotel.
Tanu and Warren had dragged the bulky wolf and gargoyle
outside and left them in the garbage bin.

The wiry goblin was currently bound and gagged in the
other room with Seth and Warren. Tanu had left them with
extra sleeping potion to administer to the grotesque prisoner.
Their rooms did not adjoin this time, although they shared
the same hallway.

Kendra heard the shower stop running. She fought free from her tight sheets and slid out of bed.

"Awake?" Grandma inquired from the neighboring bed.

"Yeah. You too?"

"I've been up for some time, resting in the dark. Something about hotel rooms has always made me lazy."

Kendra pulled the shades open, flooding the room with cloud-dimmed light. "Any word from Grandpa?"

"He phoned earlier. The raid on the Sphinx failed. The house was vacant except for a series of traps and a few old men."

"They found Haden?"

"Yes," Grandma said. "Don't fret about your friends. The Knights have a substantial fund set aside for victims of circumstances like these."

"So the Sphinx and Torina and all of them got away?"

"Vanished without a trace."

"Did they take the stingbulb?" Kendra wondered.

"No phony Kendras were found, so probably."

"How was Midwinter Eve?"

"According to your grandfather, boisterous but safe. Considering what happened, we may have been wiser to sit tight at Fablehaven and endure the commotion. Of course, most decisions are simpler in hindsight."

Tanu came out from the bathroom in a T-shirt and shorts, his hair damp. "We lived to see a new day," he said with a broad smile.

"Good work," Grandma said. "Stan thinks we may as well head home."

"Warren and I monitored the hotel and the surrounding grounds all night," Tanu said. "Everything stayed quiet. Seth's ability to see the goblin assassin really foiled their plot. The wolf and the gargoyle were only there as backup."

"You think we're under the radar?" Grandma asked.

"Looks like the Society has lost track of us. Still, we'll all be safer back inside the walls of Fablehaven."

Grandma got out of bed. "What about the goblin?"

"We loaded him into the back of the SUV, trussed up and heavily drugged. We'll press him for information once he's secure in the dungeon."

"Let's start collecting our things."

Kendra went to the bathroom and washed up. By the time she was ready, the bags were packed and waiting. She strolled with Seth to the elevator, rolling her suitcase behind her. Seth looked pensive.

She leaned into him, bumping his shoulder with hers. "So now you're seeing invisible assassins?"

"I'm relieved it was actually there. I was starting to wonder if maybe I was the only one hearing zombie voices because I was crazy."

"I wouldn't write off the crazy theory without further investigation."

"At least I wasn't kidnapped by a duplicate of myself."

"It does sound a little schizoid." They reached the elevator. Kendra pressed the down arrow button.

"Why do you get to push the button?" Seth complained.

"What are you, like three years old?"

"I'm the official button pusher. I like when they light up."

"You're a goofball."

The elevator doors opened. The car was empty. Warren hustled to catch up.

"Is it really empty?" Kendra asked, moving from side to side to examine the vacant space from various angles.

"Very funny," Seth replied. "I think so."

Warren joined them in the elevator. Seth pushed the L button. Then he pushed 5, 4, 3, and 2. "Race you down," he said, dashing out of the elevator before the doors closed, leaving his suitcase behind.

"I think he's going to beat us," Warren said, leaning against the wall.

"If he doesn't get kidnapped on his way down the stairs."

"Tanu is already down there. Ruth will be along in a minute."

The doors opened to a similar view on every floor. On the second floor somebody actually got on. When the doors opened in the lobby, Seth stood there waiting, trying to look bored.

"I got to push the most buttons," he gloated while reclaiming his suitcase.

"Plus you earned fifty idiot points," Kendra said. "A new record."

"What you call idiot points, I call awesome dollars."

Tanu had brought the SUV to the front doors of the hotel. Sparse snowflakes fluttered down from light gray clouds. Warren loaded their bags, and Kendra climbed inside. Grandma followed shortly, and insisted on driving since Tanu hadn't slept.

The ride back to Fablehaven was boring. The roads were clear, but Grandma drove cautiously. To make matters worse, they had to listen to Seth complain about the heater for the second half of the drive. Eventually Grandma turned it down.

Finally they left the road and started along the driveway. Kendra had her head down when Grandma exclaimed, "What is that?"

Kendra raised her head and saw a car smashed against the Fablehaven front gate, the hood badly crumpled, fumes flowing from the exhaust pipe into the winter air. She didn't recognize the vehicle.

"Stop the car," Warren barked. "Get Stan on the line."

Grandma slammed on the brakes and the SUV skidded to a halt. They could hear the horn of the crushed car blaring endlessly.

"This has to be a trap," Tanu muttered, opening his potion pouch.

The cell phone rang before Grandma could dial. She answered. "We're here, we see it . . . how long ago? . . . okay, we'll wait."

Grandma hung up and shifted the SUV into reverse. "The car just slammed into the gate a moment ago. Stan wants us to get back on the road until he figures out what is going on."

The passenger door of the damaged car opened and a girl tumbled out. She crawled awkwardly to the gate, using the wrought-iron bars to pull herself up. The girl looked exactly like Kendra.

"Oh my gosh!" Kendra exclaimed. "Stop, Grandma. It's my stingbulb!"

Grandma hit the brakes, making their heads tip back. "Your stingbulb?"

"The one I made when I escaped. I told her to try to get information, escape, and come to Fablehaven. I gave her the address."

"Still probably a trap," Tanu warned.

"Let me check it out," Warren offered, opening the door and leaping from the SUV. Knife in hand, he dashed toward the smashed car. Kendra scanned the leafless, snowy woods at either side of the cleared driveway, but noticed no evidence of other people or creatures.

"The car is totaled, but the gate isn't even dented," Seth observed. "How'd that happen?"

"The gate is much stronger than it looks," Grandma said. "Don't forget where we are. Appearances can be deceiving at Fablehaven."

Warren reached the crippled car. Knife ready, he stealthily peeked in the windows. The girl at the gate turned to face him, her face a mask of terror. Blood oozed from a wound on her forehead. She raised her hands protectively and sank to the ground.

Warren lowered his arm with the knife and held up an empty palm. As he spoke to the girl, her expression softened. Soon she was craning her neck to see the SUV, hope in her eyes.

Kendra scooted out the door. Grandma and Tanu followed, calling her back, but she didn't heed them. When she locked eyes with her duplicate, the beleaguered girl's face instantly brightened. Kendra ran to her, crunching over the cold gravel.

"You came," Kendra said when she got close. She had to speak loudly to be heard over the damaged car's incessant horn.

"You told me to," the duplicate answered, slumping back against the gate. "My left leg is broken. Same with my left wrist."

"Why did you bash the gate?" Kendra asked. Grandma, Tanu, and Seth caught up, listening.

"I was afraid. I have urgent information. I didn't know how close behind they were. The gate looked flimsy."

"You really messed yourself up," Kendra said.

"Most of these injuries are from before. The gash on my head reopened when I crashed."

Kendra scrutinized her duplicate. "You came here alone, of your own free will, right? This isn't a trap?"

"I can't be certain if they're chasing me or not. I don't think so. I've traveled a long distance."

Grandpa, Dale, and Coulter were approaching from the far side of the gate. Dale and Coulter rode on ATVs. Hugo carried Grandpa.

"Let me share my news," the duplicate said. "I'll feel better once it isn't just in my head anymore. The Sphinx used the Oculus. He had trouble, but he survived."

"What does he know?" Grandma asked.

The duplicate blinked at Grandma. "It's so strange to see you outside of my memories. Um, he was trying to find the location of the key to an artifact called the Translocator. He had previously purchased information from a member of the family that manages the Obsidian Waste preserve in Australia. Apparently Patton took the key from the preserve and hid it."

"Did the Sphinx find out where?" Kendra asked.

Dale unlocked the gate. The duplicate had been supporting her weight against it. Wincing, she leaned forward so Dale could pull it open. "Yes. The key is at a dragon sanctuary called Wyrmroost, north of Montana. He plans to send in somebody named Navarog to retrieve it."

Grandma raised a hand to her lips. "The demon prince. The dark dragon."

"The person you guys let out of the Quiet Box," the duplicate said. "Anyhow, using the Oculus exhausted the Sphinx. If he wasn't weak and in a rush, I doubt I would have escaped."

"How did you get away?" Grandma asked.

"I jumped out of a moving car," the duplicate responded. "But let me tell it in order. The Sphinx used the Oculus at Torina's house the morning after Kendra escaped. They had no idea we'd switched places. Nobody even noticed that Cody was missing. The Sphinx was excited because he thought he'd had a breakthrough on how to use the Oculus without losing his mind. He postponed their departure so he could try. They had me in the room while he did it.

"He succeeded, although it seemed touch and go at the

end. Once free of the Oculus, he was groggy but excited, and started making plans about recovering the key from Wyrmroost. They took me from the room before I heard very much. I only know the details I told you.

"About an hour after the Sphinx came out of his trance, somebody noticed that the house was under surveillance. The Sphinx was furious. They took me through an underground tunnel to a different house at least a block away. They had cars waiting, and we got out of town quickly.

"Right after our first stop for gas, I faked like I was feeling carsick and begged them to roll down the window. My hands were tied. The window came down as we were accelerating along the on-ramp, and I immediately dove through the opening. We were going fast. I broke my leg and wrist and picked up some nasty road rash. A bunch of motorists behind us pulled over, so the Sphinx kept right on going."

"What did you tell people?" Seth asked.

The duplicate grinned. "Hey, Seth. I told this big, nice trucker that my uncle had tried to kidnap me. Wasn't hard to believe. My wrists were still tied."

"Where did they take you?" Kendra asked.

"Back to the gas station. I pretended to call my family. I couldn't remember Grandpa's cell-phone number. People were talking about taking me to a hospital. I saw an old lady pull up to the gas station alone. She came inside and went straight to the bathroom. I pretended that I needed to use it too and hobbled in after her. I cornered the old lady in her stall and told her that the trucker was an abusive man who had picked me up hitchhiking. I stressed that I needed to get away from him. I asked her to pretend to be my great-aunt and take me to the hospital. She agreed."

"So you faked like the lady was your relative!" Seth said.

"They bought it enough to let us leave," the duplicate said. "The lady didn't know how badly I was hurt, although she could see where I was scraped up and bleeding. I told her that the hospital was just an excuse to get away from the trucker, then asked if she could take me to her house so I could use her phone. I lucked out. She was local, and she didn't have a cell phone.

"After we got to her place, I pretended to call Grandpa again. I told her he was coming to pick me up, but he lived over two hours away. She invited me to eat with her. She was really kind. I noticed that she had a computer, so I asked if I could check my e-mail. Fortunately, the street and number of the Fablehaven driveway lingered in my brain. When I logged on, I printed up driving directions to this address. While she was fixing dinner, I wrote a note. I explained that I was stuck in a life-or-death emergency, and promised to return the car along with a bunch of reward money. I took a single credit card from her purse, snagged her keys, slipped out the door, and stole her car."

"Let me guess," Seth said. "That's the car."

The duplicate nodded. "Her address is on the driving directions in the passenger seat. Maybe you guys can fulfill my promise to her. Either way, I had to get here."

"You've been through quite an ordeal," Grandma said.

"You're lucky you weren't apprehended by the police, let alone the Society. You used the credit card to buy gas?"

The duplicate nodded. "It didn't work the last time I tried. The tank is almost empty."

"We'll see that the woman gets a new car and a generous reward," Grandpa promised. "For now, we had best get you into the house. Tanu will see to your injuries."

Tanu scooped up the duplicate. She grimaced, then settled into his arms. He carried her gingerly.

"Good job," Kendra said to the duplicate.

"I'm relieved I found you. Getting here felt like a long shot."

The endless honking stopped abruptly. Dale and Warren had pried open the hood and stood hunched over the crippled engine.

"She seems just like you," Grandma murmured to Kendra as Tanu moved away. "It's uncanny."

"And she won't last more than another day or two," Kendra said. "The second dead Kendra this week."

＊ ＊ ＊

Seth sat on a sofa in the living room, tapping his knees as if playing the bongos. Grandpa had called an emergency council. They were all waiting for Tanu to come down from examining the stingbulb. Everybody was quiet and thoughtful.

Seth frowned as he looked around the room. With the Sphinx coming ever closer to his goal, were these the people to stop him? More than half of them looked too old or too young. Sure, they had weathered some attacks from the Sphinx, but generally he kept getting what he wanted. And nobody had launched any sort of successful counterattack against him. Seth felt certain the time had come to go on the offensive.

Tanu came down the stairs and entered the room.

"How is she?" Grandma asked.

"Her wrist is badly sprained. The leg is broken, but could be worse. A minor fracture. She also picked up plenty of road rash and a fairly severe concussion. Who knows how she managed to drive so far? She definitely has a lot of heart. I gave her some substances that will dull the pain and speed her recovery."

"Not that she'll live to enjoy a recovery," Kendra muttered.

"She's aware of her tiny lifespan," Tanu said. "She kept asking to speak to you, Kendra. She hopes there is some other way she can serve you before she dies."

"We could pack her in the Quiet Box," Seth said. "I'd rather preserve her in limbo than the evil Maddox. You never know when a duplicate Kendra might come in handy down the road."

"Wouldn't that be torturous for her?" Kendra asked.

"Seems like she's content as long as she has a purpose," Tanu said.

"Wouldn't hurt to make her the offer," Grandma suggested. "See what she thinks."

"We'll explore those possibilities with the duplicate after the meeting," Grandpa said.

"I have an unpleasant question," Warren said. "Could the Kendra stingbulb have been corrupted? Or could it be a different stingbulb than the one Kendra left behind at the house in Monmouth?"

"Stan and I have thought this through," Grandma said. "The Sphinx has clearly learned about the key at Wyrmroost. He didn't glean the info from Kendra or a stingbulb, because Kendra didn't learn that information until after she escaped. We see no strategic value he might gain in letting us know what he has discovered. In fact, the Sphinx would want to keep that discovery a secret in order to pursue the key at Wyrmroost uncontested. We'll keep an eye on the replicated Kendra, but Stan and I feel comfortable trusting her report."

"Wait a minute," Seth said, eyes widening. "What if the Kendra we rescued is just another replica? What if this isn't actually Kendra! She could have led the bad guys to our hotel room! We may not have seen the real Kendra yet! She might still be their prisoner."

Everyone turned to Kendra. "It's really me," Kendra assured them. "Isn't there some sort of test? Some way to differentiate for sure?"

"She could read the message Patton left in the hidden chamber," Grandma said. "That ability could not have been replicated by a stingbulb. Only potent fairy magic could bestow the capacity to read those words."

Grandpa nodded. "Agreed. But I appreciate your vigilance, Seth. We must remain wary. Question everything. Take nothing for granted. I want to turn our attention to the matter of the Sphinx and the Translocator." Grandpa summarized what he, Kendra, and Coulter had learned about the location of the Translocator and where Patton had hidden the necessary keys.

"What are the chances of the Sphinx acquiring the first horn of a unicorn?" Grandma mused.

"What were the chances of him finding stingbulbs?" Coulter replied.

"How rare are unicorn horns?" Seth asked.

"Unicorns are among the least encountered of all magical creatures," Grandpa said. "We believe they still exist, but there is no certainty on the matter. They are elusive creatures of extraordinary purity, and their horns exhibit potent magical properties. Long ago, they were hunted to near extinction by greedy wizards. During the lifespan of a unicorn, each grows three horns. They shed the first two as they mature, sort of like humans losing baby teeth. The horn here at Fablehaven is the only first horn I know to exist anywhere."

"But that doesn't mean the Sphinx will fail to find another one elsewhere," Coulter emphasized.

"We would be unwise to count on him failing," Warren agreed, "especially if he's gaining mastery over the Oculus. Somehow, somewhere, he'll find one."

"For all we know, he may already have one," Grandma said bleakly.

"If this is our worry," Grandpa said, "I see no other option than to try to beat the Sphinx to the key at Wyrmroost. We have all witnessed the Sphinx's resourcefulness. Knowing the location of the key to the Australian vault, he will find a way to get Navarog into the dragon sanctuary. And once he recovers the vault key, his acquisition of the Translocator will not be far behind."

"But can we protect the vault key better than the dragons of Wyrmroost?" Tanu asked.

"At least we can keep the vault key in motion," Grandpa replied. "We can use it or transfer it. Since the Sphinx knows the current location, it is only a matter of time before he claims it."

"Then our first task is to retrieve the horn from the centaurs," Grandma said.

Dale whistled. "Good luck with that one. That horn is their most prized possession. They revere Patton for giving it to them. It provides the energy that turned Grunhold into a safe haven during the shadow plague."

"Could we convince them we only mean to borrow it?" Grandpa proposed. "We could return the horn after the mission."

"Unless we're all eaten by dragons," Coulter mentioned.

"It will be tough to convince them," Grandma said.

"That's an understatement," Dale asserted.

"Why not steal it?" Seth suggested.

The others laughed darkly.

"Unpleasant as it sounds," Warren said, "it may come to that. Anybody know much about where they keep it?"

"The centaurs have a proud, private society," Grandpa said. "But as caretaker, I technically have a right to visit them without fear of harm once a year. Otherwise they have the right to slay any who venture onto their allotted land. I have only exercised the right twice. Theirs is not pleasant company."

"We would want to get as close to the horn as we can," Grandma said. "Analyze the lay of the land, so we can plan a raid if necessary. Then we can make a case for borrowing it."

"If they refuse to lend us the horn, the visit doubles as a reconnaissance mission," Warren finished.

"I'll send them word of our visit right away," Grandpa said. "We'll go tomorrow."

"I'm coming," Seth declared.

"The centaurs have no fondness for you," Grandpa reminded him. "Your impertinence led to Broadhoof's humiliation at Patton's hands. We'll want you as far from their domain as possible."

"They will blame us all for the death of Broadhoof," Grandma said.

"Which is why we should bring Kendra," Grandpa said. "Broadhoof helped her defeat the plague. Her purpose there will be to honor the centaurs for Broadhoof's sacrifice. If she can do so with sincerity, it may help our cause. We can't expect to dodge the issue."

"I'd be happy to apologize," Kendra said. "I feel terrible that he died, and he really did help save us all."

"You'll have to be careful," Grandma said. "They won't want your pity. Their pride will reject any such offering. But if you show sincere gratitude for his sacrifice, acknowledging his role in saving Fablehaven, it might make some headway."

"Would it be safe for Kendra?" Coulter asked. "Won't the centaurs blame her more than anyone for his death? She was riding him at the time."

"They may," Grandpa said. "But under the protection of my annual visitation rights, they will not be able to harm her. Furthermore, they will hesitate to openly blame a young girl for his demise. Being slain by a mighty demon has a much more heroic ring to it."

"Who else should accompany you?" Tanu asked.

"Most of you," Grandpa replied. "I'll want as many pairs of eyes assessing the situation as possible."

"Except mine," Seth muttered.

"We mustn't leave Seth and the house unguarded," Coulter said.

"Unguarded?" Seth complained. "Are you trying to destroy my self-esteem?"

"Dale has crossed paths with the centaurs more than most of us," Grandpa said. "Ruth is a talented negotiator. Warren, Tanu, and Coulter are all seasoned adventurers with experience recovering guarded items. Plus Coulter has specific expertise involving magical items."

"I can hold down the fort," Seth assured them stoutly.

"I'll stay behind," Warren, Tanu, and Coulter offered in unison.

"Warren will remain at the house with Seth," Grandpa stated. "Seth, the decision to leave you with extra protection has nothing to do with our estimation of your valor, and everything to do with your age."

"Maybe I could join you guys in disguise," Seth proposed.

"We can't take this mission lightly," Grandma said. "We must keep this visit as civil as possible. If we fail to recover the horn, the Sphinx will recover the key unchallenged. Your history with the centaurs is tainted, Seth. They may be able to get over the heroic death of Broadhoof. But centaurs never forget an insult."

"I hate how my past actions keep messing up my future options," Seth muttered.

"Then you've started down the road to wisdom," Grandpa replied.

CHAPTER TWELVE

Grunhold

Seth tromped across the yard wearing insulated boots. No snow remained on the lush green lawn or in the vibrant flower beds. The fairies had melted it away. Beyond the yard, the rising wind had shaken much of the snow from the naked tree branches, leaving the ground below blanketed by whiteness. A gray expanse of featureless clouds dulled the sky from horizon to horizon.

Last night they had transferred the stingbulb Kendra into the Quiet Box, removing the fake Maddox, who would soon expire in his dungeon cell. The stingbulb Kendra had been excited at the prospect of using the Quiet Box to prolong her life. Seth found it very weird that he had now met three separate versions of his sister.

At the edge of the yard, Seth set off into the trees,

feet punching through the icy glaze atop the snow and then sinking at least ten inches into fluffy powder. Where the snow had drifted, it rose above the tops of his boots.

"Ahoy, Seth!" Doren called from where he reclined on a hammock.

Newel slid off his hammock, hoofed goat legs sinking in a deep drift. "You got our message?"

"I saw it from my window." Somebody had stomped the words "hammocks today" in the snow beyond the perimeter of the yard outside the attic window.

"We noticed you weren't among the group that left earlier," Doren said. "Where were they heading?"

"To the centaurs."

"Lucky day for you!" Newel said. "They'll get nothing but high heads and dirty looks from that lot."

"I wanted to go. I know centaurs can be jerks, but they're just so cool."

"Don't believe the cool part for a second," Doren said. "The extra set of legs turns them into pompous nimrods."

"You'll fare much better in our company," Newel avowed. "Two hooves are glorious. Four are overkill."

"I'm glad to see you guys," Seth said, smiling for the first time that day.

"Your hammock is waiting," Newel offered. "Make yourself comfortable. We've been thinking about our prior discussion, and we have a new proposition for you."

"I think you'll like this one," Doren said.

Seth sat down on his hammock, kicked his boots together to knock the snow off, then swung his legs up. "I'm listening."

"We've been trawling the tar pit some more," Newel began.

"We know you feel uncomfortable about removing valuables from Fablehaven," Doren said.

"But what if we found something you could use here?" Newel proposed. He rummaged in a large, coarse gunnysack and removed a metal breastplate, smoky gray, with a rich sheen.

"Whoa," Seth said, sitting up.

"I know," Doren said. "How cool is that?"

"Seth, this spell-forged breastplate is composed of adamant," Newel explained, turning it over in his hands. "The lightest, strongest magical alloy ever devised. In bygone days, wars were waged to obtain armor of this quality. A wealthy lord would have gladly emptied his treasury in exchange for a piece like this."

Doren motioned toward the armor. "These days, an article like this is considerably rarer. The breastplate is absolutely priceless."

"What do you want for it?" Seth asked, trying to sound nonchalant.

Newel and Doren exchanged a glance. Doren nodded and Newel spoke. "We were thinking 96 size C batteries."

Seth had to resist an urge to laugh. Would they really part with precious armor for batteries? "Let me see it."

Newel handed the breastplate to Seth. It felt almost as light as plastic, but when he tried to bend it, the metal was unyielding.

"What do you think?" Doren asked.

"Feels kind of flimsy," Seth said. Wearing his best bargaining face, he examined the armor suspiciously.

"Flimsy?" Newel exclaimed. "Hugo couldn't scratch it with a sledgehammer. The light weight is part of the value. Without restricting your freedom of movement, that breastplate will turn any blade, stop any arrow."

"Why do I need armor?" Seth said, deliberately giving them a hard time. "I'm not a knight. This may have been the ultimate prize back in the olden days, but guys, any object is only as valuable as a buyer is willing to pay."

Newel and Doren leaned together and conferred quietly.

"Seventy-two batteries is our final offer," Newel declared.

Seth shrugged. "Look, I've known you guys for a while now. And I like you. But I don't know. I bet Nero would give you some gold for this."

"Didn't you get the news flash?" Newel said, grinding his teeth. "Gold no longer buys batteries."

"We really need batteries," Doren begged. "We're missing so many shows."

Seth worked hard to resist a smile. The satyrs were desperate. They were normally much savvier negotiators. "I'll have to sleep on it."

"He's toying with us," Doren accused, eyes narrow. "He's enjoying this. Who wants to be a knight more than Seth Sorenson?"

"You're onto him," Newel agreed, holding out a hand to Seth. "Give it back."

Seth burst into laughter. "You guys need to lighten up."

"We were trying to have a serious conversation," Newel said stiffly, beckoning for the armor with his fingers. "You're right, Seth. Value is subjective. Since nobody wants it, we'll just go chuck the armor back in the tar pit."

Seth cleared his throat and assumed a serious expression. "Upon further reflection, I've decided to accept your offer."

"Ouch, too bad," Doren lamented. "The sale just ended."

Newel yanked the breastplate out of Seth's grasp. "The price just shot up to 120 batteries. Surely much more than a disinterested onlooker like yourself would be willing to provide."

"Okay, look," Seth said, trying not to sound nervous. "The breastplate is really sweet. And it could come in handy. I shouldn't have teased you. I know your lack of batteries stresses you out. I was just bored, so I was trying to be a tough negotiator."

"You're our only battery supplier," Newel said. "We've been racking our brains over this. You can't tease us like that. Not about batteries."

"The more TV we get, the more we need," Doren explained.

Seth raised his eyebrows. "Maybe you guys are spending too much time in front of the tube. It's making you grouchy. Grandpa might be right. Maybe you should take some time off and learn to appreciate nature."

"We've spent the last four thousand years appreciating nature," Newel groaned. "We get it. Plants are pretty and smell nice. For us, the new and exotic frontier is season finale cliff-hangers."

"It's your life," Seth said. "Look, of course I want the armor. But the Society is after us like never before, so it may take a couple of weeks before I can make it to a store. If you give me the priceless breastplate, I'll score you guys 120 C batteries as soon as possible."

"Done," Newel said, tossing the breastplate back to Seth.

"We fitted it with straps so you can wear it home," Doren said.

"Can I come out now?" a voice inquired from behind Seth.

"Sure," Newel replied.

"Verl?" Seth said, twisting in his hammock.

The cow-spotted satyr skipped into view, holding a large rectangular object bundled in brown paper. "I need your help."

"Where were you?" Seth asked.

"Crouching behind a snowdrift. Newel said I had to keep out of sight until they concluded business with you. What are batteries, by the way?"

"Tiny cylinders of power," Doren said. "Don't strain your brain."

"Right," Verl said, peeling back the brown paper to reveal the object in his hands. It was a canvas with a large image of Kendra's face rendered in charcoal.

"Wow," Seth said. "That looks pretty realistic. You drew it?"

"Along with many others," Verl admitted timidly. "At first I produced pictures of us together: on a carousel, rowing in a canal, waltzing at a ball. Doren warned me I was trying too hard. I finally settled on this striking vision of my muse. What better way to declare my affection than to simply revel in her beauty? Would you be so kind as to deliver it?"

"No problem," Seth said, grinning.

"I blush to think of her beholding my work," Verl confessed, handing over the canvas.

"So do we," Newel assured him.

"She'll love it," Seth said, trying to accept the canvas. Verl would not let go.

"You sure, Verl?" Doren taunted. "Pretty mushy stuff. Stan won't like it."

Verl released his hold on the picture. "Yes, I'm sure. Take it to Kendra with my highest regards."

Seth felt and heard a rumbling that built into words. *Come to me, Seth.*

Seth stared at Newel and Doren. "Did you guys hear that?"

"What?" Doren asked. "Verl guaranteeing his humiliation? Loud and clear!"

"A voice calling my name," Seth said.

Visit me tonight. There is little time. The voice was like distant thunder.

"Nothing?" Seth asked.

The satyrs shook their heads.

The faint rumbling faded.

Newel tapped Seth on the arm with his fist. "Feeling all right there, buddy?"

Seth forced a smile. "I'm okay. I keep hearing things lately. Maybe I should get back to the yard." He slid out of the hammock.

"Keep the breastplate," Newel said. "Just don't forget that you owe us—"

"—one hundred and twenty size C batteries," Seth finished.

* * *

Four stoic centaurs waited at the border of their domain, muscular torsos bare except for wolf skins draped across their powerful shoulders. Kendra recognized two of them. The silver one with the enormous bow was Cloudwing. The other was Stormbrow, whom Kendra had mostly seen as a dark centaur. The coat of his horse body was white dappled with gray. He had a high forehead and long, lank hair. One of the unfamiliar centaurs had a golden hide and was not as excessively muscled as the others. The final centaur had chestnut fur and curly auburn hair.

Hugo brought the cart to a stop in front of the centaurs. Grandpa had already explained that Hugo would not be able to enter the centaurs' realm.

"Greetings, Stan Sorenson," proclaimed Cloudwing in a clear, musical baritone.

"Good day, Cloudwing," Grandpa said. "Stormbrow. Quickstride. Bloodthorn. I take it you received my message."

"Yesterday the golem bore us tidings of your advent," Cloudwing replied. "You brought many companions."

"We need to counsel with Graymane," Grandpa said.

Cloudwing dipped his head. "Such is your right once per annum."

"You have the girl with you," Stormbrow accused, his voice deep and harsh.

"She accompanies us to offer appreciation for Broadhoof's noble sacrifice," Grandpa said.

"Her gratitude is not required," Stormbrow grated.

"Nevertheless, here we are," Grandpa replied, climbing down from the wagon.

"Stay aboard the cart," Cloudwing instructed. "We will tow you onward."

The golden centaur and the reddish centaur came forward and took hold of the handles Hugo had used to pull the wagon. Grandpa had explained that if they didn't solicit help, the centaurs might offer this service in order to shorten the duration of their visit.

They were currently on the far side of Fablehaven's marshlands. The road they had traveled had skirted the fens for the latter portion of the journey. Behind them, vapor hung above the foul, unfrozen water, where slime, moss, and tall weedy plants thrived in defiance of winter.

With no further words, the centaurs broke into a canter, towing the cart along at great speed. Kendra reviewed the instructions Grandpa had given. Unless engaged in conversation, centaurs considered eye contact a challenge. She was supposed to keep quiet unless Grandpa identified specific opportunities for her to speak. They were all under orders to accept insults graciously and without rebuttal. Given his knack for infuriating centaurs, she was relieved that her brother had stayed home.

The centaurs hauled them through an extensive vineyard and a sweet-smelling orchard populated by diverse fruit trees. Fairies flitted among the vegetation, driving back the snow and keeping the plants unseasonably fruitful. Only at the main house and near the Fairy Queen's shrine had Kendra ever seen so many. She also spotted female centaurs in the midst of the trees, effortlessly balancing huge baskets laden with fruit. Wrapped in furs, the women possessed a hard, cold beauty.

Beyond the orchard, they passed into a snowy grove of tall evergreens. Occasionally Kendra glimpsed pavilions through the trees. When the cart emerged from the grove, a tremendous block of stone loomed before them. Three times as tall as it was wide, the megalith towered thirty feet high. Off to either side, Kendra saw other monolithic standing stones, curving out of sight to form a ring around a broad hill.

"We will proceed on foot," Cloudwing announced. "Welcome to Grunhold." The centaurs who had been towing them released their hold on the wagon.

Kendra clambered down along with the others and followed the four centaurs around the megalith and up the gentle slope. Their path wound around hedges and earthworks, beneath arched trellises, up ramps, and over small, decorative bridges. As in the vineyard and the orchard, colorful fairies filled the air, keeping the vegetation in bloom. Among the terraced gardens, Kendra observed standing stones of varied shape and size, smaller cousins of the megaliths encircling the base of the hill. Here and there male and female centaurs roamed or conversed, showing little interest in the visitors. Occasionally Kendra noticed yawning entrances recessed into the hillside. Kendra wondered how far the shadowy tunnels extended.

As they neared the top of the hill, Kendra stared up at the primitive dolmen on the summit. Five massive upright stones served as columns to support an immense slab of rock, together forming a crude shelter. It looked as though an army of giants would have been required to place the enormous slab atop the other stones. Beneath the massive capstone waited a brooding centaur the color of a storm cloud. His long gray hair matched his bushy beard and the fur of his equine body. His eyebrows were the same darker gray of his tail. Although his face looked older than the other centaurs, it was not wrinkled. His torso may have carried more fat than the others, but none were more heavily muscled.

"Greetings, Stan Sorenson," Graymane intoned as they approached. "What brings you and yours to Grunhold?"

"Greetings, Graymane," Grandpa answered formally. "We are here to honor the nobility of Broadhoof and to ask a favor."

"Come forward," Graymane invited, backing away.

There was ample room inside the dolmen for the five centaurs and the six human visitors. The shelter had no furniture, so they stood facing one another, the centaurs on one side, the humans on the other. Kendra glanced up nervously at the enormous slab above them. If it fell, they would all be squished flat as tortillas.

"I am not acquainted with all of those in your party," Graymane said.

"You remember my wife, Ruth, and my assistant Dale," Grandpa said. "This is Tanugatoa, a renowned potion master. Coulter, a lifelong friend and an expert in magical relics. And my granddaughter, Kendra."

"The selfsame Kendra who sat astride Broadhoof as he perished?" Graymane asked, glancing at Cloudwing.

"The same," Grandpa replied. "Broadhoof bore her and the fairy stone into Kurisock's realm. Without his bravery, Fablehaven would have fallen into darkness."

"We feel his loss," Graymane said. "Broadhoof was like a son to me. Tell me, Kendra, how he died."

Kendra glanced at Grandpa, who gave a brief nod. Her gaze shifted to Graymane, her neck craning back. He stared down at her gravely. Her mouth felt dry. Trying to suppress her nerves, she reminded herself that the centaurs could not harm them. This was an official, protected visit. All she had to do was relate the truth in a gracious way.

"We were riding for the black tree with the nail in it. The only way to stop the plague was to destroy the nail. The stone the Fairy Queen had given me could counteract the plague. I had used the stone to heal people and creatures who were infected by the plague. She told me that uniting the stone with the nail would destroy both objects.

"All around us dark creatures attacked. Ephira, the

hamadryad who belonged to the tree with the nail, had originated the plague along with Kurisock. She attacked Broadhoof to protect the tree. Her touch could darken any creature. Just ask Stormbrow. But because Broadhoof was in contact with me, and I had the stone, when Ephira touched him, he found himself trapped between two powers. The stone prevented him from turning dark, but the strain killed him.

"Broadhoof managed to get us near enough to the tree that we ultimately succeeded. Uniting the stone and the nail cost my friend Lena her life. Without the help of Broadhoof, we would have been doomed. I'm so sorry he died. I had no idea that getting stuck between the power of the stone and the nail would kill him. I mourn for him. He was a true hero."

Kendra noticed that a cluster of fairies had gathered near the dolmen as she spoke. She tried to ignore them so she could concentrate on Graymane's response.

"I have already heard this account from others who were present. I appreciate your forthright retelling of the events, and join you in mourning." His eyes turned to Grandpa. "Was the loss of one of our finest worth rescuing the preserve? I think not. But for our present purposes, I will agree that Broadhoof died a hero, and leave it at that. You mentioned a favor?"

"We were hoping to see the first horn you keep in your possession," Grandpa said.

Graymane traded startled looks with Cloudwing and Stormbrow. His dark tail swished. "None are permitted to lay eyes on the Soul of Grunhold."

"My ancestor presented you with the first horn as a favor," Grandma reminded him.

Graymane stamped a hoof. "I am aware of the origin of our talisman. It was freely given. If we are to discuss past favors suddenly requiring compensation, I might submit the death of Broadhoof as an ample display of gratitude."

"I do not mean to suggest that we have a claim on the horn," Grandma said. "I hoped merely to point out that it is not inherently for the exclusive use of centaurs. Humans have successfully watched over the Soul of Grunhold in the past."

"To what end would you make this observation?" Graymane asked.

"Dark times have befallen the world," Grandma said with severity. "Sinister forces are gathering talismans to open the great prison Zzyzx and unleash the demons of old."

"Dire tidings, indeed," Graymane acknowledged. "Yet how is it our concern?"

"We require the horn to access a key that will enable us to safeguard one of the talismans," Grandpa said. "If we can protect the talismanic artifacts, we can prevent the prison from opening."

Graymane shared quiet words with Cloudwing on his right, then Stormbrow on his left. "You would remove the Soul of Grunhold from Fablehaven?"

"We would return it within days," Grandma said. "We ask no aid except to briefly borrow the horn."

Graymane slowly shook his head. "Should the demon horde escape Zzyzx, the Soul of Grunhold would be our only defense. We cannot accept the risk. You ask too much."

"If the demons escape Zzyzx, Grunhold will become a small island in a sea of evil," Grandpa stressed. "Under assault from the demon horde, the horn will fail and Grunhold will fall. If, however, we prevent the demons from escaping Zzyzx, Grunhold may well endure forever."

"We cannot send our prized talisman into peril," Graymane replied. "When you removed the power from the shrine of the Fairy Queen, you destroyed it, leaving her sanctuary irreparably desecrated. My decision stands. Find another method to accomplish your aims. We will not lend you or anyone the Soul of Grunhold."

"Could we at least look upon the horn?" Grandpa asked. "Another way to protect the talismans that unlock Zzyzx would be to ensure that our enemies will not be able to steal the horn from you. Such assurance is vital."

Graymane smirked dourly. "You might also appreciate the chance to scout for ways to pilfer the horn yourself."

"The horn must not be stolen," Grandma affirmed. "We have no desire to rob you."

"As you should know, the Soul of Grunhold *cannot* be stolen," Graymane said. "The first horn of a unicorn can only be found or given. The object radiates such purity that even the most jaded scoundrel would be overwhelmed with enough guilt and remorse at the thought of stealing it to render him incapable of carrying out the robbery." The imposing centaur gave Grandma a pointed look. "Even if the thief had convinced himself he only meant to borrow it."

"What if our powerful enemies found a way to circumvent such remorse?" Grandpa inquired. "With your assent, I could station guards."

"We have guards of our own, the finest inhabiting this preserve," Graymane stated. "Furthermore, the Soul of Grunhold lies deep inside the hill, at the heart of a Tauran maze."

"A maze of invisible walls?" Coulter exclaimed.

Graymane nodded. "The same as my kind used anciently. Fatal spells lace the unseen barriers. The intruder who touches any wall will be instantly struck down."

"Such contact will also raise an alarm," Stormbrow added.

"Our enemies have proven themselves unbelievably resourceful," Grandpa worried.

"You still doubt?" Graymane scoffed. "At the heart of the unsolvable maze awaits Udnar the mountain troll as a final redundancy."

"A mountain troll?" Dale exclaimed. "How did you win his loyalty?"

"We reached an arrangement," Graymane replied flatly. "It involves copious quantities of food and drink."

"What about the entrance to the maze?" Grandma asked.

Graymane fell silent, scrutinizing the humans one by one. "The entrance to the great hollow below the hill is sealed. I will refrain from relating the specifics to prevent any of you from imprudently coming to harm."

"We wouldn't dare make an attempt for the horn,"

Grandpa assured him. "As you say, it would be impossible. You give us reason to hope our enemies would be equally daunted. Perhaps we can locate a first horn through other channels."

"Wisely spoken," Graymane said. "Do not forget, any attempt to steal the Soul of Grunhold would mean war with the centaurs. We have our allotted realm, but by treaty we remain free to roam most of the length and breadth of Fablehaven, with the exception of a few private domains. War with the centaurs would mean the end of your preserve."

"Which is why we traveled here to solicit the favor according to protocol," Grandma placated.

"It disappoints us that you refuse to lend us the horn," Grandpa admitted. "Much evil abroad and at home may flow from that decision. Yet we acknowledge it as your decision to make."

"Then our parley is at an end," Graymane announced. "Return to your domain in peace."

"We have it on good authority that our enemies are interested in the horn," Grandma said. "Stay vigilant."

Graymane turned his back on them.

"We require no such advice from humans," Cloudwing clarified. "Permit us to escort you to the borders of our realm."

"Very well," Grandpa said, his voice formal. "Farewell, Graymane."

Kendra followed the others out of the massive stone shelter. She noticed that a cluster of fairies continued to hover nearby, gazing at her curiously. When she showed them prolonged attention, several of the fairies fluttered away, probably in an attempt to appear disinterested. One of the fairies who remained looked familiar. Tinier than most fairies, she had fiery wings shaped like flower petals.

"I know you," Kendra said.

The other fairies who had remained turned to jealously regard the small red fairy. "Yes," the fairy chirped, darting closer to Kendra. Rolling their eyes, the other fairies dispersed.

"You were one of the three who helped us when we defeated the shadow plague."

"Correct. I overheard your conversation with Graymane."

"Didn't go so well." Kendra noticed Stormbrow watching her surreptitiously. She doubted whether he could understand the fairy, but Kendra spoke in plain English. She lowered her voice and resolved to choose her words carefully.

"The centaurs will never part with the horn," the fairy informed her.

"Can you help us get it?" Kendra whispered, hanging back from the others, eyes on the centaurs.

The tiny fairy gave a light, tinkling laugh. "Not likely. But I do know where you can find the entrance to the maze."

"Please tell me."

"Gladly. By the way, if I refused, you could command me to reveal what I know. Just a little tip for the future. Many fairies are unhelpful. The entrance lies beneath the southernmost warding stone."

"The gigantic one?" Kendra asked, nodding her head toward the tremendous megaliths at the base of the hill.

"Yes," the fairy answered.

"They look too big to move," Kendra whispered.

"Much too big," the fairy agreed, "and bound in place by spells. But two hours before dawn, the stones march. They trade places. Takes them an hour. For that hour of the night, while the stones are marching, the entrance to the maze lies wide open. It is the only time the centaurs can enter."

"Those humongous stones move by themselves?"

"All twenty of them. It's quite a sight."

"Do many centaurs go into the maze?"

"Not often."

"Can you tell me anything else?"

"I've learned to pick up phrases in the Tauran language. I listen in on their conversations for practice. Only a few centaurs know how to navigate the maze. They only go in to bring food for the troll. They love the horn and would kill to protect it. Don't go after it, Kendra."

"Thanks," Kendra said earnestly. "We better not talk too long. The centaurs are already suspicious."

"My pleasure." The tiny fairy zipped away.

Kendra walked with the others back to the cart. She sat in silence as they passed through the evergreen grove, the orchard, and the vineyard. When they reached the edge of the dreary, steaming marsh, the centaurs handed the wagon back to Hugo, who stood waiting exactly where they had left him.

Once they were well along the path, Kendra scooted

near Grandpa. "Are we safe to talk about what happened?" she asked.

Grandpa looked around. "I think so, if we keep our voices down."

"I know where the maze begins."

"What?" Grandpa looked startled. "How?"

"A fairy told me. The entrance is hidden beneath the southernmost warding stone. That is what the fairy called the giant stones at the bottom of the hill. Two hours before dawn the stones move around, leaving the entrance accessible for about an hour."

"Well done, Kendra," Grandpa said. "Unfortunately, I'm not sure it changes our circumstances much. Few creatures have more raw power than mountain trolls. None of us can navigate a Tauran maze. And even without the obstacles, the horn can't be stolen in the first place. If they don't give it to us, we can't take it. Am I wrong?"

Everyone was now huddled close around the conversation.

"I have no idea how we could borrow the horn without permission," Tanu said.

"Nor do I," Dale concurred.

"Our best bet is to start searching elsewhere," Coulter suggested. "Somewhere in the wide world there must be another first horn."

"We'll be racing the Sphinx," Grandma said. "And he has the Oculus."

Grandpa frowned. "That may be so. But a glimmer of hope is better than none at all."

CHAPTER THIRTEEN

Shadow Charmer

The alarm on Seth's wristwatch roused him from sleep. He fumbled with the tiny buttons until the beeping stopped. Leaning up on one elbow, he watched the motionless lump on Kendra's bed. The alarm did not seem to have disturbed her.

Even so, he waited. Kendra could be crafty. She seemed to have a sixth sense when it came to preventing mischief. Minutes passed, but Seth stayed in bed. It gave his mind time to fully awaken.

Earlier that day, after the others had returned from their mission among the centaurs, they had related to Seth and Warren all they had discovered. The decision had been made to start hunting for a unicorn's first horn outside of Fablehaven.

Quietly, Seth had begun to make his own plans.

He had spent the afternoon wondering about the voice he had heard while conversing with the satyrs. At first he had assumed the speaker was some random ghost wandering the woods. Later, a more convincing possibility came to mind. He now felt confident that the voice belonged to the demon Graulas.

After that realization, the plan began to fall into place. Graulas must have been impressed that Seth had helped overthrow the shadow plague, just as the demon had been astonished with how he had defeated the revenant. Seth felt sure that the demon was summoning him.

Since Graulas was calling to him, it must mean the demon had useful information. The possibilities were exhilarating. Perhaps Graulas could explain why Seth was hearing ghostly voices. After all, dark mysteries were his specialty. And hopefully Graulas could provide pointers on how they could swipe the horn from the centaurs after all. A visit to the demon might be all it would take for Seth to save the day.

His grandparents were always encouraging him to learn from his mistakes. And Seth had learned enough about his grandparents to know they would never permit him to visit the demon. They were relentlessly overprotective. If he brought it up, they would be on guard and do everything in their power to stop him. So Seth decided he would keep his plan to himself, leaving a note under the bed in case things went wrong and he never returned.

Could this be a trap? Yes. But if Graulas had wanted

to kill him, the demon could have done so the last time Seth had visited. Could visiting Graulas place anyone besides himself in jeopardy? No, he couldn't see how. What if he was mistaken and Graulas had not been summoning him? What if the mysterious voice had an entirely different origin? If he dropped by uninvited, might the demon kill him for intruding? Maybe. But the Sphinx was on his way to collecting his third artifact, and Seth's friends and family were grasping at straws. Somebody had to make an aggressive move. Seth gritted his teeth. When all hope was gone, wasn't it his job to fix things? Of course it was.

Rolling out of bed, Seth strapped on his adamant breastplate and pulled a camouflage shirt over it. He put on jeans, laced up his boots, and grabbed his coat, gloves, and hat. Then he retrieved his emergency kit from under the bed. The kit contained odds and ends that might come in handy to someone alone in the woods on an adventure. In addition to standard equipment like a flashlight, a compass, a pocketknife, a magnifying glass, a whistle, a mirror, and various snacks, Seth had retained the gaseous potion from the hotel. In the commotion, Tanu had forgotten to ask for it back.

Seth stuffed his pillows under his covers, then crept to the door and down the stairs, listening behind for sounds of Kendra stirring and ahead for evidence of anyone else up and about. The house remained quiet, and he silently made his way to the garage, found a mountain bike, and wheeled it outside. He wished he had the guts to borrow an ATV, but worried that the noise would awaken somebody and end his excursion before it began. Somewhere in the darkness, Hugo and Mendigo were watching over the yard. Seth hoped he could slip quietly past them. Hopefully they had no direct orders to keep him out of the woods.

The night was well below freezing. Unseen clouds blotted out all light from the heavens. A few softly glowing fairies bobbed among the flowers in the yard, providing the only illumination. Seth mounted the bike and soon discovered that heavy boots were not designed for pedaling. Once he gained some momentum, the endeavor became somewhat easier.

He knew the way to the cave where Graulas lived. From what Seth had seen, Hugo had been keeping the main paths through Fablehaven relatively clear of snow. Hopefully that would hold true on his way to the cave. Otherwise he might have to ditch the bike and walk.

Seth pedaled across the lawn toward the path he needed. Squinting in the darkness, he rode through a flower bed and had to hit the brakes and turn to avoid a row of rosebushes. He decided to walk the bike until he was far enough from the house to use a light.

Just as he was passing out of the yard onto the path, a huge hand gripped his shoulder and hoisted him into the air. The mountain bike clattered to the ground. Seth cried out in startled terror before realizing he had been apprehended by Hugo.

"Late," the golem rumbled.

"Set me down," Seth demanded, legs swinging. "You almost scared me to death!"

Hugo placed Seth on his feet.

"Go home," Hugo said, pointing at the house.

"Are you under orders to send me back?" Seth asked, slipping a hand into his emergency kit.

"Guard," Hugo said.

"Right. They told you to guard the yard. Not to baby-sit me."

"Woods bad. Seth alone."

"Want to come with me?" Seth tried, jittery fingers finding the potion bottle.

"Guard," Hugo repeated more firmly.

"I get it. You have your orders. But I have mine. I have to run a crucial errand."

"Stan mad."

"You mean Grandpa wouldn't want me running off? Of course not. He thinks I still wear diapers. Which is why I'm doing this in the middle of the night. You have to trust me, Hugo. I know I've done some dumb things in the past, but I've also saved the day. I have to sneak into the woods for a little while. It isn't for idiotic reasons, like to get gold. Basically, I'm trying to save the world."

The golem stood in silence for a moment. "Not safe."

"It isn't totally safe," Seth admitted. "But I'm prepared. See? I even have this potion from Tanu. I'm going someplace I've been before. I'll stay on the path and be careful. If I try to get permission, I'll fail. They won't let me. But only I can do this. Sneaking away is my only choice. You have to trust me."

Hugo turned and looked at the house. Seth could barely see the earthen giant in the darkness. "Hugo come."

"You'll come? You don't have to join me. We don't want to leave the yard unguarded."

Hugo pointed across the yard. "Mendigo."

"Mendigo is on lookout too?" he confirmed.

"Seth go. Hugo come."

Relief flooded through Seth. This was unexpected good fortune. He wondered if Hugo would still consent once he knew the destination. There was only one way to find out.

"Hugo, take me to the cave where Graulas lives."

Hugo picked up Seth. "Seth sure?"

"We have to go there. He can give me important info. It could help save everyone. Remember last time? Grandpa didn't want me to go there, but we ended up getting information that helped us stop the plague."

Hugo loped away into the woods, moving swiftly. When traveling without the cart, the golem preferred to move cross-country rather than sticking to roads or paths. Ice and snow crunched under the golem's massive feet. Bare branches whipped past in the darkness, but Hugo altered how he cradled Seth to keep limbs from scraping him. This was so much better than awkwardly biking along icy trails in the frigid darkness!

Seth had given no real consideration to the possibility of Hugo helping him. He had heard Grandpa give the golem orders to protect the yard, and he had never known the golem to disobey a command. Hugo was becoming more of a free thinker than Seth had realized.

After pounding through the cold night long enough for Seth to start worrying about frostbite, the golem came to a halt and set him down. The night was too dark for Seth to discern any landmarks, but he figured the sudden stop meant they had reached their destination. The golem would not be able to set foot on the land allotted to Graulas. If Seth ran into trouble, he would be on his own.

Seth retrieved the flashlight from his emergency kit. The beam glittered on a snowy slope that led up to a steep hill with a cave in the side. Seth rubbed life back into his partially numb ears, then adjusted his hat and coat to cover his face better.

"Thanks for the lift," Seth said. "I'll be back soon."

"Be safe."

As Seth tromped through the snow toward the cave, he began to question the sanity of this excursion. He was walking alone at night into the cave of an evil and powerful demon. Hoping to bolster his spirits, he shone the flashlight back at Hugo. Under the single white beam, standing in the snow, the golem looked different, like some strange, primitive statue. Hardly comforting.

Clenching his jaw, Seth increased his pace. If he was going through with this, he might as well get it over with. He marched past the rotten post with the dangling rusted shackles, paused outside the spacious mouth of the cave, almost turned back, and then strode inside.

Seth hurried along the excavated tunnel, winding past a couple of curves before reaching a stuffy room with roots twisting down from the domed ceiling. The first thing that struck him was the unnatural warmth. The second was the smell, sweet and disgusting, like spoiled fruit.

After shining his light across rotting furniture, smashed crates, pale bones, and moldering books, Seth let the beam settle on a massive shape slumped against the wall. He could see and hear the shape taking slow, ragged breaths. The lumpy figure stirred, cobwebs billowing, and sat up. The flashlight shone on a dusty face dripping with wrinkled lobes of inflamed flesh. A pair of ram horns curled from the sides of the bald head, and a milky film clouded the cold, black eyes. "You . . . came," the demon wheezed in an impossibly deep voice.

"You really did call me," Seth said. "I thought so."

"And you . . . heard me." A fit of coughing seized the moribund demon, sending plumes of dust into the air. When the spasm finished, Graulas spat a shiny wad of greenish gunk into the corner. "Come closer."

Seth approached the huge demon. Even with Graulas seated on the ground, Seth stood no higher than his hunched shoulder. The foul smell intensified as he drew nearer, becoming a rancid medley of decay and infection. Seth fought the urge to puke.

Graulas closed his eyes and tilted his head back, his bulky chest laboring like a huge bellows. Seth heard a wet rattling with each strained inhalation.

"Are you okay?" Seth asked.

The demon tilted his grotesque head back and forth, wattles flopping as he stretched his neck. He spoke slowly. "I am more awake than when we last spoke. But I am still dying. As I mentioned when we met before, death comes slowly for my kind. Months are like minutes. In a way, I envy Kurisock."

"He's really dead?"

"He has passed beyond this sphere of existence. His new abode is less pleasant. No doubt he will be there to greet me." A small spider descended from the tip of one of the ram horns, suspended by a silvery thread.

"Why did you want to see me?" Seth asked.

The demon cleared his throat. "You were foolish to come. If you understood who I was, you would stay far away. Or maybe you were not so foolish, for again I mean to help you. Tell me how your abilities are developing."

"Well, I could hear you when I was in the woods with the satyrs. In the dungeon I could hear what wraiths were whispering. And I saw a goblin the other day even though he was invisible."

The demon raised a thick, gnarled finger and tapped it against a deformed hole in the side of his head. "Whether I like it or not, my perceptions reach well beyond this hovel. I can observe most of the preserve from here, all save a few shielded locations. One place I could never look was inside the domain of Kurisock. Until he died. Then the curtains came down and I could see. The nail in the revenant left a mark on you when you removed it. When the nail was destroyed, you were nearby, and some of its power fled to you, marking you more deeply."

"Marking me?"

"The nail left you empowered. Primed for even greater achievements. I understand your need. Your family discussed the object they desire from the centaurs as they traveled unshielded roads. Your grandfather should know better. I could hear every word."

"They need the unicorn horn from the centaurs," Seth said. "I was hoping you might know how we could get it."

Graulas began to cough, a violent progression of heaving and choking that left him slumped to the side, propped up by one elbow. Seth stepped back, wondering if he was about to witness the ancient demon's strangling on his phlegm. At last, gasping, creamy fluid drooling from the corner of his mouth, Graulas forced himself back into a sitting position.

"The first horn of a unicorn is a powerful object," Graulas rasped. "It purifies whatever it touches. Cures any sickness. Neutralizes any poison. Eliminates any disease."

"Do you want me to use it to heal you?"

The demon coughed again. It might have been a chuckle. "Disease has woven itself into my being. The touch of a first horn would probably kill me. I am that corrupt. I have no need of the horn. But I know how you can acquire the Soul of Grunhold. If you want the horn, you must employ your skills as a shadow charmer."

"What?"

"A shadow charmer enjoys brotherhood with the creatures of the night. His emotions cannot be manipulated. Nothing escapes his gaze. He hears and comprehends the secret languages of darkness."

"Am I a shadow charmer?" Seth asked hesitantly.

"In all but name. The nail laid a strong foundation. I intend to stabilize those gifts and formally dub you an ally of the night. It will bring your abilities into greater focus."

"Will it make me evil?" Seth whispered.

"I did not say an ally of *evil*. All power can be used for

good or ill. This power is already yours. I will merely help you harness it better. Use it how you like."

"How will it help me get the horn?" Seth asked.

The demon stared, clouded eyes weighing him. When he spoke, his voice was deliberate. "Who can navigate an invisible maze? The man who can see it. Who can get past a mountain troll? The man who becomes his friend. Who can steal the first horn of a unicorn? The man immune to guilt."

"You really were listening to Grandpa."

"It would entertain me to see the centaurs humbled," Graulas said. "You are the first new shadow charmer in centuries. Perhaps you will be the last. Few remain who could formalize the honor. You already exhibit most of the traits in embryo. Nothing will wash that away. Better to complete what was started. Darkness has touched you, much as light has embraced your sister."

"This sounds shady," Seth hedged, backing away. Did he really want favors from a dying demon? Wasn't the decaying stink of the place a hint that he should go?

Groaning, using a splintered fence post as a crutch, Graulas rose ponderously to his feet, his curled horns nearly touching the ceiling. Gesturing elaborately, as if painting in the air, the demon began chanting in a guttural language. Toward the end of the display, Seth began to understand the words. " . . . consoler of phantoms, comrade of trolls, councilor of demons, hereby and henceforth recognized and acknowledged as a shadow charmer."

Graulas lowered his arms and sat down hard. Wood splintered beneath him and dust plumed outward.

"You okay?" Seth asked.

The demon coughed mildly. "Yes."

"Why did you switch to English at the end?"

The corners of the demon's mouth twitched. "I didn't. Congratulations."

Seth covered his eyes for a moment. "I didn't give you permission to do that!" He regarded the demon somberly. "I'm scared that coming here was a huge mistake."

Graulas licked his cracked lips with a bruised tongue. "I can't make you evil any more than you can make me good. You worry that accepting aid from a demon somehow alters your identity. I was once very evil. Deliberately evil. Over time, as I weakened and deteriorated, my lust for power abated. Apathy replaced avarice. You are not speaking to an evil demon. An evil demon would have killed you on sight. You are talking with a rotting shell. My life ended long ago. When I thought I was utterly past feeling, you sparked my interest. I remain sufficiently curious to help you. I have no private agenda. You remain free to use your gifts however you choose."

Seth furrowed his brow. "I guess I don't feel more evil than before."

"Choices determine character. You made no decision to become a shadow charmer. These new abilities have been thrust upon you by circumstances beyond your control. If anything, your status as a shadow charmer should protect you and those you love from evil. You now see and hear more clearly. Your emotions can't be confused by magic. You will encounter opportunities to talk rather than fight."

"Are you speaking English now?"

"Yes." Another wild fit of coughing wracked the demon. When the hacking subsided, Graulas lay sprawled on his side, eyes closed. "I must rest."

"When should I go after the horn?" Seth asked.

"Now," the demon rasped, his voice losing power. "Tonight."

"How do I see the invisible maze?" Seth asked.

Graulas sighed. "The same way you see me. Your abilities have been stabilized."

"I have more questions. What can you tell me about the Sphinx? We know he is the leader of the Society of the Evening Star."

"I have been confined to this preserve for centuries," Graulas groaned groggily. "I lost interest in world politics ages ago. My memories are of ancient India and China. I know little of the Sphinx. When he visited Fablehaven, he seemed like a man. But it is hard to detect an avatar, even for me."

"You detected Navarog."

"I have met Navarog previously. And his avatar. It makes a difference."

"I may have to fight Navarog."

The demon snorted. "Do not fight Navarog."

"Does he have a weakness?"

Graulas opened his eyes to narrow slits. "Concentrate on the horn. Nero will teach you about shade walking and befriending trolls."

"Nero?" Seth asked.

A suave voice spoke from behind. "We meet again, Seth Sorenson."

Seth whirled, shining his light on the troll. He recognized the reptilian features, the bulging round eyes, and the glossy black body with yellow markings. "What are you doing here?"

"A shadow charmer," Nero simpered in an oily tone. "Who would have suspected? To think, I once saved you from a fall and almost had you as a servant."

"Don't you live a long way from here?"

A long, gray tongue flicked out of the troll's mouth and licked his right eye. "When Master Graulas commands, I obey."

"You're here to help me?" Seth asked.

"You need a mentor. Graulas wants me to instruct you in a few matters and accompany you to Grunhold."

"You can't enter Grunhold."

"No. But as a mortal, you can. In fact, as a shadow charmer, you might even survive."

Seth turned back to Graulas. "Are you still awake?"

The demon smacked his lips. "Awake or asleep, I always listen."

"You really want me to go to Grunhold tonight?"

"There will be no better opportunity," the demon growled, rolling over. "Now give me peace, boy."

Seth faced Nero. "Okay. How do I survive?"

The troll licked his other eye. "As a shadow charmer, you can shade walk. Away from bright light you will be nearly invisible. Very, very dim. When you keep to the shade, even vigilant eyes will pass over you. Particularly if you hold still. This will help you approach the entrance."

"Will I be able to see in the dark?"

"Turn off your flashlight."

Seth complied. He could see nothing. "Apparently not." He switched his light back on.

Nero shrugged. "Your vision may not penetrate darkness, but other talents should emerge over time. No two shadow charmers are identical."

"What types of talents?"

"I have heard of shadow charmers who could quench flames. Project fear. Lower the temperature in a room."

Seth smiled. "Can you teach me?"

"These skills will emerge naturally or not at all. Back to the task at hand. Master Graulas tells me that a mountain troll awaits inside Grunhold. Along with a reputation for immense size and strength, their breed has a deserved notoriety for stupidity. The oaf will recognize you as an ally of the night. But he also has a charge to guard the horn. Show no fear. Take his friendship for granted, and you will probably win it. Then you must convince him that you are a trickster, and that stealing the horn is a prank. Mountain trolls love jokes." The troll held out his webbed hand.

"Is that a banana?" Seth asked.

The troll tossed the fruit over his shoulder and deftly caught it behind his back. "Your prank will be to replace the horn with a banana. The troll should like that."

Seth laughed. "Are you serious?"

"Entirely."

"Where did you find a banana?"

"I have suppliers. Some of the satyrs cultivate tropical fruit."

Seth folded his arms. "Invisible or not, the maze could be trouble, right?"

"The hardest part," Nero said. "If your instincts fail, the trick with mazes is to always turn left. Only veer right when you can't turn left. Eventually you will systematically cover all the ground in the maze until you find your destination."

"The entrance will only be open for an hour."

"As I already noted, the maze will be the hardest part."

Seth sat down on a filthy keg. "If I get trapped inside, I'll have to bide my time until the next night when the entrance opens again. My family will freak. How do we get to Grunhold?"

Nero rubbed his hands together. "The best way is through the marsh. I have a raft. I can land you near the southern side of the circle of stones."

"I hope I can convince Hugo."

"I saw you arrive with the golem. If he would bear us to the raft, it would save time. We should make haste—the hour grows late."

CHAPTER FOURTEEN

Heart and Soul

U p there on the left," Nero directed. "Perfect, you can put us down. I'll take it from here."

Hugo set Seth on the ground. Seth clicked on his flashlight. The golem held Nero by his ankles. The troll hung upside down, staring into the stony hollows of the golem's eyes. "No hurt Seth," Hugo warned, the words coming out like massive boulders grinding against each other.

"You have my word," Nero pledged, placing a webbed hand over his chest.

The golem turned Nero around and placed him on the ground. He kept hold of one arm. Nero tried to tug away, but Hugo held tight.

"You can release me," Nero invited.

Leaning forward, the golem pinched Nero's neck between thumb and forefinger. "No hurt Seth."

"I'm on his side," the troll managed in a strangled voice. "I swear it."

"Let him go, Hugo," Seth said. The golem released the troll and stood up straight. "If he ends up harming me, you have my permission to squash him."

"Thanks for the vote of confidence," Nero gagged bitterly, rubbing his throat.

"Seth no go," Hugo rumbled.

"I have to try, Hugo. We've come this far. I need to finish what I've started."

"We must reach Grunhold before the warding stones start marching," Nero inserted. "You will need every second."

Seth gave Hugo a hug. The golem patted his back. "Hugo come."

Seth shook his head. "You're too big. You'll swamp the raft. And you don't hold together so well in water. Just wait here so you can take me home after we return." Seth followed Nero toward the raft.

The golem raised a hand in farewell. "Be safe."

"I'll be right back," Seth promised.

Nero pushed the raft into the water and leapt aboard. The rectangular craft was a little bigger than a king-size mattress. Without guardrails, the mooring cleats were the highest part of the vessel, a scant foot or so above the water. Clutching a long pole, the troll gestured for Seth to join him. Seth jumped onto the flat craft. Leaning on the pole, the troll shoved the raft away from the shore. Ripples spread over the dark, fuming water.

"Extinguish the light," Nero murmured. "From here on, we must avoid attention."

Seth turned off the flashlight. He could see nothing. He listened to the soft sound of water lapping against the raft. "You can see in the dark?" he whispered.

"I can."

"Can you see me?"

"Certainly."

"Shouldn't I be invisible?"

"Shade walking only works before you've been spotted. Once an observer sees you, dimness will no longer hide you."

Seth thought about that. "What if I snuck up on you later?"

"Then you might be cloaked to my eyes."

Seth sat down cross-legged. The air in the swamp felt less cold. A heavy, stagnant odor invaded his nostrils. "Why are you helping me?"

"You are an ally of the night," Nero said. "Graulas is demonic royalty. Long ago he served as the left hand to Gorgrog, the demon king. I owe Graulas a tremendous debt. He gave me my seeing stone."

"You'll wait for me while I snag the horn?"

"Whether you return tonight or tomorrow, I'll be waiting with the raft near the shore where I drop you. Silence. Something approaches." Seth listened intently, but could hear nothing. Nero crouched at his side and whispered in his ear. "Lie flat."

Seth sprawled out on his stomach. He could feel the troll lying beside him. A moment later, he heard something sloshing through the water in the distance. It was coming toward them. Seth wished for eyes like his sister so he could pierce the darkness without a light. What could it be? From the sound of it, something big. He held his breath.

The sloshing drew nearer. The rhythm of the splashes suggested a gigantic creature wading through the water. One leg sloshed forward, then the other, then the other, then the other . . .

Nero eased away from Seth. The swamp was totally black. As the sloshing continued toward them, ripples began to make the raft wobble. But then the raft began to glide forward, away from the path of the approaching threat. Seth heard noisy breathing above and behind them.

Unable to see, he closed his eyes and focused on quieting his own breathing. The creature passed directly behind them, never pausing, and soon the sloshing threat was moving away. The sound had completely faded before Nero resumed poling forward in earnest.

"What was that?" Seth whispered.

"Fog giant," Nero replied. "They don't see any better than you in the dark. They roam the marshes erratically. But if they find you, that is the end."

"It came close."

"Much too close. We're fortunate it failed to catch our scent or hear us. The brute must have had a destination in mind."

"The water isn't deep here," Seth said.

"The water is seldom deep in the marsh. Up to the thighs of a fog giant. Keep silent. Before long we will near the shores of the centaurs. If you are apprehended inside of their territory, they will kill you as surely as any giant would."

Seth stopped speaking. The anticipation of his mission helped offset the boredom. He was about to trespass alone into the centaurs' secret stronghold armed only with a banana. If the centaurs caught him, not only would he die but he would provoke a war. The thought was sobering.

Without warning, the raft ran aground, squishing against the muddy, reedy bank. "Here we are," Nero whispered. "Move away from the water. Keep to the shade. Go swiftly. The hour grows late."

"Thanks for the ride," Seth whispered back. "See you soon."

Seth sprang from the boat, reeds rustling as he landed. He froze, crouched, listening. When no furious centaurs descended on him, he crept forward, staying low and stepping with care. Up ahead, through the trees, Seth began to discern the wavering glow of firelight. He advanced toward the light.

The foliage at the edge of the swamp soon gave way to evergreens. There was little undergrowth, so Seth scurried from tree to tree until he obtained a view of a large hill. The monstrous silhouette of a colossal stone dominated the foreground. Cressets and torches burned on the hill, shedding warm auras of radiance and backlighting the megalith.

Seth took out his compass. He could barely read it by

the wavering light of the distant flames. He found north and promptly determined which of the megaliths was the southernmost. It was the second monolith to the right.

By no means did the torches brighten the entire hill. The jittery flames merely provided periodic illumination. At first the area appeared deserted. Then Seth began to spot centaurs spaced around the base of the hill, lurking in pockets of darkness away from the flaming cressets. He counted three, and assumed there would be more on the far side of the entrance. Rather than cluster around the southernmost stone, the centaurs had opted to spread out, as if simply guarding the hill. Their positions showed no preference to any particular megalith.

Clearly the centaurs didn't want the placement of their sentries to give away the position of the entrance. The deployment could work to his advantage. It gave him some room to work with. The level area between the evergreens at the base of the hill lacked cover. But it was dim. If his ability worked as Nero had described, he should be able to slink forward, then sneak along the bottom of the hill to the southernmost megalith. If not, he would be apprehended the instant he crawled out from behind the trees.

Dropping to his hands and knees, Seth inched forward, eyes on the nearest centaur. The guard stood perhaps a hundred feet away, brawny arms folded. The cover of the trees was soon well behind Seth. At times, the centaur seemed to stare right at him; then the brooding face would turn away. So far, so good.

Seth had no idea how much movement might destroy

his dimness and attract attention, so he advanced very slowly. He crawled toward the nearest megalith, stomach tight with worry. Once he was close enough to the huge stone, it would interrupt all lines of sight from the hill. Too bad the southernmost stone was still over a hundred yards away.

When he reached the megalith, Seth stood up, sweaty despite the cold. He started working his way around the gigantic stone to peek at the hill again. Just as part of the hill was coming into view, the ground began to vibrate.

Seth froze. The vibration grew into a trembling, the trembling into a quaking, and the megalith beside him began to rise. Seth fell flat and crawled on his belly toward the hill. He squirmed to the nearest bush and then held still, ready for a centaur to shout an alarm.

Abruptly the quaking stopped.

Glancing over his shoulder, Seth saw that the bottom of the stone was hovering about five feet in the air. The megalith appeared to have risen about fifteen feet, the lowest ten feet of the stone having been underground. A dark pit yawned where the colossal stone had rested. Slowly, the megalith began to drift sideways.

The clock was ticking.

Seth had one hour to get through the entrance, navigate the maze, befriend the troll, claim the horn, return through the maze, and exit unnoticed.

Rising to his knees, Seth surveyed the vicinity, making certain the centaurs had retained their previous positions and scanning for any sentries he may have missed. He saw no surprises. The nearest centaur was up the slope about thirty feet. From this angle, a torch farther up the hill made his outline obvious.

Seth began crawling along the base of the hill, trying to keep bushes and hedges between himself and the guards. Several times he had to creep across open spaces. He proceeded slowly, and no alarm was raised.

His most nerve-racking moment came as he crept across empty ground not fifteen feet in front of a sentry. He was halfway across the shadowy gap when his knee came down on a dry twig, snapping it clean. Seth halted, head down, muscles locked in panic.

From the corner of his eye he saw the centaur plodding forward to investigate. His only chance was to remain still as a statue and hope he appeared much less visible than he felt. The centaur halted immediately beside him. Had Seth stretched out a hand, he could have touched his hoof. Seth concentrated on breathing softly. Might the centaur smell him? His arms began to feel wobbly from holding the same position.

The centaur finally backed away, returning to his station in the gloom below a tall hedge. Seth slunk forward, careful to move in silence.

At last, heart pounding, Seth came even with the pit belonging to the southernmost megalith. The huge stone had now floated completely out of the way. To reach the pit, once again he would have to traverse an expanse of unshielded ground.

Clenching his tongue gently between his teeth, Seth

crawled forward, resisting the temptation to hurry across the bare area. He was well away from any cover when he heard approaching hoofbeats. He slowly turned his head. Several centaurs were approaching from his left, bearing torches and pushing enormous wheelbarrows heaped with food.

Behind him, a centaur whom Seth had failed to notice emerged from hiding. The centaur called out in a series of grunts, gargles, and whinnies. The centaur language sounded more like horse noises than human speech.

The oncoming centaurs responded to the greeting by trumpeting strange replies of their own. They were heading toward the entrance to the maze.

As the centaur behind Seth cantered over to greet his comrades, their eyes were on each other. Seth decided it might be the only decent distraction he would have before they reached him, so he rose, sprinted to the pit in a low crouch, and dove blindly into it.

Fortunately the walls of the pit were not sheer. Seth rolled to the bottom. Relieved once again to hear no cries of alarm, he regained his feet. A rounded entryway dominated one side of the pit. It had no door, so Seth dashed inside.

Below his feet the ground became firm and smooth. The long tunnel sloped steadily downward, plunging into and under the hill. Not wanting to accidentally brush against a wall, Seth switched on his flashlight, cupping a hand over the end to reduce the glare. Before long, he noticed a bluish radiance up ahead and switched off the flashlight.

Seth sprinted along the tunnel until he emerged in a vast cavern. Heavy iron chandeliers hung from the high,

vaulted ceiling, casting a diffuse glow across the room. Tall
barriers of dark iron reached halfway to the ceiling, barring
the way except for five gaps. There was no way to confirm
that the iron walls were invisible to others. They sure looked
solid to him.

Hooves clattered in the tunnel, and Seth slipped through
one of the gaps into the labyrinth, putting a barrier between
himself and the entrance to the cavern. He did not proceed
far. If he was careful, the presence of the centaurs might
work to his advantage. By following them at a distance, he
could take the guesswork out of wandering the maze. He
bounced on his toes, flexing his fingers, ready to run in case
he had accidentally chosen the correct gap and the centaurs
came his way.

Glancing at the ground, he noticed that the iron walls
cast no shadows. The mellow light from the chandeliers
dispersed evenly, with no interference. And in that moment
he realized his problem.

If the walls of the maze were invisible to the centaurs,
the iron barriers would do nothing to conceal him from
their sight!

From the sound of the approaching hoofbeats, the
centaurs were almost through the tunnel. Seth raced out
of the maze and hurried to one side of the tunnel mouth,
standing as close to the wall as he dared. The light from
the chandeliers was mild. Was it dim enough for his
shade-walking ability to function? Probably not. His mind
scrambled. He had gotten only a quick glimpse of the
oncoming centaurs. Their wheelbarrows were big, almost

the size of wagons. They were piled high with food. What if he tried to hitch a ride as the first one emerged? If he stayed low and kept in the front of the wheelbarrow, the centaur pushing it might not see him.

The first centaur had almost reached him. He could hear the creak of the first wheelbarrow's wheel and the unhurried clop of hoofbeats. As the wheelbarrow nosed out from the tunnel into the cavern, Seth hopped in front of it, sprang inside, and burrowed down as low as he could. He found his cheek nestled against something soft and covered with coarse hair. It took a moment to realize that it was the ear of a pig. In fact, the entire wheelbarrow was stacked with freshly slaughtered hogs, many of them almost Seth's size!

The dead pigs were piled high enough that Seth could not see the centaur pushing the wheelbarrow. He wriggled down as far as he could. Who knew if this wheelbarrow would remain in the lead, or what might happen after they negotiated the maze? He had to try to bury himself. The pigs were heavy and did not leave much wiggle room, but Seth managed to partially conceal his body.

The wheelbarrow entered the maze, moving ahead smoothly, turning right, then left, then veering slightly back to the right. Seth tried hard to pay attention to each turn. If he managed to avoid discovery, he would have to return through the labyrinth on his own. He wondered how the centaurs moved so surely if they could not see the walls. Either they had memorized the route with startling precision, or they were somehow navigating by secret markers, perhaps on the ground or ceiling. Focusing on the iron walls from his position in the wheelbarrow, Seth soon became disoriented by the many turns. He found that if he contented himself with watching the walls peripherally and studied the ceiling instead, he retained a better sense of where they were in the room.

They followed a serpentine route through the maze for longer than Seth liked. He tried to keep count of how many times they doubled back, approximating their position by the stationary chandeliers. At length they arrived at an open area toward the middle of the cavern. In the center of the broad space stood a stone about the size of a refrigerator. The mountain troll sat near the stone, a huge, hunched creature bristling with spikes. His back was to the centaurs, but Seth could see his thick limbs and tough hide. Seated, the troll was at least three times taller than Seth. A chain with links as thick as Seth's waist connected the creature to a huge metal ring in the ground.

Suddenly the wheelbarrow was upended, and Seth found himself participating in an avalanche of dead pigs. Lying beneath a heavy pile of swine, he heard other wheelbarrows dumping their contents. The downside of his position was that the pigs were crushing him. The upside was he could still somewhat breathe and he was utterly hidden from view.

He heard the centaurs retreating. No words were exchanged with the titanic troll.

As the hoofbeats faded, heavier footsteps drew near. The chain clanked weightily. Seth had a vivid image of the troll cramming dead pigs into his mouth, and a human boy along with them. Seth tried to squirm, but the weight of the hogs was too great. He was pinned.

"Hello?" Seth called, not raising his voice too much.

The troll stopped moving.

"Hello?" Seth tried again.

Seth heard a couple of nearby footfalls, and the porcine press began to lessen. A moment later, Seth had been uncovered. This was his chance. He had to act friendly. Show no uncertainty. He rose to his knees.

The troll towered over him, yellow eyes glaring down. His flesh was thick and folded like the hide of a rhinoceros. The cruel spikes protruding from his shoulders, forearms, thighs, and shins ranged from the length of a knife to the length of a sword. The brute smelled like a monkey house.

"Hi," Seth said brightly, waving and smiling. "I'm Navarog. How are you?"

The troll snorted and grunted at the same time. The exhalation intensified the funky odor.

Seth stood up shakily. "I'm a shadow charmer. An ally of the night. Trolls are my favorite. You sure are big. Look at those spikes! You must be the strongest troll ever!"

The troll smiled. Four of his bottom teeth jutted up almost to his nose.

"I figured we'd become friends," Seth continued, stepping away from the dead swine. "How do you like it here?"

The troll shrugged. "Why you in food?" The words came out like a controlled belch.

"I'm working on a trick. I'm going to play a joke on the centaurs."

The troll sat down, picked up a hog, and stuffed the entire animal in his mouth. Bones crunched sickeningly as he chewed. "Me like jokes."

"I have a really funny one planned. I missed your name."

The troll swallowed noisily and wiped his lips. "Udnar." He picked up another hog by the rear legs, dangled it above his upturned mouth, then dropped it in. "Pigs good."

"I like pigs too."

Udnar grabbed a third pig and held it out to Seth. "Take."

"I can't," Seth apologized. "I ate one on the way in, so now I'm full. I'm not big like you."

"You take no ask?" the troll accused, voice rising.

"No, um, not one of yours. I brought one from home. A little one. My size."

Udnar appeared satisfied. He leaned over to a different pile, snagged a pumpkin the size of a beach ball, and popped it into his mouth. "What joke?"

Seth fished out the banana from his emergency kit. "Know what this is?"

"Banana."

Seth took a steadying breath. He prayed that Nero was right about mountain trolls and pranks. "I'm going to give the centaurs a hilarious surprise. I'm going to switch this banana for the Soul of Grunhold."

The mountain troll stared at him, eyes widening. He placed one huge hand over his mouth. Then the other. The enormous creature started to shake. He closed his eyes, and

tears trickled down his cheeks. Dropping his hands, the troll released a blast of sound like a stuttering foghorn.

Seth joined in the laughter. The sight of the troll cracking up was really funny, and the rest was fueled by relief.

Eventually the laughter subsided, leaving the troll panting. "Where put Soul?" Udnar asked.

"I'm going to hide it, just for a little while. A few days. It will be a good prank."

"You bring back," the troll checked, his merriment gone.

"I'll bring it back in a few days," Seth promised. "I just need to sneak it away long enough for the prank to work."

"Centaurs mad," Udnar said seriously.

"Probably. But can you picture their faces when they look for the horn and find a banana?"

Udnar erupted in laughter again, clapping his hands. As his laughter abated, the troll gobbled down another pig. "You funny guy. Talk good Duggish. Udnar miss Duggish."

"I love Duggish. Best language in the world. So where do you keep the Soul?" Seth was keenly aware that time was slipping away.

The troll jerked a thumb at the stone in the middle of the room. "Soul in heart."

"The rock is the heart?"

"Heart of Grunhold."

Seth trotted over to the stone. Udnar began smashing open barrels and guzzling the contents. On the far side of the stone Seth found the horn conspicuously sticking out, the top half fitted in a socket.

Seth pulled the horn from the hole. About eighteen

inches long, the straight, tapering horn spiraled to a blunt point. It felt heavier than Seth would have guessed and had the smooth luster of slightly translucent pearl. He found it beautiful, but experienced no rush of guilt upon taking it. "I'll bring you back," he promised quietly.

He crammed the banana into the hole. The fruit was a little too wide to fit perfectly. He twisted and pressed until it curved up instead of down.

The troll lumbered over to join him, and collapsed to the ground guffawing at the sight of the banana. Seth moved away from the brute as he thrashed his bulky legs in ecstasy. "So, so, so funny," Udnar panted, sitting up.

"I need to get going," Seth announced, striding toward the only gap in the iron barrier.

"Back soon?" the troll asked.

"Count on it," Seth assured him. "You don't know any tricks for getting through the maze?"

"No touch walls," Udnar cautioned.

"I won't. Once they notice the banana, don't tell them you helped me. Pretend you don't know how I did it. That way they'll just get mad at Navarog the trickster. 'Bye, Udnar. Enjoy your pigs! See you soon!"

"Back soon, Navarog."

After stowing the horn in his emergency kit, Seth sped up to a jog. He wondered if the centaurs could sense that the Soul had been removed from the Heart. Regardless, time was running out. How long since the giant stones had started marching? Half an hour? More? Less? Why hadn't he consulted his watch until now?

He had tried to pay attention when they emerged from
the maze, and felt confident that his first turn was to the
right. At his next intersection he could either go left or
straight. Neither iron corridor looked more familiar than
the other.

Nero had said that the secret to a maze was to always
turn left. But Seth supposed the reverse would work just as
well—always turn right. They had spent most of their time
winding around on one side of the room, and it looked like
left turns would take him away from that side. He decided
to take every right turn, but to keep an eye on the ceiling,
and break from the pattern if the position of the chandeliers
started to look wrong.

Seth broke into a run. Because a lot of this would be
trial and error, the faster he covered ground, the more likely
he would be to get out in time. When he hit dead ends, he
reversed his course instantly. Same when he headed down
a corridor that led him to a section of the room he had not
travelled in the wheelbarrow. Soon he was panting and
sweating. The muscles in his legs began to ache.

Fatigue forced him to slow his pace. He took
encouragement whenever a particular intersection or series
of switchbacks felt familiar. Most of the time nothing seemed
recognizable.

He kept checking his watch. He may have failed to look
at the time when he had first entered the cavern, but he
knew how long it had been since he had started back to the
entrance. Ten minutes. Fifteen. Twenty. Hope began to fade
with every minute that sped by.

As he kept watching the ceiling, Seth finally found himself on the side of the room near the exit. Since he had only been in this area right at the start, he doubled back whenever corridors led him too far away. He abandoned his rule to generally turn right, and soon began to feel he was passing along the same corridors multiple times. A certain intersection with five choices began to look familiar. Upon reaching it again, he felt certain he had tried four of the five branches, so he jogged down the unfamiliar iron hall. After two more turns, he emerged from the maze, the tunnel to the surface gaping before him.

Seth glanced at his watch. More than thirty minutes had passed since he had started back. Breathing hard, Seth dashed up the steady incline of the tunnel until he reached the pit. Overhead, the giant stone was drifting into position, blocking out the light from the hillside torches. The megalith already covered more than three-quarters of the pit.

Observing no centaurs, Seth quietly climbed the side of the pit opposite the hill, hesitating just below the top. If he timed this right, he could use the giant stone to screen him from view. If he timed it wrong, he would be fatally mashed into the dirt.

The colossal stone hovered directly above the pit and began to sink. Moving slowly, Seth climbed out, then held still as the stone settled behind him. Ahead of him were evergreen trees, their needles visible at the edge of the firelight from the hill. Most of the intervening ground was shadowed by the megalith.

Seth crawled slowly forward. If he rushed now, he

might get spotted and spoil everything. Little by little, the evergreens drew near. When he paused to glance back, the centaur sentries stood at their shadowy posts, frowning into the night. They appeared to harbor no suspicions that the horn had been removed from its socket.

Once he reached the shelter of the evergreens, Seth arose and ran to the brink of the swamp. He saw neither the troll nor the raft.

"Nero," he hissed into the darkness. "Nero, I'm back." He was tempted to sweep his flashlight over the water, but decided not to risk a centaur noticing the shine. "Nero!" Seth cried in a louder whisper.

A voice from the darkness shushed him. He waited in silence until he heard water lapping against the raft. As it drew near, Seth could see the troll.

"Come aboard," Nero whispered.

Seth obeyed, the raft rocking and sloshing as he landed. Nero used the momentum from the jump to pole away from the shore.

"I can see you," Seth whispered.

"Dawn begins to color the sky. We must hurry back to the golem. If a fog giant spies us, it will not end well. You achieved your aim?"

"I got the horn," Seth said. "The centaurs haven't realized."

As if in response to his words, they heard the long, low moan of a distant horn. As other horns took up the call, sonorous wails echoed through the swamp. "They know," Nero spat, licking an eye. He began to pole them forward louder and faster. "You are now a fugitive. The golem must smuggle you to the safety of your yard as soon as possible."

"Will the centaurs be looking everywhere?" Seth asked.

"Everywhere. Fortunately, they cannot run on water. They'll have to come around the marshes to get at you. If the golem hurries, you should be fine."

By the time they reached Hugo, the east was gray and Seth could see quite well. Seth leapt from the raft to the muddy shore. "Thanks, Nero."

"Away with you," the troll urged.

"Home, Hugo! Fast as you can! Avoid centaurs at all cost!"

The golem swept Seth into his arms and loped away into the trees.

CHAPTER FIFTEEN

Horns

K endra awoke disquieted. She rolled over and squinted at the gray predawn light filtering through the attic window. Twisting the other way, she peered at Seth curled up on his bed, the blankets up over his head. She closed her eyes. No need to rise before the sun.

Then she heard the long, distant call of a horn. Was that what had awakened her? Another horn answered on a different pitch. She had never heard horns resounding from the woods of Fablehaven before.

She glanced over at Seth again. He was sure curled up tight. And he didn't normally sleep with his head under the covers.

Crossing to his bed, she peeked under his wadded sheets and found only his pillows. She checked under his bed and found his emergency kit missing.

Kendra did not relish her role as tattletale. But with a brother like Seth, what was she to do? It wasn't like he was stealing from the cookie jar. At Fablehaven, his adventurous nature sometimes led to life-threatening situations.

At the door to her grandparents' room Kendra knocked softly, then entered without waiting for an invitation. Their bed was empty. Maybe Seth wasn't gone after all. Perhaps everyone was awake but her. But why would Seth have disguised his bed?

She hurried downstairs and found her grandparents on the back porch with Tanu and Coulter. They all stood against the railing, gazing out over the yard. The sonorous moans of horns drifted to them from different parts of the woods. Some sounded nearby.

"What's going on?" Kendra asked.

Grandma turned her head. "The centaurs are agitated about something. They seldom range this far from Grunhold, and never wind their horns so freely."

Chills tingled through Kendra. "Seth is gone."

The others whirled. "Gone?" Grandpa asked.

"I don't know when," Kendra reported. "He stuffed pillows under his covers. He took his emergency kit."

Grandpa bowed his head, clapping a hand over his eyes. "That boy will ruin us yet."

"We wouldn't be hearing horns if they had caught him," Coulter observed.

"True," Grandma acknowledged.

Warren approached from behind, rubbing sleep from his eyes, his hair matted erratically. "What's going on?"

"Apparently Seth has riled the centaurs," Grandpa said.

"Would he have gone after the horn?" Grandma asked. "Surely he couldn't be so foolish."

"If he had gone after the horn, the centaurs would have him," Warren said. "More likely he was mad he didn't get to accompany us to Grunhold. He probably went sightseeing."

Grandpa was gripping the porch railing hard enough to make the veins stand out on the backs of his hands. "We'd better send Hugo after him." He raised his voice. "Hugo? Come!"

They waited. Nobody came.

Grandpa faced the others, looking sick. "He couldn't have cajoled Hugo into joining him?"

"Mendigo?" Grandma called.

A moment later, the human-sized wooden puppet came dashing across the lawn, the golden hooks of his joints jingling. He stopped near the porch.

"Did Hugo leave with Seth?" Grandma asked.

The puppet pointed toward the woods.

"No wonder the centaurs haven't caught him," Tanu said. "If he's on the run with Hugo, he should make it back."

"And I'll have to deal with the aftermath," Grandpa grumbled. "The centaurs don't smile on trespassers."

"What can we do?" Kendra asked.

Grandpa harrumphed. "We wait."

"Who would like a smoothie?" Grandma asked.

Everyone but Grandpa asked for one. Grandma was walking into the house when Tanu spoke up. "Here he comes."

Kendra looked across the yard. Hugo came loping out of

the woods at full speed with Seth tucked under one arm. The golem charged straight to the deck and placed Seth on his feet. At first her brother looked worried, but then he started trying to resist a smile. The call of horns continued to echo across the woods, the forlorn notes occasionally overlapping.

"Is something funny?" Grandpa asked in a severe tone.

"No, sir," Seth said, still wrestling against a smirk.

Grandpa trembled with anger. "The centaurs are not to be trifled with. And you are not to be trusted. You are grounded indefinitely. You will spend the rest of your time here locked in a cell in the dungeon."

Grandma laid a hand on Grandpa's arm. "Stan."

Grandpa shrugged away from her. "I'll not lighten the punishment this time. We've clearly been too gentle in the past. He is not an imbecile. He knows that this type of behavior puts himself and his family at risk. And for what? To sneak a peek at some centaurs! Frivolous amusement! Hugo, how could you have joined him in this?"

The golem pointed at Seth. "Horn."

"Yes, we hear the war horns," Grandpa said impatiently. Then he paused, his expression softening. "Are you telling me that you went to rescue Seth after you heard the horns?"

"No," Seth said, no longer smiling. He took something from his emergency kit. "He's telling you that we got the Soul of Grunhold." He held up the pearly unicorn horn.

Everyone on the deck gaped in disbelief.

"I'll be jiggered," Coulter murmured.

Grandpa was the first to recover, his eyes intently roving the trees. "Inside. Now."

Seth returned the horn to his emergency kit and climbed over the porch railing. Warren clapped him warmly on the back. "Well done!"

"Hugo, resume patrolling the yard," Grandpa said. "Your excursion with Seth never happened."

Kendra followed her brother into the house, her mind reeling. How could he have possibly gotten the horn? Had there been some sort of total centaur malfunction? What about the guards and the maze and the troll? What about the guilt that prevented the horn from being taken?

They took seats in the living room.

"So, how mad are you?" Seth asked, holding up the lustrous horn, a grin creeping back onto his face.

"Less mad," Grandpa admitted, fighting a smile himself. "At least you weren't endangering us frivolously. Although it was still unwise. How was this accomplished?"

"First I went to Graulas."

"The demon?" Grandma exclaimed.

"When I was outside with the satyrs, I heard him calling to me, summoning me, just like when I heard the wraith in the dungeon. I figured Graulas could explain what was happening to me, since dark stuff is his specialty. He told me that the nail turned me into a shadow charmer."

"A shadow charmer?" Coulter repeated, frowning.

"Yeah," Seth replied. "That was why I could see the invisible goblin at the hotel, and how I heard the voices. I already had most of the powers. Graulas just explained the details and made it official."

The adults traded uncomfortable glances.

"Finish recounting how you obtained the horn," Grandpa prompted.

Seth related the whole adventure, from the help he received from Nero, to crawling past the centaurs, to tricking the mountain troll, to his hasty retreat to the yard.

"No centaurs saw you," Grandpa said.

"Not a glimpse," Seth assured him.

"And you told the troll your name was Navarog," Grandma confirmed.

"Right."

"The centaurs will undoubtedly suspect us," Grandpa said wearily. "But without proof, they cannot go to war. Our story will be that we tried to warn them as soon as we learned that the Society might be after the horn. They will be reluctant to admit that we stole the horn out from under them, and may embrace an alternate explanation."

"Meanwhile, we should head for Wyrmroost," Warren said. "Once we retrieve the key to the Australian vault, we can return the horn to the centaurs. We'll pretend we recovered it from the Society."

"We mustn't move hastily," Grandpa replied. "We should consult with the leadership of the Knights of the Dawn. This mission to Wyrmroost must succeed. We don't have the expertise in this room to form a proper team."

"I'll second that," Coulter muttered.

"We'll need dragon tamers," Tanu agreed.

"For sure I'm going," Seth announced. "I got the horn."

Grandpa turned to him. "You aren't out of the woods yet, young man. Don't start making wild presumptions. You took a huge unauthorized risk going to the centaurs."

"Would you have ever authorized it?"

"We're all fortunate you succeeded," Grandpa continued, ignoring the comment. "Had you failed, you would be dead and we would have a war on our hands. Additionally, this shadow charmer business will require further investigation. Shadow charmers are the stuff of old bedtime stories. They are generally the villains. We have no idea what kind of access dark creatures may now have to you."

"What if Graulas can now spy on us through your eyes?" Grandma said.

"I don't think it works like that," Seth said.

"We possess little sure knowledge of shadow charmers," Grandpa reiterated. "We'll do what we can to acquire more."

"Don't hold your breath," Coulter mumbled.

Grandpa leaned forward, regarding Seth kindly. "I honestly don't know what to do with you. Facing Graulas was incredibly brave. So was retrieving the horn. I know you had good intentions, that you took a calculated risk. Moreover, you weren't wrong. You pulled it off. Recovering the horn was a major coup. But until we learn more about your status as a shadow charmer, and because you took a potentially disastrous risk without permission, I'm afraid I still have to punish you."

"Punish?" Seth blurted, rising to his feet, the horn in his hand. "Good thing I didn't find the cure for cancer—you might have had me arrested!"

"I'm with your grandfather on this," Grandma said. "We

love you and we're proud of you. The risks you took worked out this time. But how can we reward such behavior? Because we love you, we must teach you caution, or your boldness will destroy you."

"I weighed my options and made smart choices," Seth responded. "I didn't set out to borrow the horn. I only decided to try for the horn after Graulas showed how my skills as a shadow charmer gave me a realistic chance at success. It was me or nobody. What would Patton have done?"

Warren chuckled. "He would have shaved the centaurs, dipped them in honey, covered them with feathers, and hung them up like a bunch of piñatas." Kendra, Seth, and Tanu laughed. "I'm just saying."

"Very few men who live their lives like Patton Burgess die in bed," Grandma said gravely, extinguishing the snickers.

"We're not sure how to guide you, Seth," Grandpa said resignedly. "Considered in context, maybe your decisions were reasonable. Maybe if we were more willing to let you take risks, you could have come to us. I certainly don't relish reprimanding you for courage and success."

"Then don't!" Seth urged. "Just be glad we have the horn! I know you love me, but sometimes that gets in the way. Honestly, was there any chance you would have let me visit Graulas if I'd come to you and asked?"

Grandpa met Grandma's eyes. "No," he admitted.

"You guys don't like to let me take risks because you feel like you have to protect me. Even when protecting me could harm all of us. If we don't stop the Sphinx, you won't be able to protect anybody. I wasn't off goofing around. Sometimes risks are necessary."

"You'll need to give your grandmother and me some time to consider this in private," Grandpa said.

"Just keep in mind that my new abilities could come in handy at the dragon sanctuary," Seth said.

"The excursion to Wyrmroost will likely be a suicide mission," Grandma said. "The entire sanctuary is a death trap. Punishment or no, keep in mind that we'll need to send in a small team of our most experienced operatives."

Seth put his hands on his hips. "You can't just cut me out of it."

"Who we include or exclude is not up to you," Grandma stated firmly.

"The reward would be not having to go," Coulter huffed.

"Yeah, well, I'll give this stupid horn back to the centaurs before I get left out of the trip to Wyrmroost," Seth threatened. "Good luck taking it from me!"

"It isn't going to be a vacation," Coulter said.

"And it isn't about seeing cool dragons," Grandpa growled, clearly losing his temper.

"Although they will be cool," Warren murmured, earning an elbow from Tanu.

Tears brimmed in Seth's eyes. His mouth opened as if he wanted to say more; then he turned and stormed out of the room.

"What are we going to do with that boy?" Grandma sighed.

"I don't know," Grandpa said. "If he hadn't decided to go after the horn, we'd still be treading water. Maybe he's the only one of us seeing this clearly."

Grandma shook her head. "Don't kid yourself. His main interest is still the adventure. Saving the world is a happy side effect. This is all still a game to him."

"Patton was the same way," Warren mentioned. "He did a lot of good, partly because he relished the thrill."

"I think Seth cares," Kendra spoke up. "It isn't only about the fun anymore. I think he's learning."

"He went through a lot tonight," Tanu said. "And he hasn't had much sleep. His emotions are tangled."

"I could go talk to him," Kendra offered.

"No, let him brood," Grandma said. "He's a good boy. He'll settle down and find the shame in his outburst if we let him stew."

"He's right that we can't take the horn from him," Warren pointed out. "In fact, we may not be able to use it without him. It is still stolen property. He may be the only person who can withstand the guilt."

"We'll cross that bridge when we must," Grandpa said. "I swear, that boy will be the death of me. For now, let me get on the phone to Dougan. The Lieutenants should be able to help us assemble a strike force."

"I'll go and get—" Grandma began, but the sudden blast of a horn cut her off. Much louder than the other horns, this one sounded close.

Warren rushed out of the room. "They're at the outskirts of the yard," he called.

"I'll handle this," Grandpa said. "I hope Seth is right about their lack of proof."

"Let me come," Kendra suggested. "It'll look more innocent, like we were caught off guard."

Grandpa appeared ready to disagree. Then his expression changed. "Why not? You're right, we don't want to appear the least bit defensive. We want to look bewildered by their presence. But let me do the talking."

Dale came stumbling down the stairs, bleary-eyed and in his nightclothes. "What's all the racket?"

"Dale," Grandma said. "Go stand on the deck and watch Stan speak with the centaurs. We have no idea why they've come."

Grandpa escorted Kendra outside. They crossed the lawn to where Cloudwing waited beside a tall centaur with light blue fur.

"Greetings, Cloudwing," Grandpa said as they drew near. "I didn't expect to see you again so soon."

"Make no pretenses at courtesy," the blue centaur growled. "Return the Soul."

"Now, hold your horses," Grandpa responded in a less friendly tone. "What are you talking about? I'm not sure we've met."

"Skygazer is our spiritual leader," Cloudwing explained.

"When I awoke today," Skygazer said, "the power shielding Grunhold had waned. The Heart remained, but the Soul had fled. We found human tracks leading to the marsh. On the far side of the marsh we located similar tracks along with the unmistakable footfalls of your golem.

The golem's tracks were very fresh, and returned directly to your yard."

Grandpa stared at Skygazer in astonishment. "And you think that means one of us took the horn?" Kendra had never realized her grandfather was such a good actor. His disbelief seemed authentic. "One of our spies recently sent us information that our enemies might make an attempt for the horn. We relayed that information to your king. I sent Hugo out as a precaution, to keep watch for anything suspicious."

"You asked to borrow the Soul yesterday," Cloudwing reminded him.

"Right, we *asked*. It would come in useful. We knew our enemies wanted it as well. But we harbored no illusions about stealing it. If we intended to steal it, why would we draw attention to ourselves with a visit? Why would we warn you to guard it well?"

Skygazer glowered. "When necessary, we have secret means of communicating with our mountain troll, Udnar. He mentioned the name Navarog."

"Navarog!" Grandpa exclaimed. "The dragon? The demon prince? He was imprisoned until recently. We've heard he is abroad again. This bodes ill."

"A demonic dragon could not have entered Grunhold," Skygazer stated.

"Navarog can assume human form," Grandpa said thoughtfully. "He is a powerful demon lord. He might have had magic to foil your defenses. Later, if he changed form again and took flight, it would explain why his footprints vanished."

"Or he was working with you, and the golem brought him here," Cloudwing said, his posture and voice less certain.

Grandpa laughed. "Right, Navarog the dragon, the demon prince, is now our errand boy."

Skygazer scowled. "Udnar reported that the intruder moved inhumanly fast, and taunted him by divulging his name, as if fearless of retribution. He left a banana where the Soul belonged."

"These are dire tidings," Grandpa lamented. "Our enemies will employ the horn to our significant detriment."

"You claim no involvement in the thievery," Skygazer confirmed.

Grandpa shrugged. "Does it seem possible that one of us could have navigated the many safeguards protecting your Soul? If we uncover any leads, you'll be the first to know."

"Very well," Skygazer relented. "We'll be watching." The centaurs wheeled about and cantered away through the leafless woods.

※ ※ ※

Seth stalked back and forth across the attic bedroom, the horn clenched in his fist. He had felt confident that his success would override any resentment of his disobedience. And it had, to an extent. But in the end he still felt he had disappointed everyone.

Why did he want to go to Wyrmroost so badly? Were they right? Did he mostly want to go as a tourist? Was his chief motivation to see dragons? Or did he sincerely believe his presence would make a difference?

Yes, seeing dragons would be awesome. Why lie to himself? The dragons were part of the allure. But they were not his only reason for wanting to go to Wyrmroost. The Society of the Evening Star had come into his neighborhood and kidnapped his sister. The Sphinx had demonstrated that no place was safe anymore. He would never relent. He had to be stopped before he opened the demon prison and destroyed the world.

Seth had powers now. Who knew, with emotions immune to magical manipulation, he might make a fabulous dragon tamer. But nobody would know unless they gave him a chance. Gavin was supposedly their top dragon tamer, and he wasn't an adult either.

Certainly Seth could make himself useful at Wyrmroost. He always found a way. Was it any less dangerous to sit at home and do nothing while the Sphinx took over the world?

He shouldn't have gotten so angry at his grandparents. Getting them riled would not help his chances of going. They responded to reason, not threats. And they deserved his respect. It was just so frustrating having everyone always telling him what he could or couldn't do!

He heard footsteps on the stairs. The door opened and Kendra entered. She looked around the room, her eyes sweeping over him. Her brow crinkled. "Seth?"

The curtains were shut, leaving the room fairly dim. He stood a good distance from the door. But he wasn't hiding.

Kendra turned to go.

"I'm here," Seth said.

Startled, she spun around. "There you are! Where were you?"

"Here all along."

"Wow, I guess that shade walker thing really works. It isn't that dark in here."

Seth shrugged. "Did you want to scold me too?"

"Actually, I wanted to make sure you were all right. And to check out the unicorn horn."

Seth held it up. "It's heavier than it looks." He studied it appraisingly. "I'd say it's worth about ten million awesome dollars."

"Or ten million idiot points. Depending on your perspective. Can I hold it?"

Seth scowled suspiciously. "Did they send you up here to get the horn from me?"

Kendra looked at him reproachfully. "No. I don't think they're stressed about your threats. I'm just interested."

"I'm not sure I can let you handle it," Seth said. "After all, it's stolen property. What if you touch it and start feeling all guilty? You might go mental and try to return it to the centaurs."

"You borrowed it, not me. What would I have to feel guilty about, as long as you don't mind me touching it?"

Seth ran his thumb along the smooth surface of the horn. "If I'm able to lend it to you, it means I could entrust it to them as well. I won't have to be included on the team to Wyrmroost."

"We'll have to find out if you can share it sooner or later. Might as well be now. Look, if you're worried I'm trying to take it, just give me permission to hold it for a minute. Then I'll have to give it back."

Seth sighed. "Okay. You can hold it for a minute." He held out the horn.

Kendra took it. "You're right, it does feel heavier than it looks."

"No guilt?"

"None. It's so white."

Seth frowned. "Looks like they won't need me after all."

Kendra handed the horn back to him. "Who knows what they'll decide?"

"I do," Seth said. "Patton's message explained that Wyrmroost is protected by a powerful distracter spell. Which means that even though nobody will like the idea, you'll probably have to go. For the other slots they'll select old people like Warren. They'll be too worried that I'd get hurt, and that I don't have enough experience, never mind the fact that my proven abilities make me uniquely qualified."

"I don't see why you'd want to go," Kendra replied. "The thought that I might have to go makes me want to throw up."

"Even if Gavin joins the group?"

Kendra blushed. "Whatever. Why would that matter? We're barely pen pals." She bit her lower lip. "You think they might need him?"

"It's a guarantee. Wyrmroost is a dragon sanctuary, and

he's the dragon-taming prodigy. This will be your second date at a deadly wildlife park! Next time you guys should go miniature golfing."

"You're a weirdo," Kendra said. "And you dodged my question. Why do you want to go so badly?"

"Would I love to see dragons? Sure, who wouldn't? Besides you, I mean. The more important reason is simple. We have to stop the Sphinx or we're all doomed, and I know I can help do it."

"There are lots of ways to help," Kendra argued.

"Good point. Maybe I can pack your sack lunches."

"You don't have to do everything."

"Nope. Just the boring stuff. Maybe I'll write the Sphinx a stern letter."

Kendra laid a hand on his shoulder. "No matter what happens, please promise that you won't do anything stupid."

"Or anything awesome. Depending on your perspective."

"Promise."

Seth fingered the horn. "We'll see."

CHAPTER SIXTEEN

Moving Out

Christmas had always been Kendra's favorite holiday. During her younger years, it had been a day when magic overlapped reality, when the regular routine was suspended and, under the cover of darkness, visitors swooped out of the sky and snuck down the chimney with presents. She had always hoped to stay up late and catch Santa in the act, but she always fell asleep before he came and had to settle for a plate full of cookie crumbs and a thank-you note.

As she grew older, Christmas became more about seeing her friends and family. The holiday meant fancy meals with Grandma and Grandpa Larsen, eating turkey or lamb off fine china with ornate silverware, then topping it all off with as much pie as she could handle. Thanks to the gifts given and received, there remained a giddy anticipation the night before and an enchanted atmosphere on the holiday itself.

This Christmas was different.

For one thing, her parents thought she was dead. For another, the holiday had totally blindsided her. She usually looked forward to Christmas Day for weeks in advance. This year, she hadn't even remembered it was Christmas Eve until Seth mentioned it before they went to bed. How could she pay attention to the calendar when her mind was consumed with a potentially deadly mission?

Kendra had decided that her brother should become a fortune-teller. He had correctly named her, Warren, and Gavin as members of the strike force. Tanu had been included as well. Grandpa had recited the same reasons that Seth had anticipated. Her brother was also correct that he would be left out.

Fortunately, Seth had taken the news much better than she would have expected. Grandma and Grandpa seemed relieved and surprised when he had handed over the horn without a fuss. Kendra assumed it must have helped that her brother had expected the decision. Whatever the reason behind his acceptance, Grandma and Grandpa had been sufficiently impressed to forgo formally grounding him. Kendra sometimes pitied her grandparents as they tried to manage Seth. Short of locking him in a cell, how were they supposed to ground a resourceful kid who refused to stop sneaking out?

Now Kendra sat alone in the living room, enjoying the aroma of the pies baking in the kitchen. There had been no Christmas tree, but her grandparents had filled stockings with treats and given her and Seth wrapped presents. Her presents had seemed suspiciously tailored for the upcoming mission: sturdy boots, a thick coat, new gloves. At least she had had something to unwrap.

They would be eating Christmas dinner at lunchtime, so she, Warren, and Tanu could leave to catch their flight. By the evening they would meet up with Gavin, Dougan, Trask, and Mara in Kalispell, Montana. From there a private helicopter would shuttle them to their destination.

It would be strangest to see Gavin and Mara. Despite her protests to the contrary, Kendra had developed a considerable crush on Gavin as they had exchanged letters during the fall. Seeing Mara would be odd because, since they had last spoken, the Native American woman had lost her mother and her home. Grandpa had explained that after the destruction of Lost Mesa, Mara had joined the Knights of the Dawn and was rapidly becoming one of their most trusted operatives.

Seth trotted into the room, face red from the cold outside. "Kendra, somebody brought you a special present."

"What do you mean?"

"Come see."

Seth led her to the back porch, where she found Verl waiting. Clad in a turtleneck and a black top hat, the satyr looked terrified. He was leaning against the porch railing in an unnatural pose, straining to appear casual. As she opened the door, he raked his fingers through the hair above one ear and gave an awkward little smile. She stepped out onto the porch, and Seth followed.

When Verl spoke, his words came out in a rush, as if he were reciting rehearsed lines. "How good to see you, Kendra! What lovely weather today! I trust your holiday has been satisfactory? Mine has been splendid! I enjoyed a scrumptious breakfast of plum pudding and walnuts."

"Nice to see you too, Verl," Kendra said politely. "I really liked the picture you drew for me."

His smile brightened. "A trifle," he chortled, waving a dismissive hand. "I periodically dabble in the arts."

"It was very lifelike."

Verl plucked at the woolly fur on his legs. His eyes kept meeting hers, then glancing away. "I fear my humble portrait has become outdated. I must attempt another. You constantly blossom. Each day I find you fairer than the last."

Beside Kendra, Seth tried to disguise his laughter by coughing.

"You're very kind, Verl."

"I had hoped to honor the festive customs of this holiday by giving you another present."

"Oh, you shouldn't have," Kendra said.

"I cannot help myself." Verl stepped aside, revealing a mysterious object about three feet tall covered by red fabric. "I hoped to give you a gift that would complement your beauty. What more glorious present could I give you than yourself?"

With the flair of a stage magician, Verl whisked the fabric away, unveiling a statue of Kendra wearing a toga and holding aloft a cluster of grapes. Seth started coughing again. It sounded like he might choke. The statue was very artfully rendered.

"Wow," Kendra said, "that looks just like me."

Verl flashed a crooked smile. "I have never felt such a crushing weight of inspiration. My hands were guided by my admiration."

"I need to grab a drink," Seth managed, eyes watering. He slipped into the house. His laughter became audible after the door shut.

"Seth loves to rake me over the coals," Verl chuckled. "I don't mind trading jests now and again. We enjoy an almost . . . brotherly affection."

"You really did amazing work," Kendra said, crouching in front of the statuette. "It's too much. You shouldn't have. You know, I meant to get you a gift, but things have been really hectic."

Verl waved both hands. "No, stop, please, no gift is required. My lady, a soft glance, a kind word, these more than suffice. Your very existence leaves me forever indebted."

"You get that I'm fifteen?"

"All too well. I've come to terms with the sobering reality that we can never be a couple. Consider me a remote admirer, adoring your elegance from afar. All the great love stories have their tragic elements."

Kendra stood and smiled. "Thanks, Verl. The statue is beautiful. It obviously took a lot of work. Happy holidays." She took off his hat and pecked him on the forehead.

Verl's face lit up like a Christmas tree. His eyes darted and his fingers fidgeted. He met eyes with Kendra and bowed stiffly. "Merry Christmas." Turning away from her, he pumped his fist. She heard him mutter something like, "Newel owes me an hour of television." Then he vaulted over the porch railing and ran off across the yard.

She still held his hat in her hands.

Seth returned to the patio. "You just made his year."

"I can't believe he carved a statue of me."

"You need to stop blossoming into such a lovely young maiden." Kendra punched his arm. "I told you, the guy has it bad. He forgot his hat? He made that, too, you know."

"What should I do with it?"

"Leave it on the porch. Are you going to bring your monument inside?"

"I think I'll keep it out here for now. Why grapes and a toga?"

Seth opened the door. "Verl's mind is a mystery better left unsolved. Grandma said dinner is almost ready. Want to help set the table for your last meal?"

"That isn't funny! What if it really is my last meal!"

Seth rolled his eyes. "It won't be. I'm sure you guys will grab something at the airport."

Dinner consisted of a huge ham garnished with pineapple, garlic mashed potatoes, carrots sweetened with brown sugar, green beans, and hot buttered rolls. For dessert there was pumpkin pie, apple pie, pecan pie, and vanilla ice cream.

Seth ate like a bottomless pit, wolfing down his dessert quickly and excusing himself before anyone else. Kendra struggled to find her appetite. She picked at small portions and managed to finish with a warm piece of apple pie.

After the meal, Grandma and Grandpa had parting words for them, but Kendra had a tough time paying attention. Her visit to Lost Mesa with Warren had been a terrifying experience, and this had every chance of being worse. Warren was specifically charged with her care. The Lieutenants had desired a five-person team, and to that they had added Kendra, along with Warren to protect her. Theoretically she and Warren would see no action, hiding out in the caretaker's home. But Kendra had already learned the hard way how such plans can go awry. Nobody knew much about Wyrmroost. Supposedly Patton was the only outsider who had ventured there in many decades.

Kendra had put on a brave face. She understood the necessity of the mission and knew she would have to appear confident and eager in order for Grandma and Grandpa to consent to her participation. In the end, her willingness and the overall importance of the undertaking had earned permission from her grandparents.

The time to depart arrived before Kendra liked. She ascended the stairs to the attic with Dale to retrieve her bags, expecting to say good-bye to Seth. Instead she found a note on her bed atop a smoky gray breastplate with a lustrous sheen.

Dear Kendra,

Merry Christmas! This breastplate is made of a super strong metal called adamant. The satyrs gave it to me, and I want you to wear it to Wyrmroost. It should be small enough to wear under your clothes no problem. In fact, it was kind of small on me and will probably fit you better.

*I hope you'll forgive me for not saying good-bye in person.
It is hard for me to get left out. I've found a place in the woods
where I go when I need time to think. It is safe and not too far
and I won't let the centaurs get me or anything. I've made some
good friends at Fablehaven. They'll help me stop sulking. Tell
Grandma and Grandpa not to worry. I may stay there for a little
while. If they want to lock me in the dungeon when I get back,
so it goes.*

Stay safe. Don't get eaten by dragons. Have fun.
Love,
Seth

Kendra folded the note. It was so sweet and so selfish
all at once. How could he run off to the woods again after
all that had happened? Everyone had plenty to worry about
without adding another unnecessary disappearance by her
brother to the list. She picked up the breastplate, wondering
if something so light would be much protection. Judging
by the weight, it felt like the breastplate could have been
fashioned out of tinfoil. He had called it super strong. She
rapped the breastplate with her knuckles and supposed it
felt solid.

When she shared the note with Grandpa, he read it
with a frown, then rubbed his eyes. He relayed the content
of the message to the others, and asked Warren and Tanu to
go make sure Seth hadn't tried to stow away in the car or the
knapsack. Grandpa assured Kendra that he would take care
of the problem, and urged her to put it out of her mind.

Kendra showed Coulter the breastplate, since magical

items were his specialty. Coulter held the object reverently for a long while, examining it with care, then gave it back to her with a charge to keep it hidden. He warned that people would kill for an authentic piece of adamant armor, assured her that the breastplate was priceless, and confirmed what Seth had claimed about it being supernaturally durable.

Before she felt ready, Kendra was hugging her grandparents good-bye and hurrying out to climb inside the idling SUV.

* * *

Although sizable drifts of chunky snow lined the roads, the cold night in Kalispell was shockingly clear. In the moonless sky, the stars gleamed sharper and more numerous than Kendra had ever witnessed. While they were waiting outside the small airport for Tanu to bring the rental car, Warren had pointed out faint dots gradually drifting in straight lines across the star-strewn firmament, explaining that they were satellites.

As the rental car pulled into the hotel parking lot, Kendra became fidgety, drumming an anxious rhythm on her thighs. Warren had phoned ahead to confirm that the others had arrived. The thought of seeing Gavin made her edgy and self-conscious. Was this how Verl had felt earlier in the day? Suddenly his behavior seemed much less laughable.

She breathed deeply. All she had to do was act friendly. Any pressure she felt was a product of her overactive imagination. This was a dangerous mission, not a date. If romantic feelings ever arose between them, it would happen as a natural outgrowth of their friendship.

Inside the lobby, a fire roared in the hearth. The red commercial carpeting featured an unbroken pattern of gold fleurs-de-lis. A bald man with spectacles and a flannel shirt sat reading a book near the fire. Kendra eyed him suspiciously. At this point, she was ready to consider anyone a possible spy. She wished Seth were with them so he could check for invisible enemies.

While Tanu checked in at the counter, a voice hailed Kendra from across the lobby. She turned and found Gavin coming toward her with a warm smile. When he reached her he gave her a quick hug. Part of her wished the embrace had lasted longer.

He seemed even better-looking than the last time she had seen him, his naturally dark complexion slightly tanner, his cheeks more defined. He remained slim and wiry, moving with the confident grace of a dancer. Was he a tad taller? "Good to see you," Kendra said, trying to keep her manner light and casual.

"I heard you were k-k-k-kidnapped," he stammered.

"I guess word gets around. At least I got away." She glanced at the man reading his book. Was it wise to converse so close to him?

"That's Aaron Stone," Gavin said. "He's a Knight, and our helicopter pilot."

Without glancing up from his book, Aaron saluted her with two fingers.

Warren came and clapped Gavin on the back. "Ready

for some more mayhem? Didn't get your fill at Lost Mesa?"

Gavin gave him half a smile. "You have to w-w-watch it or I'm going to start associating you two with near-death experiences."

Tanu finished at the counter and waved for them to follow. In the elevator, Gavin explained that the others were ready to have an orientation meeting. Kendra dumped her luggage in her room before joining the rest of her companions in a suite at the end of the hall.

When she entered, Dougan rose from his seat, a bear of a man with bushy red hair and a densely freckled brow. He bore a strong resemblance to his brother Maddox. "Sorry you got roped into this," he said as he shook her hand.

Trask sat on a bed, polishing the absurdly oversized crossbow on his lap. Designed to fire two quarrels at once, the cartoonish weapon looked almost too large to carry. Mara leaned against a wall in a far corner of the room, arms folded, her expression inscrutable. Her tank top looked extra white against her coppery skin and flaunted the dramatic lines of her lean, athletic physique.

"Glad to see we're all here," Trask said in a low voice. "Mara?"

She struck a match and lit a fat white candle.

"While the candle burns, no outsiders should be able to eavesdrop on our conversation," Trask explained. "I don't want to blab all night, but I thought we should take a few minutes to get our heads right and make sure we're all on the same page." His eyes were on Kendra. "This mission is voluntary. It could not be more dangerous. This dragon sanctuary is closed to visitors for a reason. We know very little about how it operates or what we can expect to find inside. Patton never elaborated about Wyrmroost much, perhaps because he did not want people disturbing the key he had hidden. We can presume there will be a caretaker. Beyond that we know very little. This could be a one-way trip. We may all die. That is not the goal, but it is the reality. I don't want to be here. I'm here because I feel our enemies have made it necessary. If you still want to participate in this mission of your own free will, I want to hear you say so."

Everyone individually answered in the affirmative, including Kendra. Mara answered last, whispering her response.

Trask nodded. "Now that Charlie Rose is gone, I'm considered the lead dragon tamer for the Knights of the Dawn. I'm not in the same league as Chuck Rose. Nor do I have the innate talent of his son, Gavin. Along with Dougan, I'm one of four Lieutenants of the Knights. I have a long history as a detective. I possess many skills, but I'm no true dragon tamer. It takes everything I have to keep it together in front of a dragon. That said, I have spent time at the four dragon sanctuaries open to human visitation. I've done my best to learn how dragons behave. In my gear I have six arrows tipped with adamant. Most dragons would see them as harmless toys. And they would be right. We will not survive Wyrmroost by force. We'll survive by never getting into a fight."

"I'll s-s-s-second that," Gavin said.

Trask set aside his crossbow. "According to the plan,

Kendra will help guide Aaron to a meadow roughly two miles from the gate to Wyrmroost. If we tried to fly the helicopter over the wall into the sanctuary, none of us would survive—the magical barrier extends miles into the sky. After we leave the helicopter, Kendra will lead us to the gate, where we will use the first horn to enter. Making a guess based on the gate at Isla del Dragón, our assumption is that the gate locks from both sides, and that the distracter spell may function in both directions as well. We will probably need Kendra and the horn to get in and out. That is her main role in this mission. Warren joins us strictly as her protector.

"While Kendra and Warren stay with the caretaker, the rest of us are charged with finding this key hidden by Patton Burgess. Locating the key may be the biggest trick. All we know is that we may find a clue below the false gravestone of Patton Burgess. We may require Kendra's help to translate the clue."

Trask slid off the bed and began strolling around the room. "Throughout the coming days, we will have to rely on each other implicitly. I've said a few words about myself. I would like each of us to introduce ourselves and to sum up how we intend to be of service. Trust must unite us. When the Sphinx ran the Knights, his philosophy relied on secrets and mistrust. I never liked that system, hiding behind masks among friends. We were supposedly compartmentalizing information in case of spies, but in the end it kept us apart. That type of system made it easier for spies to operate among us and, yes, to lead us. Kendra, I know you have a big secret, and Gavin, so do you. The Society is aware of Kendra's, and has most likely guessed Gavin's by now. If our enemies can know our secrets, why not our most trusted friends? Each of you is free to choose how much you care to reveal. Try to be as forthright as possible. Let's start with Dougan." Trask sat down.

Dougan cleared his throat. "I'm a Lieutenant in the Knights of the Dawn. I am no dragon tamer, but I'm a seasoned adventurer, mountaineer, and survivalist. Trask is our team leader, and I'm here to support him."

Tanu stood. "I'm Tanugatoa, call me Tanu. I'm a potion master and I've served with the Knights for almost twenty years. The dragon sanctuary should be rich with ingredients unavailable elsewhere. Hopefully mixing potions will be my greatest contribution. In a pinch, I'm also an experienced healer."

They had been moving in a circle, and Kendra was next. All eyes turned to her as she started speaking. "I've only been a Knight for a few months. My one real ability is that I'm fairykind, which the Sphinx knows." She noticed Gavin and Mara staring at her in astonishment. "I can see in the dark, command fairies, and I can understand just about any language related to Silvian, the fairy language. Distracter spells don't work on me, which is why I'll lead us to the gate. I think we're hoping Patton may have left some clues for us in the secret fairy language, which I can read. I guess that's it."

Warren slapped his hands together. "I'm Warren Burgess, a great-great-nephew of the legendary and somewhat infamous Patton Burgess. I'm a Scorpio who enjoys badminton, snorkeling, and Chinese checkers." He paused for laughter but only earned a couple of smiles. "I'm Kendra's second cousin. I've worked with the Knights for about ten years, part of which I spent in a catatonic stupor at Fablehaven. I'm here to protect Kendra. We brought some useful items, including a knapsack which contains a fairly spacious extra-dimensional storeroom. We loaded the knapsack with lots of supplies, including powdered milk, walrus butter, and a man-sized wooden automaton called Mendigo. You're all welcome to use the extra-dimensional compartment for storage. Claims to fame? I once broke half the bones in my body slaying a giant, two-headed panther."

Mara stepped forward, standing tall and holding her head high. Her body language was defiant, as if ready for a fight, and she spoke in a serious, resonant alto. "I am Mara Tabares. I was about to inherit the stewardship of the Lost Mesa preserve when it was overthrown and my mother was killed. A dragon played a key role in the tragedy, as did a spy from the Society. I've always had an unusual connection to wild animals. I am a skilled tracker and wind watcher. Some say I may have the potential to become a dragon tamer." She fell silent.

"More than potential," Trask added. "I worked with Mara in October at Soaring Cliffs, and she remained self-possessed during a prolonged interview with a pair of adolescent dragons. No small feat. But I interrupt. Gavin?"

Gavin rubbed the back of his neck, his eyes only occasionally straying from the floor. "I guess you guys know that my dad was Charlie Rose. I b-b-basically grew up on the Frosted Peaks dragon sanctuary in the Himalayas. My dad had a tight relationship with the dragons there. After my mom died giving birth to me, he arranged for me to be accepted as a dragon brother. It is sort of like Kendra being fairykind—the dragons adopted me as one of their own and shared some power with me. I can s-s-s-speak their languages. If dragons kill me they would be challenged as if they had slain a dragon. My status as a dragon brother even affects me physically—I'm a little stronger and f-faster than I look."

He combed his fingers through his hair. "Nobody has been a dragon brother for a very long time. My dad worried that my abilities would turn me into a target, so he kept me a secret. After he was killed, my dad's best friend Arlin brought me to the Knights. Since the Sphinx was running the Knights when I joined, he knew the basics of what I could do, and so we're p-p-pretty sure the Society has guessed what I am. But we're still trying to keep the details of being a dragon brother quiet in case they don't know everything."

Trask rose to his feet. "Thanks for the candid introductions. As you can see, we have an impressive group assembled. All of you have at least been in the presence of a dragon, although a couple of you have never been to a dragon sanctuary.

"Let me convey a few thoughts about dragons, and then we'll get to bed. Gavin, feel free to jump in. Dragons are magical from the tips of their fangs to the ends of their tails. The old ones are among the most ancient creatures on the planet. Highly intelligent, they have their own unique languages, but often speak hundreds of additional tongues. No two dragons are identical. They have diverse appearances, various breath weapons, and distinct spell-casting capabilities. Much like humans, dragons have a wide array of personalities. Some are just. Others are wicked.

"Communicating with dragons is difficult. Paralyzing fear radiates from them. In the presence of a dragon, most people find that their muscles lock up and their tongues stop working. With the unique exception of Gavin, you should never look a dragon in the eye. To do so will leave you entranced and incapacitated.

"Since dragons are not accustomed to communicating with other creatures, the best way to survive a draconic encounter is to hold an intelligent conversation. They find it amusing, and will often spare your life.

"Dragon sanctuaries are unlike other preserves you may have visited. Some protections are usually afforded to the caretaker, who also serves as the gatekeeper. Otherwise, there are no protections to visitors. For those of us heading beyond the abode of the caretaker, it will be like venturing into the wild. And we will have more than dragons to contend with. These sanctuaries were founded as a home for creatures too large and powerful to cohabit with the beings at the more traditional preserves. Little is known about Wyrmroost. Who can say what we might encounter? Gavin, do you have any words of advice?"

Gavin shrugged. "We're going in there well armed. Our weapons might come in handy against some of the creatures we may encounter. But forget about your weapons if we face a threat from dragons. The first goal is to talk. The second is to flee or hide. Humans can't stand against dragons. Once upon a time there were dragon slayers. That time is long gone.

"Here's a metaphor my dad used: Dragons see us as we see mice. We're not very tasty. We're not a real threat. If they find us underfoot, they'll kill us just to keep the area tidy. But if we talk to them, they'll view us as we would a talking mouse. We become a surprising novelty, a cute pet. In the presence of a dragon, the goal is to amuse and impress. Play the role of a p-p-p-precocious mouse that no human would kill."

"Sound advice," Trask approved. "Any questions? No? Fine with me. We've gone over the basics. I'm proud to work with each of you. Let's get some sleep. Tomorrow will be an eventful day."

Mara blew out the candle.

※ ※ ※

The splintery wall of the crate pricked Seth's arm. The tin of whale butter in his pocket pressed against his thigh. He shifted position, but the movement bent his neck forward uncomfortably, nearly forcing his chin to his chest. The close, stale air inside the crate smelled of dust and rotting wood. He wished he could bore a hole in the side. Sweat slicked his skin. The carpet tented over him served as an unwanted blanket in the balmy darkness.

The saddest part was that the cramped stuffiness of the crate was almost certainly unnecessary. The odds were slim that anyone would descend the ladder until the next morning. He had clung to the ladder near the mouth of the knapsack, listening as Warren bade Kendra good night, and then descended to hide in case anyone decided to stow some final items before going to bed.

All remained quiet. It was probably safe to end the claustrophobic torture, but he refused to risk losing his chance to travel with the others to Wyrmroost. He had found a few roomier crates, but this one was up against the wall, well protected by other shabby containers. Inside this crate, with the lid on and a carpet draped over him, nobody would find him.

Tanu had missed him when he had searched inside the knapsack just before leaving. The big Samoan had thoroughly checked the room with a bright flashlight. He had even lifted the lid to the crate where Seth was hiding, but he had not looked under the carpet.

Seth wondered what Grandma and Grandpa were doing at the moment. As night fell, they would be freaking out, thinking he had roamed off into the woods and gotten lost or captured or killed. Any of those conclusions were fine with him, as long as they failed to guess the truth.

His decision to stow away inside the knapsack had not been made alone. On Christmas Eve, Grandpa had brought him into his office to deliver the news that he would not be part of the team sent to recover the key from Wyrmroost. Having already considered stowing away as a possible contingency, to allay suspicions, Seth had received the news with stoic acceptance.

After the seven members of the team had been announced to the rest of the family, Seth had retired to his room to think and found Warren waiting, spinning a basketball on the tip of his finger.

"Shame you won't be coming," Warren said, eyes on the ball.

"I'm used to it," Seth replied. "I always miss the coolest stuff."

"Think fast." Warren chucked the ball at him. Seth caught it and tossed it back briskly. "How bad do you want to stow away?" the man asked.

"Stow away?"

Warren grinned. "Don't bother with the innocent routine. I can spot fake innocence a mile away. Must be pretty tempting when you think about that knapsack. We'll have to bring it for supplies, of course. Lots of room in there. Lot of places to hide."

"You're a jerk," Seth said.

"Take it easy. I'm not here to rub it in. I kind of hope you do it."

"What?"

Warren stood, dribbling the basketball between his legs. "I think you're right. You've got unusual abilities that could come in handy. If you hadn't pulled the nail from the revenant, I'd still be a mute albino. If you hadn't been at the old manor when we went to retrieve the Chronometer, we never would have found Patton and Fablehaven would have fallen. I'm a believer, Seth. I'm not here to make you go. But if you *want* to go, I'm not going to discourage you. In fact, tomorrow afternoon, I'll leave the knapsack in the backseat of the SUV, and I'll make sure a door is unlocked."

"This is some sort of trick. Grandpa put you up to this. It's a trap."

"No trick, I swear. We can't afford to blow it at Wyrmroost. The Sphinx has the Oculus. We can't let him have the Translocator. Think what will happen if the Sphinx can see anywhere and go anywhere! What will prevent him from grabbing all of the artifacts? How long will it be before he opens Zzyzx and none of us have anywhere to hide? Like it or not, we're past playing it safe. If you want to be at Wyrmroost, I'd rather have you there than sitting idle at Fablehaven."

That conversation had been all it took to thoroughly convince Seth. He had written the note to explain his absence, and, as Warren had promised, after Christmas dinner, the back of the SUV was unlocked, the knapsack waiting.

Since Seth had entered the knapsack, Mendigo had been his only company. Unlike Hugo, the overgrown puppet had no will, no identity. It did not speak. The big limberjack existed only to carry out orders. Once, the wooden figure had obeyed orders from the witch Muriel. Now it was loyal to the Sorensons.

Seth continued to wait inside the crate, perspiring in the stifling darkness. Aside from the ample provisions packed for the others, Warren had stashed extra food inside an old trunk for Seth. When he felt certain the others were asleep, his reward would be to grab some granola bars and peanut butter. But before Seth could reach that conclusion, he heard the rasp of wood scraping against wood, as if the lid of a container had slid open. He had heard nobody descend the ladder. Peeking out from under the carpet, he saw no light. He heard the faint creak of a trunk opening, the rustle of a bag, and the crunch of an apple.

Somebody was getting into his private food stash!

The noisy munching was loudest right after each new bite. The chewing would gradually dwindle until the volume increased again with a fresh crunch. Who could be eating the apple? Certainly not Mendigo. The puppet didn't eat. Seth felt sure he would have heard somebody come down the ladder, and anyone but Kendra would require a light. Could Coulter have missed a stowaway spy from when Kendra had first obtained the magical knapsack?

Shifting his position slightly, Seth got out his flashlight. There was a wooden baseball bat near his crate that he could use for a weapon. He hesitated, worried what he might see. He would spring into action on the next new bite, he told himself.

The unseen food thief bit into the apple again, and Seth stood up, flinging off the lid to the crate and switching on the flashlight. The beam spotlighted a stocky little goblin with an oversized head; grimy, greenish skin; long, pointed ears; and a wide, lipless mouth. The goblin stared into the light, an apple core cupped in one pudgy hand, eyes flashing like bronze coins.

"Who are you?" Seth asked in a hard voice, groping for the bat.

"I might try the same question," the stout goblin replied calmly, his voice grumpy.

Seth's fingers found the handle of the bat. "You're eating my supplies."

"You're invading Bubda's home."

"This knapsack belongs to my sister." Keeping his flashlight beam on the goblin, Seth began to climb over barrels and boxes toward the uncluttered portion of the room. The squat goblin stood barely taller than Seth's waist. "If I tell her you're down here, they'll boot you out."

"But you're hiding too," the goblin said with a sly smile.

"Maybe. But I'd happily give myself up to get rid of a spy."

"A spy? You're an ally of the night. You speak good Duggish. I took it you knew what Bubda was."

"Which is what?"

"A hermit troll."

"I've heard of hermit trolls," Seth said. "You're the kind who hide out in attics and under bridges. I've never met one."

"Bubda didn't want to meet you. But you wouldn't leave, and Bubda got hungry." The troll stuffed the apple core in his mouth, seeds and all.

Seth reached the open floor. He held the baseball bat at his side. No need to act threatening if he could keep this friendly. "How long have you lived here?"

"Long time. No need to move once you find the right place. Dark. Well-stocked. Private. Places to hide. But two is a crowd."

"Your name is Bubda?"

"Right."

"I'm Seth. I'll only be here a few days. Then you can have it back. How come Coulter never found you?"

Bubda crouched, tucking in his arms. The troll was gone. He looked exactly like a barrel. When he stood up straight again, the illusion ended. "Bubda hides well."

"That was cool," Seth said. "Can you look like other stuff?"

"Bubda has lots of tricks. Bubda never shows them all."

"Did you collect all this stuff?" Seth shone his light around the room.

"Some was here. Some Bubda brought. Bubda finds what Bubda must."

"You're down here most of the time?"

"Almost always. Better that way."

"What about a rest room?"

"Careful what barrel you open."

Seth snickered. "I could use a rest room. I was thinking about sneaking out."

"Up to you. Maybe you leave for good?"

Seth shook his head. "You're stuck with me for a few days. Don't you get lonely?"

"Bubda likes to hide. Bubda likes to rest."

"We should be friends. I'm an ally of the night. We speak the same language."

"Bubda likes to be alone. Other people are a pain. You're other people, Seth. Better than some. Maybe better than most. But no people is best."

"Will we get along?" Seth asked. "Are you going to try to harm me in my sleep?"

Bubda shrugged. "Bubda didn't bother you yet. Bubda waited for you to go. Bubda can wait more."

Seth glanced at the giant wooden puppet. "Okay. Try not to eat too much of my food. And don't eat any of the other people's food. If they notice it missing, we're finished. Understood?"

"Bubda knows. Bubda only took food from where you took food. Bubda has other food."

Seth wondered what other food Bubda meant. Did he eat the spoiled goo in the old barrels? The thought triggered Seth's gag reflex. "All right. I guess we're roommates."

"More?" Bubda asked, pointing at the trunk.

"Sure, Bubda. Have a little more. You give me my space, and I'll give you yours."

The troll pursed his lips and nodded. "Deal."

Bubda was no taller than Seth's chest, but he looked heavy, and he had long, sharp fingernails. Seth sidled over to Mendigo and dropped his voice to a soft whisper. "Keep Bubda under constant watch. If he comes within ten feet of me while I'm sleeping, pin him to the ground. Same if he sneaks up on me at any time. You hear me?"

Mendigo gave a nod.

CHAPTER SEVENTEEN

Wyrmroost

The helicopter soared through the clear sky, rotors beating at the cold air. Sitting up front with the pilot, Kendra enjoyed a breathtaking view of the snowy forest below through the large, curved windows. She had never seen beauty to compare with this rugged panorama of frozen summits and icy lakes.

Not long after they had taken off, Kendra had decided she never wanted to be a helicopter pilot. The numerous dials and gauges intimidated her. Aaron Stone controlled their direction with a stick that projected up between his legs. He used a second stick to take them up or down, and foot pedals to swing the tail from side to side. The coordination and know-how required seemed hopelessly beyond her.

"Go more to the right, Aaron," Kendra said. Once

again, the pilot was veering away from the pair of lofty peaks that dwarfed all others. Trask had said the mountains were actually the two highest points in North America, but were unrecognized as such because of the potent distracter spell shielding the sanctuary.

"You sure you see two tall mountains?"

"I'm staring right at them."

Aaron lifted the visor on his helmet and squinted. "Are you looking at those summits?" He pointed away from their heading.

"No, the ones I see are much bigger. They're by far the tallest mountains out here."

He flipped down his visor. "This is odd. I can usually think my way around a distracter spell."

As they drew nearer, Kendra noticed that the shoulders of the imposing mountains were virtually clear of snow, along with much of the surrounding wilderness. She scoured the hills and valleys for dragons or other creatures, but saw none. She began to notice a faint rainbow shimmer in the air ahead of them, reminiscent of the aurora borealis. The soaring mountains drew ever nearer.

"We're getting close," Kendra said.

"You see the valentine?"

Kendra scanned the snow-choked forest below for a heart-shaped clearing. The helicopter was supposed to set down in the cordate meadow so they could continue the journey on foot. "Not yet."

They continued forward, but the helicopter began to slowly lose altitude as Aaron eased them closer to the ground.

Below, the shadow of the helicopter rose and fell with the contours of the terrain. On many slopes, the snow sparkled in the sunlight. Kendra spotted a clearing shaped vaguely like a kidney. "Could that be it?" she asked, pointing.

Aaron followed her finger to the ground. "I don't think so."

"You're veering off course again. Go back to the right."

Less than a minute later, the desired meadow came into view, an unmistakable white valentine amidst the trees, smaller than Kendra had expected. "Here we are," Kendra announced. "Aaron, bring us more to the right. See it?"

"I've got it. Sharp eyes. Good job, Kendra." He raised his head, surveying the horizon. "I still don't see those mountains."

"They're straight ahead. Their summits are much higher than we are."

"You're kidding."

"Along with plenty of lower ones," Kendra reported. "Rocky ridges and steep hills. Looks like rugged terrain inside the sanctuary. Some unfrozen lakes. It isn't snowy in there, just at the tops of the peaks."

"Weird," Aaron said.

"Think you'll be able to find your way back to pick us up?"

"We're leaving a radio and a beacon in the clearing. I've been studying the topography, scouting for landmarks outside the sanctuary. I think I could get back on my own. If not, I'll rely on Trask and instruments."

Based on how often he had swerved away from the

sanctuary, Kendra had her doubts about his ability to return unaided. Hopefully the gadgets would work.

Aaron brought the helicopter down softly in the snowy field. Once they were on the ground, the clearing no longer looked much like a valentine. Trask, Dougan, Warren, Tanu, Mara, and Gavin poured out of the helicopter and began unloading gear. Kendra climbed out as well.

The rotors never stopped spinning. Once the gear had been unloaded, Trask ducked into the cockpit to have a few words with Aaron. Afterwards, they all backed away and watched as the rotors sped up and the red and white helicopter ascended noisily into the sky, sending windy waves of snow flying across the field.

Despite the bright sun, the air was bitter cold. Warren helped Kendra adjust her hat, goggles, and collar to reduce exposed skin. Bundled in her bulky coat, Kendra felt like an astronaut. Warren helped her strap her boots into snowshoes. Dougan put a harness on her and clipped it to a climbing rope. Kendra would lead them, and hopefully the rope would help the others keep moving in the right direction.

Tanu tapped his gloved fists together. "Are we sure we don't want to just climb in the knapsack and let Kendra carry us to the gate?"

"We've been over this," Warren replied hastily. "We need to be out and ready in case of danger. There's no reason to have Kendra carry us forward alone. If all else fails, we can try the knapsack."

Tanu shrugged and nodded.

Trask came tromping over the snow. "We ready?" He had

finished camouflaging a large plastic container at the edge of the clearing. Everyone behind Kendra was now attached to the rope via harnesses and carabiners.

"Sure," Dougan said.

Trask clipped himself next in line behind Kendra. He spoke over his shoulder to the others. "Remember, don't pay attention to where you're going. Just follow the leader. You see the peaks, Kendra?"

"Yep."

"Anyone else see them?" Trask inquired. "The huge unmistakable mountains? Didn't think so. Neither do I. The more you focus on where we're trying to get, the more you'll find yourself inclined to wander the wrong way. Follow the rope. No matter what you might think, the rope is right. Kendra, lead on."

"I keep heading toward the mountains?" Kendra verified.

"That's right. Heading that way will at least let us find the wall; then we'll worry about the gate."

Kendra began trudging into the trees. The others followed. Having no specific expertise with the outdoors, Kendra worried she might lead them poorly. She concentrated on trying to find the best route through the trees, the easiest way up each slope. Her main goal was to avoid the need to double back. Since the others would be struggling against the effects of the distracter spell, she hoped to lead them by the safest, most direct route she could find.

The snowshoes made her strides ungainly, but at least they kept her and the others on top of the powdery snow.

Tall conifers towered above her, limbs flocked white. Kendra enjoyed the crisp smell of the snow and the trees. Cocooned as she was within her insulated attire, warmed by the exercise, the cold seemed irrelevant.

She plodded up slopes and around leafless thickets and deadfalls. She tugged insistently on the rope when the others started to meander in the wrong direction. Occasionally a clump of snow would tumble from a tree to land with a muffled thump. Under evergreen branches, she lost sight of the mountains for certain stretches, but she caught plenty of glimpses to keep her chain of followers properly oriented.

Based on some old hand-drawn map in the Knights' archives, Trask believed that the clearing where they had landed was a couple of miles from the gate. Kendra wondered how far two miles would feel treading cross-country through the snow, mostly uphill. She rapidly grew weary of the way her oversized soles made each step a chore.

As Kendra reached the crest of a long slope, she found she had led her team to the top of a thirty-foot face. They would have to parallel the drop-off for about a hundred yards before they could continue forward. From the elevated vantage, ahead through the trees, Kendra beheld the massive gate. Apparently wrought of gold, the gate was composed of closely spaced vertical bars and hung independent of any physical wall or fence. Instead of attaching to a tangible wall, the gate was situated in the middle of an iridescent barrier of prismatic light. Extending high into the air, the multicolored barrier shimmered like the northern lights, but inhabited a fixed position. Kendra paused at the brink of the drop, watching ropes and wheels and sheets of light flutter and fold and collide in endless combinations.

Trask tugged at the rope. "We'd best head back."

"No, we just need to move along the little cliff until we can continue forward. I can see the gate."

"You've lost the route," Dougan mourned. "We've come the wrong way."

Everyone holding the rope was looking backwards, away from the gate and the impressive light display. They began to pull against her together, and Kendra found herself stumbling away from the gate.

"Don't trust yourselves," Kendra said.

"We've reached an impassable cliff," Trask argued.

"Stop!" Kendra shouted, struggling against them. "Your instincts are blind. I won't let us get hurt. I see how we can get to the gate."

"Close your eyes," Warren demanded. "Close them tight and follow her lead."

"That's right," Kendra agreed. "I'll keep us well away from any edges. Let me guide us."

Mumbling uncertainly, the others closed their eyes. Kendra leaned into her steps now more than before. The others kept trying to stray and, even with their eyes shut, continued to second-guess their heading. She led them to where the sheer drop-off dwindled and started directly toward the gate.

"Stay with me!" Kendra commanded as the others started hauling her in the wrong direction.

"You're leading us into an avalanche zone," Dougan cried in alarm.

"He's right," Mara agreed.

They pulled against her so hard that Kendra fell. They dragged her across the snow, away from the prismatic barrier. Kendra called out to them in desperation, "Stop! Guys, stop! You're going the wrong way!"

"Ignore your instincts," Gavin called.

"Go where she pulls us," Warren agreed.

Tanu dug in hard, and they stopped moving in the wrong direction. "Keep your eyes closed," the Samoan bellowed.

"I can sense the danger," Mara insisted.

"Your senses are messed up," Kendra said with conviction. "We're right by the gate. Don't think, just follow."

"Blind faith," Gavin said.

"Blind faith," Trask agreed.

Kendra arose and plodded in the right direction again, trying to move fast to keep their momentum flowing toward their destination. They were close. It was time to sprint to the finish.

They emerged from the forest into a wide, clear snowfield. Now nothing impeded a full view of the high golden gate and the scintillating wall. Kendra charged forward, breathing hard, straining against the rope. Her eyes drank in kaleidoscopic swirls of light stretching to the edge of sight in either direction. Slow spirals rippled and curled. Glancing back, she saw that even with their eyes closed, her companions kept their faces averted. They followed her on stiff, hesitant legs. But they followed.

It was strange to approach the shimmering radiance of the barrier. The colorful wall looked too much like a rainbow or a mirage, an illusion that should recede when an observer drew near. Instead, the barrier inhabited a fixed position, flashing and gleaming, filling Kendra's field of vision as she approached the gilded gate.

"Stand still," Kendra called at last, a step or two from the shiny gate. Glancing back, she saw that the others were trembling.

"Hold your ground," Trask growled.

Gavin and Warren dropped to their knees. Mara moaned and grimaced. Dougan hummed a simple tune in a strained voice, beads of perspiration on his brow. Tanu took deep, cleansing breaths, wide nostrils flaring, broad chest expanding and contracting.

Kendra unzipped her coat and felt for the inside pocket where she had stashed the unicorn horn. Her gloves made her fingers clumsy, so she pulled one off, and soon held the smooth horn in her bare hand.

"Forward," she encouraged, leaning against her companions to grind out the final steps to the gate. Seeing no keyhole, she touched the tip of the horn to the center of the gate. Upon contact, the metal gleamed brilliantly and the gate swung silently open. Even upon close inspection, the hinges of the gate were apparently anchored to nothing more than the translucent barrier of light. Legs churning, she towed the others through the opening.

On the far side of the barrier, she no longer had to pull. Opening their eyes, the others gathered around her, wearing befuddled expressions as if they had just awakened. The frigid bite had gone out of the air. Tiny wildflowers bloomed in the tall grass. No snow clung to the trees here, nor to the ground, save a few meager patches in the shade. Ahead of them stood a gray stone wall with round towers at the corners and a raised drawbridge in the center, dark timbers studded with iron. The broad, crenellated wall reached maybe twenty feet high, the corner towers an extra ten feet taller. None of the buildings beyond the wall reared much higher. No visible guards or sentries manned the battlements. The stronghold looked timeworn and dreary, more like an abandoned fort than an occupied castle. Behind them, the golden gate clanged shut.

"Welcome to Wyrmroost," Trask murmured.

Kendra found the sturdy, silent fort disquieting. "Do we go knock?" she wondered.

Tanu scratched his head, staring up at the tremendous mountains. "How did we miss those?"

A roar like a thousand lions exploded from the nearest stand of trees, making Kendra start and turn. A gold and red creature snaked up from the grove, long body twirling and winding like a ribbon. Two sets of gold-feathered wings fanned out, propelling the serpentine dragon toward the gate.

"Stay calm," Gavin urged. "Stand your ground. Don't reach for weapons. Don't make eye contact."

Kendra stared away from the dragon, watching it approach from her peripheral vision. The great wings spread wide, creating a rush of wind as the dragon alighted near them. Paralyzing fear washed over Kendra, the terror instinctual and overpowering. Was this how a rabbit felt when it saw a hawk swooping down? The dragon had a head like a giant lion, with red-gold fur and a crimson mane. Eight sets of legs supported the scaly body, the large feet each a hybrid of dragon claw and lion paw. The dragon stood half again taller than Trask, and stretched longer than two school buses.

"Visitors," the dragon purred in a rich, interested voice. "We seldom have visitors. This is a dangerous domain. I prevent the unworthy from entering. Are any of you capable of speech?"

"I can converse with you, mighty one," Gavin said.

"And look me in the eye. Impressive. What of your companions?"

"I can speak," Trask said. "We seek the caretaker."

"I can speak as well," Mara added.

Kendra trembled. She doubted she could move her arms or legs, but forced some words past her lips. "As can I."

The dragon inclined his leonine head. "An impressive group of humans. Four of seven retaining some semblance of control. One with true self-possession. Who can move?"

Mara and Trask went to stand at either side of Gavin, who saluted the dragon casually. Kendra tried to override the paralysis in her limbs but failed. The dragon shook his head, fluffing up his shaggy mane. "Three? Why not the fourth? I see, although she harbors a strange energy, she is not a true dragon speaker. What errand brings you to Wyrmroost?"

"We s-s-seek audience with the caretaker," Gavin said.

"Fair enough," the dragon replied. "You will find Agad

inside Blackwell Keep. I am Camarat. I work with Agad. I have not screened visitors for many years." Camarat prowled forward and sniffed Warren, then took a whiff of the knapsack. "More in there than one might suspect. But nothing too alarming." The dragon moved in front of Trask, exhaling blue-white fumes from his nostrils. "What brings you to Wyrmroost?"

"We seek the key to a distant vault," Trask said, scowling after the words left his mouth.

"A key? Interesting." The dragon moved to Mara, exhaling on her. "What else do you hope to accomplish?"

"We want the key and we want to survive," she replied.

The dragon reared up like a cobra, towering over them, two sets of legs pawing at the air. "Very well, you may pass. Be forewarned. Wyrmroost is not for the faint of heart."

The gilded wings spread wide and with a rush of air the dragon took flight, elongated body curling and snapping like a whip. Awed by the fluid grace of the magnificent creature, Kendra watched it corkscrew into the sky. With a clacking of gears and the clang of heavy chains the drawbridge in the wall began to swing down. A hard-packed path wide enough for a wagon led directly from the golden gate to the drawbridge. Trask marched toward the fort.

"Is there often a dragon at the gate to welcome visitors?" Kendra asked Gavin, falling into step beside him.

"I've n-n-n-never seen such a thing. We would have warned everyone. I haven't met a dragon quite like Camarat either."

"Was he breathing truth serum on Trask and Mara?"

"Or something like it. Hey, good job dragging us through the gate. I was feeling pretty foggy."

"We all have our specialties." She hoped she sounded casual instead of proud.

They reached the drawbridge and passed over a shallow, dry moat choked with thorny shrubs. The iron teeth of a raised portcullis hung menacingly above as they strode through the thick wall and out into a flagstone courtyard. A solid gray building topped by battlements stood before them. No light shone within the high, narrow windows. Three figures awaited them in front of the single heavy door to the stone structure.

In the center, the tallest minotaur Kendra had ever seen leaned on a long-hafted battle-ax like a staff. His shaggy fur was the silky chestnut of an Irish setter, and a black patch covered one eye. To the left stood a creature like a centaur, except with the body of a moose. Several scars defaced his brown skin, the most gruesome angling down from one ear and curving halfway across his throat. He carried a black bow and wore a quiver of arrows. A polished horn hung from one shoulder by a leather strap. On the right, a thin, hairless woman with four arms and skin like a snake tested the air with her slender tongue. Her lower hands held daggers with jagged blades.

The minotaur stepped forward, twisting his head so he could better regard the newcomers with his good eye. "What brings you to Blackwell Keep?" he asked gruffly.

Trask held his hands at his sides, palms outward. "I am Trask. We come as friends, hoping to lodge here for the night. Are you Agad?"

The minotaur snorted, nostrils flaring. "Agad will receive you in the High Hall." He gestured at the snakelike woman. "Simrin will escort you. Leave your arms and gear in the guardhouse." With his ax, he pointed at a structure to the side of the main entry. "The alcetaur will assist you." The moose-bodied centaur came toward them.

"Let's do it," Trask muttered, heading for the guardhouse.

The silent alcetaur showed where to pile their gear. Warren checked with Trask before setting down the knapsack, then complied after receiving a curt nod. Kendra kept the unicorn horn inside her coat pocket.

With their belongings stored, Kendra and the others followed Simrin through a cavernous hall where crows roosted in the rafters. Shorter than Kendra, the serpentine woman moved with a fluid, slithery stride. She led them out a door at the rear of the hall, up two flights of stairs, and across an enclosed walkway to an adjacent building. Kendra peered down through a window at a courtyard overrun by ferns, bushes, and gnarled trees. Chipped statues spotted with lichen watched over the vegetation, marble faces all but worn away.

Simrin guided them up a few steps and through a large set of doors into a narrow chamber with a barrel-vaulted ceiling. Daylight shone through leaded lancet windows onto a long stone table with twelve seats on each side. At the head of the table in the largest and most elaborate chair sat a plump, elderly man whose flowing gray beard reached his lap. A black cloak trimmed with sable hung from his hunched shoulders, mostly covering the silky red robes beneath. Jeweled rings adorned each finger. He was eating moist chunks of meat out of a hollowed heel of tough, dark bread.

The old man motioned to the nearest chairs. "Please join me," he invited, licking his thumb.

Trask and Dougan claimed the chairs nearest the elderly man. They all sat down. "You are Agad?" Trask asked.

"I am Agad, custodian of Wyrmroost." The old man dipped his fingers in a wooden bowl of water and wiped them on a linen napkin. "You seek the key deposited here by Patton Burgess."

They hesitated to respond. The bearded man regarded them coolly. "Correct," Dougan finally said.

Agad took a sip from a heavy goblet. "Patton was a friend of this sanctuary until he and a colleague smuggled a dragon egg off the premises. The exploit proved fatal."

"I heard he has a grave here," Kendra blurted.

Agad gave her a prolonged stare. "Not common knowledge. But yes, his bones are interred here at Blackwell. Only bones remained." The old man turned to Trask. "These are no environs for charming young girls. You will not find the key. My counsel is for you to depart immediately."

"We mustn't turn back," Trask said. "We were hoping to leave the girl and her protector here at the keep while the rest of us pursue the key."

"Alas," Agad lamented, folding his hands, "your intention is in vain. For us to maintain peace with the dragons, visitors may only seek shelter within the walls of Blackwell Keep during the first and last night of their stay."

Kendra and Warren exchanged a worried look.

"Surely we can arrange an exception for the child," Dougan said.

"I am afraid the terms of our truce allow for no exceptions," Agad sighed. "However, if you would indulge me, I would like to speak to the girl alone."

"We intended to ask for some assistance—" Trask began.

Agad held up a hand. "I oversee the keep and watch the gate. I have little involvement with the diverse inhabitants of this sanctuary, and virtually no interest in the agendas of visitors. The girl has clearly been adopted by fairies, and I have long taken an academic interest in such rarities. Your best chance to garner any advice from me would be to allow us some words in private."

Laying a comforting hand on Kendra's shoulder, Warren arose. "How do we—"

"I am master of this keep and custodian of this refuge. As visitors, you live or die by my word. She will be safer with me than in your company. I pledge that I intend the young woman no harm." Agad did not raise his voice, but his manner left no room for argument.

"I'll talk with him," Kendra said. "Go on, I'm not worried."

Agad smiled as if her words had officially settled the matter. "Simrin will show you to your quarters. The girl's gallant protector can wait outside this hall."

Kendra whispered assurances to Trask and Warren, remaining in her seat while the others shuffled out. Simrin

closed the large doors at the end of the chamber as she exited.

"Come nearer," Agad offered. "Would you care for food?"

"I'm not hungry," Kendra said, moving to the nearest seat.

"Do you mind if I continue my meal?"

"Not at all. Go ahead."

Keeping his elbows tucked close to his chest, the old man resumed transporting slimy chunks of meat from the bread bowl to his mouth with his fingers. "I have long wondered when you would appear."

"What do you mean?"

"Patton told me that one day a girl who was fairykind might show up searching for the key. Are you here of your own free will? These companions are not captors, I hope."

"They're friends," Kendra assured him. "I'm here on purpose."

"And you expect to retrieve the key?"

"We must. Our enemies know about it. They haven't come for it yet, have they?"

Agad shook his head. "No. You seven are our first guests in a great while."

"How did you know I was fairykind?"

"I would scarcely be half a wizard were I blind to such telltale brilliance as accompanies you, my dear Kendra."

"You know my name."

"Patton spoke of you in considerable detail." Agad packed another pinch of dripping meat into his mouth, the red juice staining his whiskers.

"I thought wizards were extinct," Kendra said.

"You are not far from the truth. Very few true wizards survive. Oh, you can find pretenders, magicians and witches and the like, but my kind have become an extremely rare breed. You see, all true wizards were once dragons."

"You're a dragon?"

"No longer. Many mature dragons can assume human form. Most are content to transform back and forth on occasion. Ages ago, a very wise dragon named Archadius discovered that by permanently assuming human form, he significantly increased his magical abilities. Others of us, those most interested in magic, followed suit."

"I guess that makes you a good caretaker for a dragon sanctuary."

Agad dabbed at his lips with a napkin. "Yes and no. I certainly have a profound understanding of dragons. Enough to realize that dragons have little fondness for those of us who embraced permanent humanity. To some extent they view us as weak, to some extent they are jealous, and to some extent they blame us for the general decline of dragons."

"Why blame wizards?"

"With good reason. Wizards were among the greatest dragon slayers. Like humans, dragons have alliances and enmities. Those battles raged on after various dragons took human form, and in the process, humanity discovered how to slay dragons. Furthermore, wizards played an instrumental role in confining dragons to sanctuaries." He wetted his fingers in the bowl of water, then dried his hands on the napkin.

"Can other dragons tell you used to be a dragon?"

"Only by witnessing the extent of the spells I can work. Or if anciently they had seen me transform. Under normal circumstances, the metamorphosis is so complete that even a fellow dragon cannot identify a dragon in human form. A human avatar serves as a virtually perfect disguise."

"Do you like being human?"

The wizard gave her a lopsided smile. "You ask difficult questions. A dragon prefers being a dragon when he is a dragon. We can only tolerate being human while clothed in human form. Changing back and forth is disorienting. The form we assume affects our minds. Here, now, I cannot fully recall the experience of being a dragon. I enjoy the mastery of magic I have achieved. I mostly enjoy how a human thinks and perceives the world. Do regrets linger? Indeed. Yet overall, with no way of rewriting history, I am content with my decision."

"You made the choice a long time ago?"

Agad exhaled sharply. "Thousands of years ago."

"So you age slowly?"

"Almost as gradually as a dragon." He sipped from his goblet. "But we digress. I meant to talk with you about Patton."

"It sounded like you hate him."

"I must present that façade. It is true that he was unpopular among the dragons here, even before he snatched an egg. But I know the truth. The egg he took belonged to a dragon named Nafia who had fallen into a pattern of eating her young. Dragons breed infrequently, and I wanted her most recent offspring to survive. Patton smuggled the egg to a safe location. To appease the dragons, I feigned outrage, invented a ruse that Patton had perished, and pretended to inter his remains in our churchyard."

"Do you know where he hid the key?"

Agad shook his head. "He did not trust that secret even to me—although, if you dig, you will find peculiar markings on the portion of his headstone below the ground. I take it you can decipher the secret fairy language."

"Yes. Can you help us retrieve the key?"

"Sadly, I can offer almost no assistance. The dragons have no love for me. Potent magical defenses reinforced by an ancient truce protect me while I remain at Blackwell Keep. Should I stray beyond these walls, the dragons would devour me and my assistants. Same if I broke our truce by letting you lodge here longer than is allowed."

"How can you be caretaker if you never leave?"

"My assistants venture beyond these walls as my eyes and ears. Not an enviable job. And I can discern much by magical means." The wizard settled back in his chair. "I was not lying to your companions when I told them they would fail."

"We have to try," Kendra said. "Our enemies are resourceful."

"Even if you somehow manage to remove the key, can you guard it better than dragons?"

"Now that they know it's here, our enemies will find a way to get it. We have to move it."

"They have the Oculus. They'll find it again."

Kendra stared at him. "How do you know they have the Oculus?"

"I could feel when they spied here. I could not identify the watcher, but I felt the gazing. I have been studied through the Oculus before."

"Could one of your assistants help us?" Kendra tried.

"I can't risk any of my personnel assisting you. Dragons are unforgiving. Beyond this castle, you are trespassers, and I cannot let your mission upset our fragile truce. Besides, none of my aides are very trustworthy. I know some of them spy on me for certain dragons. I do not think my assistants would harm you against my orders within these walls, but I harbor doubts even about that. It takes a hard sort to survive in a place like this."

Kendra crossed her arms on the table. "Okay. When should I check out the gravestone?"

"I'll instruct Simrin to show you the churchyard. Later tonight, steal down there with a comrade or two. Try not to let my assistants see. Cover your tracks when you leave." Pushing off the armrests of his chair, the old wizard stood. "Do not reveal my friendship with Patton to anyone, including your friends. Blame my candor on my interest in your status as fairykind. I will supply counsel to you and three companions of your choosing on the morrow. At this juncture, the best help I can offer will be advice."

"We'll appreciate anything you can do."

The wizard patted her arm. "I wish I could say I thought it would be enough."

CHAPTER EIGHTEEN

Blackwell Keep

Covering the plastic cup with his hand, Seth felt the dice tickling his palm. "Come on, sixes," he murmured, uncovering the cup and dumping five dice into the lid of the Yahtzee box.

"Three fives," Bubda announced.

"No sixes." Seth studied his score sheet. "I already have my fives. I still need four of a kind. Fives will do." He scooped up the dice and rolled a three and a four. Then he rolled a one and a six.

"No four of a kind," Bubda said. "You claiming the six?"

"I'd miss my bonus for sure. And I already used my chance slot. I better take a zero for Yahtzee."

Bubda scooped the dice into the cup and grinned as he rattled them briskly. The hermit troll had already recorded a

Yahtzee this round, and had assured his upper section bonus. Boredom had driven Seth to comb through the junk in the storeroom. The Yahtzee box had an old-fashioned design, as if it came from the fifties or sixties. Some of the score cards had been used, but plenty remained blank, and there were two little golf pencils as well. Seth had started playing by himself, and the troll eventually came to watch over his shoulder. Bubda's reluctant curiosity had mushroomed into a Yahtzee marathon.

The troll tossed the dice into the box lid.

"Four ones," Seth announced. "You already have your ones. You have four of a kind, and that would be a really low three of a kind. You can try for a full house."

Bubda shook his head and picked up a single die, leaving the four ones. "Yahtzee bonus is a hundred points."

He rolled a six. Grumbling, he snatched it up and rolled a one.

"Yahtzee!" Bubda crowed, raising both fists.

Seth could only shake his head. "You're the luckiest guy in the world." Bubda had already won nine of thirteen rounds.

Bubda capered in a circle, slapping one hip while twirling a finger over his head. Seth regretted having shown the troll that every Yahtzee deserved a victory dance.

Above and behind him, Seth heard the flap of the knapsack open. Bubda dove over to a pyramid of crates. Tucking his head and scrunching up his limbs, he suddenly looked uncannily like a wooden trunk. As feet started down the ladder, Seth backed into a corner, hoping his shade walking abilities would keep him out of sight. How had he let a game of Yahtzee become a security risk?

When the figure descending the rungs came into view, Seth breathed easier. "I'm alone," Warren called in a hushed voice. Seth liked how his questing eyes swept over him without any recognition.

"Here I am," Seth said, coming forward.

"Not bad," Warren approved. "You appeared out of nowhere."

"What's the latest?"

"Sorry I haven't been able to get down here until now. I didn't want the others to get wise to you yet." Warren glanced at the floor. "Were you playing Yahtzee?"

"I don't cope well with boredom. It's nighttime, right?"

Warren nodded. "We're inside a keep. Sort of a little castle."

"I know what a keep is."

"Kendra and some of the others are investigating the churchyard for clues. I didn't relish leaving her side, but I wanted to check on you." Warren explained to Seth about meeting Agad and how they would all have to move on together in the morning.

"We're here now," Seth said. "Should I just come out and reveal myself?"

"I'm not sure how the others will take it."

"I won't throw you under the bus for helping me. I'll pretend I acted alone."

"I'm not worried about that. I just want the team to stay cooperative and focused. Your appearance could be divisive. You'll be safer in here than anywhere, and once we leave the keep, you'll always be with us. I think we might be smart to quietly hold you in reserve. If we get into a jam where you can help, you can be our reinforcements."

"Okay. I guess that makes sense."

Warren stooped and picked up the red dice. He shook them in the brown cup and dumped them into the box lid. "Look at that. Large straight." He straightened up. "I've never felt more over my head than with this one. I'm tempted to try hiding the knapsack in some obscure corner of the keep, then hunkering down in here with you and your sister."

"Why don't you?"

"Agad is a wizard, and he can't have us here. He'd get wise to us if we tried to stash the knapsack. Camarat, that dragon at the entry gate, sniffed out the knapsack as soon as he met us. I don't think there's a safe place to hide in the whole stinking sanctuary. We need to achieve our objective and get out."

Warren went to one of the supply boxes and took out a granola bar. He tossed a second one to Seth. They peeled the wrappers and started munching.

"Whatever you do," Seth said around a chewy mouthful, "try not to leave me down here too long. You can only play a certain amount of Yahtzee games in a row before you become a lunatic."

"I'll keep that in mind."

※ ※ ※

The night was still and not nearly as cold as Kendra would have expected. She doubted that the temperature had even dipped below freezing. Overhead, stars glittered in such quantity that even the most familiar constellations became lost in the abundance.

The gravestones in the churchyard behind the keep's modest chapel stood in various states of disrepair. Many were cracked or chipped. Some had been worn smooth. Some leaned drunkenly. Several graves were simply marked by piles of stones. Three were designated by rough-hewn granite spheres the size of beach balls. Kendra could see well enough to read most of the headstones without light, so Trask and Gavin followed blindly, trusting her eyes.

The headstone for Patton Burgess was more solid and legible than many of the others. It rose to her waist and read:

Patton Burgess
Word to the Wise
Tread Lightly Among Dragons

Kendra read the words aloud, then walked around to look at the other side. "Nothing on the back." It was strange to think that in her hometown, she had her own false headstone. Her parents still believed she was buried there. But it was for the best. If it would keep them safe, it was worth it.

Trask and Gavin crouched and began scraping at the hard earth with spades. Kendra surveyed the churchyard. Mara, Dougan, and Tanu were keeping watch somewhere, while Warren kept the lights burning in some of their sleeping quarters.

"This is like digging through iron," Gavin complained.

Trask paused, uncapping a vial Tanu had lent him and sprinkling some of the contents on the ground. After a moment they resumed digging and seemed to make faster headway. Kendra felt tense. The keep had an oppressive atmosphere. Designed to house a small army, the sturdy complex felt too large and too empty. There were too many parapets, too many obscure windows and alcoves, too many places to hide. She could not help wondering who might be watching. As her friends chopped deeper into the defiant earth, the sounds of their excavation were magnified by unnatural echoes. Kendra scanned the surrounding walls for unfriendly eyes.

Simrin came to mind. Earlier in the day, she had glimpsed the snake woman climbing straight up a wall to a catwalk, palms flat against the stone instead of gripping, moving up the vertical surface like a gecko. Was Simrin spying on them right now, peering down from a gloomy perch, ready to convey information to the dragons?

During the day, Kendra had run across other creatures besides the minotaur, the snake woman, and the alcetaur. She had seen a huge hunchback ogre with meaty forearms and a pruned face crossing a courtyard with an anvil under one arm. The lumpy brute had one eye larger than the other, and a scabby bald head fringed by thin yellow hair. She had also noticed a small man no taller than her waist springing around on slender legs like a grasshopper. Who knew what other unusual assistants Agad had enlisted?

"This headstone does reach deeper than one would suspect," Trask panted.

"Any words yet, Kendra?" Gavin asked.

Kendra crouched and saw the first lines of a message. "Yes." Kendra got out the pen and paper she had brought. They had decided to have her write down the inscription to avoid discussing the clue out in the open.

Trask and Gavin grunted as they prodded and scraped deeper into the ground, revealing more of the deeply rooted tombstone. Trask sprinkled more of the potion Tanu had provided, and Gavin began attacking the soil with a small pickax. A flare of light made Kendra glance up, and she caught the end of a shooting star streaking across the sky.

By the time the entire message was exposed, a ring of rocks and dirt surrounded the sizable hole. Perspiration glistened on Trask's hairless head. Although the inscription was written in small letters, Kendra could read the message without difficulty. Sitting at the edge of the hole, she copied the words.

The object you desire is an iron egg the size of a pineapple, the top half crowned with protuberances, hidden inside the treasury of the secret Dragon Temple, alongside other items sacred to the dragons. Access is heavily guarded. Success is unlikely. Retrieve no extra items. Ignore the gauntlets. Enmity with dragons is no minor concern. Tell no dragon you seek the temple, including Agad. Directions to the temple can be had at the Fairy Queen shrine near Split Veil Falls.

"Got it," Kendra said, folding the note.

Trask and Gavin set about refilling the hole, packing the

rocks and soil back into place as best they could. While she waited, Kendra reread the message several times. Kendra had not suspected the Fairy Queen would have a shrine here at the sanctuary. She hadn't seen a single fairy. Apparently Kendra would have been joining the others whether or not Agad had allowed them to stay. If the Fairy Queen shrine at Wyrmroost was anything like the shrine at Fablehaven, Kendra was the only person who might survive trespassing there.

She tried not to imagine what obstacles might await if they managed to locate the Dragon Temple. It was already clear that when Patton had set out to make the Translocator hard to find, he had meant business.

※ ※ ※

Seth tried to resist, but the voices were so insistent. He hung near the top of the ladder for several minutes, listening to the whispery pleas, trying in vain to stifle his curiosity. The gibbering chorus reminded him of the Hall of Dread. The indistinct voices overlapped so much that most words were hard to catch—he most frequently heard "hunger," "thirst," and "mercy."

Warren had trusted him to stay put. Seth didn't want to make a stupid blunder, not here at Wyrmroost, with so much at stake. But once the whispers had begun, he had found them impossible to ignore. What if the hushed voices led to important secrets that only he could uncover? This could be his chance to prove he belonged on the adventure.

Pushing up the leather flap of the knapsack, Seth climbed out into the guardhouse and crouched in silence. The dark, still courtyard awaited beyond the door. Outside of the knapsack, he could discern that the babbling whispers originated from a single direction, reaching his ears from a source deeper inside the keep.

Keeping to the walls, Seth crept out into the gloomy courtyard, eyes wandering up to the starry firmament. Considering the lack of light, his shade walking abilities should make him nearly invisible to onlookers. Leaving the knapsack was a risk, but the possibility of gaining useful information about the sanctuary was too attractive. He might even be able to create an alliance with a powerful being. Desperate situations sometimes called for extreme measures.

And to be honest, if nothing else, it was a reasonably good excuse to get out of the stuffy storage room. The crisp mountain air was already rejuvenating his spirits.

Closed portcullises and a raised drawbridge barred an excursion beyond the wall. Across from the gateway, the main building loomed, dimly visible by starlight, accessible by a single heavy door. Staying near the walls, tense and watchful, Seth took the long way around the courtyard before reaching the iron-bound door. To his delight, he found it unlocked.

In the cavernous room beyond, Seth debated taking out his flashlight. It was too dark to see, but he decided that even a muted glare would be too risky in such a prominent room. Instead of navigating by sight, he followed the confused babble, the voices increasing in volume as he inched across the room, shins, toes, and outstretched hands occasionally bumping against unseen obstacles.

Finally Seth reached a wall and then a doorway. Briefly risking his flashlight with a hand cupped over the bright side, he found a stairway that went up and another that went down. The whispers were definitely coming up from a lower part of the building. Maybe the stronghold had a dungeon like the one at Fablehaven.

Upon hearing a gritty scrape from above, Seth extinguished his flashlight and backed against the wall. The scuffing sound had been unnatural. A moment later he heard faint footfalls carefully descending the stairs. The unseen person reached the bottom steps and then stopped. Seth could hear steady breathing.

"They were in the graveyard," a low voice said, "digging up Patton's grave."

"Did they take anything?" a quiet female voice answered.

"No. They seemed interested in markings on the headstone."

"They have returned to their rooms?"

"Far as I could tell."

"Keep an eye out. I'll check their wing."

Seth remained rigid in the darkness, an anxious hand squeezing his flashlight. From the timbre of the voices, he suspected the snake lady Warren had described and the minotaur. But there was no way to be sure. He heard soft steps shuffling away across the cavernous room.

Once he thought he was alone again, Seth considered returning to the knapsack. If he had expected the keep to be crawling with spies, he would have stayed in his hiding place. But the gibbering whispers persisted, and now that he was out and about, it would be a shame not to finish what he had started. It didn't sound like either of the speakers had descended the stairs, so Seth moved blindly forward to the vicinity of the downward staircase. Probing ahead with one foot, he found the lip of the first step and started down.

Advancing with as much stealth as he could manage in the darkness, Seth descended two long flights of stairs, passed through a door, down a hall, through a doorway, and down a winding stairwell. All the while, the volume of the whispers increased, until he worried whether he would be able to perceive any other sounds.

His hands found a door of solid iron, the surface rough and flaky with corrosion. His fingers located a catch, and with a clang the door squealed open, releasing an even more boisterous flood of cryptic whispers. The clangorous door made Seth uneasy. Others who were not saturated by the whispering might have heard the metallic racket from a considerable distance.

Heart hammering in his chest, Seth lingered in the doorway, working up the courage to proceed. The blackness ahead felt too ominous and too loud, so he took out his flashlight again. This deep below the keep, the light shouldn't glare out any windows. The glow revealed a short corridor that led to the curved wall of a partially visible chamber. Advancing cautiously, Seth emerged into an oval chamber with a circular hole in the floor, a shadowy mouth of unfathomable darkness. The babbling voices rose from the well, hissing and begging and threatening. A pervasive coldness in the air chilled Seth to his center.

No railing protected the hole. Had he failed to use a light, Seth might have stumbled into it unawares. The thought sent chills racing across his shoulders. The hole was perhaps ten feet across, the room no more than thirty. A single long chain snaked around the floor, forming several heavy piles of coils along the way. One end was anchored to the wall, the other ended near the circular well. Each oxidized link contained two holes, one for the previous link and another for the next.

Seth advanced to the brink of the hole, uncapped the flashlight, and shined the beam down. He could see a long way, but the light did not reach the bottom. As soon as he uncovered the light, the whispering rose to furious levels.

"Quiet," he muttered.

The whispering stopped.

The abrupt silence seemed much more unnerving than the prior clamor. A mild breeze wafted up from the depths of the hole.

Worried that the owners of the hushed voices could see him, Seth switched off the flashlight, plunging the room into impenetrable darkness.

"Help us," whispered a plaintive, parched voice. "Mercy."

"Who are you?" Seth whispered back, trying to keep his teeth from chattering.

"We are those confined to the depths," the thirsty voice answered.

"What kind of help do you—"

"The chain!"

A chorus of other ghastly voices repeated the request. "The chain, the chain, the chain, the chain."

Seth cleared his throat. "You want me to lower the chain?"

"We will serve you for a thousand years."

"We will fulfill your every wish."

"You shall never know defeat again."

"You shall never know fear."

"All will kneel before you."

More voices kept adding promises until Seth could no longer make out any specifics.

"Quiet," Seth demanded. The voices complied. "I can't hear you when you all speak at once."

"Wise lord," a raspy voice began, speaking alone, "we have lost all sense of time and place. We do not deserve this abyss. We need the chain. Send us the chain. Where is the chain?"

Other spectral voices took up the cry. "The chain. The chain. The chain . . ."

"Hush," Seth said. Once again, the voices fell silent. "We're going to play the quiet game. The first person to talk loses. I need a second to think."

Seth clicked on the flashlight. He shone it on the rusty chain. Fully uncoiled, it would reach deep into the hole. Once lowered, the metal chain would be far too heavy for him to raise alone. He walked around the perimeter of the hole. None of the unseen entities spoke. Seth's parents sometimes made him play the quiet game when they were driving together. He hadn't even needed to promise the winner a treat!

"Okay, I have some questions," Seth said. "I'm going to need a single spokesman to respond."

"Me," an avid voice answered.

"Fine. We're at a dragon sanctuary. What do you know about Wyrmroost?"

There came no reply for a moment. "We know little of sanctuaries. But we can kill dragons. We shall slay hundreds of dragons on your behalf. Their treasures will adorn your hall. No enemy shall stand against you. Give us the chain."

"I have a feeling if I lower the chain, you'll come up here and eat me."

"Not far from the truth," said a voice behind Seth.

The comment startled Seth so badly that he nearly fell forward into the hole. He lost his grip on the flashlight and it spun down into the blackness, illuminating an increasingly distant section of the endless pit, skipping twice against the side as it descended. The light vanished without Seth glimpsing the bottom, and without any far-off crunch of the bottom being reached.

A torch flared, driving back the momentary darkness in the chamber. An old man with a long beard and a heavy cloak held the firebrand aloft. Seth edged away from the gaping hole. "You must be Agad," Seth said. "You almost gave me a heart attack."

"And you must be the interloper from the knapsack,"

Agad replied. "Camarat could sense you inside, along with a hermit troll and an unconventional automaton. The dragon had it right. You are young, and you are a shadow charmer."

"I don't mean any harm."

One of Agad's eyes twitched. "Interesting that the first place you came was the Blackwell."

"I was following the whispers. I haven't been a shadow charmer for very long."

"Well, this is easily the most dangerous room in the keep, and probably one of the most dangerous in the entire sanctuary. I wondered if you might be drawn here. Patton said you have a penchant for mischief, though he neglected to mention your full-fledged status as a shadow charmer!"

"Patton mentioned me?" Seth asked.

"He told me to expect you as well if the girl showed up. I'd like to think you would not have lowered the chain."

"The chain? No way! You kidding? I was just hoping I could get info from them or something."

Agad walked over to the nearest pile of coils and sat down. He gestured with the torch and Seth sat as well. "The entities inside the Blackwell would say anything to gain freedom, at which point their promises would evaporate. Do not treat with these types of beings, Seth. They do not give. They only know how to take."

"Why do you have a chain in the first place?"

The question earned a reluctant smile. "If one knows how to manage them, to guide them, to liberate them temporarily and under strict conditions, the inhabitants of the Blackwell have their uses. But even I would employ them only as an absolute last resort."

"In the future, you might want to lock the door."

Agad smiled more broadly. "I left the room accessible in anticipation of your visit. Truth be known, you and I are the only people in Blackwell Keep who could have entered this room, locked or not. A pervasive fear more potent than dragon terror shields the Blackwell from the unworthy."

"Could I learn to control them?"

The wizard considered him. "Perhaps. But should you try to learn? I think not. These unholy fiends will turn on you given the slightest opportunity. Seek more savory allies than these. With thousands of years of experience, I have rarely attempted to use them, and still consider myself perilously vulnerable."

Seth could feel the cold of the links through his pants. "Could you skip telling the others about this? Most of them don't know I came along yet. I'm hiding out in reserve. You know, for emergencies."

"To cause them or repair them? Presumably your friends would be cross if they knew you came to the Blackwell."

"They already think I'm an idiot."

Agad coughed into his fist. "Patton did not share that opinion. He recognized a lot of himself in you. But that worried him, because of how many times he narrowly avoided a premature death. I also see great potential in you, Seth Sorenson. Most shade walkers are evil to the core. You strike me as quite the opposite. Take care here. A dragon sanctuary is no place for the reckless. Properly applied, courage may serve you well. Curiosity, daring, a thirst for adventure—these will likely lead to your demise."

"I'll try to remember that."

Agad smiled sadly. "I have learned not to get too attached to visitors. Whether or not you accomplish your aim here, mere survival would be a noteworthy triumph. You had best get back to your knapsack."

"Okay. Thanks for the advice."

The wizard arose. "I suppose it goes without saying that I expect never to discover you near the Blackwell again."

"I'll keep away from the voices. By the way, about telling the others . . ."

Agad winked. "I won't tell if you don't."

※ ※ ※

Threatening clouds blotted out much of the morning sunlight as Kendra strolled along the top of the keep's wall. Above her, the sky was blue and clear, but leaden clouds massed on all sides, as if the sanctuary sat in the eye of a hurricane. Light breezes stirred the air from unpredictable directions.

Ahead of her, Simrin led the way with sinuous grace, the supple scales on her back subtly rippling with each stride. Behind Kendra came Trask, Gavin, and Tanu, the three she had chosen for this final interview with Agad. Simrin had explained that Agad wanted to meet inside one of the keep's corner towers.

Kendra had awakened with a raw, scratchy throat.

She had hoped the soreness would fade once she was up and about, but if anything, the sensation was getting more irritating. Each swallow seemed less comfortable than the one before. She reminded herself to ask Tanu for a remedy.

Where two walls intersected at a rounded tower, Simrin opened a heavy oak door banded with iron and stood aside. Kendra led the way into a circular room about twenty feet across. Thin arrow loops interrupted a wide section of the wall. Off to one side, a wooden ladder accessed a trapdoor in the ceiling. Simrin closed the oaken door without following.

Agad waited at the far side of the room holding a long, slim rod. Between them, a relief map of Wyrmroost covered the floor, complete with the two towering peaks, plenty of hilly forests, several valleys, a few lakes, many streams, and a tiny model of Blackwell Keep.

"Good day," Agad said. "I thought the Lesser Map Room might be an appropriate venue for this discussion. I considered the Greater Map Room, but the detail is too exquisite. A custodian must protect some secrets."

"Looks like we may be in for foul weather today," Trask observed.

Agad fixed him with a shrewd gaze. "Is that a comment or a question? No doubt you have noticed the disproportionate lack of snow at Wyrmroost." He tapped one of the lofty peaks with his rod. "The sky giant Thronis lives atop Stormcrag. Not only is Thronis the largest living giant on record, he is a gifted sorcerer. He chooses to view Wyrmroost as his domain, and tempers the climate with sorcery. The dragons despise him, but his stronghold is unassailable, and they appreciate the reduced winds. Gales and dragon flight do not mix well."

"I had no idea any sky giants remained in the world," Tanu said.

"Welcome to Wyrmroost." Agad smiled. He tapped the other mountain with his rod. "Near Moonfang, the higher summit, lives Celebrant the Just, widely acknowledged as king of all dragonkind. You would need wings to scale these mountains. Give them a wide berth. The entire sanctuary is perilous, but no foes are more deadly than the entities atop these mighty peaks."

"What other creatures can we expect to encounter?" Gavin asked.

Agad stroked his beard. "Dragons, firedrakes, wyverns, basilisks, griffins, giants, mountain trolls, rocs, and phoenixes are among our more powerful inhabitants. Even the small game can be most hazardous. After centuries dwelling here, not even I can name all that lurks under sky, leaf, and stone at Wyrmroost. Needless to say, visitors do not enjoy long life expectancies. Keep your visit short."

"Perhaps you can help us shorten our stay," Trask said. "We know we'll be looking for the Fairy Queen's shrine."

Agad glanced at Kendra. "I suppose that might help explain the presence of our young friend. Although I'm sorry to say the shrine lies on the shoulder of Stormcrag, within the boundaries most jealously watched by Thronis. You say your errand must take you there?"

"Unfortunately," Trask confirmed.

The wizard winced. "The immediate surroundings of the shrine should offer shelter from Thronis or any other foes. Unfortunately, most who tread there are instantly obliterated. On the chance any of you should be taken alive by Thronis, beware his mind. The giant is no fool. There are reasons he has endured so long, residing in comfort on sacred land coveted by all the dragons of Wyrmroost. Those reasons extend far beyond his incomprehensible brute strength. I take credit for installing his greatest weakness— an irremovable collar that will constrict and strangle him if he speaks a lie. Do not utter my name to the sky giant. Thronis has no love for me. Where else might your errand take you?"

The companions looked at one another. "We're unsure," Kendra finally confessed.

Using his rod to point for emphasis, Agad described the best route from Blackwell Keep to the shrine of the Fairy Queen. The way was not straight, but he detailed how the circuitous course would avoid the most rugged terrain and circumvent the lairs of the most fearsome creatures. He went on to point out other dangerous locales: a gorge frequented by mountain trolls, a wooded vale home to dozens of wyverns, a high pass near the nest of a roc, and numerous dragon lairs. Kendra hoped the others had better memories than she did.

Finally Agad stepped away from the map, leaning his rod against the wall. "That orientation should give you a slightly better chance out there. Remember, nothing is certain. Trouble can happen anywhere, anytime. This is a sanctuary for predators, and they are often in motion."

"Thanks for the guidance," Kendra said.

Agad closed his eyes momentarily, a slow blink. "Thank me by surviving. Try not to smash any hornet nests. I have enough problems without visitors stirring up new ones."

"How do we leave Wyrmroost when we're done?" Kendra asked.

The wizard rubbed his mustache. "You were admitted through the gate, you must exit through the gate. Use the same key. If you wish, you can seek refuge here on your final night. Any final inquiries?"

"Could you spare any potion ingredients for me?" Tanu asked boldly. "I could particularly use substances derived from dragons. It would be a way for you to help us discreetly."

The wizard cocked his head and scratched behind his ear. "True. It would be hard to trace any ingredients back to me. Come with me after we terminate this meeting. Perhaps we can barter. You must have some items rare to Wyrmroost."

"I'd be happy to do some trading," Tanu said.

"Are there rules to slaying d-d-d-dragons?" Gavin asked.

The wizard shot him a hard look. "Are you expecting a fight?"

"I'm asking hypothetically."

Agad scowled. "Unlike some sanctuaries, there are no formal penalties affixed to the murder of a dragon here. But as you must know, no dragon looks upon a dragon slayer with a kind eye unless the death occurred within the mutually accepted parameters of a formal duel."

Gavin nodded.

The wizard shook his head slightly. "Please do not lose your life and doom your friends by engaging a dragon in combat."

"I have no intention of fighting dragons," Gavin assured him. "I just like to know the ground rules."

"Camarat said you seemed experienced with dragons," Agad said.

"I'm young, but my dad taught me a lot. Chuck Rose."

"Never heard of him." Agad started toward the door. "We need to get you outside the wall before midday. After that, you may do as you will, but I recommend stealth and haste."

"I wish I could bring Mara and the others to see this map room," Trask said. "I would love to repeat some of your instructions."

Passing through the doorway, Agad glanced at the sky. "You have my permission. Be quick about it." The old man patted Kendra on the shoulder. "Good luck to you. I hope you find what you are seeking, and that the price is not too steep."

Agad strolled away with Tanu at his side.

Kendra turned to Trask and Gavin. "Helpful?"

Trask gave a small shrug. "The more we learn about what we'll face here, the less I like it. But I'd rather be scared than blind. We better get the others."

Walking with Trask and Gavin, Kendra considered

their leader. Trask seemed to be the most capable of all of them. He was tall, strong, skilled, worldly. He moved with confidence. He made swift decisions. He carried himself like a man who had seen it all.

She did not enjoy hearing that he was scared.

CHAPTER NINETEEN

Dragon Tamer

By the time Kendra started across the drawbridge with her companions, the entire sky had gone cloudy. The gray ceiling directly above the sanctuary looked lighter than the murk surrounding Wyrmroost, but flurries of snowflakes had begun to fall, pushed by inconstant breezes. When Kendra cast her eyes beyond the rainbow barrier, the snowfall outside the sanctuary looked much heavier.

Kendra glanced regretfully back at the wall enclosing Blackwell Keep. She and her friends were out in the open now. Vulnerable. Back at the hotel, Gavin had related how dragons viewed people much as people saw mice. At the moment, she felt like a mouse dropped into a cage of snakes. Within the boundaries of Wyrmroost, dragons or other mystical predators could await beneath any tree, inside any cave, beyond any rise. No viable shelter remained. It was only a matter of time before they attracted attention.

They started up a slope, moving in a loose cluster. Tanu had given her a lozenge for her throat, but it still felt raw. As Blackwell Keep shrank behind them, Kendra watched the others. With his long, purposeful strides, Trask seemed determined and confident. Tanu and Mara wore serious, thoughtful expressions. Dougan appeared calm, as if on a casual stroll to enjoy nature. Warren repeatedly tossed a stick in the air, apparently trying to see how many times he could spin it end over end before catching it. Gavin brought up the rear, anxiously rubbing his palms with his thumbs, eyes in constant motion.

They passed beneath tall cedars and pines, the capricious wind stirring the limbs overhead. Beneath the trees Kendra saw dry accumulations of old needles, tangles of twigs, a few jutting boulders, and periodic patches of old, dirty snow. The tiny flakes falling at the moment were not sticking to the ground. In fact, under the trees, not many flakes managed to reach the forest floor.

"Should we break out the puppet?" Warren asked. "Might as well have Mendigo scout for threats. He does us no good in the knapsack."

"We'll pause at the top of this ridge and get him out," Trask said.

Toward the top of the ridge the terrain grew steep. Kendra used both hands while scrambling to the crest. On the far side, the ground fell away even more sharply. The snow flurries had ended for the moment, although the breeze had picked up. Above them loomed higher ridges and hills, stony spines, wooded ledges, rocky faces, and eventually the bald, sheer cliffs of Stormcrag. Off to the left and farther away, Moonfang soared into the sky, the summit obscured in mellow gray clouds.

Kendra recalled looking down on the sanctuary from the helicopter, as well as the map at Blackwell Keep. Using the mounting ranks of high ground for reference, she tried to visualize some of the unseen ravines, valleys, meadows, streams, and lakes.

"Look across the gulf," Dougan said.

A dark, lumbering shape emerged from the trees on the next ridge over. Built like a bear, the creature had the shaggy fur of a yak and a thick, hawklike beak. The beast reared onto its hind legs, standing twice the height of any grizzly, and emitted a sound halfway between a screech and a roar.

"What is it?" Kendra whispered.

"Not sure," Trask muttered. "Might be past time we got our weapons out."

Trask and Warren opened the knapsack and descended into the storeroom. The bearlike monstrosity continued up the opposing ridge and then disappeared over the far side, swishing a hairless tail with a bulbous knob at the end.

"Look above the shoulder of Stormcrag," Mara said, eyes skyward.

Kendra followed her gaze and saw two distant silhouettes reeling through the air, widespread wings canting sharply. They lacked the long necks and tails of dragons, but the airborne creatures were large, with four legs.

"Griffins," Tanu said.

As they watched, the creatures swooped and circled acrobatically. Then they plunged out of sight together.

"They found prey," Dougan commented.

A minute or two later, Trask and Warren emerged from the knapsack, followed by Mendigo, the golden hooks of his joints jingling. Besides carrying his huge crossbow, Trask wore a pair of matching swords across his back and twin daggers at his waist. Warren held the sword he had claimed at Lost Mesa. Mendigo toted an eight-foot spear and a heavy battle-ax. Mara took the spear and Dougan accepted the ax.

"No weapons for you guys?" Kendra asked Tanu and Gavin.

Tanu twisted, showing Kendra the blowgun tucked into his belt. "Sleeping darts and potions for me."

Gavin twirled his walking stick. "This will do for now. Avoidance will be our best friend. But it's good to be armed in case of smaller threats."

"Like giant hawkbears," Kendra said.

He grinned. "Exactly."

"Mendigo," Warren said, "scout our perimeter. Don't range too far from us. Alert us of any possible threats. Don't let any creatures take us unawares. Our goal is to avoid encounters. Should trouble break out, guard Kendra as your first priority, then the rest of us. Get her into the knapsack if the danger becomes extreme. Our first goal is to flee conflicts, but use violence in our protection as required. As a last resort, if you must kill to protect us, do it."

The wooden humanoid bobbed his head and skipped

down the far side of the ridge, moving with a loose, jangling grace. Kendra soon lost sight of him under the trees.

"We'll follow this ridgeline for a time," Mara said, "then drop into a wooded valley."

"Off we go," Trask said, resting his great crossbow over one shoulder.

The hike took them across a variety of terrain. They picked their way across stony scree, forded narrow brooks, traversed brushy meadows, and skirted an oblong lake. Near a shaded pond, they fell flat behind a fallen log as a dragonlike creature with black wings, two scaly legs, a scorpion's tail, and a wolfish head guzzled down gallons of water. They saw more griffins wheeling high above, but never up close. At one point, near the crest of a hill, Mara pointed out a column of dark smoke rising in the distance.

As night fell, they took shelter in a shallow gully against a concave wall of clay beneath a rocky outcrop. Mara built a campfire and they ate well from the plentiful stores in the knapsack—tinfoil dinners of salty beef and vegetables, complemented by dried fruit and applesauce. After the meal, they broke out graham crackers, chocolate bars, and marshmallows to make gooey s'mores. Gavin and Tanu let their marshmallows catch fire and ate them charred, but Kendra preferred to patiently roast hers to a golden brown.

Warren offered to set up a small dome tent for Kendra, but the others were content sliding their well-insulated sleeping bags into waterproof bivouacs, so she opted for a bivouac as well. Despite having Mendigo prowl the area as a sleepless sentry, they decided to keep watch one at a time as well. Dougan mentioned that they might take shelter in the knapsack, but Warren pointed out that they could get cornered inside and should consider the knapsack a last resort.

Kendra took the first watch. She sat beside the coals of the banked fire, staring out into the dimness of the surrounding trees as sporadic snow continued to fall, still not noticeably sticking to the ground. She tried not to dwell on what terrors might patrol the night beyond her field of view. Hopefully Mendigo would alert her before anything deadly came too close.

Midway through her watch, fierce growls reached her ears, echoing along the gully. Branches snapped and stones tumbled. It took several minutes to relax after the vicious snarls subsided. Later, when Dougan came to relieve her, the air grew calm, and they listened together to the slow beats of huge wings high above them, like the rhythmic flapping of some enormous tarp.

The next morning dawned cold and frost-crusted. Clouds still ringed Wyrmroost, but no longer formed a solid ceiling, nor retained such a threatening color. After her watch, Kendra had slept quicker and better than expected. The hot chocolate Tanu had prepared helped her gain the courage to abandon the toasty cocoon of her sleeping bag. Kendra plopped in a marshmallow and watched it melt into foam as she sipped. The beverage had been made with powdered milk from Fablehaven in order to keep magical creatures visible for the others.

Throughout the morning and early afternoon, Mara led

the way. She had an uncanny knack for keeping the map of Wyrmroost in her mind and matching it to the surrounding landscape. Whenever debates arose regarding which direction they should head, they relied on her judgment as the final word, and invariably they would encounter a landmark that proved her intuition right. They crossed a ravine on a natural bridge of stone. They traveled through a defile too narrow for two of them to walk abreast, a thin strip of sky visible high above. They crept around the edge of a tranquil valley crossed by a winding brook, hoping to avoid the attention of the basilisks who, according to Agad, resided there.

Having snacked throughout the hike, they stopped for a late lunch on a craggy hilltop. Stunted conifers covered the shoulders of the hill, but only jagged boulders crowned the summit. Huddled among the stones, Kendra ate a sandwich, a slightly overripe banana, and a hearty granola bar. She drank two boxes of fruit punch through tiny straws.

As they were packing up lunch, Mendigo came clattering across the rocky hilltop, pointing back the way he had come. The puppet waved for them to run the other way.

Swiftly chimneying up between two boulders, shielding her eyes with a long brown hand, Mara peered in the direction Mendigo had come from. "I see a peryton," she reported. "No, several; no, a whole herd. Coming fast! Run!" She half climbed, half fell from the boulder, rolling over unforgiving stones when she landed, rising with a badly skinned elbow and a deep gash in her knee.

"To the trees," Trask urged, holding his crossbow ready.

Dougan grabbed Kendra's hand and they clambered across the stony summit until they reached dirt and trees. Looking back, Kendra saw a large winged stag gliding about fifty feet above the hilltop. The stag had a massive rack of black horns, golden fur, and feathered wings and hindquarters. Other perytons promptly soared into view. Kendra counted more than a dozen before she tripped and went sprawling onto a moist mat of old pine needles.

A tremendous roar exploded behind them, an earsplitting imitation of thunder and jet engines, exceeding even the mighty bellows Kendra had heard from the demon Bahumat. A peryton hit the ground near Kendra, sharp hooves gouging the earth, jaws snapping at her, razor teeth missing by inches. Without pause, the peryton bounded skyward, wings unfurling. Another landed near Dougan, antlers lowered, and he sprang aside, putting the trunk of a tree between himself and the cruel prongs. Again, rather than stay to fight, the peryton returned to the air. The attacks seemed halfhearted, done in passing.

Kendra lunged behind the bole of a tree, hoping the cover would shield her from horns, hooves, and fangs. Other perytons skipped off the ground to her left and right, wings folding temporarily and then flapping as they climbed. Apparently there were limits to how far they could remain airborne—the creatures moved in gigantic, gliding jumps.

One frantic peryton became tangled in the branches halfway up a nearby tree, bleating and squealing, antlers thrashing and feathers falling until it crashed through a jumbled ladder of limbs and flopped awkwardly to the ground. The cervine creature arose with a pronounced limp and turned to face Kendra, lips peeled back to reveal wicked yellow teeth dripping with foam.

The stampeding herd thumped off the ground on all sides, showing little interest in the humans, but the injured peryton charged Kendra, dragging one hideously askew leg. The tree beside Kendra had no reachable branches, so she scooted to the far side of the trunk. As the snarling peryton drew near, Mendigo dove beneath it, wrenching and jerking the injured leg. Frothing and snapping, the mutant stag struggled forward. Dougan came at the ferocious creature from the side with a snarl of his own, burying his ax in the top of its neck. The deerlike legs buckled, and man and peryton collapsed to the ground.

Overhead, a second explosive roar drowned out all other sound. Glancing up through the limbs of the trees, Kendra saw a tremendous blue dragon soar overhead, flying at great speed. The perytons had not been attacking! They were fleeing!

Suddenly Mara was at her side, yanking Kendra to her feet. "The dragon is overtaking the perytons," she said, leading Kendra perpendicular to the downhill route the herd had taken. "They may double back this way."

Glancing back, Kendra saw Dougan trailing after them. She glimpsed Trask moving parallel to them farther down the hill. Where was Warren? Tanu? Gavin?

Kendra, Mara, and Dougan raced diagonally down the hillside. The lower they went, the taller the pines became. There was little undergrowth to contend with, just the inherent unsteadiness of moving fast over uneven terrain. The dragon roared again, the deafening volume striking Kendra like a physical blow. Lightning flashed and thunder boomed.

"Here they come," Mara warned, raising her spear.

Perytons came gliding and bounding up the hill, some above the treetops, others swerving adroitly between the conifers. The herd had fanned out, some going straight up the hill, some coming at diagonals. There seemed to be at least fifty.

A blinding bolt of lightning hit the top of a tree farther down the hill, splitting the trunk in a dazzling shower of sparks. The booming thunder came instantly, followed by a louder, more prolonged roar.

Kendra ran by instinct, heedless of the danger of falling, trying to match Mara's inhuman speed. She could hear Dougan pounding along behind her, breathing hard. Mara slid to a stop beside a particularly thick tree and Kenda skidded into a crouch beside her. On all sides, hooves thumped briefly against the forest floor as perytons kicked off the ground. Overhead, winged stags filled the air at various altitudes. Then the dragon blocked out the sky, scales shining blue and violet. The great jaws snapped, and the rear half of a peryton plummeted to the forest floor trailing wet streamers.

"Go," Mara whispered, and they bolted straight down the hill. Trask lingered beside a tree until they caught up with him.

"They're coming back around," he predicted, bald head shiny with sweat.

The dragon roared again from well behind them. Kendra, Trask, Mara, and Dougan sprinted down the hill, drawing to a halt at the edge of a broad meadow.

"Down," Trask said, kneeling beside a trunk, crossbow held ready.

Kendra squatted beside Mara. Panicked perytons came streaking down the hill, leaping and gliding out over the meadow, some quite high, others skimming along just above the brush. Kendra gasped as the immense blue dragon circled into view some distance off, curving toward the clearing. The perytons in and above the meadow tried to veer away from the oncoming threat, but the dragon swooped across the far side of the meadow, batting perytons from the air with claws and tail.

As it passed the clearing, the dragon's head turned. For an instant, Kendra glimpsed a glaring eye, bright as a sapphire. The dragon wheeled and broke hard, wings thrust out like parachutes. Dipping below the treetops, the immense predator plowed through the tall pines, bulky body noisily felling trees as it smashed to a halt.

"It saw us," Mara and Trask said with one voice.

"Heads up," Dougan warned. Many of the perytons in the meadow had reversed their course and were now coming back toward them.

Most of the perytons landed between thirty and fifty yards from the edge of the meadow, springing and flapping hard in the attempt to clear at least the initial treetops. Kendra saw one peryton stumble badly. Instead of jumping, it skimmed forward just above the ground, feathery wings spread wide.

As it neared the trees, the peryton lost momentum and crumpled, flattening a strip of brush.

As the creature staggered to its feet, Mara darted from cover, casting her spear aside and seizing the peryton by the base of the antlers. The lean muscles in her arms tensed as the peryton swayed and jerked in her grasp, but soon the creature calmed, and she pressed her forehead to its muzzle. With the woman and the creature standing together, Kendra glanced down and noticed that the peryton cast an incongruently humanoid shadow.

Farther across the meadow, the dragon emerged from the trees on foot, wings folded, neck craning up like some nightmarish dinosaur. Elaborate spines and ridges projected from the horny head. Even from a distance, Kendra felt numbing fear wash over her. Wings still tucked, the immense dragon galloped toward them, burnished scales gleaming metallic blues and purples.

Trask scooped Kendra into his arms and ran out into the meadow. Mara now sat astride the elk-sized peryton, and Trask heaved Kendra in front of her. Mara dug in her heels and the peryton lunged forward, running along the border of the meadow parallel to the trees, taking them away from the charging dragon.

The volcanic roar behind them made Kendra clamp one hand over an ear. She needed the other to hang on. The peryton jumped, and Kendra's stomach lurched like she was on a roller coaster. The wings flapped, but they did not rise very high. Over her shoulder, Kendra saw the dragon taking flight in pursuit. Dougan and Trask waved their arms, trying to distract the raging beast, but the dragon ignored them.

Mendigo crashed out from under the trees into the meadow, holding the knapsack by a leather strap. The puppet flung the knapsack at Kendra, and Mara caught it as the peryton sprang again, climbing a little higher this time.

A huge shadow fell over Kendra, and Mara leaned toward the trees. The peryton swerved, and suddenly they were weaving through a slalom course of pines. Lightning flashed and a trunk off to one side burst asunder. Mara handed Kendra the knapsack. The next time the peryton hit the ground, Mara leapt off, rolling to a stop.

Without Mara's weight, the peryton climbed higher. Kendra caught glimpses of other frightened perytons racing through the woods. Above the trees the dragon bellowed again.

Kendra and her peryton burst from the trees, losing altitude over a pond in a grassy clearing. Instead of helping her get away, fleeing astride the peryton seemed to attract the dragon's attention, so she flung herself from the winged mount, skipping twice on the surface of the frigid water before coming to a stop in the shallows. Her peryton splashed down in the shallows, then took flight again, vanishing into the trees.

When Kendra stood, the water came to her thighs. Slowed by the water, she sloshed toward the shore, fumbling with the flap of the knapsack. If she climbed inside, the dragon might miss her. But as she exited the water, the dragon alighted in the grassy area beside the pond, filling the field. This dragon was ten times the size of Chalize, the coppery dragon that had ravaged Lost Mesa. Kendra found herself gazing up into eyes like burning sapphires.

"You shine brightly, small one," the dragon said. Each word sounded like three female voices shouting a dissonant chord.

Dripping, shivering, Kendra could not move. She wanted to reply, but her jaws felt glued shut. Her lips twitched. A response awaited in her mind. She wanted to say, "Not as bright as you," but her mouth refused to make the words. Kendra groaned feebly.

"No last words?" the dragon said. "How disappointing."

※ ※ ※

Seth dangled from the ladder near the top of the knapsack. He looked down at Bubda. "The dragon got her. Kendra can't speak."

"Nothing you can do," the troll advised. "Live to fight another day."

With the flap closed, Seth had seen nothing, and the room felt none of the motion during the pursuit, but he had been listening to the frantic chase. He had no idea what perytons were, but he could tell there had been many of them, and that a dragon was chasing them. The thunderous roars had sent Bubda scurrying to the farthest corner of the storage room, where he now cowered.

"I'm a shadow charmer," Seth said. "I may be able to talk to the dragon."

"Better if we play a game of Yahtzee."

"Wish me luck." Seth pushed up the flap and climbed out of the knapsack. He was in a field beside Kendra, near a rippling pond. The dragon was bigger than he would have imagined: the horny head larger than a car, the claws longer than swords, the body a massive hill of flashing scales comparable in size only to a whale.

"Another one?" the dragon exclaimed in its ringing triple voice. "Similar aspects—siblings, I would suppose, but opposites, one dark, the other light. Have you a sharper tongue than your sister?"

Seth was no longer aware of Kendra beside him. He was unafraid, his muscles felt no paralysis, but he found himself utterly fascinated. Those eyes—jewels enlivened by a radiant inner fire. He lost all sense of urgency beneath the mesmerizing gaze.

"Double disappointment," the dragon lamented. "I take it silence runs in the family? Whom shall I devour first? Light or darkness? Perhaps both together?"

The dragon shifted its gaze back to Kendra, and Seth glanced over at his sister. Had the dragon said it meant to eat them? His head was swimming. He didn't want to die. He didn't want his sister to die. Bracing himself for dragon teeth, he took her hand. All of a sudden, cold clarity rushed through Seth's mind.

"Neither!" Kendra blurted, squeezing his fingers. "Shouldn't we get acquainted first?"

"She speaks," the dragon exclaimed, eyes narrowing. "Why the delay?"

Seth stared the dragon in the eyes. "We were overwhelmed

at first." The dragon still looked impressive, but whatever spell had clouded his thinking no longer bothered him.

"We've never seen such a spectacular dragon before," Kendra agreed.

The dragon lowered her head near them. They could feel the humid exhalations from her wide nostrils. "You have spoken to dragons before?"

"Only a couple," Kendra said. "None so impressive as you."

"You interrupted my hunt," the dragon snapped. "I have not seen humans in ages. The novelty distracted me. You do not belong here."

"We don't plan to stay long," Seth said.

The dragon made a melodic humming that Seth took for a chuckle. "You disrupted my plans. Perchance I should return the favor."

"We don't taste good," Seth warned. "Kendra is bonier than she looks, and I don't bathe much."

"How about a game," the dragon proposed. "I shall round up the rest of your party. There were six others, I believe. I will devour the four dullest, and find a use for the others as servants in my lair."

"I think not!" called a stern voice. Seth turned and saw Gavin striding from the woods. He had previously seen him only in a photograph.

The dragon looked up. "A third speaker, nearly as youthful as the others. Neither light nor dark. I could sandwich you between the other two. What sadistic human sent younglings to Wyrmroost?"

"Kendra, Seth, get in the knapsack," Gavin commanded.

The dragon hooked a claw into the strap and flung the knapsack away. "Unacceptable."

Opening his mouth wide enough to show his molars, Gavin began to shriek and squeal in what sounded like magnified dolphin chatter. The dragon responded in louder tones, a cacophonous symphony of tortured string instruments. They screeched back and forth several times before the dragon turned her blazing gaze back to Kendra and Seth.

"You have a unique protector," the dragon acknowledged. "I had no idea that dragon brothers persisted in the world. Out of respect for his singular status and surpassing eloquence, I will spare you and your friends. Enjoy your reprieve. Do not linger here."

The dragon sprang skyward, vast wings unfolding. Seth raised an arm to shield his eyes from the brief windstorm. Once aloft, the dragon passed swiftly out of view, heading back toward the larger meadow.

Gavin jogged over to them. "You all right?" he asked Kendra.

"I'm fine. This is my brother."

"I s-s-s-suspected," Gavin spluttered.

Kendra grabbed Seth by his upper arms and shook him. "What are you doing here?"

"Easy!" He shrugged away from her. "What did you think? That I wandered off into the woods at Fablehaven to pout? Give me a little credit. I stowed away. Good thing I did. Don't you get what happened? Together we're a dragon tamer!"

"I was impressed," Gavin said. "You were looking Nafia in the eyes and speaking naturally. None of the others would have been capable of that. I watched for a moment before speaking up."

"How are the others?" Kendra asked.

Gavin winced. "T-T-Tanu took a hard fall. I think it knocked him out. Warren was gored. He got hung up on the antlers of a peryton right at the start. It d-d-dragged him quite a ways. Sorry I lost track of you for a while. I was trying to help him."

"Will he be all right?" Kendra asked.

"He's hurt, but he'll recover."

"What did you tell the dragon?" Seth asked.

"I just talked tough. They think it's cute. And of course I used my claim as a dragon brother. I told Nafia you were all here under my protection." Gavin looked Kendra up and down. "You must be cold."

"I wasn't feeling it before," she said. Her arms were curled up against her chest. Seth could see her shivering.

Gavin trotted over and retrieved the knapsack. "Get inside and find a change of clothes. Things are b-b-b-bad enough without you catching pneumonia."

Kendra nodded and climbed into the knapsack. Seth closed the flap.

"Should we go find Warren and the others?" Seth asked.

"You read my mind."

CHAPTER TWENTY

Griffins

They found Warren concealed underneath the tangled deadfall where Gavin had left him. Kendra was still changing her clothes inside the storage room. Dougan, Gavin, and Seth heaved rotten limbs out of the way. Looking up at Seth, Warren gave a wan smile, the right side of his shirt soaked dark with blood. "Looks like the cat's out of the bag," he muttered.

"You knew about Seth?" Dougan asked.

"I might have caught wind of his presence."

Gavin crouched, examining the wounds in Warren's shoulder and upper chest. Warren winced when Gavin fingered the sodden fabric near one of the punctures. "Ugly," Gavin said.

"Sharp antlers," Warren gasped. "Not a very impressive way to go. Stabbed by a deer. Don't put that on my tombstone. Blame the dragon."

"You'll be all right," Dougan assured him, his eyes less confident than his voice.

"Where's Tanu?" Warren asked.

"Big guy took a spill," Dougan said. "Lost consciousness. Mara and Trask are trying to revive him."

"What stopped the dragon?" Warren asked.

"Gavin spoke to her," Seth said. "He used dragon talk. It was freaky. He calmed her down and sent her away."

"Seth and Kendra were holding their own," Gavin approved.

"Sorry to be the weak link," Warren muttered. "The deer gored me and kept on running. I was spitted on those antlers for a long time. Long enough to really notice, you know? To think about it."

Trask and Mara came jogging down from higher on the hill, led by Tanu. The brawny Samoan glared at Seth. "What are you doing here?"

"You missed me during your inspection," Seth replied.

"Perfect," Tanu muttered. He dropped to his knees beside Warren. "Sorry I'm late."

"Heard you banged your head," Warren said.

Wearing an embarrassed grin, Tanu smoothed a hand over his thick, dark hair. "Don't know what happened. Must have tripped and hit a rock." Tanu produced a knife.

Warren grimaced as Tanu began to cut away his shirt. "I feel sorry for the rock."

Tanu shrugged. "It smacked me pretty good. I've never been knocked out before. Thick skull." He slashed away a wide section of fabric.

Warren eyed the knife. "You're not dizzy or anything?"

"I do my best work dizzy." Tanu ripped away another portion of the bloody shirt. He set aside the knife, rummaged in his satchel, fished out a small bottle, uncapped it, and took a sip.

"How about some of that for me?" Warren carped.

Tanu squinted and clenched his teeth, then shook his head briskly. "You don't want this stuff. This is to clear me up, sharpen my senses. Trust me, you're going to want things dulled."

"You're the doctor."

Tanu scrabbled through his satchel again. "Not strictly speaking."

"Right, well, you're the medicine man."

"Try some of this." Tanu poured a small amount of potion onto a cotton ball, then wafted it beneath Warren's nostrils.

"Whoa," Warren said, going slightly cross-eyed. "That's more like it."

Tanu leaned forward and began meticulously applying a paste to the puncture wounds.

Kendra pushed open the knapsack's flap. Gavin stooped and gave her a hand up.

"How's Warren?" Kendra asked, emerging.

"He should be all right," Tanu said. "We'll have to rest him in that knapsack of yours, and get out the unicorn horn."

"Will it heal him?" Seth asked.

Tanu shook his head. "The horn doesn't heal. It only purifies. Keeping the horn in his grasp should prevent infection and counteract any toxins."

Kendra nodded. "How about you?"

Tanu shrugged. "I have a little headache. My pride took the biggest hit."

"*Your* pride?" Warren griped, his speech slurred. "I was vanquished by a deer!"

"A giant magical flying deer with fangs," Seth said, parroting a description Gavin had shared earlier.

"That sounds a little better," Warren conceded. "Seth is in charge of my tombstone."

"Don't speak," Tanu soothed. "Relax. Breathe. You need to rest."

Gavin and Kendra had wandered away a few paces. Seth joined them. His sister glowered at him. "What?" he asked.

"You shouldn't be here," Kendra snapped.

"How about thanks for saving—"

"Gavin would have saved me. That's his specialty. Look at Warren. He's a wreck and we're barely getting started. I don't want you dead."

"N-n-not to interrupt," Gavin said, "but Seth may very well have saved you, Kendra. I'm not sure I would have made it to you in time. Nafia was in hunting mode. She would have struck quickly."

Kendra rolled her eyes. "Seth doesn't belong here. He hitched a ride uninvited. Wyrmroost is a death trap. Whether I die or not, I don't want him getting killed."

"I don't want to get killed either," Seth said agreeably.

"I'd much rather live. Partly because I know you'd write 'I told you so' on my gravestone. Believe it or not, I don't want *you* to die, either. I know what it feels like to bury you, and I'd rather not go through it again."

Kendra folded her arms and shook her head. "I'm glad you helped me. I am. Too bad Grandma and Grandpa are going to kill you."

"We'll have to make it out of Wyrmroost first," Seth responded. "Please, one crisis at a time."

"Did you two know that holding hands would make you dragon tamers?" Gavin asked.

Seth shook his head. "No, but it kind of makes sense. I've been thinking about it. At Fablehaven, when Ephira was attacking us, as long as I touched Warren, he shared my immunity to fear."

"When I faced the dragon, my mind was clear," Kendra recounted, "but I couldn't make my mouth move. I was paralyzed. As soon as Seth touched me, I was free."

"And I wasn't scared or frozen," Seth said, "but the dragon had me mesmerized. I couldn't think. Except, when the dragon glanced away from me, and said she would kill us, some instinct made me grab Kendra. Half to comfort her, half to get comfort. I didn't want to die alone. Then all of a sudden I could think clearly."

"Amazing," Gavin said. "I've never heard of anything like it."

"I've never heard anything like you speaking the dragon language," Seth chuckled. "When you first started, I thought you'd lost your mind."

"It made me self-conscious to have you guys watching," Gavin said. "I know how I look. And how I sound. Like a demented rooster."

"A demented rooster who saved our lives," Kendra said. "Thanks."

Gavin shrugged. "That's why I'm here."

"Know what makes me mad?" Kendra said. "I could talk to Chalize. I was frozen, but I managed to speak. And I talked to Camarat too. But with Nafia glaring down at me, my jaw would not work."

"Chalize was young, and I was distracting her," Gavin explained. "Camarat wasn't pushing us very hard. Dragons can deliberately exert their will to dominate us. The older ones are better at it. With Nafia, you got a full dose of dragon terror. But when you were holding hands, it didn't seem to bother either of you."

"I felt fine after we held hands," Seth said. "But I was still worried she would eat us."

"She might have," Gavin confided. "There are no guarantees with dragons. Flattery is good for the young ones. The older ones prefer spunk and personality. Most of the time."

Trask came up to them. "You three all right?"

"We're good," Kendra said. "Except it's hard to make my brother feel as guilty as he deserves when he saved my life."

Trask nodded. "Seth will have to deal with the consequences of joining us. I can't say he made a wise choice, but there's no way to undo it, so we'll make the best of his presence. Tanu has Warren stabilized. We better load him in the bag and move out."

Kendra tossed Trask the knapsack.

"There's a hermit troll in there," Seth said. "I think he's lived in there a long time. He seems pretty nice. His name is Bubda. We've played a lot of Yahtzee. He wouldn't pose a threat to Warren, would he?"

"Thanks for the tip," Trask said. "Hermit trolls aren't usually much trouble. They're scavengers. They mostly want to be left alone. I'll have a chat with this one, size him up. Bubda, you say?"

"Could he be spying for the Sphinx?" Kendra asked. "I got the knapsack when I left Torina's."

"Doubtful," Trask said. "Hermit trolls are the vermin of trollkind. They work no harmful magic. They make no allies. They have a talent for worming into cramped spaces and hiding—little else."

Getting Warren into the knapsack proved to be tricky, since he had lapsed into medicated unconsciousness. Trask clung to the ladder while Tanu handed Warren down. Dougan and Mara waited at the bottom.

Seth wanted to be down there to hear the conversation with Bubda. He hoped they wouldn't hurt him. The troll might be grumpy and aloof, but Seth felt sure he posed no threat. Bubda just wanted solitude. When Trask emerged, he told Seth not to worry. Bubda had been everything he had expected, and in return for some food he had vowed not to go near Warren.

The hike that day took them across increasingly rocky terrain. They navigated through and around tumbled boulders and other detritus. They hiked up a steep slope covered with stunted trees, half walking up the incline, half using the wind-warped vegetation to climb. For a time, they walked along a ridgeline with a sheer drop-off at either side.

Seth enjoyed being outside—the smell of the pines, the cool thin air, the ice-fringed streams full of smooth, glossy pebbles. He relished the glimpses of circling griffins, and the sight of a monstrous, bearlike creature devouring a recent kill, stringy scraps of meat dangling from a curved beak. The others seemed generally accepting of his presence, although Tanu gave him some disappointed looks.

With dusk coming on, the scant trail they had been following ended at a tall crack in a stone cliff.

"Sidestep Cleft," Mara recognized.

"Cuts through the rock for almost half a mile," Trask said. "Agad said a couple of sections are barely wide enough for big humans to squeeze through. Sidestep Cleft is only a few miles from our first destination. We should reach the shrine tomorrow."

"Do we camp on this side?" Dougan asked.

Trask checked the sky. "Starting at the far side of the defile, we'll be on ground claimed by Thronis the sky giant. No place is safe at Wyrmroost, but I take it this side might be a tad more hospitable than the other."

Backtracking a little, they set up camp in the midst of a grove of short, thickly needled evergreens. The long, irregular clearing had just enough room for them to build a fire and lay down their sleeping bags together. They dined on canned chili, corn bread, and baked potatoes, finishing the meal with chocolate bars.

When they bedded down, Seth used Warren's sleeping bag and bivouac. Mara had the first watch. Tucked into his sleeping bag, Seth gazed up at the stars, amazing himself with how far away they were. It was so easy to shrink the distance by thinking of them as little pricks of light on a black ceiling. But if peering off a cliff could make his knees a little wobbly, why not staring out across billions of miles of empty space? When he thought about it, the jaw-dropping vastness of the gulf separating him from those stars almost made him dizzy. How strange to think that the whole universe was arrayed above him like his own private aquarium.

He considered climbing out of the sleeping bag and helping Mara pass the time. Living inside a knapsack had thrown off his sleep schedule. Telling himself that he would regret staying awake now when his watch came later, he closed his eyes and forced himself to relax.

※ ※ ※

Kendra had the third watch that night. Dougan woke her gently and reminded her that she was to awaken her brother next. Nodding, she slithered out of her sleeping bag, wrapped herself in a blanket, and moved closer to the small fire.

Sitting alone, she wondered why they bothered keeping watch. No matter who was awake, Mendigo would raise the alarm first. And once he did, it would do little good. They had all been awake when the puppet had warned them about the perytons, and that had still turned into a mess.

Wyrmroost was not Fablehaven. The creatures here were huge. If a dragon like Nafia wanted them dead, they would die. They had escaped the dragon only because Gavin talked her out of killing them. He could not force her. They had relied on her generosity, and she had opted to let them go. What did it matter if they kept watch for creatures they had no chance of defeating?

She stared up at the sky, searching for satellites moving among the stars. The moon was up and getting fuller, its light making the stars look dimmer than they had of late. But after a few minutes, the slow, steady motion of a dim pinprick of light caught her eye.

Her gaze returned to the earth when she heard the jangle of Mendigo approaching. He was not coming fast, but he was coming. She had neither heard nor seen him the last time she was on watch.

The puppet strode into view through the evergreens alongside a tall, beautiful woman. The lovely stranger had aristocratic features—chiseled cheekbones, flawless skin, imperious eyes. A flowing, gauzy gown hung from her lithe frame, and golden sandals clad her feet. Most striking was her hair, a lustrous cascade of silvery blue. Aside from her air of casual confidence, nothing about the woman suggested that she should be roaming a dangerous mountainous sanctuary in the middle of the night. Her age was hard to gauge. Despite the silver in her hair, at first glance Kendra would have estimated mid-twenties, but the stranger carried herself with a stately grace well beyond those years. Mendigo walked beside her, holding her hand.

"We have a visitor," Kendra announced loudly, rising to her feet. She thought that the woman might be a dryad, but she had no intention of confronting the stranger alone.

"I mean you no harm," the woman called, her voice musical and gentle.

Kendra heard her companions stirring in their sleeping bags.

"Who are you?" Kendra asked.

"Let me handle this," Gavin grumbled, crawling out of his sleeping bag and pulling on a coat.

Trask had a hand on his crossbow.

The woman stopped a few paces from Kendra. In her flat sandals, she stood more than six feet tall. "Have you no guess? We've met before."

"Nafia?" Kendra whispered.

The woman blushed. "I go by Nyssa in human form. I'm here to help."

Gavin came up beside Kendra. "How might you help us?" he asked.

Nyssa's gaze became shrewder as she met his eyes. "I know the lay of the land."

"I'll b-b-believe that much," Gavin said.

"What an adorable stutter," Nyssa said, almost flirtatiously.

Gavin pressed his lips together. "Why would you want to help us?"

Nyssa smiled, perfect lips spreading wide. "I miss humans. Taking their form is a novelty I had nearly forgotten, until all of you showed up. Who knows when humans will come again? The closest thing we have at Wyrmroost is that old turncoat Agad."

"You're a dragon lonely for human company?" Gavin asked dubiously.

"Not just any humans," she said, stepping closer to Gavin. He was not quite as tall as she, so she was looking down. "A dragon brother." She glanced at Kendra. "And several dragon tamers. My kind of people."

Gavin glanced at Kendra. He looked disturbed. Kendra thought she understood. Their end destination was the Dragon Temple. No dragon would let them go there.

"You may not wish to come everywhere we mean to go," Gavin said weakly.

Nyssa laughed. "And where is it you humans mean to go that dragons would not be welcome? Perhaps you hope to make friends with Thronis the Terrible. Not a likely prospect. Yet you're heading into territory that he watches closely."

"We have a secret mission," Gavin said. "We can't accept your company."

Nyssa narrowed her eyes. "This is a peculiar troop of humans indeed, where the protection a dragon could offer is unwanted."

Gavin folded his arms. "I imagine that in dragon form you would not be half so accommodating to our needs."

Nyssa produced a humming response by laughing without parting her lips. "You have that right. As a dragon, I see the world through less generous eyes. Shall we experiment?"

Gavin held out both hands. "N-n-n-no, please."

Nyssa wrinkled her nose. "I love that stutter."

"We mean no offense," Gavin said, a hint of pleading in his tone. "We just need to be careful and—"

"—and a dragon in your party is one dragon too many," Nyssa said, eyes sparkling. "I understand. I do not wish to force my society upon you. If it is your wish, I will leave you in peace so you can march to your deaths on the morrow. You will soon discover that not all the inhabitants of Wyrmroost are as . . . accommodating as I am. In fact, if the rumors are true, even I would not relish being caught in your company, regardless of my form."

"Rumors?" Kendra asked.

"She speaks!" Nyssa laughed. "Is that permissible, dragon brother? I can tell you prefer to do the talking. Yes, rumors. Word has it Navarog was sighted outside the gates of Wyrmroost."

"Navarog?" Gavin cried.

"You have heard of him, I trust," Nyssa said. "A dragon so evil they made him an honorary demon! He has a fearsome reputation. He was one of the few of us who avoided being herded into a dragon sanctuary. Visitors are normally a rarity here. Could his sudden interest in Wyrmroost have anything to do with my new human friends?"

"This is horrible news," Gavin admitted. "He wasn't seen inside the sanctuary?"

Nyssa gave a sly smile. "Not to my knowledge. If the demon prince is here for you, why not let me devour you instead? Less hassle. Less drama. I'll be gentle."

"Thanks for the offer," Gavin said. "I think we'll take our chances."

"The gates to Wyrmroost are strong," Nyssa said. "If he lacks a key, even Navarog will not get past them. Perhaps you should solicit Agad for employment. With Navarog at the only exit, you might wisely opt to stay longer than planned."

"W-w-w-we'll take that under advisement," Gavin said.

"The brave little stutterer," Nyssa replied lightly. "You have just been told your death is certain, yet you hang on to your composure. Maybe you actually deserve to be a dragon brother."

"I would like to think so," Gavin said, lowering his eyes.

Nyssa embraced Kendra. "Meeting you has been a delight," Nyssa said. She extended a hand to Gavin, who clasped it and then lightly kissed it. "How chivalrous. This has been nearly as diverting as I had hoped, albeit I would have preferred to partake of your company a while longer. So it goes. I will not intrude. Sorry to bear unhappy tidings. If it comes as any consolation, your demise was almost certain even without Navarog lurking about the gates. Enjoy the remainder of your visit."

Nyssa turned and strode away into the night without looking back.

Kendra grabbed Gavin's hand, squeezing it tightly. He squeezed back.

"Could she help protect us?" Kendra whispered.

Gavin shook his head. "Considering where we're

headed, our surest death would have been to invite her to join us."

Trask came up beside them, crossbow in hand. "I had an easy shot."

Gavin snorted. "You could have done it. She was vulnerable. Of course, we would have died shortly thereafter. Nothing would dissuade the dragons who came to avenge her."

"That crossed my mind," Trask said. He sighed. "I'm not glad to hear Navarog is on our tail. I suppose it's no less than we expected."

"But it's a good deal less than we hoped," Gavin replied.

Nobody argued.

✳ ✳ ✳

The next day Kendra awoke with a sense of foreboding. The news borne by Nyssa had left her unsettled. Kendra had a hard time recalling the details of her dreams, but they had involved beautiful women morphing into dragons, and lots of running. At least the first part of the day should be relatively safe. While they journeyed inside of Sidestep Cleft, no huge monsters would be able to reach them.

Kendra brought Warren his breakfast. He seemed in good spirits, although his breathing was shallow and labored, and whenever he shifted position his face showed reactions to twinges of pain. Together they drank hot chocolate. Kendra also ate an energy bar, but Warren passed, contenting himself with some slices of an orange.

After breakfast, they loaded their sleeping bags into the knapsack and walked to the cleft. The tall crack in the rock wall stretched at least a hundred feet high, narrowing as it rose, ending before it reached all the way up. Kendra had never seen such a tall, narrow cave.

They marched into the fissure with Trask and Gavin in the front. Dougan and Tanu brought up the rear. For a good distance two people could comfortably walk abreast. Before progressing far, they switched on flashlights. Kendra shone hers up and stared at how the gap tapered to an end high above. Eventually they had to proceed single file. At one point, Tanu and Dougan had to turn sideways to fit through a tight section. Kendra tried not to picture the walls closing in, crushing their little group to jelly.

The cleft did not extend quite as high at the far side, maybe thirty or forty feet at most, but the gap ended wider than it had started. For the last couple of hundred yards, four of them could have marched shoulder to shoulder.

Beyond Sidestep Cleft they found themselves following a rocky ledge with a steep drop to one side and a sheer rise on the other. The width of the ledge fluctuated, sometimes many yards wide, sometimes only a few feet. Kendra bit her lip and leaned toward the rock wall as she passed the narrowest sections, tracing her fingers across the cold, rough stone. She tried to avoid fixating on the dry gorge far below. Gradually the ledge descended and became wider, until they reached an area haphazardly strewn with boulders the size of trucks.

Trask abruptly halted and raised a fist. Gazing forward,

Kendra saw a griffin atop a wide, flat boulder up ahead. Standing taller than a horse, the creature had the head, wings, and talons of an eagle attached to the body and rear legs of a lion. The long, hooked beak looked made for tearing, and the golden brown feathers shimmered in the sunlight.

Astride the griffin sat a dwarf on a crimson saddle of tooled leather. He had bronze skin, black eyes, and a stubbly beard, and he wore a dented iron helm. A short sword hung from his belt, and he bore a battered shield emblazoned with a yellow fist. The small man raised to his lips a megaphone made from a furry black hide. "Today is the day you were captured by a dwarf."

Trask leveled his crossbow at the little man.

"Lower your weapon, sir," the dwarf demanded, without a trace of concern.

"Unlikely," Trask growled. "I'm not half bad with this. Slide off the griffin toward me."

The megaphone partly concealed the dwarf's grin. "In the realm of Thronis the Magnificent, trespassers do not issue orders. If you lay down your arms and come quietly, you will not be harmed. Initially."

Trask shook his head. The crossbow remained steady. "Open that mouth again and you'll eat a quarrel. I have another for your mount. Fly away, little man. We don't mean you or the giant any harm. We're just passing through."

The dwarf lowered his megaphone and lightly kicked the griffin. The creature pounced behind the boulder.

Kendra heard the rush of wind an instant before a

riderless griffin swooped into view from behind, huge claws clamping hold of Trask's shoulders. Powerful wings swept downward, and the creature jerked Trask off the ground. A second griffin grabbed Dougan in similar fashion, and a third snagged Tanu.

Gavin tackled Kendra flat to the ground. Mara whirled and thrust her spear up into the belly of the griffin reaching for her. The creature screeched and swerved away, the long spear deeply attached. Several other griffins swept by, talons grasping.

"Into the backpack," Gavin insisted in Kendra's ear. He pulled the knapsack from her shoulder and lifted the main flap. "You too, Seth," he called. "Get in here."

The griffins who had missed on their first pass were wheeling around for another run. Kendra counted seven, not including the one behind the boulder and the ones who had already snatched people.

Gavin grabbed her shoulder and shoved her into the knapsack headfirst. It was an awkward way to start down a ladder, but she grasped the rungs and managed to twist around and descend correctly. Kendra hurried down to make way for her brother. She heard several of the griffins screaming—deeper, louder screeches than should come from any bird.

"Nice nosedive," Warren said, leaning up on one elbow. An electric lantern shone beside him. "What's going on out there?"

"Griffin attack," Kendra gasped, staring up at the mouth of the sack. "Lots of them."

"Griffins don't normally come after humans."

"They already carried off Trask, Tanu, and Dougan."

"Oh, no."

Kendra watched in suspense as the mouth of the knapsack closed. Someone had shut the flap.

* * *

Seth scrambled over to Gavin and started to climb into the knapsack. He had one leg inside when a griffin slammed into him with great force, sending him spinning and rolling across the ledge. Elbows and shoulder aching, it took Seth a moment to realize he had not been the target. The griffin had snatched Gavin and was soaring skyward with him.

Three griffins dived at Mara in formation. She cartwheeled away from the leader and twisted to barely avoid the outstretched talons of the second, but the third one snagged her. Her legs flailed as the creature bore her away.

Seth heard a jangling. Mendigo had been scouting ahead, but Seth saw the puppet sprinting back to them. "Mendigo!" he yelled.

Two griffins swooped at Seth, but he rolled flat next to a boulder. Although he felt the wind of their passage, the grasping talons came up empty. Instead of coming fast, the next griffin landed beside Seth, scolding him with a harsh squawk. The limberjack was only a few paces away.

"Escape with the knapsack!" Seth cried, waving the puppet away. "Keep Kendra safe!"

Claws seized Seth by the shoulders, strong wings beat down, and he rose into the air. Craning his neck to look down and back, Seth saw Mendigo beat a griffin to the knapsack, snatching the bag and somersaulting out of the way. The wooden man dodged another griffin on the way to the brink of the cliff and then jumped off, falling out of sight into the gorge.

Could Mendigo survive a fall from such a great height? What about Kendra? Seth knew from experience that the storage room didn't feel the movements of the knapsack. No matter how much the bag was jostled or handled, the room inside remained stable. He hoped that held true for flinging the knapsack off a cliff!

Turning his eyes forward, Seth saw that they were climbing fast, heading toward Stormcrag. Mara, Gavin, Tanu, Dougan, and Trask dangled from griffins ahead of him. None of the other griffins besides the one with the dwarf had riders. Even through his winter jacket, Seth could feel the sharp talons, although they had not broken his skin. Glancing down, Seth saw the distant rocky ground beyond his boots, with hundreds of feet of empty air in between. If the griffin dropped him, he would be skydiving without a parachute. Fortunately the giant claws seemed to have a secure hold.

The sensation of flying with the griffin was undeniably exhilarating. The creature curved left and right as they ascended, sometimes banking steeply and making Seth's stomach tingle. At times the wings beat hard; at other times they glided, the wind whistling in his ears. Higher and higher they rose, until it felt like he was looking down at a map of Wyrmroost, complete with miniature trees, ridges, cliffs, lakes, and ravines.

Stormcrag grew snowy as they gained altitude. He tried to look up, but they were too near the mountain for him to see the top. The air steadily became chillier. The morning had been relatively warm, so he had worn no gloves. He managed to zip up his coat, but even so, the wind created by their speed continued to steal warmth away. He massaged his ears and alternated between jamming his hands in his pockets and rubbing them together.

Eventually, Seth laid eyes on the summit of the mountain. Just below the peak, resting on a jutting expanse of rock, Seth beheld a huge mansion, partly supported by an array of pilings and struts. The sprawling edifice had steep roofs shingled with slate, massive chimneys, and broad stone patios. The closer they got to the unlikely building, the more impressive the scale of the mansion became. The railings around the terraces were taller than his house—the front door considerably taller still.

As his griffin followed the others to the spacious patio before the colossal door, Seth realized that the vastness of the dwelling should have been expected. After all, this was the home of the largest giant in the world.

❋ ❋ ❋

Kendra listened to the tumult from near the top of the ladder. The fierce cries of griffins mingled with the shouts of her friends. She heard Seth command Mendigo to grab the knapsack, heard the windy hiss as they plummeted from the cliff, and heard the sharp crack of wood on stone when they landed.

Gripping the ladder desperately, Kendra had braced herself for impact, but inside the storage room she felt nothing. The room never tilted or wobbled or trembled. She heard jingles and clicks as Mendigo scrambled over the rocky floor of the gorge, then heard the rasp of leather against stone.

Griffins shrieked again. Desperate to know what was happening, Kendra moved to the highest rung and poked the top of her head out of the knapsack until she had a view. She found herself peering out of a small cavity of rock. Missing an arm and with a deep crack visible across his torso, Mendigo ducked and spun and sidestepped until the claws of a griffin locked hold and carried him out of view. A second griffin retrieved his arm. Then a third reached grasping talons into the cavity, but the claw could not reach the knapsack. The creature shrieked and Kendra ducked her head back inside the room.

"What's going on?" Warren asked.

"Mendigo jumped off the cliff with us. We landed in a ravine. He stuffed us in a crevice in the rocks. Seems like the griffins can't reach the knapsack."

"Sit tight," he advised. "Don't peek again."

"I'm not sure we can get out on our own. The little cave is pretty small. I don't know if I can crawl out of the bag."

"Wait until they're gone to try."

"What if the dwarf comes down here?" Kendra asked. "He might be small enough to fit into the crevice and reach us."

"The fissure is small?" Warren asked.

"Close and narrow," Kendra said. "I'm not even sure if Mendigo could have fit. He must have tossed us in. Even the dwarf might be too big."

"Inside those close confines, you could give the dwarf an eyeful of that javelin over there."

Kendra glanced over at the slim, sharp-tipped weapon. "Right. Okay. I don't hear anything. Should I check again?"

"Be careful. Wait a few minutes. Make sure they're really gone. If they are, you'd be smart to move us to a different hiding spot."

Kendra retrieved the javelin. Returning to the top of the rungs bolted to the wall, she pushed up the flap and gazed out the mouth of the cavity at the dry, empty gorge. She saw no sign of enemies. Of course, there could be a griffin standing off to one side of the crevice, claw poised to rip her head off the moment she stuck it out. She waited, watching and listening. At length, she decided to check whether she could get out of the knapsack.

Kendra tried for several minutes. She was unable to move the knapsack by pushing the walls and floor of the cavity with her hand. And she could barely get her head and shoulders out of the bag. In the end, she climbed down the ladder defeated. The crevice was too cramped. Even if she somehow managed to get out, her body would fill the snug space, crammed inside a rocky womb, unable to move.

She and Warren might be safe for the moment.

But they were trapped.

CHAPTER TWENTY-ONE

Giant Problem

A freezing gust blew across the expansive patio as Seth huddled with Trask, Tanu, Mara, Dougan, and Gavin. The griffins had set them down but remained close at hand, beaks and claws ready. The griffin mounted by the dwarf landed on the first step leading to the colossal door of the mansion.

The small man raised his shaggy megaphone. "You are now utterly at the mercy of Thronis and his minions! Even without accounting for the invincible giant and his griffins, there is no way down the mountain on foot. Lay down your arms. Humble cooperation is your only reasonable option."

Trask set down his bulky crossbow, unsheathed his swords, removed the daggers from his waist, and pulled a throwing knife from his boot. He nodded at the others.

Dougan let his battle-ax fall from his fingers to clang against the patio. Tanu dropped his blowgun. Mara threw down a knife. Gavin and Seth held no weapons.

"Wise decision," the dwarf proclaimed. "There is no shame in submitting to a pride of griffins. Or the cunning dwarf who leads them."

"You better not tell us you're Thronis," Dougan groaned.

The dwarf chuckled. "I am the giant's dwarf. His Magnificence will appear when it suits him."

The great door behind the dwarf swung open. "It suits me now," a mighty voice boomed, not particularly deep, but very powerful.

Out strode an impossibly large man, several times bigger than the fog giants at Fablehaven. Seth was not half as tall as his shins. His proportions were not deformed like an ogre's—he looked like a regular man in everything but scale. His head was bald with a few liver spots and a close-cropped fringe of graying hair. His astute face was lined in places but not overly wrinkled, with a wide mouth, a longish nose, and salt-and-pepper eyebrows. Seth would have guessed he was sixty. He wore a white toga and was slightly overweight, with a bit of loose flesh below his chin and some softness around the middle. A slim silver collar encircled his neck.

Two more griffins swooped down to the patio. One dumped Mendigo to slide and roll across the hard surface. The limberjack's gashed torso came apart, cleanly split into two halves. The second griffin dropped a wooden arm.

"It has been a long while since I have gazed on humans,"

the giant commented in a voice more thoughtful than gruff. "You were foolish to stray into the shadow of my mountain. I do not take intruders lightly, no matter how tiny or naïve they may be. Come inside, so I can size you up."

Thronis withdrew from the doorway.

"You heard his Magnificence," the dwarf barked. "I'll see to your weapons. Get your sorry carcasses inside."

Mendigo had dragged his top half over to his arm and was attaching the limb with its golden hooks. Seth crouched beside the puppet. "Wait for us here," he whispered. "If we die, try to find Kendra and help her."

"On your feet, boy," the dwarf snarled.

Trask led the way. Three steps led up to the front door, each one taller than Seth could reach. Off to one side, ladders granted easier access for smaller people. They climbed the three ladders, crossed to the door, and climbed across the threshold.

They paused in the doorway to marvel at the enormity of the sparsely furnished room beyond. A tremendous bonfire blazed on a stone hearth, flames fluttering and leaping, the wood snapping and shooting out sparks. A gargantuan suit of plate armor the size of Thronis stood in one corner. On the wall beside the armor hung a shield, a spear, a spiked mace, and a sheathed sword, all on a scale to be wielded by the giant. Thronis himself sat in a monstrous chair beside a table larger than a tennis court. Leaning forward, hands clasped, he regarded them pensively.

"Come closer," he urged, beckoning. "A diverse group of heroes, as might well be expected, though a couple of you look younger than I would have anticipated. Closer, draw closer, on the double! That's better. Who would be your leader?"

"I am," Trask proclaimed loudly.

"You needn't shout," the giant said. "I know I seem far away, but I have excellent hearing. I am Thronis. Tell me your names."

Trask recited their names.

"Well met. Tell me, Trask, what brings you to Wyrm-roost?"

"Our business is private."

The giant raised an eyebrow. "*Was* private. Now I have captured you, and you had best respond to my inquiries."

"We mean no harm to any at Wyrmroost, least of all yourself," Trask said. "We are here to recover a nonmagical artifact that could help ensure the prolonged imprisonment of many foul beings."

Thronis stroked his jaw. "Foul beings? Giants, perhaps?"

"Not giants," Trask said. "Demons."

"Few of us get along with demons," the giant acknowledged. "A prudent answer, but insufficient. Would you care to elaborate?"

"I can say no more."

The giant shook his head in disappointment. "Very well. Six of you will make for a meager pie, but I suppose an undersized delicacy is better than no treat at all."

"We don't want to be pie filling," Seth protested.

Thronis pursed his lips. "What, then? A soufflé? Hmmm. You may be onto something."

"As food, we're gone in a moment," Seth said. "As entertainment, the fun could go on and on."

"Sensible reasoning," the giant admitted. "Seth, how old are you?"

"Thirteen."

"The youngest in the company, I take it."

"Right."

The giant crinkled his brow. "You have a peculiar aspect. Were you not so young, I might suspect you for a shadow charmer."

"Trust your instincts. I'm a shadow charmer."

"Which might explain why you can speak Jiganti."

"What's he saying?" Trask asked.

"I was just observing that Seth can speak the tongue of the giants. I'll try to keep the conversation in English, Seth, for the sake of your friends, but afterwards we should commune in my native tongue. I do miss Jiganti. Where were we? Pies? Soufflé? No, entertainment. Speaking Jiganti with you would be entertaining, and I would be interested to hear how a child became a shadow charmer. Perhaps I could settle for a five-person pie with a side of stimulating conversation."

"No," Seth said. "Tanu is a potion master. Mara can tame wild animals. A bunch of us are dragon tamers. Gavin is a real pro. We could be at least as useful as that dwarf."

"More useful than Zogo? Perhaps, but it wouldn't have the same ring. The giant's dwarf. I have enjoyed the sound of that since day one. Answer me, Seth, whom would you consider the most attractive of your companions?"

Seth glanced over at Mara. With one woman among them, it was an easy contest. "Mara."

"I would have to agree," Thronis said amiably. "Too bad she isn't about ten times taller. Or maybe good thing she isn't, considering how she must be feeling toward me at present." The giant rose, stepped forward, crouched, and picked up Mara. He sat back down with her on his thigh. She stared up at him defiantly. "You look Hopi."

She said nothing.

Thronis regarded her silently. "Not one for conversation, I gather. Am I not wild beast enough for you to tame? No matter. I was not counting on words from you." He pinched her head between his thumb and forefinger. "Seth, you have spirit, a trait I admire. Maybe your vigor can help rescue some of your friends. I want you to explain in detail why you are here at Wyrmroost. Should you fail to do so, your loveliest companion will perish tragically. Then another. And another. All of them, in quick succession. But not you. You I will keep for a time. Perhaps you can help me prepare the crust."

Seth's mind raced. Was it worth keeping their mission a secret if it meant getting everyone killed? The Society already knew about the key. Navarog was at the gates. A quick decision was required. If information might spare them, why not spill it?

"Okay," Seth said. "I'll tell you. But put the lady down." He avoided eye contact with the others, not wanting to see disapproval.

"A civil decision, young man," Thronis said, bending

down to place Mara on her feet. "Sorry, my dear, nothing personal. I am cursed with an inquisitive nature. Come here, Seth, I want you on the table."

Seth trotted over to the chair. Thronis scooped him into a huge hand and set him gently on the tabletop. When he glanced down, the others appeared far away, as if he were standing atop a bluff.

"Tell me your business at Wyrmroost," Thronis prompted.

"We're after a key."

"A key to what, exactly?"

"The key to a vault on an enchanted preserve far from here."

"What lies within the vault?"

"An artifact."

"What artifact?"

Seth hesitated. "We're not sure. We think it might be a thingy called a Translocator. The artifact is one of the keys to Zzyzx."

"Oh-ho," the giant exhaled. "And how will unearthing the keys to Zzyzx protect us from demonkind?"

"Others are after the keys to Zzyzx," Seth explained. "Bad people who want to open the prison. We're moving the keys to keep them hidden."

Thronis challenged Seth with a suspicious glare. "And how do I know you are not in fact the wrongdoers? You are, after all, a shadow charmer."

"Good point. I guess that is hard to prove. But I'm not lying. It's why we're here."

Thronis cracked his knuckles. "So you're hunting for a key in order to access a different key. Did you expect to find this key on my mountain?"

"I don't think so."

"Then why make the imprudent mistake of coming near?"

"We were trying to find our way to where the key is hidden."

"Where might that be?"

"We're . . . um . . . not totally sure."

The giant eyed him. "You're becoming evasive. Do not try my patience. Do you need me to demonstrate that I am serious about squashing your friends? Tell me what you know about where the key you seek is hidden."

Seth sighed. He glanced down at his friends. Their expressions were unreadable. At least the giant was not a dragon. "The key is inside the Dragon Temple. We're not sure where that is. Honestly."

The giant's eyes flashed. "You intend to brave the guardians of the Dragon Temple?" Thronis turned to address the others. "Is this spoken in jest, Sir Leader?"

"The boy speaks the truth," Trask said.

Thronis turned back to Seth. "Then you are more courageous than I am. Or more reckless. Or simply uninformed. Have you any idea the chore that lies before you?"

"We're sort of winging it," Seth said.

Now the giant laughed heartily. Seth watched in silence. As the flood of mirth abated, Thronis brushed a tear from his eye. "Any dragon at Wyrmroost would immediately slay you for planning to enter the Dragon Temple, let alone actually treading there. Not to mention the three implacable guardians."

"Who are the guardians?"

The giant shrugged. "I understand that the first is a hydra. Hespera is her name. I have no idea regarding the other two—not that their services would be needed. What are the odds of getting past a hydra?"

"We'll figure out something," Seth said stoutly.

The giant laughed again. "I am amused. Truly diverted. I would even use the word *delighted*. This is far better than any pie. It may even exceed a soufflé. I find the absurdity exquisite!"

"I get underestimated a lot," Seth said.

Thronis composed himself. "I meant no insult. Apparently your need is great, or you would not undertake such a desperate task. You are thirteen, and a shadow charmer, which means there is more to you than meets the eye. No doubt your comrades have hidden talents of their own. But you were taken by griffins! If dragons were hawks, griffins would be sparrows. And the hydra would be a hawk with twenty heads!"

"We have to try," Seth said simply.

"You get to try only if I opt not to include you in a recipe," the giant affirmed. "It would be a shame to waste such uncommon ingredients. But perhaps we can reach an accord." He fingered the silver collar. "You see this ring around my neck?"

"Yes."

"You have not by chance spoken with Agad the wizard?"

"I have."

"You have?" Dougan exclaimed.

"Long story," Seth shot back.

The giant went on, ignoring the interruption. "Are you aware that if I tell a lie this collar will constrict and crush my windpipe?"

"Agad didn't tell me personally, but I heard the rumor."

"Good to know that word of my curse reaches the ears of every newcomer," Thronis said dryly. "Agad is very smug about the accomplishment. As well he should be. I am something of a spell weaver myself, and not easily duped. I wasted years trying to get the collar off, to break the spell, until I finally decided it might be simpler to always be truthful. What I am saying is that if we make an arrangement, I will hold to my end. I must, or I will die."

Seth placed his hands on his hips. "How do we know the spell is real? Or that you haven't found a way around it?"

"I suppose that is hard to prove. Nevertheless it is true. And, to be candid, you are in no position to doubt me."

"What sort of agreement?"

Thronis favored Seth with a sly grin. "Indulge me for a moment while I paint the picture. A giant of my size is a fearsome opponent, even knowing no magic. Granted, at a glance I am intimidating. But a glance would not reveal the millennia I have lived, the spells I have mastered, my deceptive agility, my skill with arms, or the true strength in me, a raw power that goes well beyond the predictable capacity of my large frame.

"Most are aware that the hide of a giant is shockingly resilient. Pause to consider my additional mail." He indicated the battle gear in the corner. "Reflect upon the quantity of steel required for such magnificent armature, and the additional security it provides. Have you ever heard of a giant with a suit of plate? Array me in full armor, grant me my weapons, and I could prevail against any dragon of this sanctuary in open battle, save perhaps Celebrant.

"Yet despite these advantages, I have never braved the Dragon Temple." Thronis gazed pointedly at Seth. "This is not because the location of the temple is a mystery. I have two orbs in a neighboring chamber, one white, the other dark. The dark helps me adjust the climate. The white is for gazing. From my manse on Stormcrag, I can behold most of Wyrmroost, and much of the world beyond the walls. Although I cannot penetrate the Dragon Temple, I know precisely where it lies.

"Dragons are notorious for hoarding treasure. I protect an enviable hoard myself. How many Dragon Temples do you suppose exist in the wide world?"

"One?" Seth tried.

"There are three, one in each of the forbidden sanctuaries. Each temple houses the preeminent treasures of all the hoards, the most powerful items amassed by the dragons of the world. And each temple contains a certain talisman the dragons particularly want to keep out of mortal hands. It was partly in exchange for these three talismans that dragons agreed to come to the sanctuaries in the first place. Do you know what talisman resides in the Dragon Temple here at Wyrmroost?"

"Gauntlets?" Seth guessed. Warren had informed him about the message Kendra had copied from Patton's grave.

"Precisely. The famed Sage's Gauntlets. According to legend, when the man who wears them commands, dragons must obey. Do you suppose such gauntlets might come in handy for me?"

"Probably, since you live at a dragon sanctuary."

Thronis shook his head. "No. They would not fit on my little finger. The Sage's Gauntlets are meant for mortal wizards. Mastering them would be a complex endeavor even for Agad, let alone for you or your comrades. If you were to steal them, no dragon on the planet would rest until you were eviscerated."

"We're not after gauntlets," Seth insisted. "We're after a key."

"I see. Answer me this. The dragon temple is ancient. How did your key get inside?"

"A man put it there."

"Slipped by the three guardians, did he? How extraordinary."

"This guy did lots of impossible things."

The giant leaned an elbow on the table. "Who was this puissant trickster?"

"Patton Burgess."

Thronis nodded. "I have bothered to learn the names of only a few mortals. But his I know. Perhaps he did hide your key inside the Dragon Temple. Perhaps he gave you knowledge that will help you gain access. The odds are poor, but the prospect intriguing. Which is why I mentioned an accord.

"I have not ignored the Dragon Temple for lack of interest. There is nothing inside to tempt me to risk all, yet there are a few items I would like. Precious figurines. A set kept together. A dragon worked in red stone. A snow giant crafted from white marble. And a jade chimera. There are two other pieces to the set—an onyx tower and an agate leviathan. Bring those as well. Yes, bring all five figurines, and perhaps you will glimpse my generous side."

Seth tried not to let his dismay show. "Won't the dragons be furious if we steal those things?"

Thronis waved an impatient hand. "They'll be furious you enter the temple at all. Taking only these few figurines will not incite them to significantly greater rage. The gauntlets are another matter. Leave the gauntlets where they lie."

Trask raised his voice. "If we vow to bring you the figurines, you will let us go?"

The giant held up a finger. "I will do more than let you go. In preparation for the endeavor, I will feed you, equip you, and have my griffins fly you to the entrance of the Dragon Temple. But one problem remains. I am unable to lie. You should not be able to deceive me, either. While fruitlessly studying how to relieve myself of my collar, I learned how to devise a similar choker. I will make one for each of you to wear. Should you bring back the figurines, I will remove the collars and provide you with safe conduct to the gate of Wyrmroost. Should you play me false, you will all strangle."

"What will you give us?" Seth asked. "You know, to equip us?"

"If I am to surrender my pie, I want some hope of a return on my investment. I can give you a dose or two of precious dragonsbane. Maybe a sword edged with adamant, or a spear tipped with the same. Rare items that I would rather not lose, to be sure, but what good is a hoard of objects never used?"

"This sounds better than being baked in a pie," Seth confessed.

Thronis regarded Trask. "What say you, Sir Leader? This is the only bargain I intend to offer. Remember, I do not lie. You will not receive a second chance. These terms strike me as absurdly generous. Those of you who do not accept have reached the end of your lives."

Trask conferred briefly with the others in a quiet huddle. "You offer us a better alternative than certain death," Trask acknowledged. "We accept."

Thronis slapped a hand down on the table. Seth staggered and fell to his knees, ears ringing. "Let us adjourn to my treasury and get you outfitted," the giant enthused. "I will place chokers on you to make sure the story the boy shared was true. Nothing will save you if he was fibbing about your purposes. As long as the tale proves to be true, tonight I will feast with my tiny champions, and in the morning, you shall sally forth to win whatever glory chance will allow!"

CHAPTER TWENTY-TWO

Raxtus

Bubda sat on the splintery barrel, ankles crossed, arms folded, wearing a grouchy expression. "Bubda think about it," he said. "Ask again next week."

"We need you to try now," Kendra insisted. "If those griffins come back, they'll kick us out of here. You'll lose your home."

"Kick you out. No find Bubda."

"We found you," Warren pointed out.

Bubda waved a dismissive hand. "You cheat. Knew Bubda was here. Poke Bubda with rake."

"If they take us, we'll tell them about you," Kendra threatened.

The hermit troll scowled. "Where Seth? Bubda miss Seth! Seth speak Duggish. Seth play Yahtzee."

Kendra tried hard to keep her tone sincere and sweet instead of frustrated and angry. "If you want to see Seth again, we need you to try to move the knapsack out of the little cave."

Bubda hopped down from the barrel. "No! Bubda hate sky! Bubda no leave! Bubda hide." He squatted, curled up his arms, tucked his head, and suddenly looked like a shabby wooden cask.

"How about a game of Yahtzee to decide?" Warren proposed.

Bubda raised his head. "Yahtzee?"

"The three of us," Warren continued. "If Kendra or I win, you try to move the knapsack."

"If Bubda win?"

"You get to play us again," Kendra said cheerily.

Bubda scrunched his face. "Bubda no fool. Bubda win, you nag no more."

"Fair enough," Warren conceded.

Bubda brightened. "You no win. Bubda Yahtzee champion." He waddled over to the Yahtzee box.

Kendra had learned to play Yahtzee with her Grandma and Grandpa Larsen. She could remember nights around the kitchen table with her parents, grandparents, and Seth, eating chocolate-covered pretzels, drinking root beer, and playing round after round. Grandma Larsen had always seemed to win more than anybody, but Kendra knew that, aside from adhering to a few basic strategies, the outcome of the game was based on chance.

As long as either she or Warren won, Bubda would

have to try to get the knapsack out of the crevice. It was disheartening to put their safety into the custody of a plastic barrel of dice, but at least they had a two-against-one advantage.

In the end, nobody got a Yahtzee, and chasing five of a kind ruined Bubda. He missed his upper-section bonus, missed his large straight, and penciled in a low four of a kind. Both Kendra and Warren ended up with higher scores through more conservative play.

"Dice broken," Bubda spat after failing to roll a fifth three on his last turn. "Play again."

"We had a deal," Warren reminded him. "We can play again, but first you need to do us a favor."

Grumbling unintelligibly, Bubda tottered over to the rungs in the wall and climbed up. He slipped out through the top of the knapsack with no apparent difficulty. Seconds later he came back down, still mumbling to himself.

"You put it outside?" Kendra asked.

The troll gave a curt nod.

"That was fast!" Kendra gushed.

Grinning, Bubda raised one arm, cocked his head, and began to dance in place. For a moment, as he turned and swayed, he looked as slender and flexible as a serpent, his body almost elastic. Then he dropped his arm and the illusion ended. "Play Yahtzee again."

"I'll play you," Warren offered. "Did you see anything out there, Bubda?"

"Rocks," the troll answered.

"Any creatures? Anything alive?"

Bubda shook his head.

Warren turned to Kendra. "You ought to head topside and see if you can find a better spot for the knapsack."

Kendra hustled over to the ladder.

"Be watchful," Warren advised. "Move quickly. Don't stay up there too long."

"I'll be careful," Kendra promised.

She pushed through the flap and found herself on the floor of a deep gorge just outside the cavity of rock. Above her stretched a high, sheer cliff, with an equally steep face on the far side of the gorge. The floor of the gorge generally sloped down away from Stormcrag, winding out of sight in either direction.

A brief scan of the area revealed no enemies, nor did she see a particularly good place to stash the knapsack. They appeared to be in no immediate peril. Squatting, she noticed a long fragment of brown wood, clearly a piece splintered from Mendigo. She picked it up.

Clutching the long splinter under the blue sky in the lonely gorge, the weight of what had happened with the griffins came crashing down on her. Tears stung her eyes, but she resisted. Why was she going to stash the knapsack? Who was going to come rescue them? Her brother and her friends had been carried off by flying lions. They were most likely dead.

Kendra sat down hard. At least the griffins had carried away Trask, Tanu, and Dougan alive. She had seen that much. The ferocious creatures had not instantly begun to slaughter them. The conflict had not seemed like a bloody feeding frenzy. The dwarf had called for surrender. There was reason to hope that Seth and the others were alive somewhere. There was also reason to suspect they were being fed to baby griffins in gigantic nests.

Warren had urged her to be quick. Why? So she could find a new place to stash the knapsack before the griffins returned. Right, but why? So they could hide until their food finally ran out? Who was going to come rescue them? If they were still alive, the others were probably in greater need of rescue.

Warren was injured. He probably wanted to hide until he healed enough to help. But Kendra did not believe they had much time. There was no way to track where the griffins had gone. Wings did not leave footprints. That left her with two options. Try to make her way back to the gate. Or try to make her way to the fairy shrine.

Navarog was supposedly waiting at the gate. Plus, turning back would mean abandoning Seth, her friends, and their quest. She had to go forward. According to Mara, they had been near the fairy shrine when the griffins attacked. If she could find a way back up to the top of the cliff, she might have a chance. Maybe if she worked her way up the gorge, the walls would get lower or more climbable.

She should inform Warren. It wasn't fair to leave him down there wondering if she was alive. He might get stupid and try to go up the ladder despite his injuries.

Kendra went back into the storage room. Warren was blowing into the little plastic barrel and shaking the dice. "Warren?" Kendra asked.

He stopped rattling the dice. "Find a spot?"

"I think we'd better try to make it to the fairy shrine."

He frowned. "I might be more helpful in a few days."

"They're not coming back. Seth and Gavin and all of them."

Warren was silent for a moment. "You never know. They may. But we shouldn't plan on it."

"I'm going to see if I can get us back up to where we were before we fell."

"Don't go scaling any cliffs," Warren cautioned. "This is no place to take a fall."

"I'll be careful."

"At the first sign of trouble, hide the knapsack and duck inside. If we have to, we can defend the mouth of the bag."

"Okay."

"Less talk, more Yahtzee," Bubda griped.

Warren started rattling the dice again. "Be careful."

"I will." Kendra went back up through the top of the knapsack.

The rocky floor of the gorge made her footing treacherous, so Kendra took her time picking her way up the gradual slope toward Stormcrag. As the sun climbed higher, neither wall of the gorge offered much shadow. The faint warmth felt good, but she also felt exposed. Any unfriendly eyes gazing down into the gorge could not miss her. Nevertheless, she made good progress. And she saw no creatures, except for a trio of large dragonflies.

Kendra was getting ready to break for lunch when, coming around a corner, she gained a view of where the gorge abruptly ended. Now she not only had impassable stone walls to her right and left but a new one, as insurmountable as the others, directly in her path. There was no way out of the gorge in the direction she had headed all morning.

At first Kendra wanted to scream, but she realized the noise could attract predators. She wanted to punch the nearest wall of the gorge, but decided it wouldn't be worth cutting up her knuckles. Instead she sank to her knees, bowed her head, and cried.

Once she let them start, the tears came hot and fast. Her body shook with sobs. She was glad her brother couldn't see her grief. He would have laughed over her tears. But she didn't want to think about her brother. That just made it worse. More tears flowed.

"Don't cry," a kind voice said behind her.

Kendra rose and whirled, wiping tears from her wet cheeks, and found herself staring into the eyes of a dragon. Legs numb, she backed away. It was the smallest dragon she had seen yet, with a body the size of a large horse, although the long neck and tail added greatly to its length. Its gleaming armor of silvery white scales reflected a glimmering rainbow sheen, and the head was bright as polished chrome. Overall, the dragon had a lean, sleek build, as if designed for speed. Strangely, Kendra realized that she felt none of the paralysis she had experienced when confronted by other dragons.

"Don't worry," the dragon said. "I won't eat you." He had a male voice, somewhat like a confident teenager, but the words came out richer and fuller than any human could have managed.

"I don't feel scared," Kendra said.

"I've never inspired much terror," the dragon replied, almost sadly. "I'm glad you're not afraid."

"I mean, I don't feel paralyzed like with some dragons," Kendra explained, not wanting to belittle him. "I'm plenty startled. I'm sure you could rip me to shreds if you wanted."

"I mean you no harm. You shine like a fairy. More than a fairy, to be accurate. And more than a fairy friend. I've actually been looking for a chance to meet you."

"What?"

"You've been surrounded by other people." The dragon swung his head away. Was he shy? "You caught my eye right when you entered Wyrmroost. I've followed you from Blackwell Keep."

Kendra scrunched her brow. "You're a little too shiny to blend in much. How did we miss you?"

Suddenly the dragon was gone, as if he had been wiped from existence. Then he was back. "I can go nearly invisible."

"Wow. That would explain it."

"Luckily, I have a few talents besides being a runt."

"You'll grow."

"Will I? Hasn't been going very well the past several centuries."

"Centuries?" Kendra said. "You're not young?"

"I'm a full-grown adult," the dragon said with an edge of bitterness. "Dragons never completely stop growing, but the process slows down as you get old, and I'm well past the age when it slows down. But enough about me. You were crying."

"I'm having a bad day," Kendra said.

"I saw. The griffins carried off your friends."

"One of them was my brother."

"Seth, right? I've been eavesdropping a little. I'm Raxtus, by the way."

"Nice to meet you." Kendra glanced up at the walls of the gorge. "I'm trying to get out of here, but it looks like I'm boxed in."

"You really are," Raxtus agreed. "Only winged creatures can access this box canyon. If you head the other way, you'll hit a huge drop-off, the top of a cliff. There is no way to climb down. A stream used to cut through here. Sometimes it comes back and makes pretty waterfalls, but mostly the water runs a different way now."

"So I'm trapped."

"You would be trapped, yes, but I have wings. I could carry you, no problem."

"Really?" Kendra said.

"Where are you going? You guys always speak low when you discuss your plans. Not a bad idea, by the way. But bad for eavesdropping."

The dragon seemed nice, and he was clearly her only hope. Would he object to taking her to the fairy shrine? Only one way to find out. "The Fairy Queen has a shrine here," Kendra said.

"I knew it!" the dragon exclaimed. "You're fairykind, aren't you? I could tell. Well, I thought I could tell. I wasn't a hundred percent sure, but I would have bet on it. Too bad I didn't."

Kendra was not normally open about her status as fairykind, but there seemed to be no point in trying to hide it from Raxtus. "Yes, I'm fairykind. Do you know where the shrine is?"

The dragon laughed softly. "You can't begin to guess how familiar I am with the Fairy Queen's shrine. I'm probably the only dragon in the world who can go there. I don't mean near the shrine, in the vicinity, I mean actually right up to the shrine itself."

"Other dragons can't?"

"No. Almost nobody can. The Queen would strike them down. I'm guessing you can, though."

"Yes. I mean, I have before, but only at the shrine at Fablehaven. A different preserve."

"I'm familiar with Fablehaven," Raxtus said.

"But I'm not sure if I can visit the shrine here. If the Fairy Queen doesn't want me there, she might turn me into dandelion seeds."

"Right. You have to be careful. You don't just hang out at the shrine without a purpose."

Kendra chuckled. "You don't talk like a dragon."

"I'm unusual. I'm not a dragon of Wyrmroost."

"You're not?"

"I'm at Wyrmroost, but not of Wyrmroost. I was never admitted formally. I'm under no obligation to remain here. I come and go. I'm at Wyrmroost a lot, though, partly because my dad lives here. But I travel all over, mostly incognito, you know, invisible. I really like drive-in movies."

"I've seen a dragon outside of Wyrmroost," Kendra said.

"I've heard of many others. I've never heard of one like you."

"There are no other dragons like me," Raxtus admitted. "See, when I was still in my egg, a cockatrice got into the nest. My dad wasn't around, and my mom had just gotten herself killed, so there was nobody to protect us. Three eggs were eaten. Had they hatched, they would have been my siblings. But before the cockatrice got to the last egg, some fairies intervened and rescued me. By the way, I don't remember any of this; it was told to me later. Even for a dragon in an egg, I was young when this happened. The fairies who saved me brought me to one of the Fairy Queen's shrines for protection. I was incubated and hatched by fairy magic, and I came out . . . unique."

"You're beautiful," Kendra admired. "And nice."

The dragon gave a snuffling, annoyed laugh. "I get that a lot. I'm the pretty dragon. The funny dragon. Problem is, dragons are supposed to be fearsome and awe-inspiring. Not witty. Being the funny dragon is like being the bald mammoth. Being the pretty dragon is like being the ugly fairy. Get it?"

"You get teased?"

"I wish I only got teased! Mocked would be more accurate. Scorned. Berated. Shunned. Who my dad is only makes it ten times worse, although it also explains why I'm still alive."

"Who is your dad?"

The dragon didn't answer. He looked up at the sky. "I've known you for like five minutes and I'm already confessing my problems. Laying out my whole life story. Why do I always do this? It's like, I want to get it out there at the start so I don't get hurt later on. But I just come off as needy and pathetic. Here you are with real problems and I keep turning the conversation back to me."

"No, it's okay, I'm interested, I want to know."

Raxtus pawed at the ground. "I guess I have to continue now that I've led you on. My dad is Celebrant the Just. He's basically the king of dragons. The biggest, the strongest, the best. And I'm his greatest disappointment. Raxtus the fairy dragon."

Kendra wanted to give him a hug, but realized that might prove his point. "I'm sure your dad is proud of you," Kendra said. "I bet most of this is just in your head."

"I wish you were right," Raxtus replied. "It's no delusion. Celebrant has basically disowned me. I have two brothers. Half brothers. They came from a different clutch, obviously. Each of them rules one of the other forbidden sanctuaries. I look way more like Dad than either of them do—going by shape and color, I mean. I'm the miniature version of Celebrant. He has these glossy platinum scales, a lot like mine, but harder than adamant. On him they look awesome. He's built thicker than me, all muscle. He has like five breath weapons, and knows tons of offensive spells, but he's no thug. His mind is keen as a razor. He has it all. Dignity. Majesty."

"He can't hate you just because you're small!" Kendra asserted.

"Small is only part of it. Guess what my breath weapon

does? Helps things grow! You know, makes flowers bloom. And the only magic I can do is defensive stuff like hiding, or else healing. Again, like a fairy. It doesn't help that I look so much like my dad. I know it shames him. He hasn't utterly disavowed me, though. Somewhere deep inside, he feels guilty that my siblings were killed, that he wasn't there to stop the cockatrice, and that he didn't know I had survived until years later. For that, I remain under his protection, which means that as much as other dragons shun me, none of them want to fight me. No dragon on Earth is eager to risk the wrath of Celebrant."

"See! He loves you."

"No. Guilt is not love. Dad has made it clear he doesn't want me near him. And he's right. My presence discredits him: the humiliating contrast between the most magnificent dragon in the world and his absurd jester of a son."

Kendra could think of nothing to say. Again she resisted the urge to hug him.

"Anyhow, now you know my sorry background. The full confession. I don't want to be feeble and useless; I'm not proud of it. I love action movies. My fondest dream is to be a hero. To be fierce and brave, to somehow prove myself a real dragon. But when the opportunity arises, I cringe. Like when the griffins took your friends. I could have charged to the rescue. Come on, they were griffins! But there were a lot of them, and I knew who must have sent them. I decided to lie low for a minute, and before I knew it, the opportunity had passed me by."

"Who sent the griffins?" Kendra inquired eagerly.

RAXTUS

"Thronis, the sky giant up on Stormcrag. He keeps griffins like people keep hounds. The dwarf was Zogo. The giant's dwarf."

"You know where Thronis lives?"

"Sure."

"Here's your chance for heroics!" Kendra said. "We can rescue my brother and the others!"

"You're right, that would be valiant. Too valiant. I'd get us both killed. If I was lucky, maybe I'd invigorate some of his houseplants along the way. I'm barely half a dragon, Kendra. The rest of me is glitter and fairy dust. Even the bravest dragons stay far from Thronis. He is both giant and sorcerer. Powerful spells protect his stronghold atop Stormcrag. True, I yearn to be a hero, but I'm a coward at heart. Want an example? I followed you all morning trying to work up the courage to say hello. I only found the nerve once you started crying."

"But you could go invisible," Kendra suggested. "Sneak up there in the dead of night."

"Spells," Raxtus said. "Thronis would know. He'd slay me before I could help anyone. Look, as a friend, I'm the ideal dragon. As a hero, not so much."

"Can you turn into a human?" Kendra wondered.

"Like an avatar? A human version of myself? Not really. I mean, I've tried. But it doesn't work out well. I can't manage to look like a person."

"What do you look like?"

The dragon glanced away. "Maybe we should change the subject."

[407]

"What?"

Raxtus looked back at her. "I look like a boy fairy with butterfly wings."

Kendra did a poor job stifling her surprised laugh.

"Like a foot tall," Raxtus went on. "You can laugh, I know how it sounds—believe me, I know—just don't spread that one around, please. It isn't common knowledge."

"It just caught me off guard," Kendra apologized.

"Caught me off guard too. For years I took consolation that one day I could escape to human form, once I learned the trick, and maybe become part of a community. No luck. I'm a freak in any form. I'm polluted by fairy magic down to the core."

"You're not a freak," Kendra said firmly. "You're the coolest looking dragon I've ever seen. You're like a sports car. The only dragons I've seen or heard of are harsh and mean. It's easy to be mean when you have sharp teeth and claws. It would be much harder to be likable. I've never even pictured a likable dragon until right now."

"You're very kind. You know, we dragons don't get to air out our feelings on talk shows. We don't have therapists. But talking to you has been helpful. Thanks for listening. Hey, you mentioned you've been to Fablehaven."

"Right. I've been there a lot."

"And you can talk to fairies."

"Yes."

"I wonder if you might have met my foster mom. Her name is Shiara."

Kendra brightened. "Silver wings? Blue hair?"

"That's her!"

"She's the best fairy at Fablehaven!" Kendra gushed.

"You don't have to lay it on quite so thick," Raxtus said.

"No, I'm serious. Shiara stands out. She has helped me. Most fairies are flaky, but Shiara is actually reliable and smart."

"She saved me from the cockatrice and nurtured me. It wasn't at Fablehaven. This happened long before Fablehaven was founded. I don't visit her as often as I should. It feels too much like embracing the sissy side of my nature. As if anyone cared! Sometimes, though, I sneak into Fablehaven at night and visit her."

"How do you sneak into Fablehaven?"

"Same way I sneak into Wyrmroost. I may be less than half a dragon, but I have a few tricks. One is traveling from one fairy shrine to another. Anywhere the Fairy Queen has a shrine is open to me."

Kendra felt almost too excited to ask her next question. "Could you take me home?" If she could only get back to Fablehaven, she could return with reinforcements.

"Sorry, Kendra. I don't think I could transport a passenger. Maybe someday, with study and practice. Even if I could, the last time I tried to visit Fablehaven, the way seemed barred."

Kendra frowned. The shrine at Fablehaven had been destroyed, so it made sense that Raxtus would not be able to use it. She should have thought of that before she asked. Still, there were other ways the dragon might be of service.

"Could you take me to the Fairy Queen's shrine here at Wyrmroost?"

"Sure. It isn't even far. Especially flying."

Kendra glanced at the knapsack. "You said you have healing powers. My friend is hurt."

"Warren? A peryton gored him, right? I don't know what it is with those antlers. They must be slightly poisonous. They make ugly wounds. Well, I could try. I mean, I'm better with plants. But why not? I could give it a shot. Can he get up here? I'm not the biggest dragon, but I doubt I could fit through the mouth of a knapsack."

"I'll be right back," Kendra said. "You won't leave?"

"I'm a coward, not impolite! Oh, did you mean would I run if trouble shows up? If I run away, I'll take the knapsack with me. Not that I sense any danger. I've been paying attention. I think we're good. So I'll be here."

Kendra descended the ladder. Warren was asleep. She could not see Bubda. Kneeling beside Warren, she prodded his cheek. "Hey, you awake?"

He smacked his lips and his eyelids fluttered up. "Huh? We okay?" His voice sounded thick.

"Did you take more medicine?"

"Sorry, I'm a little loopy. The pain."

"It's okay. That's why you have medicine. I made friends with a dragon."

Warren blinked. He rubbed his eyes. "Sorry. Feels like my head is stuffed with cotton. I think I misheard you."

"No, really. A nice dragon. He was raised by fairies, and he might be able to heal you."

"This is my most messed-up dream yet."

"Do you think you could climb the ladder?"

"You're serious?"

"He's too big to fit down here. But he's not super big. For a dragon, at least."

Warren leaned up on one elbow. "You really think he can heal me?"

"Worth a try."

"Unless he eats us." Warren winced as he sat up. "You'll need to be my crutch."

"Can you make it up the ladder? Should we wait for the medicine to wear off?"

"This is the best time. The medicine numbs me. Up we go."

Kendra took his hand and helped him rise. He leaned on her as he hobbled over to the ladder. Clinging to a rung, he hesitated for a moment, gathering his strength, then started up. Kendra followed.

When Kendra emerged from the knapsack, Warren was on his back on the ground, sweating and panting. Shielding his eyes with one hand, he stared at Raxtus. "That has got to be the shiniest dragon I've ever seen."

"He doesn't look very well," Raxtus commented.

"Thanks, Doc," Warren mumbled.

"Can you try to heal him?" Kendra asked.

"I can try." Craning his neck forward, Raxtus stared down at Warren. Squealing softly, the dragon exhaled over the length of his body, glittery sparks twinkling silver and gold. Warren squirmed and shivered, as if taken by a sudden chill.

The hair on his head began to flutter, and the stubble on his jaw sprouted and lengthened. A moment later, Warren had long, flowing hair and a heavy beard.

Grimacing, Warren patted his injured chest. Then he raked his fingers through his hair. "You've got to be kidding. Who is this joker?"

"Sorry," Raxtus said. "It didn't take."

"Oh, it took," Warren complained, sitting up. His beard reached halfway down his chest. His thick hair hung past his shoulders. "It just didn't cure anything. On the bright side, I think I popped open some scabs."

"Thanks for trying," Kendra said.

Raxtus hung his head.

"Hey, don't look down," Warren said. "I appreciate the effort. I do feel a little more lucid. And my breath tastes slightly mintier." He scooted toward the knapsack.

"I rarely work with humans," Raxtus apologized.

"He's going to carry us to the fairy shrine," Kendra said.

Warren turned and placed a foot on the ladder. "Now, *that* would be a huge favor. Sorry to be a bear. Excruciating agony makes me cranky. Kendra, you know where to find me." Grunting and wincing, he disappeared into the bag.

"Humiliating," Raxtus muttered.

"You warned us it might not work," Kendra said.

"Did you notice how he wasn't scared of me? At all?"

"I told him you were nice. Besides, he's on pain medication."

"I'm about as intimidating as a puppy. Wearing diapers.

With a pacifier in its mouth. Well, one thing I can do right is fly."

"How do we do this? Should I get on your back?"

"No. I'm too spiny and sharp. You'd need a saddle. Not that any dragon worth a nickel would wear a saddle. They would die of shame. But shame is where I live. I own the whole neighborhood. I'd wear a saddle if we had one. But we don't. So I'll have to carry you. Would you feel safer inside the knapsack?"

"Would I be safer?"

"I won't drop you, if that's what you're implying. You can trust me on that."

"Okay," Kendra said, shouldering the knapsack. "Take me flying."

CHAPTER TWENTY-THREE

Shrine

Raxtus really was quite adept at flying. He gripped Kendra snugly around the torso with a single foreclaw and ripped through the air with dizzying maneuverability. Because of the way he held her, Kendra was free to spread her arms and legs and pretend she was flying all alone. The speed, the cold wind in her face, the exhilaration of swift turns and sudden dives, all combined to fill Kendra with surprising joy. Soon she was laughing.

"I could set us down," Raxtus said, "but it seems like you're having fun."

"I am!"

"Flying is one of my great escapes. How's your stomach holding up? Want to try something fancy?"

Kendra had never been a daredevil. But she felt so secure

in Raxtus's grasp, and he flew with such smooth competence, that she found herself saying, "Go for it."

First Raxtus swooped into a huge loop. The sky became the ground and the ground became the sky, and then everything was right again. After verifying that Kendra was still enjoying herself, he climbed high, then plunged in a corkscrewing dive, spiraling through space at tremendous velocity. To the spirals he added more loops and lightning turns, tracing pretzels in the sky. Kendra lost all sense of up and down as everything blurred into a wild rush of motion.

When Raxtus landed and set Kendra on her feet, she held her hands out to balance herself, took a wobbling step, and fell sideways. The dragon caught her and laid her down. The ground seemed to tilt and spin.

"Are you sure you're all right?" Raxtus asked.

"I'm great," she said. "I loved it. But you've ruined roller coasters for me. They'll never impress me again! Aren't you dizzy?"

"Flying only clears my head. It never leaves me dizzy or sick."

She did feel a little queasy. But not horribly. Now that she was on solid ground, the motion sickness was fading. Kendra looked around. She was crouched on a high shoulder of rock, one of the mounting folds of land that led up to Stormcrag. The steady hiss of rushing water reached her ears. Crawling to the nearest edge, she peered down at the top of a lofty waterfall divided into two halves by a mossy outcrop. She liked the peculiar perspective, above and somewhat in front of the falls, similar to the last view a person might have as he plunged off the brink. The water plummeted white and misty to a pool far below.

"Careful," Raxtus said. "I'm fast, but not that fast."

"I won't fall. I'm not woozy anymore." Kendra backed away from the edge. "Where's the shrine?"

"Just up the slope from here a ways. I figured you would want a minute to make sure you still felt good about treading there. I'll walk with you."

Kendra scrambled over the jagged terrain, using her hands to steady herself. As they worked their way around an upthrust formation of dark gray stone, a wide ledge came into view ahead. A trickle of water flowed off the ledge and across the rocks to join the stream before it plunged over Split Veil Falls.

A dozen golden owls with human faces perched on the ledge, all gazing unblinkingly at Kendra. "Astrids," Kendra said.

"All twelve," Raxtus affirmed.

"Are there twelve total?" Kendra asked.

"Twelve who hang around here," Raxtus said. "There are ninety-six in the world. Can you hear them?"

Straining, she heard only the whisper of the falls. "No."

"Listen with your mind," Raxtus suggested.

Kendra recalled how the Fairy Queen had spoken to her with thoughts and feelings instead of audible words. She tried to open her mind to the astrids.

"They're laughing," Raxtus reported.

The faces on the golden owls remained expressionless. "Could have fooled me," Kendra said.

"They want to know if you plan to destroy this shrine as well," Raxtus relayed in a more serious tone. "What is that about?"

"Tell them I was following orders from the Fairy Queen last time. She had me do it to save Fablehaven from an evil plague."

"They're not thrilled with your answer," Raxtus chuckled grimly. "They have no way to verify with the Queen. But I think they believe you."

"What exactly are they, Raxtus?"

"You don't know about the astrids?"

"They're one of many things I know nothing about," Kendra said.

"I just assumed since you were . . . never mind."

"Since I was fairykind?"

"Well, yeah. Wasn't there an orientation?"

"I wish."

The dragon swung his head toward the astrids. "Theirs is an ancient story. Long ago, the astrids were among the most trusted agents of the Fairy Queen. As a reward for their outstanding service, they were selected as the honor guard for the Fairy King."

"There's a Fairy *King*?"

"There *was* a Fairy King, although the Queen was easily the more powerful of the two. Her astrids failed to protect the Fairy King from Gorgrog, the king of demons. When the Fairy King fell, so did the male counterparts of the Queen's fairies. Thus the imps were born.

"It's hard to say how responsible the astrids were for the

tragedy, but the Queen blamed them, and she cast them out of her service. Six turned away and went dark. The other ninety remain faithful, clinging to the wish of one day earning her forgiveness."

Kendra regarded the astrids with new eyes. "You can hear their thoughts?"

"I can. But they no longer commune with the Fairy Queen or the fairies. They lack much of their former splendor. Yet despite their limitations, they strive to watch over the Queen's interests."

"Will they prevent me from reaching the shrine?"

"I can't say."

"Ask them."

"They say the shrine guards itself from those who don't belong."

"Well, I feel good about it." She started forward, then turned to look back at Raxtus. "You coming?"

"I better wait here. You go on ahead."

Kendra went back and set the knapsack by his forelegs. "Keep an eye on that. I don't want Warren getting zapped for my trespassing."

"You got it."

As Kendra approached the ledge, she got her closest view ever of the astrids. They were big birds, nearly as high as her waist. The gilded feathers had faint brown markings. The human faces possessed creamy, flawless skin and displayed no abnormal features. The various astrids differed only slightly from one another. Their eyes remained fixed on her—mostly dark brown eyes, but two had deep blue irises. The largest had light gray eyes the color of old quarters. Kendra could not determine the gender of the faces. Forced to guess, she would have gone with female, but without any certainty.

The Fairy Queen had once warned Kendra that before approaching a shrine, she should search her feelings to check if her presence would be acceptable. Aside from the creepiness of the staring astrids, she felt calm and confident. And she had a genuine need, not only to find the directions to the Dragon Temple that Patton had left, but hopefully to get some additional advice. With no sixth sense warning her away, she boosted herself onto the ledge and looked to the far side where water bubbled up out of the rocks. The water trickled into a shallow pool, hardly more than a puddle, before drizzling off the ledge. Near the spring stood a tiny white statuette of a fairy beside a golden bowl.

Where could Patton have left the directions? At first glance she observed no sign of a message. How might he have conveyed the information? It was almost certainly written in the secret fairy language. He might have jotted it on paper and stored it in a container. Or chiseled it onto a rock.

Kendra glanced at the miniature statue. The thought of petitioning the Fairy Queen suddenly made her shy. The astrids had a point—the last time she had solicited help from the Fairy Queen, it had led to the destruction of the shrine at Fablehaven. She worried the Queen might be resentful.

But this was no time to be bashful. At best, Seth and the others had been captured. At worst, they were dead. Navarog lurked outside the gates of Wyrmroost. Or perhaps inside by now. She could not let him get the key. The Sphinx had too many artifacts already. Kendra needed help. Surely the Fairy Queen would appreciate the severity of the situation.

Kendra knelt beside the tiny statue. "I need help," she whispered.

The air stirred. A cool breeze ruffled her hair, smelling as though it had passed over snowy slopes to reach her. The refreshing scent intensified, then became richer and more varied. Kendra smelled pine sap, wildflowers, decaying wood, honeycombs. She inhaled the earthy aroma of a cave and the salty tang of the sea.

Kendra Sorenson. The words entered her mind almost as if they had been spoken aloud. A distinct feeling of comfort accompanied the thought.

"I hear you," Kendra whispered. "Thanks for saving me when I was peering into the Oculus."

A risky endeavor. Not only can your mind drown amid the flood of stimulation, but as you peer through the Oculus, you leave yourself vulnerable to be observed by others, as I saw you.

"I never wanted to use it," Kendra said earnestly. "The Sphinx made me."

A dangerous man.

"Did you see him when he used the Oculus?"

Yes. His mind was temporarily open to my scrutiny.

"What did you learn? Did you find a weakness?"

I was surprised to discover that he is a man, not a creature in disguise.

"How could he be so old?"

Magical tampering, how else? I could not identify the exact means. But I saw that he truly believes his cause is just.

"Freeing demons? Is he nuts?"

Misguided. He knows that no prison can stand forever. He fears that one day, others less capable than himself will release the demons and fail to bridle their power. He trusts himself to do it right, to hold their ferocity in check. But his motives are impure. In connection with his other motivations, he craves the power. He thinks he can bend the demons to his will, but he is mistaken. The world will pay if he breaches Zzyzx.

"What else did you see about him?" Kendra asked, fascinated.

Little else. With more time I could have learned much. Someone helped him awaken from his trance, as I helped you. Not someone near him. One who reached him from afar. I could not sense who roused him. As soon as the Sphinx released the Oculus, my link to him was sundered.

Kendra wondered who might have helped the Sphinx awaken. No candidates came to mind. Her thoughts turned to her present situation. "I need help. Navarog is trying to get the key to a vault in Australia that holds part of the key to Zzyzx. The vault key is inside the Dragon Temple here at Wyrmroost. We're trying to get it before our enemies have a chance, but a bunch of griffins nabbed Seth, Trask, Tanu, Mara, Dougan, and Gavin. Warren is with me but he's badly injured. A dragon named Raxtus is helping us."

I understand your need. Beholding the Sphinx's ambitions helped illustrate the gravity of this predicament. Sadly, I am nearly blind at Wyrmroost. Very few fairies dwell there, most of them reclusive and sullen. I did not know you were at the sanctuary until you approached my shrine.

"What about the astrids? Maybe they could help."

Rage washed over Kendra. She felt angry and hurt, the bitter residue of an unforgivable insult. It took her a moment to realize the furious emotion was not her own. It emanated from the Queen.

I have no interest in their manner of aid. You would do well to ignore them.

Kendra struggled to separate herself from the wrathful emotions conveyed by the Queen. She wanted to punch somebody. "How long ago did they mess up?"

Eons ago. Their failure did irreparable damage. Time has not dulled my agony. The consequences of their negligence were permanent, and so shall be their exile.

"But after all this time they keep serving you. What about forgiveness?"

The hot fury ebbed, replaced by a cooler, more cerebral emotion.

Your desire to extend mercy is a tender product of your innocence. You cannot conceive of all that was lost. The tragedy was so painfully preventable.

"Did they betray you on purpose? Was it deliberate?"

No. Careless. Weak. Devastating. But not premeditated.

"Weren't they some of your best servants?"

My elite champions. My most able agents. Pride blinded them to their vulnerabilities. A small amount of caution would have prevented the disaster.

"I bet they've learned that lesson."

Not all have remained loyal.

"Don't forgive those six, then."

A cold, suspicious emotion took hold of Kendra.

You speak out of self-interest. You are desperate for any aid, even theirs.

"I'm desperate for aid because I'm trying to save the world. Not because I'm selfish."

The emotion warmed into weary indifference.

My astrids would not be the servants they once were. I stripped them of their power. They are hardly shadows of their former selves.

"You could give it back."

No, I cannot. Their energy now resides elsewhere.

Kendra tried to gather her thoughts. She had run out of words. It seemed stupid to let a grudge persist for eons. She fought with Seth all the time, but they were smart enough to make up afterwards, and they were only kids.

When at my shrines, you need not speak for me to hear. You have expressed yourself eloquently on behalf of the astrids, and, despite my potent emotions to the contrary, I deem it sound counsel. Unpleasant, infuriating, but sound. My people have not been able to communicate with the astrids since the King was taken. I will remove that barrier.

"Raxtus could hear them."

Correct. Raxtus is not formally a member of my kingdom, although he was my ward for a time, and I regard him as a friend. Perhaps he can aid you here at Wyrmroost. The dragon has more strength than he realizes.

"Can the astrids help me too?"

Spells and treaties prevent all but dragons and mortals from entering the Dragon Temple. Furthermore, in my astrids' present state, the help they can lend you will be limited. You must arrange any assistance from them on your own. I remain unready to contact them directly. The barrier between myself and the astrids will endure.

"Is there any other help you can give me?"

You seek the location of the Dragon Temple. Patton inscribed instructions on a stone tablet and threw it into my pool. But I can show you better. The temple is not far. Climb down from here toward the east, and then continue toward the tallest pinnacle to the northeast.

For a moment, everything went black, although Kendra's eyes remained open. Then a vision unfolded. She soared down a slope away from the shrine, then curved toward a vertical finger of rock. The vision dissipated into mist, and her regular sight returned.

"I see where to go."

Drink from the spring.

Kendra intuited that the Fairy Queen meant for her to use the golden bowl. She collected water from the bubbling fountainhead until the bowl was halfway full. Lifting the cold metal to her lips, she drank. The fresh water was flavored by minerals and had a slight metallic tang. But then the fluid tasted like citrus juice, and honey, and saltwater, and grape juice, and milk, and raw eggs, and apple juice, and cream of wheat, and carrot juice—all those flavors at once but somehow separate and distinct.

Now my astrids will hear your mind, and you will hear their thoughts in return. But they will not hear mine. Go in peace, Kendra.

Warm feelings buoyed Kendra better than a physical hug. "Thank you."

Kendra stood and turned. The astrids perched on the brink of the ledge, regarding her solemnly. Raxtus waited farther down the slope. Stepping between the astrids, Kendra hopped off the ledge, then swiveled to face them.

"How do I talk to you?"

That will suffice. Multiple voices responded together in her mind, the same way she heard the Fairy Queen. *Thank you for advocating our cause. We have waited so long for some acknowledgment from our Queen.*

"Happy to do it," Kendra said. "Did you hear about my problem?"

We could hear you, but not the Queen.

"Do you always speak in unison?"

We are a cadre of twelve. We have shared our minds for so long that it requires little effort to think as one.

Their telepathic voices were different from the Queen's. No emotions accompanied the words, and the tone came across more grim and masculine even without Kendra's physically hearing anything. Now that Kendra could perceive their inner voices, she decided the smooth faces must be male after all.

"You can think on your own as well, though."

We can do what we will.

"I need your help."

We are indebted to you, but we cannot enter the Dragon Temple. Raxtus could, in theory.

"But he's a dragon. We shouldn't tell him I mean to go there."

He hears our thoughts. He already knows.

Kendra turned and looked down the slope at the gleaming dragon.

He says not to be afraid.

"Why can't I hear his mind?"

Who can say? He can't hear yours, either.

Kendra bit her lower lip. "Can't you do anything to help me?"

You will have what support we can lend.

"Thanks." The twelve somber faces were unsettling. Did she even want eerie mutant owls as allies?

We are not all we once were.

"I'm sorry," Kendra blurted. "I didn't mean to think ungrateful thoughts."

We understand.

Kendra turned and hustled back toward Raxtus, regretting that the owls could read her mind, and feeling embarrassed that they could perceive those regrets. She heard wings flapping, and glanced back to see several astrids flying away in different directions.

"You mean to enter the Dragon Temple," Raxtus said. "I should have known you were up to something terrible. That's how my luck goes. Kendra, if I fail to stop you or at least report your intentions, I become an accomplice and could be killed for treason."

"I'm only trying to recover something a friend hid there," Kendra explained. "I have no other motives."

"The astrids told me telepathically. They can hear your mind now. I trust them, and I trust you. You must be an incredible person to be fairykind. You're very personable. I'm sure you and your friends really need this key. However, no other dragon will care about your motives. The Dragon Temple isn't casually off-limits—access is strictly forbidden. Don't fret, I won't turn you in. But I would love to talk you out of it."

"I have to try," Kendra insisted.

"Alone? Have you any idea the obstacles you would have to overcome to reach the treasure vault? Three invincible guardians block the way."

"Do you know any tricks to get by them?"

Raxtus laughed nervously. "Nobody knows anything about the guardians. Except there's a widespread rumor that the first is a hydra. Which is almost worse than not knowing. How could you possibly hope to get past a hydra?"

"What's a hydra?"

Raxtus lowered his head and closed his eyes. "You don't even know? Kendra, you have no business going up against these kinds of creatures alone. Even with your whole team, going into the Dragon Temple will be a one-way trip. Just leave the key in the treasury. Let your enemies die trying to get it."

"The Sphinx has Navarog on his side, and he knows the key is here. If I do nothing, the Sphinx is sure to claim the key."

"Navarog is bad news," Raxtus conceded.

"The owls relayed our dilemma to you?"

"The basics, yeah."

"What if you help me? This isn't just for me or my friends. We're trying to save the world from a man who wants to unleash a horde of demons."

The dragon turned away. "Honestly, you're nice, and your reasons sound legitimate, but you don't understand me. I tried to explain what a coward I am. I wasn't being modest. And I'm not only afraid of us dying. It would be so illegal for me to venture into the Dragon Temple. It would be a betrayal of my whole species." He swung his head back around to gaze into her eyes. "I may be pathetic, but I've never lost my honor. My involvement in this would end poorly. On top of losing my honor, I would be useless to you. It would be a disaster."

"The Fairy Queen said you have more strength than you realize."

He perked up. "Really? She said that?"

"Her words."

"Well, that's encouraging. Although, she's basically my fairy godmother. An endorsement from a parental relative is nice, but hard to put on a résumé. Look, I'll pretend I never heard where you were going. I'm pretty good at deluding myself. But don't ask me to join you. I just can't go into the Dragon Temple. Life is short enough without chasing certain doom. Kendra, you seem determined, I can read it on your face. If you insist on going through with this, I won't stop you, but my involvement will have to end. I've already shamed my dad by what I am. I can't risk shaming him further by what I do."

"Will you at least carry me to the entrance?"

"I'll carry you to a spot *near* the entrance. None of the other dragons pay attention to me, and I can be fairly stealthy, so I'm not too worried about getting identified near the temple. But then I'll have to take off."

"I understand," Kendra said. She tried to keep her voice even. She had asked Raxtus to risk death and humiliation, and he had denied her. Could she really blame him? At least he would provide a lift to her destination. He had already been more help than she had any right to expect. Even so, she felt disappointed. "You never explained about hydras."

"Right. Sorry. I'm always wandering off onto tangents. Picture a really big, mean dragon with lots of heads. If you chop one off, two grow back. Hydras technically aren't dragons. They don't work magic or have breath weapons. They're famously hard to kill. I can't guarantee the first guardian is a hydra, but that is the rumor. I have no clue about the other guardians."

How was she supposed to get by a hydra? Let alone the other guardians. She was alone. Raxtus was right. Going to the Dragon Temple would be suicide. Inside the knapsack, Warren had the unicorn horn. Should she ask Raxtus to take her to the main gate of Wyrmroost? Navarog might be there, but maybe she could hide in the knapsack and have Raxtus turn invisible. They might be able to slip away.

It would mean deserting her team and abandoning their quest. Seth would never run away. Would any of the others abandon her? No, she could at least investigate the Dragon Temple and the first guardian before utterly forsaking the mission. She owed everybody that much.

"I'm ready," Kendra said. "Should we go?"

"Should we? No way. But I'm willing to take you."

Raxtus grabbed her with one of his front claws and soared into the air. This time he performed no fancy tricks. He turned invisible and flew low to the ground, staying near cover whenever possible. Kendra saw the finger of stone approaching just like in the vision the Fairy Queen had shown her. When they landed in a grove of tall pines, Raxtus set Kendra on her feet. The dragon remained invisible.

"It's getting late," the dragon murmured. "Why not sleep on it?"

"If I'm doing it, now is as good as tomorrow."

"You're the boss. You're so dead, though. No offense, but you really are. I mean, I could almost cry. Anyhow, just go down this slope, walk around the nearest bluff, and you'll see the entrance. Can't miss it."

"Is it hard to get inside?"

"No doors. You just stroll in. I have no idea how far in the first guardian will be situated. Careful, getting out may not be as simple as entering. These types of places tend to be designed that way."

Kendra nodded. She had received similar advice back when she had ventured into the vault containing the Sands of Sanctity at Fablehaven. The reminder sort of wrecked her idea of tentatively peeking at the first guardian. She would have to consult Warren.

"Thanks, Raxtus. I appreciate your help. I better go talk to Warren about our next move."

"I hope he talks you out of this. Tell him I'm sorry about the beard. Be careful. Nice to meet you."

The air stirred as he beat his invisible wings.

And then she was alone.

Kendra sat down. Did she really want to go down and talk to Warren? He would tell her to wait to enter the temple until he was healthier. Would he be wrong? They could hole up in the knapsack for a few days—even weeks, if necessary. They had plenty of food. The main drawback would be the risk of Navarog catching up.

She stretched out on her back and stared up at limbs bristling with green needles. The trees provided good cover. The air was cool but not frigid. Her mind wandered. She vaguely hoped a brilliant idea would occur. Inspiration refused to strike.

Eventually she sat up. She should find a place to stash the knapsack while she talked with Warren. Was it good enough to set it beside a tree? What if some creature came along? Maybe she could dig a shallow hole. Or at least cover the knapsack with some branches. Maybe she could stow it on a tree branch. If so, would she still be able to climb inside?

Kendra wandered the grove looking for an ideal spot. Nothing jumped out at her. Most of the trees lacked low branches. The ground had no usable irregularities, and it was too hard for digging.

Fluttering wings caused her to turn and crouch beside

a tree. She fumbled with the flap of the knapsack, hoping to hide before she was spotted, but relaxed when an astrid glided into view. The golden owl perched on a branch above her.

Your friends are with Thronis.

"My brother?"

They are alive and well. Apparently the giant plans to help them.

She felt hope awaken inside her. "How did you learn this?"

Two of us flew into the mansion and spied.

"I thought Thronis was protected by spells."

Astrids have been ignored for centuries. The sky giant has warding spells against dragons and other perceived threats. We are beneath his notice.

"Then I should just sit tight?"

We will continue to scout for you. If you go into the hidden room, I can transport the bag somewhere safe.

Kendra began to weep with relief. The astrids could help her hide the knapsack, her brother and friends were alive, and she might not have to face the Dragon Temple alone. Deep down, she had been quietly resigning herself to the fact that she would have to retrieve the key on her own. Her problems remained far from solved, but at least she no longer felt entirely hopeless.

CHAPTER TWENTY-FOUR

Temple

S eth had never seen so many dragonflies. Ranging from the length of his pinky to half the length of his forearm, the streamlined insects hovered and darted above the reedy pools near the entrance to the Dragon Temple. One landed on his arm. He glanced down at the compound eyes, the transparent wings, and the slim, multihued body. After a moment, the dragonfly took flight, joining the swarms.

Had he not drunk powdered milk from Fablehaven that morning, Seth might have suspected the insects were magical creatures in disguise. But these were the real thing, shimmering in every color of the rainbow. Until now, he had never made a connection between dragons and dragonflies.

The yawning entrance to the Dragon Temple loomed before him. The temple was basically a natural ravine covered by an arched stone roof. Matching granite dragons nearly the size of Thronis flanked the mouth of the gloomy gorge, fierce jaws agape.

Seth caught sight of a griffin skimming over some distant treetops. After covertly dropping them off beneath a stand of pines, the griffins had flown off to continue the search for Kendra. Earlier that morning, Mara had found tracks in the gorge where Kendra had fallen the day before. Those tracks went a long way up the gorge until they tangled with the tracks of a very young dragon. Fortunately, there had been no blood or other evidence of a struggle. Mara had identified more of Kendra's tracks near the Fairy Queen's shrine, once again converging with dragon markings. From there, the trail went cold.

As unlikely as it sounded, Mara's best guess had been that the dragon was transporting Kendra. Trask agreed. Since Kendra had already visited the Fairy Queen's shrine, she presumably knew where to find the Dragon Temple. But at the entrance to the Dragon Temple, they had discovered no further traces of Kendra or a young dragon. Could she have braved the temple alone? Maybe the dragon had learned where Kendra was heading and turned on her. Trask, Mara, and the others had all fanned out to search the vicinity, leaving Seth near the entrance with their gear.

"I've got her!" Gavin called.

Seth spied Gavin scrambling down the scree beside the bluff to the right of the entrance, causing little rockslides as he went. Kendra followed behind, picking her way more carefully, the knapsack over one shoulder. Seth checked the sky, relieved to see no dragons. While searching for Kendra, they had been exposed. If a dragon spotted them this close to the Dragon Temple, their adventure would end before it began.

While waiting for Gavin and his sister to reach him, Seth considered the immense temple. What kind of creatures raised a roof over a canyon and called it home? With an entrance that big, and such vast space inside, who knew what might await them? The stone dragons out front seemed like a not-so-subtle hint.

"I'm so glad you're all right," Kendra said as she approached Seth.

"We lucked out," Seth admitted. "Thronis wants some stuff from the treasure room."

"We're not going to steal for him," Kendra said, turning to check with Gavin.

Gavin fingered the silver chain around his neck. "If we d-d-d-don't, these will strangle us."

Kendra glanced at Seth. "You all have one?"

Seth shrugged. "It was the only way to avoid getting baked in a pie. Seriously."

"The dragons won't like it," Kendra warned.

"At least the dragons will have to catch us to kill us," Seth reasoned. "Thronis had us for sure."

"Makes sense," Kendra allowed.

Seth studied Kendra. "While we were following your tracks, they said it looked like you were with a dragon."

"I made friends with a small dragon named Raxtus. Small for a dragon, I mean. He was fully grown. He refused to take part in anything related to entering the Dragon Temple. But he dropped me off nearby and wished me good luck."

Gavin frowned. "Let's hope he doesn't repeat what he knows to less friendly ears."

"I think he'll keep quiet," Kendra said. "I haven't seen Raxtus since yesterday, and no dragons have flocked to bar access to the temple."

Trask jogged over to them. "Kendra, good to see you. Is Warren well?"

"He's hanging in there."

Trask ran a hand over his bald scalp. "I'm sorry to say, but you'll probably want to enter the temple with us."

"I was planning on it," Kendra assured him.

Trask nodded. "We have no idea what wards protect the temple, but we could easily trip magical safeguards or alarms simply by entering. If word of our intrusion gets out, it will likely be safer inside than out here. I prefer we stay together."

Mara approached. Dougan and Tanu could be seen returning as well, trotting doggedly toward them.

Kendra looked down at some of the gear piled near Seth.

"Big enough sword?" she asked, raising her eyebrows.

The sword in question had a thick blade at least eight feet long. Beside it lay an assortment of other armaments.

"Weapons from Thronis," Seth explained. "The huge sword is edged with adamant. The spears are tipped with adamant. Some of the smaller blades have adamant edges as well. They're all too small for him to use, so he was willing to risk them. But he wants them back if we survive."

"Now all we need is somebody who can lift the sword," Kendra joked.

"Between Agad and Thronis," Seth said, "Tanu managed to gather ingredients to make two of his giant potions. You know, like the one he used at Fablehaven to fight the resurrecting cat."

"The sword is too small for Thronis," Trask said. "But just right for me if I were a little bigger."

Seth hefted a coarse brown sack. "We have three of these. Each contains a dose of dragonsbane, the only poison that works on dragons."

"Does it work on hydras?" Kendra wondered.

"Why hydras?" Seth asked suspiciously.

"The dragon I met heard a rumor that the first guardian is a hydra."

"Thronis came across the same story," Seth said. "He thinks dragonsbane would work on a hydra, and so does Tanu, but neither of them is certain."

Kendra lightly kicked one of the sacks with her toe. "How do we get dragons to eat it?"

"One way is to hang onto a sack if one of us gets gobbled up," Seth said.

"Cheerful thought," Kendra muttered. "Do we know whether any of the guardians are dragons?"

"Pretty safe bet," Trask said. "Dragons have access to dragons, and no guardian would be more formidable."

"Except maybe a hydra," Seth chimed in.

"Whatever happens in there," Trask said, "if we get into

serious trouble, you and Seth are to duck inside the knapsack and Mendigo will try to escape with you."

"Where is Mendigo?" Kendra asked.

"Scouting," Seth replied. "He got busted up when he jumped off that cliff with you, but Thronis repaired him. He's good as new."

"Together we have a wide array of expertise and abilities," Trask said. "We'll find a way to get past these guardians and get out with the key."

"Afterwards you have to take some treasure back to Thronis?" Kendra said.

"His griffins will meet us at a rendezvous point," Seth said. "It should be smooth sailing if we can survive the temple."

"Except that Navarog might be waiting at the main gate," Kendra reminded him.

"Right," Seth said pensively. "Well, hopefully we'll have some dragonsbane left over."

Tanu reached them, panting lightly. Dougan arrived a moment later.

"You guys are all warmed up," Seth said. "I hear a brisk jog is just the thing before fighting dragons. Should we do some stretching?"

"We about ready to go inside?" Tanu asked, ignoring Seth's comments.

Trask gave a nod.

Tanu rummaged in his satchel. "Time for me to earn my keep." He pulled out a bunch of small plastic cylinders capped by little rubber stoppers. "These are the closest I could come to creating dragon insurance. For three hours after swallowing a dose, we'll be fire resistant and have some protection against electricity. There is also some liquid emotion in the mix, a jolt of courage to help against dragon terror. I have a second dose for each of us in case three hours isn't enough."

"Fire *resistant?*" Seth asked. "How about fire*proof?*"

Tanu shook his head. "Against dragon fire, resistant is the best I can claim."

"Fire is the most common draconic breath weapon," Gavin said. "But the guardians of the Dragon Temple may not be very common."

"Protection against fire is better than nothing," Trask said, accepting a cylinder, uncapping it, and downing the contents. The others followed suit. Seth found that the clear liquid tasted sugary at first, then spicy hot, then cool and tangy.

"Anything else?" Seth asked.

"A gaseous potion for each of us," Tanu said. "As a last resort, chug it and try to drift away. Use it wisely. As a gas, you'll move slowly, and a direct blast of dragon fire would probably sear you into nothing." Tanu handed a small bottle to each of them.

"You have the smoke grenades?" Trask asked.

"I was getting to them." Tanu pulled out small glass bulbs full of purple fluid. "This liquid turns to smoke when exposed to air. The vapors will smell nasty to us but much worse to creatures with more highly developed olfactory senses. Like dragons, for example. The fumes should basically blind their noses. Trask and I will take charge of these grenades."

"Call back Mendigo," Trask prompted Seth.

"Mendigo!" Seth cried. "Return to us!"

"I can turn two of us into giants," Tanu said, holding up a pair of crystal vials. "I vote for Trask and Dougan, our two most tested fighters. Any objections?"

"Makes sense to me," Gavin agreed.

Trask nodded and accepted a vial. Dougan claimed the other. "Let's get ready to move out," Trask said. He picked up his heavy crossbow and a large oval shield that covered more than half of his body.

"Mendigo, take the big sword," Seth ordered as the man-sized puppet joined them.

Mendgio picked it up, staggering for a moment before balancing the preposterous weapon against his wooden shoulder. Tanu pulled on a heavy shirt of overlapping metal rings and strapped on a sword. Dougan seized his battle-ax. Gavin and Mara each lifted a spear. Seth buckled a sword around his waist and claimed a crossbow. He handed Kendra a sizable knife in a sheath.

"What am I supposed to do with this?" Kendra asked, pulling the knife out.

"Stab," Seth suggested.

Kendra sheathed the knife and opened the knapsack. "We're going in," she called down.

"Good luck," Warren responded from below, his voice hoarse.

"If we see a dragon, let me try to talk first," Gavin advised. "I may be able to negotiate or trick it. If nothing else, I should be able to calm it."

"You'll get your chance to talk," Trask said. "Meanwhile, I'll be aiming."

As they marched toward the entrance and the stone dragons, Seth drew his sword. The weight felt comforting in his hand. He envisioned himself slashing a dragon across the snout.

Walking beside him, Kendra leaned over. "We should stay close in case of dragons."

"Right." He had almost let himself forget how Nafia had muddled his mind. He supposed he could cling to Kendra with one hand and wield the sword with the other.

They passed between the granite dragons and into the shadow of the high, arched roof. Several dragonflies flitted through the air. Nothing decorated the ground or the walls but the natural stone and dirt of the ravine. Trask led the way, crossbow held ready. Next came Gavin and Tanu. Mendigo strolled beside Kendra and Seth. Dougan and Mara had the rear.

Up ahead, the ravine curved. Just prior to the curve, the ground fell away almost vertically for roughly thirty feet. The precipice stretched from one wall of the ravine to the other.

"Rope," Trask said.

Gavin disappeared into the knapsack.

Edging forward, Seth peered over the brink. The smooth slope was not quite ninety degrees, but it might have been eighty.

Gavin emerged from the knapsack with a sturdy length of knotted rope. Dougan fastened one end around a tall boulder and tossed the coil off the edge. The rope reached the base of the slope with several feet to spare.

Slinging his crossbow over his shoulder, Trask picked up the rope. "If you lean away from the wall," he instructed Seth and Kendra in a low voice, "you can walk down. Or if you prefer, you can descend from knot to knot with your hands and feet."

Leaning away from the precipice, trusting the rope, Trask began walking backward. Keeping his body perpendicular to the slope, step by step, hand over hand, he walked confidently to the ground. Gavin hurried down next in similar fashion, followed by Tanu.

Copying their technique, Seth grabbed the rope and leaned out over the drop. Part of him wanted to embrace the rope and descend knot to knot, but once he started walking backwards, he could feel how his grip on the rope kept his feet planted against the slope, and realized that this way was superior.

When Seth reached the bottom, he glanced over at Gavin, eying the silver chain around his neck. It would be a shame to let such a remarkable object go to waste.

Seth pulled Gavin aside. "Level with me. Are you interested in my sister?"

"I'm not sure this is the t-t-time to get into that," Gavin responded, eyes straying to the top of the steep slope.

Seth fingered his own silver collar. "Seems like the perfect time."

"Since when are you a matchmaker?"

"I'm just curious."

Gavin flushed a little. "If you must know, yes, I am very interested in Kendra. I can't wait to see where our relationship goes."

"I thought so," Seth replied smugly. "For the record, I think she likes you, too."

Growing redder, Gavin started distancing himself. "She'll come down any minute. We can talk more later."

Seth looked up, waiting for Kendra. Mendigo descended one-handed, clutching the enormous sword in the other, releasing and grabbing the rope at such a pace that he was practically running backwards. Mara came down next with the knapsack. While Dougan worked his way down, Kendra emerged from the knapsack.

"You cheated," Seth whispered.

"Dragons and hydras are stressful enough," she replied.

"I think somebody has a crush on you," Seth mentioned casually.

Kendra's eyes widened. "You didn't say anything to him?"

Seth shrugged. "He didn't get strangled. I think he's got it bad."

Kendra grabbed Seth's arm tightly. Was there a flicker of excitement in her gaze? It took her a moment to find words. "Don't talk to boys about me. Ever. For any reason."

"I was just trying to ease your stress."

Her grip tightened more. "I sort of appreciate the intention, but it does not make me less stressed."

"You should just kiss him and get it over with."

Kendra released him in disgust. Seth suppressed a laugh.

As they came around the first significant bend in the ravine, the daylight from the entrance grew dim. Glowing white stones set in the walls and distant ceiling provided sufficient illumination to see, although the uneven radiance left the cavernous room cloaked in pockets of shadow.

Ahead of them, a lake covered the floor of the ravine, the light from the luminous stones reflecting off the dark, glassy surface. Shaped like a trapezoid, the far side of the lake was much narrower than the near side. Just beyond the lake, the ravine tapered to a tall, narrow passage not unlike the Sidestep Cleft. A ledge running for hundreds of yards along the left wall of the ravine provided the only route around the lake.

"I don't like it," Trask murmured. "We're going to get ambushed. We'll be trapped on that ledge over the water with no way to maneuver."

"We should cross the lake in groups of two," Dougan recommended. "That way at least we can cover one another."

"And avoid getting everyone wiped out by a single blast of dragon breath," Trask agreed. "Okay, me and Gavin first. Then Mara and Seth. Then Kendra and Tanu. Then Mendigo and Dougan."

Seth wrung his fingers as Trask set out along the ledge with Gavin, moving in a low crouch, treading lightly and quickly.

"Keep that crossbow handy," Dougan murmured in

Seth's ear. Nodding, Seth unslung his crossbow and made sure it was ready to fire.

When Trask waved his crossbow over his head at the far side of the lake, Mara and Seth set out. They descended near to the water to boost themselves onto the ledge. The stone shelf angled upward, so they were soon a good ten or fifteen feet above the dark and silent lake. In places, the ledge narrowed to only a few feet wide, but most of the way falling was not a concern. They moved swiftly, trying to step lightly. Seth winced whenever dirt or pebbles crunched grittily underfoot.

The last section of the ledge descended like a ramp to deposit them at the far side of the lake. When they arrived, Trask signaled with his crossbow again and Kendra started across with Tanu. Seth watched the murky lake and listened, but detected nothing threatening.

Finally Dougan and Mendigo started across at a brisk pace. Seth and the others had backed away toward the narrow passage that led deeper into the roofed ravine. Trask remained nearer to the water, a pair of adamant-tipped quarrels ready in his oversized crossbow.

Seth began to relax as soon as Dougan and Mendigo reached the near shore. And then shrieking heads came boiling up out of the water.

With water raining down on them, Dougan and Mendigo broke into a run. Fumbling the giant sword, the limberjack dragged the tip behind him, the metal scraping and clanging against rocks. Unflinching, Trask took a step closer to the lake, aiming his crossbow. Tanu shepherded Kendra, Seth, and Mara deeper into the passage. Gavin dashed toward the lake, waving one arm, shaking his spear, and screeching the dragon language.

As the dark green hydra scooted its bulky body onto the shore, Seth gawked in amazement. The massive creature had no fewer than fifteen heads swaying at the end of as many serpentine necks. Three shorter necks ended in charred stumps. The draconic heads were roughly the size of coffins, varying somewhat one from another in size and shape. Several bore scars.

As Gavin continued to wave his arm and shriek, all the heads gradually fixated on him, malevolent eyes glittering. Breathing heavily, Dougan reached Seth and the others at the mouth of the narrow passage. Mendigo arrived behind him.

"We don't care who you are," the heads spat together, harsh voices ringing in unison. "All who enter this temple must die."

"We're not after the g-g-g-gauntlets," Gavin called, switching to English. Seth wondered if Gavin also stuttered when speaking the dragon tongue.

"You think we care what you're after?" the heads cried. "We have killed since the dawn of time, and we shall kill well into the dusk."

The hydra looked old to Seth. Compared to Nafia, the heads and necks seemed wasted, more skeletal. One was missing an eye. Another lacked a lower jaw. One head dangled listlessly at the end of its neck, either dead or unconscious. Missing patches of scales left bare spots on the scarred necks. Lank scarves of scum glistened wetly.

"You call yourself a killer?" Gavin taunted. "I name you a slave! A broken-down old watchdog!"

The heads screamed. Seth covered his ears, and even so the wails resounded with tremendous volume. "We are Hespera! We guard sacred treasures!"

"You cower in a muddy pit reeking of slime," Gavin laughed. "Elsewhere in this same sanctuary a younger hydra roams a glorious swamp, hunting fat prey as it pleases!"

"Liar!" the heads snarled together.

"Oh, these dragons really pulled one over on you. Listen to yourselves! So many sad voices singing the same sorry tune." Gavin pointed to one head. "Say something on your own." He gestured to the head missing an eye. "How about you, cyclops?" Gavin shook his head. "Your minds are further gone than your body! Pathetic!"

Two of the heads on the right began to hiss at each other. Another head began to squeal. A head on the left stretched toward Gavin, fangs bared, but he skipped out of reach.

"Silence," demanded a single head toward the center, yellower than the others.

Gavin pointed at the speaker. "That one."

Trask loosed a quarrel at the yellow head, and one of its eyes went dark. The head reared up, jaws opening, and Trask launched a second quarrel into the mouth. Using undersized forelegs and semicircular fins, the hydra scooted farther out of the lake. Trask tossed his crossbow to Gavin, who caught it as he sprinted away from the lake. Several heads lashed toward Trask. Casting aside his shield, he drew a pair of swords, and the blades rang against tooth and scale as he whirled and slashed, moving generally away from the water.

Seth fired his crossbow, but could not tell where the arrow landed. Tanu threw glass bulbs that began to fill the air with smoke. The hydra flopped farther onto the shore. After hacking off part of a tongue, Trask turned and ran. Everyone stampeded deeper into the passage. Behind them the hydra flailed and bellowed. The echoing wails seemed to come from all directions.

"Slow down," Trask panted. "Don't rush, we're out of danger."

"We should stop here," Tanu suggested in a stage whisper. "The passage widens again not much farther on. We could stumble unprepared into an equally deadly foe."

"The creature is too big to reach us here," Trask said, leaning against a wall. "Anyone hurt?"

Nobody responded.

"Could have been worse," Dougan said.

"The hydra isn't there to keep us out," Seth said. "It's there to trap us inside."

"It would appear that way," Trask agreed. "The creature didn't show itself until all of us were past."

"Between the narrow approach and the vulnerable ledge, we'll have a tough exit ahead of us," Gavin lamented, handing Trask back his crossbow.

"What was with the trash talk?" Seth inquired.

"I was trying to get some of the heads out of sync," Gavin said. "I wanted to identify the g-g-governing head. I think we succeeded. Hespera is ancient. Some of those heads looked unwell. Senile or nuts or something. I hoped some might resent their role as guardian. If we could take out the governing head, and incite the others, the monstrosity might end up trying to go ten different directions at once."

"Trask got an eye," Dougan said. "How's that for marksmanship under pressure?"

"We injured the main head," Gavin agreed. "Might have injured it badly. The second quarrel went in the mouth and out the top of her skull."

Trask crouched, winding and reloading his crossbow. "We'll deal with her when the time comes. Those shrieks alerted everything with ears to our presence. We should keep moving. Stay on your toes."

Trask took the lead again. As Tanu had observed, the passage widened until they were advancing along a broad ravine once again. Seth paid attention to his footing on the uneven floor. The sporadic glowing stones left much of the ground in shadow.

"Who have we here?" uttered a slow, deep voice from a cave in the wall of the ravine about thirty yards ahead. The cave mouth had looked like a patch of shadow until Seth saw a huge gray head emerge.

His mind went blank. He couldn't even clearly see the shadowy eyes, but he found himself stupefied, unable to move. Gavin grabbed his hand and placed it into Kendra's, and the sensation passed.

"Weary travelers," Gavin answered.

"I will give you rest," the morose voice answered.

Opening his mouth wide, Gavin shrieked and squealed. The dragon hooted a brief response.

"Glommus!" Gavin cried. "Run! Hold your breath!"

Trask fired both arrows at the head as it came farther from the hole and swung toward them. Stumbling alongside Kendra, Seth heard a mighty whoosh, then felt a fine spray against his skin. A thick mist muted the light from the glowing stones. Gavin appeared at his side, wrestling the knapsack from Kendra and tugging open the flap.

As commanded, Seth had not inhaled. His eyes were itching, and the strength seemed to be draining out of him. He lost hold of Kendra as Gavin tried to stuff her into the knapsack. Seth had never felt so drowsy. Was there something he was supposed to be doing? Was he on the ground? How did he get there? The rocky floor of the ravine felt like a pillow-top mattress. Wasn't he in the middle of something important?

His lungs clenched insistently. He heard another loud whoosh. His eyes felt heavy, his mind drowsy. Was he holding his breath for a reason? Seemed like it was important. He exhaled what remained in his lungs. Some instinct deep inside warned him not to inhale. But if he didn't inhale, wouldn't he suffocate? He risked a small breath, and oblivion swallowed conscious thought.

CHAPTER TWENTY-FIVE

Slayings

K endra thought she heard a fuzzy voice in the distance. The words made no sense, but the speaker sounded insistent. She wished he would go away. She felt so tired.

One word began to register. The speaker kept repeating her name. She began to notice a sharp, piquant smell. Her eyes started watering and the voice became less muddy. Somebody was slapping her gently.

Her eyes opened and she sat up with a jerk. Tanu held her steady. Her sinuses felt raw. Wetness dribbled from her nostrils. She wiped her nose on her sleeve.

Tanu moved a small bottle away from her nose and capped it.

"What's that?" she asked.

"It's like smelling salts," he explained.

Kendra looked around. They were alone, in a dim ravine. She was forgetting something. "The dragon!" she exclaimed.

Tanu shushed her. "It's all right. I killed it."

The last thing Kendra remembered, Gavin had been trying to force her into the knapsack. She had gone limp, lost contact with him, and dreamless sleep had overwhelmed her.

"Where are the others?" Kendra asked.

"Still out cold," Tanu said. "I dragged you well away from the fumes, but even so it took almost twenty minutes to wake you up."

"The dragon drugged us?"

"Some kind of sleeping gas. Potent stuff. I became alerted when Tanu and Seth fell into a deep sleep at the same time in the middle of the day."

"Tanu fell asleep? But you're—"

Tanu was shaking his head. "Vanessa."

Startled, Kendra reflexively scooted away.

Tanu held up his hands innocently. "Be glad I showed up. That dragon would have killed all of you. Where are we?"

Kendra hesitated. "I probably better not say. Just in case. How did you kill the dragon?"

Tanu grinned. "When they sleep, I can sense everyone I've ever bitten. As I mentioned, I was curious about the unusual way Tanu and Seth had suddenly lost consciousness, so I took control of Tanu, studying the situation through half-closed eyes. At first I was merely investigating a hunch, but once I glimpsed how Dougan lay sprawled next to me, I knew that something was truly wrong. Fine mist permeated the air, and I observed a dragon sniffing around. I would never label myself a dragon tamer, but I have stood in the presence of dragons and kept my wits. The fear assailed me, intense and irrational, but the dragon had not noticed me, and I managed to resist. I noticed a sword beside me on the ground. I've always been useful with a blade in my hand. When the great head swung over to sniff at me and Dougan, I sat up and slashed his throat. Imagine my surprise when the blade cut deep, parting his scales as if they were made of cardboard. I've never wielded such a sword!

"My attack caught the dragon completely off guard. When I rose to my feet and cut him with a return stroke, I left the beast nearly decapitated. The dragon reeled away, belching sweet fog and bleeding profusely. He retreated into a gloomy cave and died. I went in after him to verify his demise, and finished parting his head from his body."

"You killed a dragon," Kendra said in awe.

Tanu laughed. It may have been the Samoan's voice, but the laugh belonged to Vanessa. "I suppose I did." It was strange to hear Tanu speaking with Vanessa's inflections. "I may be the sole living dragon slayer. Not that I deserve to brag. That was handed to me. You don't often find the exposed neck of a dragon moving sluggishly overhead. And there I was, with a sharp sword in my hand. It hadn't occurred to the beast that any of us could possibly be conscious. He was carelessly taking his time."

"Should I help you get the others?" Kendra asked.

"No. The sleeping gas still hangs heavy in the air. I'll have to bring them. You can wait here and help wake them." Tanu handed Kendra the tiny bottle that had helped her snap awake. He craned his head back to study the lofty ceiling. "This is no simple dragon lair. Where are we? You place us in greater danger by not telling me."

"On what side of the ravine was the dragon's cave?" Kendra asked.

"That side," Tanu pointed. "Back that way."

The answer helped Kendra orient herself. "There's a hydra back beyond the dragon cave. And somewhere up ahead an unknown guardian awaits."

Tanu scowled. "Is this a Dragon Temple? What have you gotten yourselves into?"

"Long story," Kendra said.

"I'm sure you have your reasons," Tanu muttered. "Look, I'll collect the rest of your team. You'd better put in a good word for me with your grandparents when you get home."

"Is it far to the others?" Kendra asked.

"A good distance. The mist is widely dispersed."

"There's a knapsack. It has a room inside. If you're strong enough to carry people down into the room, it might be faster. Maybe not."

"Thanks for the tip. I'll be back."

Kendra waited alone, trying to muster her courage. They had survived a dragon. Maybe they would actually make it out of the Dragon Temple. Uncapping the small bottle, she tried a little sniff and felt a spicy tingle penetrate her sinuses, triggering tears. The invasive smell left a metallic aftertaste on the roof of her mouth. She was just beginning to wonder what was taking so long when she heard Tanu returning. He dragged Trask over to her and laid him on his back. The knapsack hung from his shoulder.

"Anybody in the sack?" Kendra asked.

"Mara, Gavin, Seth, and Warren," Tanu said.

"Was Warren asleep as well?"

"And badly wounded. I found him crumpled at the bottom of the ladder."

"He was already injured," Kendra said. "He was inside the knapsack when the dragon put us to sleep. He must have tried to climb out and help us."

"When he tried to emerge, the sleep gas knocked him out and he fell," Tanu finished. "Serves him right. Warren was always so cocky. I'm not going to try to lug any of them back up the ladder."

"Right," Kendra said. "I'll climb down to wake them up."

"I'll go back for Dougan. He was too heavy to move into the knapsack. When we're done, I'll relinquish my hold on Tanu and you can wake him as well."

Tanu walked away.

Kendra squatted beside Trask, uncapping the bottle and waving it beneath his nostrils. She recalled how her name had been the first word to register. "Trask," she said. "Trask, wake up. We're in the temple, Trask. You have to get up. Trask. Come on, Trask."

He did not stir. Kendra took another quick whiff from the bottle. Her eyes immediately teared up and her sinuses burned. How could he sleep through that sensation? Wiping away tears, she returned the mouth of the bottle to his nostrils. He showed no reaction. "Trask! Trask, come on, get up. Trask, dragons! Hurry, Trask, wake up!" She prodded his cheek. She pried open an eye only to see it languidly roll back. She shook him. She shouted. Nothing elicited a response.

Kendra continued to speak and shout persistently. When Tanu returned with Dougan, Trask still had not stirred.

"Is there a trick to this?" Kendra asked.

"It took a good twenty minutes to awaken you," Tanu said. "Time away from the fumes must be part of the equation. Once you get Trask awake, I'm sure the others will rouse faster."

"How did you know which potion to use?" Kendra asked. "Can you see Tanu's thoughts?"

Tanu shook his head. "Trial and error. I knew he must have some compound akin to smelling salts."

Kendra put the bottle beneath Trask's nostrils. "Wake up, Trask. Come on, get up, we have dragons to fight. Trask? Trask?" She jostled his shoulder.

"I'll wait to release Tanu until Trask wakes up," Tanu said. "I don't want to leave you here alone."

"Thanks, Vanessa. I really appreciate it."

"Don't forget to put in a good word with your grandparents."

"I will," Kendra promised. "If we ever make it out of here." She returned to trying to rouse Trask.

Kendra had no way to confirm how long it took for Trask

to start awakening. It felt like more than twenty minutes. At last he began to hum and moan as she shook him. Not long after that his eyes opened. With her hand on his shoulder, she felt him tense up.

"What happened?" he asked.

Kendra explained. By the time she was done, Trask was on his feet.

"Vanessa Santoro," he said grudgingly, shaking hands with Tanu. "We're indebted."

"Believe it or not, I'm actually on your side these days," Tanu replied. "Now that you're awake, Lieutenant, I'd best return your potion master to you. I'll be watching. If you should fall asleep unnaturally again, I'll be back." Tanu reclined on the ground. "You should have good luck awakening those in the knapsack by now. Save me and Dougan for last. 'Bye, Kendra."

"'Bye."

Tanu closed his eyes and his body slackened into a deep sleep.

Trask stood guard while Kendra descended into the storage room. It took only a few minutes to awaken Seth. Gavin and Mara woke even faster, and Warren sat up on his own. It turned out the fall had broken both bones in his forearm. The others carefully helped him back to his resting place.

After everyone in the storage room understood what had happened, Kendra led the way up the ladder. Using the pungent scent from the little bottle, she awoke Dougan and finally Tanu. The Samoan had a big grin on his face by the time they finished recapping what had transpired.

"Glommus was an old dragon, and blind," Gavin said. "I had heard of him. His reputation was renowned. He was truly one of a kind. Once I understood who we were facing, I knew we were in trouble. That b-b-breath of his will put anything to sleep—even other dragons!"

"I managed to break a smoke grenade before I went down," Tanu put in.

"Which explains why Glommus had to get so close to smell us," Gavin said. "We really lucked out. Without that narcoblix, we would be dragon food."

"I know Vanessa gets the credit," Tanu said, repressing a grin, "but it's pretty cool to think I took down a dragon. My body, at least."

"Good thing you had one of the adamant-edged swords," Seth observed.

"We're not out of the woods yet," Trask reminded them. "We have another guardian ahead of us, and the hydra behind. We've overcome a major obstacle, but now we have to refocus."

They set about getting their gear in order. Tanu descended into the knapsack to check how Warren was faring and discover what additional attention he might need.

Seth wandered over to Kendra. "So why do you think Vanessa picked Tanu instead of me?"

"Would you have wanted her to pick you?" Kendra asked.

"Well, I would have sort of been a dragon slayer."

"You know, I don't think Vanessa meant it as an insult. She's controlled Tanu before. Plus Tanu is bigger."

Seth looked mopey. "She bit me too."

Kendra rolled her eyes. "Cheer up. You may not have killed dragons, but you've gotten to see dragons. And who knows, you might still get eaten by one!"

"I'm glad I've seen some," he admitted.

Kendra huffed. "Are you really glad? Truly? It freaks me out. We almost died."

"Don't get me wrong. I'm not trying to pretend I wasn't freaked out too. I thought we were doomed. But if dragons weren't freaky, they'd be . . . disappointing."

Kendra patted his shoulder. "Don't worry. There should be plenty of freaky stuff ahead of us. We still might not even survive."

Trask decided their group had been too clustered when Glommus had attacked, so he strung them out more as they resumed their journey. He and Gavin took the lead. Mara and Tanu followed fifty yards back. Then Kendra, Seth, Mendigo, and Dougan stayed back another fifty yards at the rear.

They traveled a long distance, generally sloping upward. The ravine narrowed and widened. It became deeper and shallower. It turned several times.

Kendra scrutinized every shadow, worried about another cave or offshoot containing a hidden dragon. Up ahead, Trask and Gavin searched the walls of the ravine high and low with bright flashlights. Kendra stayed ready for disaster to strike at any step. She knew that any minute Trask and Gavin could be engulfed in a fiery inferno.

She tried to guess what the final guardian might be.

Another dragon? A giant? A huge demon like Bahumat? Some more deadly creature they had never heard of? The possibilities were endless.

When they rounded another corner, steps became visible up ahead. The beige stone stairs reached from one side of the ravine to the other, leading up to a pillared structure. Bronze statues of dragons flanked the top of the steps. The massive building had no front wall, and was plenty large enough to accommodate dragons or giants.

Trask and Gavin waited for the others to catch up just short of the wide stairway. "Looks like we've reached the temple proper," Trask said. "Gavin has volunteered to scout ahead. We're assuming the third guardian awaits us inside."

"He's scouting alone?" Kendra asked.

"I'll follow twenty yards back," Trask said. "I'll keep him covered with my crossbow. Tanu, trail along behind me. The rest of you hang back and await my signal."

Kendra watched Gavin mount the steps and disappear into the gloomy building. Trask was halfway up the steps when Gavin came running back out, waving Trask away. Gavin raced down the stairs two at a time and sprinted toward Kendra. She involuntarily drew back as he came into the light of the nearest glowing stone. His skin had taken on a bluish cast, almost black around the neck and lips. He gazed at her with horribly bloodshot eyes. "The horn," he murmured, collapsing.

"He's poisoned," Seth realized, diving into the knapsack.

Kendra could have hugged her brother for moving so

quickly. Sitting beside Gavin, she took his hand to console him. It felt cold. Black eyelids had hooded his eyes. A buttery discharge leaked from below the closed lids like gooey tears. He began to quiver and twitch. His veins were becoming increasingly visible, black lines beneath his blue, clammy skin.

Tanu knelt beside the knapsack, his head and one arm inside the storage room. She heard him call, "Throw it!" A moment later the Samoan was approaching with the unicorn horn in his fist. He touched the tip of the horn to Gavin's blue-black throat and held it there.

The convulsions stopped instantly. The black veins faded and the blue hues drained from his skin. Gavin coughed and opened his eyes, a sweaty hand closing around the horn. "That was close," he breathed.

"Is he all right?" Trask asked.

"The horn purifies," Tanu said. "If it was poison, he should be fine."

"I'm great," Gavin said, sitting up. "It was p-p-poison. We're in serious trouble."

"What did you see?" Trask asked.

"Not much. I barely glimpsed her. I didn't speak with her. Didn't have time. The poison hit hard and moved fast. But I didn't need a conversation to know who she was. The third guardian is Siletta."

"The poison dragon," Tanu groaned.

Gavin nodded. "She didn't breathe on me or anything. The whole atmosphere in there is tainted."

"I've never heard of a poison dragon," Trask said.

"Many thought she was just a legend," Tanu explained. "Or if not, long dead. Dark potion makers fantasize about her. She is utterly unique."

"Poison to the core," Gavin said. "I once spoke to a dragon who knew her anciently. Her breath, her flesh, her blood, her tears, her excretions, everything is deadly poison. You saw how I looked? That was simply from being in the same room with her. Everyone should touch the horn. Even out here we may be getting exposed."

They all crowded together to place a hand on the horn.

"What do we do?" Tanu asked.

Gavin laughed grimly. "We give up. There is no way past Siletta. I couldn't conceive of a better guardian. Even if you held the horn to protect yourself from the poison in the air, she's still a dragon, with teeth and claws and a majestic aura of terror. She saw me. She's ready for us. Besides, who knows how long the unicorn horn would protect you? All magical items have limitations. Siletta is a living fountainhead of the most potent venoms ever known."

"We're pinned between a hydra and a poison dragon," Dougan muttered.

"We need to figure this out," Trask said. "She could emerge at any moment."

"I'll take care of her," Seth said.

"Don't be ridiculous," Tanu replied.

Seth scowled at the dismissal. "I'm not. I have a plan. I'll need Kendra."

"What do you mean?" Trask asked.

"We won't use the horn just to keep us alive while we

fight Siletta," Seth said. "We'll use the horn to kill Siletta."

"How so?" Kendra asked.

"When Graulas was helping me get the horn, I suspected that he wanted it for himself. But then he told me that his diseases had become so much a part of him that curing them would probably kill him. If this dragon has poison blood and poison flesh, wouldn't the horn kill her?"

"Maybe," Gavin said thoughtfully. "But I doubt the horn contains enough energy to counteract so much poison. Unicorns possess tremendous purity, but we have no unicorn, just an old horn. You'd be pitting the power of a discarded horn against a live dragon."

"We have Kendra," Seth argued. "She's like a battery full of magical energy. If she holds the horn, she'll keep it charged. And of course I'll have to go with her or the dragon terror will freeze her."

The adults exchanged glances.

"It might work," Gavin admitted.

"They're children," Trask objected.

"Children or not," Tanu vouched, "they've done some astounding things."

"Let me take the horn," Gavin volunteered. "It might have enough potency to d-d-defeat the dragon without jeopardizing Kendra."

"No," Kendra said, her voice quavering. "If anyone should use the horn, it should be me. Seth is right. We can't risk the horn running out of energy. We'll only get one shot at this."

"I'll not have children sticking their necks out for me,"

Dougan said. "Neither of them are even supposed to be here. Kendra should be back at the keep, and Seth should be at Fablehaven. We can't risk losing Gavin. We need him as our ambassador to the dragons. If Tanu can bolster me against the dragon terror with a potion, I'll do it."

"Let me take this risk," Mara said. "I'm quick. I'm nimble. And I'm a dragon tamer."

"What about Mendigo?" Tanu proposed. "The puppet won't react to the poison. And he's uncannily agile."

"Mendigo could come with us," Seth said. "You know, as backup. But Kendra has to be there to make sure the horn stays energized. We all know it probably won't have enough power otherwise. And I have to be there for Kendra to be there."

"You just want to kill a dragon," Kendra accused.

Seth fought to stifle a guilty smile. "Maybe a little. But mostly I want to get that key and go home."

"Do you really think you can do this?" Trask asked, eyes flicking back and forth from Seth to Kendra. "The dragon won't sit still and let you touch her. If her poison doesn't take you out, you'll probably be clawed to death or eaten."

"I should carry a bag of dragonsbane," Seth said. "In case she swallows me."

Gavin shook his head. "Siletta is composed of poison. I wouldn't count on dragonsbane to do more than amuse her."

"We can pull this off," Kendra said stoutly. "Mendigo will have orders that if we fail, he's to pick up the horn and hold it against the dragon. This is easily our best chance. Since I want to live, that means I should do this. It needs to be me. It isn't as if Seth and I would be much safer waiting here while somebody else tries to fix the problem. Everything depends on this."

"We won't blow it," Seth promised.

"They make a solid argument," Trask said. "Objections?"

Gavin sighed. "If we mean to keep going forward, it's our best bet."

"If we try to retreat, Siletta may follow," Mara warned.

"They're so young," Dougan protested weakly.

"All right," Trask said. "Do it."

"At the top of the stairs you'll see a tremendous room with pillars throughout," Gavin described. "Use the pillars as obstructions to keep the dragon from leaping at you easily. When you make your move, go in hard and fast. Keep hold of each other."

"I have handcuffs in the knapsack," Tanu said. "Should we cuff them together?"

"Yes," Seth and Kendra answered at the same time.

Tanu climbed down into the storage room. Gavin handed Kendra the unicorn horn. Pulling Mendigo aside, Trask handed the puppet a sword and a flashlight.

"Mendigo," Trask began, "you will enter the temple ahead of Kendra and Seth. Tanu will give you four smoke bulbs. You will smash them in different parts of the room. You will stay in motion, cavorting around the room, but keeping the flashlight on the eyes of the dragon. As needed, you will use the sword to defend Kendra and Seth. Should they get killed or otherwise lose the horn, you will retrieve the horn and hold it against the dragon. Understood?"

Mendigo nodded.

Tanu emerged from the knapsack. "We'll put the horn in Kendra's right hand," Tanu said, cuffing Kendra's right wrist to Seth's left one.

"To avoid being poisoned, you'll both need to keep in constant contact with the horn as well as each other," Gavin said. He adjusted their grip until he was satisfied. Seth ended up holding the horn a little higher than Kendra, with his hand overlapping hers.

"My good hand is free," Seth said. "Should I bring my sword?"

"No," Trask said. "If you get close enough to use a sword, you'll need to be using the horn. But you could bring your crossbow."

Gavin gave Seth the weapon.

"Don't dwell on the crossbow," Dougan cautioned. "The horn is everything."

"Right," Seth agreed.

"Off you go," Trask said.

"Good luck," Tanu added.

"Come on," Seth urged, tugging Kendra forward.

"Settle down," Kendra complained.

Mendigo trotted ahead, reaching the stairs and bounding up them fluidly. Kendra glanced at Seth. "Don't stress," he said with a smile. "No matter how big the dragon is, all we have to do is touch her."

"Before she touches us with her claws or teeth," Kendra amended.

"Right. And we had better hope the horn works quickly."

Kendra's hand felt damp to Seth. Was it his perspiration or hers? Wouldn't that be wonderful if the horn slipped from her grasp? He and his sister would die blue, handcuffed together.

They started up the large steps. The bronze dragons glared down from above. As Kendra and Seth cleared the highest steps, the room came into view. Glowing stones in the walls and ceiling provided dull light. Smoke billowed inside the vast chamber where Mendigo had shattered bulbs. The left and right sides of the room were forests of wide pillars, with a spacious central aisle leading to a distant doorway.

Most of the way across the room, the dragon crouched among the leftmost pillars. Mendigo pranced along a good distance away from Siletta, keeping a bright flashlight trained on the dragon, the beam interrupted at intervals when blocked by columns. Lacking visible scales, Siletta looked like a giant salamander with translucent skin. Networks of dark blue veins tangled with purple and green organs. Large enough to swallow a car, her wide mouth contained multiple rows of slim, pale teeth, sharp and slightly curved.

In a flurry of motion, the dragon scurried toward Mendigo, long body lashing. The puppet danced away from the attack. Only now that Siletta had moved closer to a luminous stone did Kendra notice her incredible length, the elongated body supported by at least ten sets of legs.

Seth led the way to the nearest pillar on the left side of the room.

"I see you two," the dragon hissed in a voice like fierce, overlapping whispers. "Did you send this ludicrous puppet to pester me?"

Kendra shook her head at Seth, warning him not to answer.

"We're here on vacation," Seth yelled. "We're touring the world's weirdest dragons. The puppet is our guide. Do you charge for photos?"

Tugging Kendra forward, Seth ran ahead to another pillar. As they dashed across the open space, Kendra saw the dragon slinking toward them.

"Why aren't you choking?" Siletta asked.

"We're not in the mood," Seth replied. "We were wondering if you could give us directions to a dragon named Glommus. All we could find was a big stupid gray dragon with its head chopped off."

Siletta gave a rattling snarl. A purple fog filled the air. The particles smoked when they touched Kendra's skin. Again, Seth led the way as they ran to the next pillar. Squinting through the purple haze, Kendra could barely make out the dragon crouched only two pillars away.

"What counter spell are you using?" Siletta accused.

Seth peeked around the pillar, raised his crossbow, and fired.

The dragon roared. They could hear her scuttling toward them. Peering around the pillar, Kendra saw that instead of coming straight at them, the dragon was looping around to a neighboring pillar.

Seth and Kendra adjusted to keep their pillar between

themselves and the dragon. "Stop slinking around," Siletta hissed, her voice thick with irritation.

"We'll stop hiding when you stop being poisonous," Seth called. "Seems like you're the one stalling. Come on out so we can get our photo and go home."

They heard Mendigo jingling nearby, then the great head of the dragon came around the side of the pillar not ten feet away. Kendra had heard no hint of Siletta's stealthy approach. Apparently the dragon could move silently when it suited her. The huge mouth opened and a geyser of warm sludge sent them sprawling backwards. Kendra clung desperately to Seth and the horn as they fell. The tarlike substance spat and sizzled, vaporizing off of their skin and clothes. Kendra used her free hand to wipe the sludge away from her eyes as Seth hauled her to her feet.

Sword in hand, Mendigo was hacking at the dragon just behind the head. Twisting and snapping, Siletta trapped the limberjack in her mouth, leaving only the wooden legs hanging out.

Holding the horn out in front of them, Kendra and Seth charged. The mouth opened again, regurgitating more inky liquid. Mendigo flopped out onto the floor, but this time there was not as much pressure behind the foul outpouring. Keeping their footing, Kendra and Seth sloshed forward, the horn outstretched, reaching for the dragon's snout.

As the tip of the horn drew near, Siletta reared away. They charged her, but her long body flexed and twisted away from them. Dozens of squishy, webbed feet backpedaled. Even as the front half of her sinuous body curved out of reach, her tail swung around and whipped Kendra and Seth across the ankles, sweeping their feet out from under them. They hit the floor hard.

"Now I see," Siletta hissed angrily. "Yes, yes, the wicked children brought a nasty thorn to prick me."

Rising together, Kendra and Seth chased the retreating tail. The front of Siletta went behind a fat pillar up ahead and seemed to disappear, her tail the last part of her to vanish. Heedless of the danger, Kendra and Seth raced toward the dragon, coming around the pillar in time to see that Siletta had been climbing the far side. Her head and front legs had already reached the top and started across the ceiling. Leaping forward, Kendra and Seth raised the unicorn horn and pressed it to the end of the dragon's tail just before it rose out of reach.

The tail froze and went rigid. Kendra heard a wet, tearing sound. Looking up, she saw splayed feet peeling away from the wall. The dragon was starting to fall! Breaking contact with the tail, Kendra yanked Seth sideways. They lunged to the other side of the pillar as Siletta slapped heavily to the floor. Coming back around, they found her flapping and flailing. Pouncing toward her rear section, they stabbed the horn against her gummy body.

The writhing stopped. Siletta held very still. The horn grew hot in Kendra's hand. As the dragon began to vibrate, the horn became scorching, but Kendra and Seth kept it firmly in contact with the dragon, even after her legs went limp and her head drooped to the floor. Underneath the translucent skin, the black lines of her veins spread into inky clouds. The strangely visible organs lost their shape and blurred together. Her insides began to boil, and her skin split open, emitting rank plumes of the deepest blues and purples.

Kendra covered her mouth with her free hand and pushed the unicorn horn against the dragon. As Siletta started to shrink and wither, she and Seth adjusted to keep the horn in direct contact. After a few moments, they held the horn against a dry, shriveled husk not a tenth of the dragon's previous size. After Siletta had remained brittle and motionless for a long minute, with no new vapors steaming out of her, Seth said, "I think we're good."

Keeping their hands on the horn, they stepped back. The grotesque dragon husk did not twitch. Kendra looked over her shoulder. Some distance away, a pool of black liquid covered the ground, but she did not see Mendigo.

"Where's our puppet?" Seth asked, voicing her thoughts.

Kendra walked to the black pool, crouched, and dipped the tip of the unicorn horn in the foul fluid. Bubbling and smoking, the tarlike puddle turned to vapor. On the bare floor rested the sword, a flashlight, and numerous small golden hooks.

"What the heck?" Seth exclaimed. "He's gone!"

Kendra considered the evidence. "That black sludge must have dissolved the wood."

Seth picked up a hook, examining it closely. "Not even a splinter left." Tears shimmered in his eyes. "That sort of takes the fun out of everything. Think we could rebuild him?"

"With only hooks left? I guess we can gather them up, just in case."

Maintaining his grip on Kendra and the horn, Seth crawled around the area, meticulously collecting every hook and clasp he could find. Kendra gathered hooks as well. She told herself not to cry, that Mendigo was not a person. The puppet had no identity, no will; he was just a tool. A mindless wooden robot. When he had worked for Muriel, Mendigo had put Kendra and her family in grave danger. But since his loyalties had been altered by fairies, the puppet had saved Kendra's life multiple times. And now he had been destroyed trying to protect them. He may have only been a mechanical servant, but he had been reliable and true. She and Seth would be less safe without him. Kendra found herself wiping moisture off of her cheeks.

"Kendra!" a voice hollered from outside the chamber. "Seth? Are you all right?" It was Tanu.

"Think we got them all?" Kendra asked.

Seth scanned the floor. "Looks like it. We'd better go let them know what happened."

Together they walked to the top of the stairs. Their companions waited not far from the bottom step.

"We killed Siletta," Kendra announced. She and Seth started down the stairs.

The others cheered and shouted congratulations. At the bottom of the steps, she and Seth had to recount all the details. Everyone kept hugging them and clapping them on the back. By the exuberant expressions of relief, Kendra could tell that most of her comrades had doubted that she and her brother would succeed. They were all saddened to hear Mendigo had been disintegrated, but no further tears were shed. Tanu said that the magic animating Mendigo had most likely been in the wood, but that he was no expert on such things, and keeping the hooks couldn't hurt. The Samoan used a key to remove the handcuffs.

"Do you think the horn sanitized the air in there?" Seth asked.

"Touch a unicorn horn to a pond and the whole pond will be purified," Tanu said. "I'm not sure how the horn would affect a gas. The vapors you saw rising from the dragon and the poison pool would be harmless, but the preexisting gasses in the chamber might still have potency."

"We'll take no needless risks," Trask said. "Three of us will proceed to the treasure room, each with a hand on the horn. Kendra should be one, to be certain the horn remains active. She should also be there in case Patton left another message."

"I want to come too," Seth said. "I remember the descriptions of the figurines."

"And I'll come for protection," Trask said.

"I'm going to head back to the hydra," Gavin announced.

Trask shook his head. "We'll face Hespera together once we retrieve the key."

"No, I have a p-p-p-p-plan," Gavin insisted. "Let me borrow Seth's crossbow. I'm going to visit the corpse of Glommus and dip my spear and some quarrels into his vital juices. I may be able to put the hydra to sleep."

"You'll probably just fall asleep yourself when you return to the area where Glommus lies," Tanu cautioned.

"If I do, you guys can wake me," Gavin insisted. "I'm inspired by Kendra and Seth. A small, focused attack has advantages. If I approach the hydra alone, I think I can soothe her and get close enough to prick her. Don't worry, I won't throw my life away. But if I can clear the path for our escape, why not?"

"I'll trust your judgment," Trask said. "You don't want somebody to accompany you?"

"My best chance of getting close is to go in alone," Gavin said. "If I succeed, you'll find me waiting. If I can't pull it off, I'll come back. Or you'll find me unconscious near Glommus. If you don't find me at all, you'll know what happened."

"I don't like this," Kendra said.

"I feel good about it," Gavin replied.

"None of our options are pleasant," Trask said. "Gavin, I think this is worth a try. If you can get close and put the hydra to sleep, we might beat the odds and see daylight again. You're free to go. In case Gavin can't subdue the hydra, the rest of you should make ready to face Hespera and dash to our rendezvous with the griffins. Kendra, Seth, come with me."

CHAPTER TWENTY-SIX

Ambush

The dragons had evidently placed a lot of confidence in their guardians. Beyond the chamber where Kendra and Seth had slain Siletta, a short, spacious hall led to the doorless treasure room. Trask took his time carefully probing and investigating, but detected no traps. With Siletta and Glommus dead, and the hydra pinned back near the entrance, the treasury was left unguarded.

Beyond the giant doorway, the treasury contained three wide aisles bounded by rows of stone tables. An endless variety of items cluttered the tables, ranging from the opulent to the primitive. Elegantly cut gemstones the size of billiard balls rested alongside rough-hewn stone mallets. Walking along one row of tables, Kendra noticed an elaborate pagoda carved from lucent jade, a rusted iron helm, a ten-foot ivory tusk inlaid with gold, a bucket of crude nails, delicate baubles of colored glass, ragged books decorated with arcane glyphs, a rotting leather birdcage, a collection of large lenses inside a compartmentalized wooden trunk, fanciful bronze masks, a tattered cape, a corroded candelabrum, and a pile of copper coins with holes in the center.

Trask, Kendra, and Seth each kept hold of the unicorn horn. Seth towed them across the aisle so he could pick up a gleaming sword.

"Pure adamant," Trask noted reverently.

"Can I keep it?" Seth wondered.

"We should take nothing more than we must," Trask admonished. "We don't want dragons after us to reclaim stolen treasure."

"They'll already be after me for killing Siletta," Seth said.

"We should still avoid causing any extra harm," Trask said. "Combating the guardian dragons was unavoidable. But we don't need to inflame the insult by pillaging their treasure. We owe Thronis the figurines, so we'll pay that debt. If the dragons want them back, they can take it up with him. The key was never theirs to begin with, so, in a sense, we'll have stolen nothing."

"All right," Seth conceded. He replaced the sword and they moved farther down the aisle.

A raised dais spanned the rear of the room, supporting an extra row of stone tables. Toward the center upon a pedestal higher than the surrounding tables rested a pair of gauntlets—lobstered steel embellished with gold and platinum scrollwork.

"Look at those gloves," Seth said.

"Almost certainly not the Sage's Gauntlets," Trask surmised. "On display so prominently, they must be decoys. I wouldn't be surprised if poisoned needles awaited unwary fingers."

"I don't know," Kendra said. "Aside from the dragons and the hydra, they didn't do much to guard the room. They may have been cocky enough to leave the gauntlets in plain view."

"Maybe we should grab the gauntlets," Seth proposed. "We can give them back in the end, but meanwhile we can use them to distract the dragons. If we get in a tight situation, maybe we could bargain with them."

"Not terrible thinking in principle," Trask acknowledged. "But to disturb the gauntlets would enrage the dragons beyond any hope of bargaining. I repeat, our best chance for success is to move quickly and take only what we came for. Kendra, did Patton leave any hint at the Fairy Queen's shrine concerning where in the room he hid the key?"

"I didn't see a hint," Kendra said, being deliberately vague about not having actually read Patton's message at the shrine. Her cheeks felt hot. She hoped she wasn't blushing. In hindsight, she should probably have fished the tablet out of the pool in case he had included any extra tidbits. "And I haven't noticed any writing here in the treasury either. Patton said the key looks like an iron egg the size of a pineapple, with a bunch of protuberances on the top half."

They climbed up onto the dais.

"The figurines," Seth said almost instantly. He led them

over to where five statuettes were positioned on a circular mat. "Red dragon, white giant, jade chimera. Is onyx black?"

"Can be," Trask said. "And the blue fishy thing is the agate leviathan."

"Can I let go of the horn?" Seth asked.

Trask sniffed probingly. "I think so. If you start to feel ill, make sure you get a hand back on it."

Seth opened a pouch. "Thronis gave me this," he told Kendra. He pulled squares of silken fabric from the pouch and wrapped each figurine individually, then placed them together inside the small bag.

Trask left Kendra holding the horn alone and proceeded down the long row of elevated tables, pausing beside the glittering gauntlets. He looked behind the pedestal on which the fancy gloves were situated. "I've found the key," Trask announced. "He stashed it behind the gauntlets."

"Good job!" Kendra cheered. She and Seth joined Trask, who struggled to pick up the egg-shaped mass of black iron.

"Big pineapple," Trask grunted. "Patton didn't mention the key was *solid* iron. This must weigh at least eighty pounds. Tough to get a grip."

"Use both hands," Kendra recommended. "I'll follow behind and keep the horn in contact with your skin."

They shuffled in an awkward train back across the treasure room, down the hall, and through the pillared chamber, passing Siletta's shrunken corpse. Tanu, Dougan, and Mara awaited them at the bottom of the steps.

"Success?" Dougan asked.

"We have the key and the giant's figurines," Trask reported.

"The key looks heavy," Tanu remarked.

"Or I'm getting really weak," Trask said.

"I'll lug the key down into the storage room," Dougan offered. "I already hauled the giant sword down there."

Trask gratefully handed off the iron egg. "Once you're back up, I want to move out. I hope Gavin fared all right. I'm not sure I should have let him go alone."

Face red with exertion, Dougan managed to descend the rungs into the storage room cradling the egg in one arm. When he came up, they hurried back toward the hydra. Kendra tried not to fret about Gavin. She told herself that he was fine, that he wouldn't have taken needless risks. But she knew how brave he was, and how deadly the hydra had appeared.

As they neared Glommus's cave, Tanu went forward alone to sample the air. He came back and reported that the air was breathable, and that he had found no sign of Gavin. "We might do well to raid the dragon's corpse ourselves," Tanu added. "We could smear our weapons with sedatives, and it would be a once-in-a-lifetime chance to acquire potion ingredients."

"We need to hurry," Trask pointed out, "but prepping our weapons could pay dividends. Mara, come with me and Tanu."

While waiting outside the cave, Kendra saw Gavin walking back to them with a slight limp. Squealing with relief, she ran to him, and he caught her in an embrace. He was soaking wet, his clothes were torn, and he bled lightly from several cuts and scrapes.

"What happened?" Kendra asked, pulling back.

"I got her," Gavin said with a shy smile. "I found a g-gland in the neck of Glommus and drenched my spear and a few quarrels. You know how Trask shot out one of the yellowish head's eyes? I pierced the other one with a tainted quarrel. The heads started to thrash, and I got in a few stabs with the spear."

"You're hurt," Kendra said.

"A couple of the heads jostled me as Hespera went down," Gavin said dismissively. "Nothing major. No bad cuts, no broken bones, at least for now. She's beneath the water. We should hurry."

Trask, Mara, and Tanu shortly emerged from the cave, and Gavin recounted his battle with the hydra as they jogged toward the lake. Trask made the others hang back as he and Gavin advanced through the narrow passage to survey the dark water. They returned promptly, and then all of them hurried through the passage and across the ledge in two separate groups.

Kendra walked quickly, ready for shrieking heads to rise from the depths at any moment, but the murky lake never stirred. With the slumbering hydra behind them, they climbed the knotted rope and hustled between the enormous stone dragons out into the late afternoon sunlight. Clouds of dragonflies drifted near the reedy pools.

"What now?" Kendra asked.

"We rush to the rendezvous," Trask said, picking up the

pace. "It will take over an hour. From there, the griffins will transport us to Thronis. The giant has given his word to help us, and he cannot lie. We'll weather the night in his mansion and then plan how to get out of Wyrmroost. Maybe some of his griffins can scout to see if Navarog is truly at the gates."

They marched single file, following a trackless route beneath tall conifers. Nobody spoke. With the woods around them quiet except for sporadic breezes rustling through the branches, Kendra supposed nobody wanted to jinx the group by disturbing the silence. They had survived the Dragon Temple. They had the key and the figurines. Now if only they could reach the griffins without attracting the notice of any passing Wyrmroost predators!

At one point Mara made them stop and crouch low as she watched a far-off dragon gliding in the sky. The creature showed no sign of having observed them and soon drifted out of view.

The trees thinned as they scaled the side of a rocky spine. About halfway up the long slope, Trask assembled the group below an overhang.

"Our griffins should await us just over this skinny ridge," Mara explained.

Trask nodded. "I'll cross over first with Gavin. If things look good, I'll whistle."

Kendra and the others huddled under the overhang and listened to loose rocks clack and shift as Trask and Gavin ascended the ridge. Not too long after they passed over the crest, a brief whistle shrilled twice. Mara took the lead as the rest of the group clambered up the stony slope. As Kendra picked her way up the loose rocks, she better understood why Trask and Gavin had climbed so noisily. No matter how she stepped, the rocks shifted and slid.

Near the top of the knifelike ridge, Kendra heard a flutter of wings. An astrid alighted on a rocky projection near the crest of the ridge, and words spilled into her mind. *This is an ambush. Two dragons lie in wait. Run!*

Cautiously regarding the expressionless human face of the golden owl, Mara held her spear ready. "What does it want?" she asked Kendra.

"He's warning us," Kendra said, placing a calming hand on the spear. Kendra studied the astrid. "Are you sure?"

Run! They will strike at any moment. Warn your friends. The astrid took wing.

"It's a trap!" Kendra yelled. She hurried to the top of the ridge and peered over at Gavin and Trask descending the far side. They had turned toward her in response to her shout. Several griffins had emerged from the trees below, including one ridden by the dwarf. "Dragons! Run! It's an ambush!"

The dwarf barked an order and the griffins took flight. At the same time, a pair of enormous dragons soared over the far ridge. One had green scales and a bony frill framing its angular head. The other was a monstrosity in scarlet, with lumpy knobs on its snout and a club-shaped tail. The red dragon swept low over the trees, a roiling inferno jetting from its jaws to set a long strip of pines ablaze. The green dragon wheeled out wide, curving and climbing to approach from a different angle.

The griffins scattered. Some fought to gain altitude; others stayed near the ground. They darted in every direction. The griffin with the dwarf snatched Gavin in one claw and Trask in the other. Wings beating furiously, the overburdened griffin flew up the ridge, depositing Trask and Gavin near Kendra and the others.

"We'll come back around," the dwarf promised, his words trailing off as his griffin carried him away.

Trask grabbed Kendra's arm and guided her down the back side of the ridge, rocks rolling underfoot. After a few steps, he dove with her into the lee of a boulder, shielding her with his body. Overhead a dragon bellowed. Heat washed over Kendra as a fervent downpour of flame scorched a field of scree off to their right.

After the dragon had passed over, a pair of griffins streaked low along the slope. Seth sprang out from hiding and a griffin snatched him up and angled skyward. The other one grabbed Tanu. Above her and to the left, silhouetted against the setting sun, Kendra saw the green dragon diving toward a trio of griffins, fire spurting, but the griffins split up and maneuvered aggressively to evade the larger predator.

The scarlet dragon seemed to have been coming back around for another fiery pass, but then it swerved away to follow the griffin carrying Tanu. The griffin dropped into the trees for cover as the dragon released a searing stream of fire. Below the wide, red wings, the forest erupted into a raging conflagration.

"Into the bag," Trask commanded, seizing the knapsack from Kendra. As she stepped inside, a charred, one-winged griffin crashed onto the rocks less than twenty yards down the slope. Kendra hastily descended the rungs.

Warren was propped up on one elbow. "What now?"

"There were dragons waiting when we went to meet the griffins," Kendra said, eyeing his new splint. "How's your arm?"

"Messed up, just like the rest of me. At least Tanu dressed it and gave me painkillers. Are we going to make it?"

"We'll see."

From inside the storage room, the battle seemed far away. Kendra heard the shrieks of griffins and the roars of dragons, but the stationary room remained otherwise unremarkable.

Dougan rushed down the ladder, followed by Gavin. A moment later Mara entered, but she stayed on the top rungs. "Trask found a griffin," she reported. Mara poked her head up through the mouth of the knapsack. "We're airborne."

Gavin sidled up to Kendra. "How are you?"

"I don't know."

"We'll be all right." Taking her hand in his, he offered a reassuring squeeze.

"The green dragon is tailing us," Mara called down. "It's gaining. We're swerving. We're plunging. We're close to the cliff! I think we might—" She flinched, ducking her head, then looked up after an instant. "No, we made it. This griffin can really fly!"

Staring up at Mara, Kendra and the others could see the wind whipping her long, black hair. "We're diving," she reported. "We're rising. I think I know where we're going.

We're upside down. Now we're rolling. Rising. Oh, no. No, no, no. No! Trask is falling! We're falling!" Tugging the flap down, Mara tucked her head and clung to the rungs.

They all heard the knapsack slap against the ground. Mara climbed up out of the room. Grabbing a sword, Gavin followed, then Dougan. Kendra scaled the rungs as well.

"You could wait in here," Warren suggested.

"I have to see," Kendra said.

She emerged on a long ledge near the brink of a high drop-off. Behind her rose a sheer cliff. Above her, the green dragon glided high in the sky, chasing other griffins. The red dragon pursued a distant griffin heading for Stormcrag. Mara, Gavin, and Dougan were staring upward. "What happened to Trask?" Kendra asked.

"He's coming down," Gavin said, pointing.

It took Kendra a moment to catch sight of the ghostly shape of Trask slowly descending toward them, his body a swirling mass of vapor. "He swallowed a gaseous potion!" Kendra exclaimed in relief.

Trask was waving for them to go.

"He wants us to head toward Sidestep Cleft," Mara said.

"How close are we?" Dougan asked.

"Not far," Mara said, snatching up the knapsack. "I think the griffin was trying to make it there. A griffin would fit much deeper inside the gap than a dragon. And a person could fit in deeper than any of them. The cleft is our best chance. We should be relatively safe there." They set off at a brisk run over the rocky ground.

"What about Trask?" Kendra asked.

"He'll try to hide," Dougan said. "Going gaseous saved him from the fall, but now he can't move very fast. We have to leave him. Our presence would only draw more attention to him."

"Trask will find a place to hide," Gavin said. "He knows we have to make it to the cleft. He and Mara are right—the dragons shouldn't be able to reach us in there."

Heedless of the treacherous footing, Kendra raced along the ledge. The green dragon remained in view whenever she looked back, but it seemed intent on chasing griffins. She was surprised the dragon didn't swoop over and kill them. They were such easy prey on the ledge. Perhaps the dragon had failed to notice them.

"The cleft should be around this bend," Mara announced.

"Here comes the dragon," Gavin warned.

Risking a glance, Kendra saw the dragon soaring straight at them, still a good distance away. They picked up the pace to a full sprint.

"Should we put Kendra in the bag?" Dougan asked.

"No time to slow down," Gavin replied. "We have to make it to the cleft."

Mara pulled away from them, her long legs eating up ground like a track star. But as she rounded the bend, Mara skidded to a stop. When Kendra and the others caught up, they saw why.

A huge dragon blocked the entrance to the Sidestep Cleft. The dragon had an underbelly as pale as cream and dimpled yellow scales with a texture almost like linoleum. A pair of forked antlers crowned the long head. The beaklike mouth opened and closed, clacking ominously.

Kendra felt the dragon terror take hold of her. Her muscles locked. Beside her Dougan had become equally immobile. Mara glanced back toward the green dragon, then ahead at the yellow, her dark eyes panicked. They were trapped. Gavin shrieked violently in the dragon language. The dragon responded sharply, prowling forward like a cat stalking a mouse. The huge creature did not seem interested in what he had to say. Despair took hold of Kendra. They had trespassed in the Dragon Temple, and now they would pay the price.

Kendra willed her muscles to move, but they refused. What a sad way to die! Cornered by dragons after enduring so much. At least Seth might escape. And Tanu. Maybe the dragons would fail to check inside the knapsack, and Warren would make it out as well. Hopefully Trask would quietly drift to a safe place.

The yellow dragon had almost reached them. The green dragon had to be closing in as well. Kendra wanted to close her eyes, but her eyelids refused to operate. Although her body would not move, she seemed to shake inside with fear.

Casting his spear aside, Gavin broke into a run, charging straight at the yellow dragon. Kendra did not want to watch the creature destroy her friend, but her head could not turn away.

And then Gavin transformed. The change was not

gradual. He swelled suddenly, swiftly tripling in size again and again, sprouting wings and a tail, horns and claws, until he ballooned into an immense black dragon, abruptly dwarfing his yellow opponent. The silver collar stretched, remaining in place around his scaly neck.

A blinding holocaust of liquid fire erupted from the black dragon's mouth, blasting the yellow dragon off the ledge and bathing the whole vicinity in scorching heat. Spreading his wings, the black dragon leapt and turned to meet the green dragon overhead. The green dragon exhaled fire at Gavin, but the breath he shot back looked more like molten gold than actual flame. The green dragon veered away. The black dragon returned and landed on the ledge, rocks crumbling beneath his bulk.

Kendra still could not move. Could that really be Gavin? He was gigantic! An armor of dark, oily scales plated his sides and back, and his belly looked crusted with black jewels. Cruel spikes protruded from his massive tail and along his spine. His claws curved like huge scythes, and his ferocious eyes burned like magma. Her friend was no dragon brother. He was an actual dragon!

Kendra saw the yellow dragon rising on the far side of the gorge. One side of the creature had been blackened, and the wing on that side looked tattered, but the dragon was still flying. The yellow dragon banked toward them. The green dragon appeared to be wheeling back around as well. The black dragon regarded the returning adversaries, then arched his great head down and swallowed Dougan in a single quick bite.

Through frozen lips, Kendra screamed in disbelief.

Mara tossed the knapsack to Kendra. It hit her shoulder and fell to the ground.

The black dragon swiped a foreleg at Mara, who failed to dodge the quick blow and went tumbling across the ledge and off the edge. The other foreleg swung at Kendra, a razor claw slicing across her chest and knocking her backwards. Wings spreading, the black dragon sprang to engage the oncoming adversaries.

With dragon roars thundering in her ears, Kendra dazedly examined the tear in her shirt. Beneath the torn material, the breastplate Seth had given her felt unscratched. Her mind reeled, trying to comprehend what had happened. Her breaths came quick and shallow. Not only was Gavin a dragon, he had turned and attacked his friends! He had eaten Dougan and killed Mara!

As her fingers rubbed the adamant breastplate, Kendra realized she could move. When Gavin had taken flight, the dragon terror had faded. As the dragons reeled and battled above, Kendra sat up. The knapsack lay beside her. And the Sidestep Cleft was now unguarded.

Shaking with adrenaline, Kendra snatched the knapsack, looped a strap over her shoulder, and ran for the cleft, avoiding the depressions where simmering pools of liquid gold had puddled. As the crack in the mountain loomed large before her, she peered up and back to where the two dragons contended with Gavin. The sun had just gone down. Fountains of flame brightened the dusky sky. Gavin's opponents stayed away from each other. No matter which way Gavin turned, one of his opponents would swoop in behind and try to roast him. Kendra lingered at the entrance to Sidestep Cleft, enthralled by the deadly dance. The difficulty of scoring a direct hit with dragon fire while attacker and target both careened through the air soon became apparent.

As the aerial combat wore on, the participating dragons became increasingly distant. But Kendra knew they could come plunging back at any moment. Turning her back on the dragon battle, she scurried into the cleft. The passage promptly grew much too narrow for any of the dragons, but, wanting to make sure she was out of range from dragon breath, Kendra continued onward, reminding herself not to proceed too far or the fiery exhalations might be able to reach her from the far side.

Kendra traced her finger along one wall until she felt she had traveled far enough. Setting down the knapsack, she lifted the flap and descended the ladder.

"I heard a lot of commotion," Warren said.

"Gavin is a dragon," Kendra managed in a broken voice. Skipping the last few rungs, she dropped, landing in a crouch.

"What?"

"A huge black dragon. He ate Dougan. He killed Mara." As she spoke, Kendra felt like she was listening to the words instead of saying them. How could those words be true? "He tried to kill me. He swiped me across the chest before he flew off to fight some other dragons. The breastplate I have under my clothes saved me." By the light of Warren's electric lantern, Kendra started rummaging through their gear.

"I don't believe this," Warren murmured.

"Believe it," Kendra said, testing a flashlight. It worked. "We're inside Sidestep Cleft, alone. Seth and Tanu may have gotten away with the griffins. We left Trask behind. He was gaseous." She grabbed a primitive staff with rattles at the top.

"The rain stick from Lost Mesa?" Warren asked.

"We need bad weather," Kendra said. "Who knows how long Gavin will be off fighting other dragons? Who knows how many other dragons could show up? I'm going to shake this thing until we have the biggest storm Wyrmroost has ever seen." Kendra crossed the room to the ladder of rungs bolted to the wall. "I'll be back."

"Why not shake it down here?" Warren asked.

"I'm not sure if shaking the stick down here will count up there," Kendra said. "I'm worried enough that Thronis might be able to offset the weather I summon."

"Good luck," Warren said. "At the first sign of trouble, you hide the knapsack and get down here."

"You got it," Kendra said, already at the top rung. Squirming out of the knapsack, she switched on the flashlight and started vigorously shaking the staff. Outside, the day had been relatively mild, with some light wind and a few nonthreatening clouds in the sky. She had no idea how long it would take to conjure up a big storm, especially if Thronis resisted. It might not work before Gavin or other enemies came for her. It might not work at all. But she was sick of hiding, sick of feeling afraid. This was much better than cowering in the knapsack.

CHAPTER TWENTY-SEVEN

Navarog

All Seth could do was dangle. He couldn't even hang on. The griffin had him by the shoulders. If the claws dropped him, he would fall. If the tenacious scarlet dragon killed the griffin, Seth and the griffin would fall together. If the dragon torched them with his fiery breath, Seth would get to sample the rare experience of simultaneously burning and falling.

Looking down and back, Seth had watched the red dragon chase Tanu, setting the forest ablaze. When the griffin had emerged from the trees without the Samoan, the dragon had turned to follow the griffin carrying Seth.

Legs swinging freely, Seth had shouted to the griffin that he had the figurines for Thronis in his pouch. He hoped the knowledge might give the griffin an extra reason not to drop him. He had no way to tell whether the griffin understood.

After having caught a ride with a griffin to the top of Stormcrag and then back down again the next day, Seth thought he knew something about flying. But now Seth was learning that to convince a griffin to *really* fly, you had to chase it with a dragon.

At first the griffin had resolutely climbed, wings beating hard to ascend ever higher into the cold, thin air. While they rose, drawing nearer to the steep shoulders of Stormcrag, the dragon had steadily gained. As the red dragon neared, the griffin veered close to the mountain, sometimes climbing, sometimes diving, sometimes doubling back, always using the stony crags of the mountainside to create obstacles. As the griffin banked and swooped and soared, Seth swung back and forth in its grasp, occasionally having to lift his legs or twist his body to avoid spires of stone.

Although they sometimes plunged to avoid dragon fire, they ascended more than they fell, gradually spiraling up toward the summit. At one point, with the dragon in close pursuit, the griffin careened around a corner and ducked into an ice cave. When the dragon sailed by, they flew out, climbing in the opposite direction.

Finally, as they came within range of the highest peak of Stormcrag, the griffin soared far away from the mountain, wings beating frantically to gain altitude. Out in the empty sky, the dragon closed in. The griffin faked a dive, and the dragon took the bait, plunging to intercept them. While the dragon recovered and came back around, the griffin climbed higher. Looking back toward the mountain, Seth could see that they now sailed well above the mansion.

When the dragon came close again, the griffin tucked its wings and went into a wild dive that left Seth's stomach in his throat. Presumably fearing another feint, the dragon hesitated to follow at first. By the time the dragon realized the dive was authentic, the griffin had spread its wings and Seth was rapidly gliding toward the mansion, half blinded by the wind of their speed.

The dragon surged after them, gaining until it became clear that the massive predator would overtake them before they reached the mansion. Seth hoped his griffin was not out of evasive maneuvers. Just as the dragon was almost within range to blow fire, Seth heard a deep *thrum*. An arrow the size of a telephone pole lodged in the dragon's chest. Wings limp, the dragon rolled onto its back and plummeted from the sky like a boulder.

Gazing ahead at the mansion, Seth saw Thronis manning an enormous crossbow out on the patio. The sky giant arose and went to his front door just in time to admit Seth and the griffin. Gliding to the table in the front room, the griffin dropped Seth, then landed, trotting to a stop. Heaving sides lathered with foam, the griffin bowed its aquiline head.

"Good job," Seth told the griffin, unsure whether it could understand. He walked over and stroked the damp, red-gold fur.

"I regret your discomfiting encounter," Thronis apologized, taking a seat by the table. "By the time I recognized the ambush, it was too late to warn you. I'm happy you won your way free, young Seth."

"Nice shot with the crossbow."

"Let us hope the example will motivate other dragons to think twice before venturing near my abode."

"I have your figurines," Seth reported, opening the pouch.

The sky giant grinned. "Then I am especially glad you survived! Set them near the edge of the table."

Seth unwrapped the five figurines and arranged them in a line. The giant leaned in close, examining them with one eye shut. "Hmmm," he murmured. "Well done, indeed, you have brought the figures I requested."

"Why did you want them so badly?" Seth asked.

"I wanted three of them. If I say the proper words and put the red dragon into a fire, it will grow into a true dragon that will heed my every command. Buried in snow with the correct words spoken, the marble giant will expand into a hardy snow giant, a servant with tremendous potential. And the jade chimera can likewise be transformed into an actual chimera obedient to my desires."

"I guess they will come in handy defending your mansion," Seth said.

"They should prove immeasurably useful."

"What about the tower and the fish?"

The giant cracked his knuckles. "You are welcome to keep the other figures, Seth Sorenson. Placed upon solid ground, after the designated incantation, the model tower will enlarge into an actual tower. The stronghold is designed to be inhabited by men, not giants, so it is of no use to me. Put in the sea with a few words, the fish will swell into a leviathan. I live far from the sea, with no intentions to visit."

"Could you tell me the magic words?" Seth asked.

"I will have my dwarf write them down for you upon his return. They are not complicated. The spells necessary for the transformations are ingrained in the items. The words merely set the spells into motion, like igniting a magical fuse."

"Could you look in your globe and check on my friends?" Seth asked.

"Absolutely," Thronis said, rising. "I shall return promptly."

Seth sat down, fingering the tower and the fish. Having his own tower would be pretty cool. He hoped Kendra and the others were all right. Since the red dragon had chased him and been shot from the sky, the others only had to contend with the green one. Surely most of them, if not all, would escape.

Thronis returned looking sober. "While I was away from my globe manning the ballista, Navarog joined the fight. I'm not sure when he arrived at the sanctuary. I'm afraid your friends are scattered, and it looks like some have perished. My griffins have fled. They lost track of your comrades. Three griffins have already fallen, and two others are wounded. Navarog is currently contending with a pair of dragons. And there seems to be a powerful enchantment summoning foul weather, using old magic that is foreign to me."

"Calling rain?" Seth asked.

"Essentially."

"That must be Kendra using the rain stick. She must need bad weather to help her escape the dragons."

"The dragons trust me to keep the weather relatively fair," Thronis said.

"They also trust you not to send thieves to steal from them," Seth countered. "And you trust them not to attack your griffins. This seems like a day for bending some of the rules. Why don't you help summon a big storm?"

The sky giant stroked his chin. "My griffins are nimble. They can handle harsh weather much better than the dragons. Perhaps an ugly storm is just what we need to remind the wyrms of my worth."

"If Kendra is calling one, I'd really appreciate it. Also, since you have the little statues, can we lose the chains now?"

The giant spoke a strange word and snapped his enormous fingers. The silver chain snapped and fell from Seth's neck. "We had a bargain. You have earned my appreciation. Your sister and I will call up a storm such as Wyrmroost has not seen in many a season. If you will excuse me."

Seth motioned for the giant to proceed. "Have at it."

"When the storm has been called, I shall return with some victuals."

"If that means food, count me in."

Freezing gusts howled through Sidestep Cleft, carrying the smell of snow. Thunder crackled and boomed. And Kendra relentlessly kept shaking the staff, hoping that if she shook hard enough, long enough, the dragons would be forced to seek shelter while her remaining friends got away.

Although she could see in the dark, Kendra could see farther with the flashlight lit, so she kept it on, repeatedly shining it in both directions to avoid being taken by surprise. Consequently, she identified Gavin while he was still a good distance off, approaching along the tall, narrow passageway. A dragon no longer, he bled freely from a wound on his neck and walked with a pronounced limp. Her flashlight beam reflected off the sword in his hand. As a heavy gust tore through the passage, he lifted his free hand to shield his face.

"You can stop shaking the stick," Gavin called.

"I'd rather not," Kendra replied.

"I was trying to be polite," Gavin said, coming closer. "What I mean is, stop shaking the stick or I'll kill you."

Tears stung Kendra's eyes. A disturbed laugh threatened to fly from her lips. Gavin had killed Dougan. He had killed Mara. "Won't you kill me anyhow?"

"As a dragon I would," Gavin said, limping nearer. "In this form, I'd rather not."

"Who are you, Gavin?"

He grinned. "Haven't you guessed? You're no dummy. Give it a shot."

She knew. She had tried not to admit it to herself, but she knew. "Navarog."

"Of course."

"How can you be Navarog?" He had been her friend! He had protected her! She had hoped he might become her boyfriend! She had held his hand and written him flirty letters! Kendra felt ill. She wanted to curl up into a ball and weep.

"A better question might be how the rest of you missed it. I thought it was obvious after Lost Mesa. I guess oftentimes we only perceive what we expect to see."

Kendra shook her head, horrified and baffled and curious all at once. "So you were the hooded prisoner inside the Quiet Box?"

"Despite how the hood masked my senses, I can still remember the smell of your nervousness. Not unlike the scent I'm picking up at the moment. The Sphinx got me out, and then turned me loose just before he exited Fablehaven. I went and found the nail Seth had pulled from the revenant and gave it to Kurisock."

"And then you left," Kendra said.

"My business at Fablehaven was done. I went to a dragon sanctuary in the Himalayas."

"You were the dragon who ate Charlie Rose. He never had a son, did he?"

"I knew you could piece this together. The Sphinx recommended I visit Chuck Rose. Chuck's longtime friend Arlin Santos is a Knight of the Dawn and a traitor. Chuck would disappear in the wild for many months at a time. Arlin helped me find Chuck. Killing him was simple. After the deed was done, Arlin helped me pretend that his death happened longer ago than it actually had, and helped establish my avatar as Chuck's secret son. Gavin Rose, the stuttering w-w-w-wonder."

"I liked your stutter."

"It served a purpose. Made me seem more human, more vulnerable."

Kendra scowled. "What really happened at Lost Mesa?"

"What do you think?"

She knew it was bad, but there was too much to process. "You could talk to Chalize because you were a dragon."

"Before the rest of you entered the room, I showed Chalize my true form. Scared her to death. She almost tried to fight me. Once I established my dominance, I warned her that I'd kill her if she tried to attack you guys. Then I promised that if she would let us pass, I would free her. She was so young and inexperienced that I was worried she would do something stupid. But it worked out."

"You released Chalize? You destroyed Lost Mesa."

Gavin grinned. "And I framed poor Javier, the guy with no legs. He wasn't a traitor. I ate him. Then I stole the decoy artifact, slashed some tires, and moved a pickup truck. That same night I released Chalize, but commanded her to wait until after we were gone before wreaking havoc. Freed from confinement, Chalize was powerful enough to overthrow the treaty. She breached the gate and got Mr. Lich involved freeing the zombies and animating the dead."

"I can't believe it," Kendra mumbled numbly. "You're the demon prince of dragons. And now you're in the perfect position to help the Sphinx steal the next artifact."

Gavin seemed to relish her astonishment. "By now you must realize that the Sphinx deliberately let your duplicate escape. The stingbulb version of you, the one you left behind. He knew she was a fake when her touch failed to restore energy to an item he wanted recharged. He had given the item to her casually, so she had no idea he knew."

Kendra shook her head sadly. "So the phony Kendra was accidentally helping him?"

"The Sphinx made sure she knew exactly what he wanted her to know. She thought she escaped on her own, but he was deliberately sloppy. Had she failed to make a move, he would have been even sloppier. Once the stingbulb got away, he had an agent follow her to ensure she made it back to Fablehaven. You're very resourceful, Kendra, even as a clone. The duplicate required no help. The Sphinx knew that once your grandfather heard the Society had discovered where Patton hid the key, the Knights would have to send a team to Wyrmroost to recover it. The Sphinx felt certain they would include Gavin Rose, the dragon-taming prodigy. He had it right."

Kendra bowed her head into her hands. "We brought Navarog with us to Wyrmroost. We opened the gate and let him in."

"A simple plan, but effective," Gavin said. "I got nervous when we bumped into Nafia. She knows me. Fortunately, she's a fairly dark dragon. We had met before, ages ago, and she knew my reputation, so she helped me instead of blowing my cover. When she showed up at our camp in human form, she was teasing me. At first I was scared that she meant to reveal my secret, but in the end she helped my cause, pretending I had been spotted outside the gates, further clouding my true identity."

"We're so stupid," Kendra groaned miserably.

"You keep doing a lot of our work for us," Gavin agreed. "This whole scenario has played out almost perfectly. I would have preferred to keep my identity a secret until we had left Wyrmroost. I would have preferred to devour Trask and all of them right outside the front gates, then fly away with you, Seth, and the key. But this will serve."

"Why spare me and Seth?" Kendra asked. "Didn't you try to kill me?"

Gavin shrugged. "When I slashed at you outside of here earlier tonight, I was in a rush, and worried about you escaping with the key. You and your brother are very likable. Despite being young and innocent, the two of you are surprisingly capable. I could hardly believe it when you killed Siletta. I mean, she was a legend. A dragon of no small renown. I had no idea she was a guardian here. Seth pulling the nail from the revenant was another shocking coup. The shadow plague should have swallowed Fablehaven, but you stopped that as well. Together you have accomplished some astounding feats. When the moment to reveal myself arrived, I may have changed my mind, but I felt sorely tempted to spare the two of you. Naturally, I would have eaten all the others."

"Instead you just ate Dougan," Kendra said bitterly.

"Just him for now," Gavin grinned. The grin looked wrong on his face. Too knowing, too sharklike. The boy she had once liked would never have grinned that way.

"Have you eaten any of the others?" Kendra asked.

"I couldn't find them," Gavin admitted. "Seth may have escaped to Thronis. I found the red dragon on the slopes of Stormcrag skewered by a huge arrow. Hard to guess where your storm blew Trask. Mara may have survived as well—I couldn't locate her body. She's an agile woman. She may have somehow caught herself after going over the edge. Or maybe I just missed her corpse. Don't worry, none of your friends will be coming to help you. I collapsed part of the ledge outside of the cleft, and Nafia is standing guard."

"What's going to protect you from me?" Kendra asked, shifting her stance, clutching the rain staff like a weapon.

Gavin laughed condescendingly. "You're brave, Kendra, but I see no need for you to humiliate yourself." He swished his sword a few times for emphasis. "Granted, I'm more powerful as a dragon, but even in this ungainly mortal shape, I have superhuman strength and reflexes. You glimpsed what I can do when we were swept up in that battle on Lost Mesa, and even then I was holding back, trying not to blow my cover."

Kendra lowered the staff. "You killed the dragons that were fighting you? Just now, I mean."

Gavin smirked. "They were no match for me. A third dragon joined the fight against me as well, a gray beast with curved horns. But they all fell. The wind you conjured worked to my advantage. I have always outperformed other dragons in foul weather. In the end, Nafia aided me, not that I needed her assistance."

"I had hoped the wind might prevent you from reaching me."

"With enough wind, it can get risky for the best of us to stay airborne. But we can always tuck our wings and walk."

"You must have fought the hydra as a dragon," Kendra realized.

"Why else would I have gone off alone?"

Kendra scowled. "But you said you fought her with arrows and a spear. Why didn't the collar strangle you?"

Gavin grinned. "I did fight her with arrows and a spear . . . at first. I changed to dragon form after that. The hydra was a dangerous obstacle. Even as a dragon, the outcome looked dicey for a time. She put up a good fight. The collar was a nuisance. It even stayed on in dragon form. It only fell off just before I came here, meaning Seth must have made it back to Thronis."

Relief swept through Kendra. At least her brother might make it out alive.

"Anyhow, enough reminiscing. I know the key is in the bag as well as the unicorn horn. We'll need the horn to open the gate, and of course I'm not leaving without the key."

"I'm not going with you," Kendra said firmly.

"You're mistaken," Gavin said. "You have no choice in the matter. I'd rather not knock you unconscious. As a dragon, I think I could tolerate you. As a person, I actually like you. Let's try to keep this civilized."

Kendra chuckled incredulously. "You don't like me. You want me along as your puppet in case you need to recharge any magical items."

"There's that, too."

"All right," Kendra said, slouching against the wall. "I guess I don't have much choice."

"Hand over the knapsack," Gavin said.

Kendra picked up the knapsack and held it out to Gavin. As he reached for it, she swung the staff at his head with all of her strength. He blocked the blow with the flat of his sword, wrenched the staff from her grasp, and used it to swat her on the shoulder, knocking her to the ground.

"Really, Kendra, don't, this is embarrassing." He opened the main flap of the knapsack. "After you."

Kendra bent over the knapsack and screamed, "Warren, Gavin is Navarog and he—"

She managed nothing more before Gavin shoved her aside and dropped into the knapsack, ignoring the rungs on the wall. Kendra hesitated. Should she follow him and try to help Warren? Or should she run? If she ran, he would catch her. Or Nafia would catch her. Had he collapsed the ledge outside of both entrances? She probably couldn't escape Sidestep Cleft without wings.

Kendra climbed down the rungs. By the time she reached the bottom, Warren was unconscious.

"This has been a tough week for Warren," Gavin commented. "Should I just put him out of his misery?"

"No, please," Kendra begged.

"Why should I heed your wishes?" Gavin asked. "You tried to club me in the head!"

"I'll be good if you leave him alone," Kendra promised.

"It really doesn't matter if you behave. But, sure, I'll spare you having to watch me kill your friend. Go on up the ladder." He already held the unicorn horn. He crouched, easily picking up the iron egg in his other hand.

Kendra scaled the rungs. If good behavior might spare Warren, she would behave. Besides, Gavin was right. If she resisted, all he had to do was knock her out and drag her wherever he wanted.

Gavin exited the knapsack, set aside the egg and the horn, and removed a flask from a pocket. Unstopping the flask, he began drenching the knapsack with a pungent fluid.

"What are you doing?" Kendra asked, fear creeping into her voice.

Producing a lighter, Gavin set the knapsack on fire.

"No!" Kendra cried, lunging toward the burning knapsack.

Gavin grabbed her, firmly holding her back. She struggled, staring in horror as the flames rapidly consumed the backpack. Eventually the fire began to burn lower. Flinging Kendra to the ground, Gavin poured more fluid on the fire, the resurgent flames throwing devilish highlights across his features. As the fire burned down a second time, he hacked up the blackened knapsack with his sword.

"You said you wouldn't hurt him if I behaved," Kendra sobbed, hands trembling.

"No, I said it didn't matter if you behaved. And I said I wouldn't make you watch me kill your friend. Instead, you watched me trap him in an extra-dimensional space forever. He has provisions, and the room is magically ventilated. I bet Warren will get really good at Yahtzee."

"You're a monster!" Kendra yelled.

"You're finally catching on. I'm much worse than most monsters, Kendra. I'm a dragon, and a demon prince."

Kendra huffed. "And a servant of the Sphinx. How do you like taking orders from a human?"

Gavin's face hardened. "The Sphinx may be a brilliant strategist, and it may serve my purposes to aid him for a time, but before the end, the Sphinx will learn that no mere mortal is my master."

"Why not teach him by switching sides and helping me?"

Gavin snorted derisively. "No, Kendra, I will not be helping you. I want the demon prison open."

We're coming, Kendra. She did not hear the words with her ears. They were chanted in her mind. Although a thrill of hope raced through her, Kendra tried to keep her face composed. She needed to keep Gavin talking.

"You want to open the prison on your terms, not the Sphinx's."

"We should not be having this conversation." Gavin turned and raised his sword. A screeching astrid flew toward him. The blade flashed, and the owl fell. A second astrid came behind the first, talons outstretched, human face set in a determined expression. Gavin cut it down as well. A third astrid streaked along the passage from the opposite direction. Gavin pivoted and slew it with a well-timed slash.

Kendra covered her eyes, unwilling to look at the three dead astrids. "Stop!" she cried. "Stop, he'll kill you!"

"Astrids?" Gavin asked, looking up and down the passage.

No other owls flapped into view. "Even as a human, I could kill astrids all day! Nowhere easier than in a narrow passage like this. Send them all and let's be rid of them! Whose help will you summon next? Chipmunks? Snails?"

"I didn't call them," Kendra said.

"We had best get going."

"If Nafia is standing guard, how did the astrids get through?"

"The same way chipmunks would get through," Gavin said. "Nafia is guarding against threats, not pathetic owls."

"I'm not coming willingly," Kendra said. "You'll have to knock me out or kill me."

"Easily done," Gavin said with a shrug.

Then a dragon with silvery white scales materialized behind him. The dragon was not particularly large, hardly twice as tall as Gavin, but even with its wings folded, the streamlined creature barely fit in the passageway. Raxtus stared at Kendra, then glanced from her to Gavin uncertainly.

Gavin quickly checked over his shoulder. Raxtus disappeared just in time to avoid detection, then reappeared once Gavin turned back to face Kendra.

"You're overacting," Gavin remarked, "but it never hurts to be sure. You can save the theatrics. If you want me to look away from you again, you'll have to do better than comically gawking over my shoulder."

Kendra returned her gaze to Gavin. Raxtus loomed right behind him. Gavin kept his eyes fixed on hers.

"I don't blame you for wanting to take a swing at me,"

he went on, "but try to show a bit more ingenuity. I have excellent senses. If something tried to creep up behind me, I would know."

Raxtus shook his head.

Kendra fought the urge to stare at the dragon. He had Gavin trapped! The hallway was much too cramped for Gavin to transform. All Raxtus had to do was strike. As she watched him peripherally, the silver-white dragon looked hesitant. He leaned his head forward, mouth opening slightly, then stopped himself, pulling back a tad.

"At least now you're looking over my shoulder more subtly," Gavin complimented. "Had you glanced that indirectly the first time, I would have been much more startled. You might have even earned a chance to land a cheap shot." He snorted as if the idea of resistance were ridiculous.

Kendra had to motivate Raxtus. She had to do it without directly talking to him, and it had to happen now.

"Maybe I should stop trying to fool you," Kendra sighed.

"Now you're making sense," Gavin replied. "I wish you meant it."

"What about the other dragons?" Kendra asked. "Won't they be mad you took the key we got from the Dragon Temple? Won't they be angry you killed the dragons who came after us? What about Celebrant?"

Gavin chuckled. "We'll be long gone before any of them really know what happened."

"But Celebrant is supposed to be the toughest dragon

alive," Kendra said. "Aren't you worried he'll want revenge?"

Gavin shook his head. "Celebrant is the one who should be worried. After I open the demon prison, I'll be able to descend on him with an army of such power as the world has never seen. Trust me, there will be a new king of dragons before long. Kendra, you're staring way too obviously again."

Raxtus bared his fangs, his brilliant eyes brimming with rage. His neck coiled slightly, then his head darted forward, teeth flashing, and with one swift bite, a large portion of Gavin went missing. The sword clattered to the ground. The dragon's forelegs propped Gavin up, and with three more bites, he was gone.

Kendra gawked at Raxtus in stupefied wonder.

"You know," the dragon said, still chewing, "for such a bad guy, he tastes pretty good."

"You did it!" Kendra gasped. "Where did you come from?"

"The astrids alerted me to your predicament." The dragon examined the dead astrids on the ground. "After so many centuries, these are the first of their kind to perish. My fault, as usual. I came here, invisibly of course, and saw Nafia standing guard. I chickened out. So three of the astrids went in. When I heard them die, something snapped, and, well, here I am. Better late than never. Sorry I hesitated. I've never slain a dragon before."

Kendra remained stunned. "You must be the only dragon who can fit inside Sidestep Cleft."

"Even I can't squeeze through all the way. But I could hear the thoughts of the astrids, and knew you were on this side of the narrowest gap."

"You ate Gavin. You ate Navarog."

"Not very gentlemanly to ambush him while he was trapped in human form by a narrow cave. But then again, he was no gentleman."

She wanted to hug Raxtus. Unable to resist, she strode forward and wrapped her arms around his neck. His scales felt hard and cold. As Kendra clung to him, the dragon began to shimmer and gleam as if sunlight were reflecting off of his bright scales.

"Whoa," the dragon said, his voice amazed. "What are you doing?"

Kendra pulled away. "You're shining."

Raxtus blinked. "I feel really good."

"I'm full of magical energy," Kendra said. "When I touch fairies, they glow brighter."

"Feels like you lit a fire inside of me."

"You've touched me before," Kendra said, somewhat befuddled.

"I've touched your clothes, like when I carried you. But never skin to scales until now. Hug me again."

She threw her arms around him, squeezing tightly. Raxtus shone brighter and brighter. His scales began to feel warm.

"Okay, enough," he finally said. She backed away. "I feel like I could explode."

"I can hardly look at you," Kendra said, eyes squinting.

Suddenly the dragon was gone. "I can still turn invisible," he said. "We should go."

"Let me check something." Kendra used the rain staff to probe the smoldering remains of the knapsack, hoping some connection to the room might remain. As she prodded aside the charred remnants, she found no evidence of an opening. The mutilated knapsack had lost all shape.

"Your friend is trapped inside?" Raxtus asked.

Kendra nodded, not trusting her voice to hold if she spoke.

"I don't think we can access the room anymore, but I'll bring what is left of the backpack. Maybe someone smarter than me can find a way in." He grabbed up the burned flaps of shredded leather. "Where should we go?"

"I think Seth made it back to Thronis," Kendra said hesitantly. She knew Raxtus was afraid of the sky giant.

"The griffins proved he was on your side," Raxtus said. "But the spells protecting his stronghold still might harm us if I try to fly there."

"Should we just stay here?" Kendra wondered.

"No. Not counting whatever happened to the guardians, four dragons are dead. Five, including Navarog. We need to get away from the scene of the crime."

"Where? Blackwell Keep?"

"You don't want to get Agad involved," Raxtus warned. "He won't like all of these dead dragons one bit. If he sheltered you, other dragons would probably attack seeking vengeance, plunging Wyrmroost into chaos. I'll take you to my lair. It is far from here and well hidden."

Kendra picked up the unicorn horn, her rain staff, and her flashlight. "The egg is too heavy."

"Not for me," Raxtus replied. "All four of my claws are useful for grabbing. Follow me. Walk this way. Keep that light turned off. Toward the end, when the passage widens, I'll pick you up. If the rain keeps falling, and we're quick and lucky, we'll slip away right under Nafia's nose."

Kendra followed the dragon along the passage. Once the passage grew wide, she felt his claw take hold of her waist, and then they were soaring up into the rainy night. Since she had stopped shaking the staff, the storm had lost some of its fury, but the winds continued to gust, and the rain felt icy cold against her face. How could water that cold not be frozen?

Glancing up and back, Kendra saw a looming shape through the rain that might have been Nafia perched on a craggy outcrop. The shape did not give chase.

Kendra felt like she had parachuted into a hurricane. Swirling winds buffeted them, coming from above and below. Even a small, aerodynamic dragon like Raxtus seemed overmatched by the turbulent gales. Sometimes he fought the gusts, sometimes he used them, zooming and stalling, twisting and plunging, curving and rising. As they gained altitude, the rain turned to hail, pinging off the dragon's invisible scales. Kendra's winter attire offered some protection against the cold and wetness, but eventually she began to shiver. She lost all sense of direction as erratic winds propelled them through the frigid darkness.

At last they alighted in a small grotto. When Raxtus

made himself visible, his brightness lit up the room better than a bonfire. Flowstone covered the walls and floor like frozen caramel. On a stone shelf near a glittering patch of calcite roosted an astrid.

"Is this your lair?" Kendra asked.

"This hole in the wall?" Raxtus laughed. "No, my lair isn't grand, but it isn't quite this tiny and bare. The astrid summoned me."

Your brother is well.

"Seth?" Kendra asked. "Have you seen him?"

Others in my cadre have seen him. He is with the sky giant. Now that we can speak to fairies, two of us brought a fairy to Thronis to serve as an interpreter. Your brother and the giant know you are here. They suggest you wait here until morning.

"Then what?"

The giant will slacken the weather long enough for you to dash to the exit with the other survivors from your party.

"What about Trask? And Tanu? And Mara?"

Those three are well. The giant has been using his seeing stone to locate them. Griffins are recovering them as we speak. They will take shelter around the preserve. In the morning, a griffin will come for you, and you will rendezvous with your friends at the gate.

"I'll stay with you until morning," Raxtus promised. He raised a wing. "You can sleep up against me. Your energy made me warm."

"Okay," Kendra said. "Thank the giant for me."

I'll stay with you as well.

Kendra crept underneath the upraised wing, and Raxtus

lowered it over her like a blanket. The dragon was right—
he was warm. Almost immediately she stopped shivering. It
was actually quite cozy.

Closing her eyes, Kendra tried to shut down her mind.
At least Seth was all right. And some of the others had lived.
Even Mara, who had looked like a goner.

Kendra licked her lips. Against all odds, she had escaped
Navarog. She might actually live through this. She might
see her parents and grandparents again. She might grow up.

Kendra tried not to picture Navarog devouring Dougan.
She tried not to envision Warren, injured and trapped
in the storage room. She tried not to visualize Mendigo
disintegrating. She tried to forget what she had learned
about Gavin, and tried to ignore that she had seen him
eaten right in front of her.

Where was sleep? When would it come for her?

She tried not to worry about what the morning would
bring. She tried not to wonder what new problems would
arise on the way to the gate. She tried not to stress about
what might await beyond the colorful walls of Wyrmroost.

Where was a nice, strong sleep potion when she needed
it?

Outside the wind howled. Beside her the dragon breathed
softly. She focused on the wind, listened to the breathing,
and sleep overtook her.

The New Knights

Feeling the vibrations of the road, Kendra tried to rest her eyes. Occasionally she would peek out the window at the leafless trees blurring by, or across the SUV at her brother. They would soon be back at Fablehaven.

Tanu had hinted that Grandpa had a secret he wanted to share. It had not sounded like happy news. She and Seth had pressed him for info, but the Samoan had remained tight-lipped, insisting that her grandfather wanted to relay the information in person.

Tanu sat up front at the wheel. Elise sat beside him on the passenger side. She had met up with them at the airport for added security.

Their departure from Wyrmroost had gone smoothly. The griffin had appeared on schedule, Kendra had bid farewell to Raxtus, and the others had been waiting for her after a swift flight to the gate. Mara had broken a few ribs, but Trask, Tanu, and Seth had survived relatively unscathed. When they exited, the distracter spell did not repulse them, and the horn functioned perfectly as a key.

Outside the gate, they returned to the heart-shaped clearing, where Trask contacted Aaron Stone. The helicopter had found them some time later, and, without any real hardship, they had flown back to civilization. The following morning, they started a series of airline flights that had led Kendra to her present situation.

Tanu turned the SUV into the driveway. The sky was overcast, but no snow fell. Kendra bowed her head. She did not want to see Fablehaven again. She was sick of magical creatures hunting her. She was sick of fear and betrayals. If one of her best friends had secretly been a demonic dragon, who could she trust?

Kendra glanced across the car at Seth. She could trust her brother. He might be dumb and reckless sometimes, but he was also heroic and reliable. Then again, what if the person in the SUV was not her brother? What if Thronis had replaced Seth with a stingbulb? Or some other form of duplicate, even more evil and longer lasting?

She knew she was being silly. Or was she? One of her best friends had turned out to be an evil dragon. The Society of the Evening Star had proven they would stoop to anything to set a trap. They would lie, they would steal, they would kidnap, they would kill. And they were patient. Could Tanu be biding his time, waiting for the perfect moment for the ultimate betrayal? How well did they know Elise? How could they ever place any confidence in Vanessa?

Kendra was beginning to understand why Patton had wanted to hide the artifacts beyond the reach of anyone, why he trusted only himself with their location. In a world full of traitors, how did you confide in anyone?

Of course, Patton had trusted her. Had that been wise? They had recovered the key to the vault where the Translocator had been hidden. But no matter how they tried to hide the Chronometer and the key, wasn't it just a matter of time before the Society stole them?

The SUV passed through the gate to Fablehaven and pulled to a stop in front of the house. Grandpa, Grandma, Dale, and Coulter came out to greet them. Seth jumped out of the SUV in a hurry, producing a white horn to wave at them. By telephone, Tanu had explained how Seth had stowed away, and how he had helped win the day at Wyrmroost.

"I brought it back," Seth said, rushing toward them. Reaching the cement walkway to the house, he tossed the horn into the air and caught it. When he tossed it a second time, he fumbled the catch. The horn fell and shattered against the cement.

Everyone froze. Seth looked stricken. Coulter paled. Grandpa scowled. Tiny white shards littered the walkway.

Kendra found herself choking on laughter. The look on Grandma's face was priceless. But it was unfair to prolong the prank. Kendra got out of the SUV.

"I have the real horn," Kendra said, producing the unicorn horn.

Seth was cracking up. The others looked relieved. "There was a glass unicorn head in an airport souvenir shop," Seth giggled. "The horn was just the right size. We bought the head and broke it off. So worth it!"

"For a young man on thin ice," Grandma said, "you sure enjoy stomping around."

Seth kept laughing. He couldn't seem to help himself.

Grandpa smiled. He came forward and hugged Seth. "After all you've been through, I'm glad you can still laugh. Kendra, Seth, I know you just got home, but we have a few urgent matters to discuss. Would you come with me to my office? Then you can rest."

"Should I grab our bags?" Kendra asked.

"Others will worry about your bags," Grandma said, embracing Seth after Grandpa released him.

Grandpa caught Kendra in a tight hug. "I'm glad you made it back," he whispered.

Fighting back tears, she embraced him fiercely. Grandma hugged her, and Coulter and Dale did too. Then she followed Grandpa into the house and into his office.

Kendra and Seth took seats in the big armchairs, and Grandpa sat behind his desk. She wondered for a moment whether they could be in trouble. No—Seth, probably, for stowing away, but she had done nothing wrong.

"I am so sorry for the terrible events at Wyrmroost," Grandpa said, studying Kendra. "Gavin's betrayal must have come as a horrible shock."

Kendra did not trust herself to speak. Her emotions felt too close to the surface.

"I understand you'll need time to recover," Grandpa added. "We don't need to dwell right now on the bad things that happened. Know that we will do all we can to figure out a way to recover Warren."

"What are the chances?" Seth asked.

"Honestly?" Grandpa responded. "Not good. The extra-dimensional space of the storage room is not even part of our reality. Once the connection was severed with the knapsack, the room was left adrift."

"Can he even breathe in there?" Seth asked. "The room had air vents, right?"

"The room had vents for circulation, and we have no reason to believe the vents were damaged. They would have had a connection to the outside world separate from the mouth of the knapsack."

"Could there be a way to rescue Warren and Bubda using the vents?"

"Possibly, if we can find where the vents connect to our world. But, by design, the connection point will be well hidden. The creators of the knapsack did not want enemies entering through the vents."

Seth nodded. "We'll try, though."

"Of course we'll try." Grandpa did not sound optimistic. "Warren has plenty of food and healing potions. We'll find a way to free him. Enough tragedy. I can hardly believe that I am in the presence of dragon slayers, and that another resides in the dungeon."

"You heard what Vanessa did?" Kendra asked.

"Tanu filled me in on the phone," Grandpa said. "She

was under strict orders not to inhabit any of you, but under the circumstances it is hard to view her as anything less than a hero. Not that I am ready to trust her. She could have known she was also helping Navarog."

"How can we ever trust anyone?" Kendra muttered.

"We experienced yet another painful betrayal at Wyrmroost," Grandpa acknowledged. "Admittedly, none of us saw it coming. But that does not mean we lack true allies. We can trust each other. We can trust Ruth. And it would be hard to doubt Tanu, Mara, Trask, Coulter, or Dale."

"What about stingbulbs?" Kendra asked. "Or what if more of our best allies are just really patient enemies?"

Grandpa studied Kendra thoughtfully. "We must always be on guard, I suppose. But we can't stop trusting each other, or our enemies win. We are still in the midst of a crisis. None of us can handle it alone."

"Am I busted?" Seth asked.

"A fair question," Grandpa replied, shifting his attention. "What do you think?"

"I'm probably busted. But I shouldn't be. You should have sent me along in the first place. I'm as good as any of the other Knights. Better than some. And my new abilities make me really useful."

Grandpa folded his hands on the desk. "Would you like to join the Knights?"

"Is that a trick question?"

"No," Grandpa said seriously.

"Of course!"

"It is hard to argue with your accomplishments," Grandpa

said. "I don't think your judgment has fully matured, but these desperate times require courage like yours, Seth. Rise."

Seth stood up.

"Raise your right hand," Grandpa said.

Seth complied.

"Repeat after me: I pledge to keep the secrets of the Knights of the Dawn, and to aid my fellow Knights in their worthy goals."

Seth repeated the words.

"Congratulations," Grandpa said.

"You're allowed to make me a Knight?" Seth inquired hopefully.

"I have been asked to come out of retirement," Grandpa said. "Considering the threats we're facing, I consented. I am the new Captain of the Knights."

"And now I'm a Knight," Seth said, glancing over at Kendra, hardly able to contain his excitement.

"You have made questionable decisions in the past days," Grandpa said. "But they were not foolish decisions. You took risks because the stakes were high, and, when challenged, you provided adequate reasons. You were right that when the fate of the world hangs in the balance, perhaps it is better to be active than passive. In some ways, the Knights as a whole have grown too conservative. To avert the coming crisis, I am afraid we may have to take some risks and go on the offensive."

"Did they tell you Arlin Santos is a traitor?" Kendra asked.

"Trask called it in," Grandpa said. "We moved to apprehend him, but he had already fled."

"What is the next step?" Kendra asked.

"We have the Chronometer and the key from Wyrmroost," Grandpa said. "Keeping the key safe will prevent our enemies from obtaining the Translocator. The question is whether we can protect the key while the Sphinx wields the Oculus. Part of our strategy must be to keep the key in motion, never at the same spot for too long. We'll need to get decoys in motion as well. The Translocator could serve as a powerful tool in our offensive efforts. Perhaps we should put together a mission to retrieve the artifact from Obsidian Waste. I'll be considering the issue with my top advisors, including you two, over the coming days."

"And you'll give back the horn to the centaurs," Kendra said.

"We'll do that today," Grandpa said. "Our story will be that we managed to recover the horn from the Society. When Gavin apprehended you, it was in their power for a short while, so it won't even be a complete falsehood."

"What about the fifth secret preserve?" Seth asked. "The one with the final artifact."

"We have no leads," Grandpa lamented. "But we will keep searching. And Coulter will keep trying to figure out the Chronometer. There will be much need for urgent planning in the days and weeks to come."

"Meanwhile, what happens to us?" Kendra wondered.

Grandpa shifted uncomfortably in his seat, averting his eyes. "The world thinks you are dead, Kendra. It might be simplest to let them persist in that belief until this crisis is over."

"So I'll go home alone?" Seth asked.

Grandpa looked him in the eye. "No, the two of you will have to remain here. Normally those without knowledge of magical creatures are kept out of events pertaining to the magical community. But the Society has crossed another unthinkable boundary." Grandpa frowned at them, then sighed. "After all you've been through recently, I don't know how to tell you this. I hesitated to share the news, but after giving the matter a lot of thought, your grandmother and I decided it would be both unfair and impossible to conceal the truth for long."

Kendra felt fear awaken inside, a cold hand squeezing her throat. His tone and manner suggested that something tragic had transpired. She had an uneasy suspicion regarding what boundary Grandpa meant.

Grandpa hesitated, reluctant eyes flicking from Kendra to Seth and back again. "The Society has abducted your parents."

THE ADVENTURE WILL
CONCLUDE IN BOOK FIVE
Keys to the Demon Prison
HERE'S A SNEAK PEAK . . .

A Dying Wish

Seth knew he should not be here. His grandparents would be furious if they found out. The dismal cave smelled more rancid than ever, like a nauseating feast of spoiled meat and fruit. Almost steamy with humidity, the wet air forced him not only to smell but also to taste the putrid sweetness. Every inhalation made him want to retch.

Graulas lay on his side, chest swelling and shrinking with labored, hitching breaths. His infected face rested against the rocky floor, inflamed flesh flattened in a sticky mass. Although the demon's wrinkly eyelids were shut, he twitched and grunted as Seth drew near. Groaning and coughing, the bulky demon peeled his face away from the floor, one curled ram horn scraping the ground. The demon did not fully arise, but managed to prop himself up on one elbow. One eye opened a fraction. The other looked fused shut by congealed goo.

"Seth," Graulas rasped, his formerly rumbling voice weak and tired.

"I came," Seth acknowledged. "You said it was urgent."

The heavy head nodded slightly. "I . . . am . . . dying," he managed.

The ancient demon had been diseased and dying since Seth had first met him. "Worse than ever?"

The demon wheezed and coughed, a cloud of dust rising from his lumpy frame. After spitting out a thick wad of phlegm, he spoke again, his voice little more than a whisper. "After . . . long years . . . of dwindling . . . my final days . . . have arrived."

Seth was unsure what to say. Graulas had never tried to hide his nefarious past. Most good people would be relieved to hear of his demise. But the demon had taken a liking to Seth. After becoming intrigued by Seth's unusual exploits and successes, Graulas had helped him figure out how to stop the shadow plague, and had further assisted him in learning to use his newfound abilities as a shadow charmer. Whatever crimes Graulas may have committed in the past, the moribund demon had always treated Seth well.

"I'm sorry," Seth said, mildly surprised to find he really meant it.

The demon trembled; then his elbow collapsed and he flopped flat against the ground. His eye closed. "The pain," he moaned softly. "Exquisite pain. My kind . . . dies . . . so very slowly. I thought . . . I had sampled . . . every possible agony. But now, it burrows . . . twists . . . gnaws . . . expands. Deep inside. Relentless. Consuming. Before I can master it . . . the pain increases . . . to new plateaus of anguish."

"Can I help?" Seth asked, doubting whether anything from the medicine cabinet would do the trick.

The demon snorted. "Not likely," he panted. "I understand . . . you will leave tomorrow."

"How did you know that?" His mission the next day was supposedly a secret.

"Confide . . . no plans . . . to Newel and Doren."

Seth had not provided the satyrs with details. He had just told them he would be leaving Fablehaven for a time. He had been at the preserve for more than three months, ever since he and the others had returned from Wyrmroost. He had enjoyed several adventures with Newel and Doren in the interim, and felt he owed them a good-bye. Grandpa would only let them discuss the mission in his office with spells to help prevent spying, so Seth had shared no specifics, but he probably should not have said anything at all to the satyrs. "I didn't give them details," he told Graulas.

"No . . . but I heard them mention your departure . . . as they moved about the woods. Although . . . I can't see into your house . . . I can deduce . . . you seek another artifact. Only such . . . a mission . . . would prompt Stan to risk . . . your safety."

"I can't really talk about it," Seth apologized.

Graulas coughed wetly. "The details are unimportant. If I heard and guessed . . . others may have heard. Though I cannot . . . see . . . beyond the preserve . . . I can sense much outside attention focused here. Mighty wills straining to spy. Be on your guard."

"I'll be careful," Seth promised. "Is that why you called me here? To warn me?"

One eye cracked open and a faint smile touched the demon's desiccated lips. "Nothing so . . . altruistic. I am soliciting a favor."

"What?"

"I may . . . expire . . . before you return. Which would render my wishes . . . irrelevant. After all this time . . . my days are truly numbered. Seth . . . not only . . . my physical pain . . . troubles me. I am afraid to die."

"Me too."

Graulas grimaced. "You do not understand. Compared to me . . . you have little to fear."

Seth scrunched his brow. "You mean because you were bad?"

"If I could . . . evaporate . . . into nothing . . . I would welcome death. But this is not the case. There are other spheres awaiting us, Seth. The place prepared for my kind . . . when we exit this life . . . is not pleasant. Which is partly why demons cling to this life for as long as we can. After how I lived . . . for thousands of years . . . I will have to pay a steep price."

"But you're not the person you were," Seth said. "You've helped me a lot! I'm sure that will count for something."

Graulas huffed and coughed differently than he had before. It almost sounded like a bitter chuckle. "I meddled with your dilemmas . . . from my deathbed . . . to amuse myself. Such trivialities will do little to offset centuries of deliberate evil. I have not changed, Seth. I am merely powerless. I have no drive left. As much pain as I am now enduring, I fear that the afterlife . . . will hold far greater agonies."

"So what can I do?" Seth wondered.

"One thing only," Graulas growled through clenched lips. His eye squinted shut and his fists tightened. Seth heard teeth grinding. The demon's breath came in sharp, ragged bursts. "One moment," he managed, trembling. Creamy tears oozed from his eyes.

Seth turned away. It was too much to watch. He had never imagined such misery. He wanted to run from the cave and never return.

"One moment," Graulas gasped again. After a few grunts and moans, he began to breathe more deeply. "You can do one thing for me."

"Tell me," Seth said.

"I do not know the purpose of your mission . . . but should you recover the Sands of Sanctity . . . that artifact could greatly alleviate my suffering."

"But you're so diseased. Wouldn't it kill you?"

"You're thinking of . . . the unicorn horn. The horn purifies . . . and yes . . . its touch would slay me. But the Sands heal. They wouldn't just burn away my impurities. The Sands would cure my maladies and help my body survive the process. I would still be dying of old age, but the pain would be lessened, and the healing might even buy me a little more time. Forgive me, Seth. I would not ask . . . were I not desperate."

Seth stared at the pathetic ruin the demon's body had become. "The Sphinx has the Sands," he said gently.

"I know," Graulas whispered. "Even the thought . . . that there is some small chance . . . gives me something to dwell upon . . . besides . . . besides . . ."

"I understand," Seth said.

"I have nothing else to hope for."

"Of course we're trying to get the Sands back," Seth soothed. "I can't say this mission will do that, but of course we hope to recover all of the artifacts. If we can get the Sands of Sanctity, I'll bring the artifact here and heal you. I promise. Okay?"

Discolored tears gushed from the eyes of the demon. He turned his face away. "Fair enough. You have . . . my thanks . . . Seth Sorenson. Farewell."

"Is there anything else I can—"

"Go. You can do nothing more. I would rather not . . . be seen . . . like this."

"Okay. Hang in there."

Flashlight in hand, Seth exited the cave, relieved to leave behind the humid stench and the naked agony.

Acknowledgments

An unread book does nobody any good. Stories happen in the mind of a reader, not among symbols printed on a page. I am grateful to the many readers who have been bringing Fablehaven to life in their minds. I love hearing that a whole family has embraced the series, or that an entire class has read one of the books aloud, or that a reluctant reader has used the books to discover that reading can actually be fun. As an author, the best news I get is when people are reading and enjoying the stuff I write.

I'd like to thank those who are spreading the word about Fablehaven. People discover new books when friends tell friends, when teachers tell students, when students tell teachers, when librarians tell patrons, when booksellers give recommendations, when bloggers make comments, and when families share their enthusiasm with one another. I have a job as a writer because of you guys.

Many people have directly impacted the creation of this book. My thanks go out to early readers like Chris Schoebinger, Simon Lipskar, Emily Watts, Tucker Davis, Liz Saban, Jason and Natalie Conforto, Mike Walton, the Freeman family, and Jaleh Fidler, along with Pam, Cherie, Summer, and Bryson Mull, for their insights and feedback. My young nephew Cole Saban deserves a special nod for the idea of a dragon who was poisonous down to her blood. My wife, Mary, helped more than ever with her editing and as I discussed ideas with her before writing. Once again, my brother Ty meant to help. At least he finally started *Grip of the Shadow Plague*.

I'd like to thank Chris Schoebinger for overseeing all things Fablehaven, Emily Watts for her astute editing, and my agent Simon Lipskar for his wise guidance. I'm grateful to Sheri Dew, CEO of Shadow Mountain, for her visionary leadership and support of this project. Once again Brandon Dorman provided awesome images to accompany the text. I'm excited for everyone to discover *Pingo*, our first picture book together, coming in the fall of 2009. Thanks again to Richard Erickson for his art direction, and to Rachael Ward and Tonya Facemyer for the typography. I'm grateful to the entire Shadow Mountain team for their work marketing the series, including Patrick Muir, Roberta Stout, and Gail Halladay. The sales team deserves a nod as well: Boyd Ware, John Rose, Lonnie Lockhart, and Lee Broadhead.

My friends at Aladdin have done a great job with the paperbacks and expanding the Fablehaven brand.

Since the audio book producers do their work after the book is written, I have failed in the past to sufficiently acknowledge their amazing efforts. Kenny Hodges has created all of my audio books, with help from the voice talents of E. B. Stevens for the *Fablehaven* series and Emily Card for *The Candy Shop War*. The audio books have turned out really well, thanks to their great work.

I would also like to thank some of the families who have hosted me during my latest round of touring: the Gillrie family in Florida, the Flemings in Arizona, the Benders in Long Island, the Benedicts in Virginia, and the Andrews in Texas. I'd like to thank the many booksellers who have made extra efforts to help the cause, including Tracy Rydell, Jackie Harris, Donna Powers, Joel Harris, Lisa Lindquest, Angie Wager, Deborah Horne, Nancy Clark, Laura Jonio, and Nathan Jarvis.

Some authors have gone out of their way to give me advice and on occasion to spread the word about my books. Such authors include Richard Paul Evans, Orson Scott Card, Shannon Hale, Brandon Sanderson, Obert Skye, and Rick Walton. Christopher Paolini was kind to read the books and write a review.

You especially have my thanks, dear reader, for sticking with the *Fablehaven* series this far. One more to go. I'm excited about it. Swing by BrandonMull.com to get on my e-mail list for news and updates. And feel free to track me down on Facebook.

Reading Guide

1. Kendra has faced multiple betrayals over the course of the series. Which do you think was the worst and why? Have you ever felt betrayed by a friend? How did you handle the situation?

2. During this story, Vanessa made some efforts at restitution for past betrayals. How much do you feel she can be trusted? Explain.

3. Why did Seth steal the unicorn horn from the centaurs? What might have happened had he failed? Do you feel he made a good choice to go after the horn? Have you ever taken a risk that made others uncomfortable? If so, what were the circumstances?

4. What makes Raxtus feel like a failure as a dragon? What makes Raxtus a good friend for humans? Are some of the things he dislikes about himself actually desirable qualities? Explain.

5. If you had possession of and could operate the Oculus—the All-Seeing Eye—how would you use it? Who would you spy on? What would you look for?

6. Why did Thronis help Seth? Do you think the giant is a good person? Why or why not?

7. If you had a stingbulb, how would you use it?

8. The key at Wyrmroost was well guarded. Why did the Knights choose to go after the key? Do you agree with their decision? Why or why not?

9. So far, three artifacts have been found, The Sands of Sanctity, the Chronometer, and the Oculus. Which do you think is most valuable? Why?

10. Grandma Sorenson is deadly with a crossbow. Perhaps your own grandparents have some secret weapons or skills you don't know about. What could they be? Use your imagination and create an adventure story about one of your grandparents, making him or her the hero. Then send your grandparent the story.

11. Raxtus feels he can never live up to what his father expects him to be. Have you ever fallen short of the expectations others had for you? How can high expectations be helpful? How can they be hurtful?

12. If you were playing a game of Capture the Flag with your friends at night, would you rather be able to see in the dark like Kendra, or shade walk like Seth? Which might give you the better advantage?

13. Graulas tells Seth, "Choices determine character," who we are and who we become. Can you think of a choice that you've made that has improved your character? How important is character? What are the most important choices you make every day?